PRAISE F

"*Doll Parts* is the most mesmerizing and original book I've read in a long time. It's eerie and addictive, a story that pulls you in and won't let go. Penny Zang has a gift, and I would read anything she writes."
—Samantha Downing, international bestselling author of *My Lovely Wife* and *Too Old for This*

"*Doll Parts* is a dark, atmospheric exploration of friendship, exploitation, and female rage. Delving into the most vulnerable and turbulent stages of womanhood, it's perfect for fans of Megan Abbott and Ashley Audrain."
—Robyn Harding, international bestselling author of *The Drowning Woman*

"Haunted and haunting, *Doll Parts* is an exquisite exploration and scathing critique of our cultural obsession with pretty dead girls as well as a riveting mystery pieced together by two fascinating and complex protagonists. Like a beloved collection of poetry, this story is worth carrying around, dog-earing, highlighting, returning to again and again. I loved this book from its very first sentence."
—Megan Collins, author of *Cross My Heart*

"Sad Girl Cult but make it crime fiction: the genre-blending *Doll Parts* is as dark and evocative as tear-smudged eyeliner, as rebellious and moody as a song by Hole. Part mystery, part bildungsroman, and part paean to female friendship, Zang's debut examines

our cultural obsession with beautiful dead women—and, against a world that might prefer them silent, cold, and pretty, the lengths to which two best friends will go to remain vital, messy, and true to themselves, their bravery reverberating across timelines."
—Ashley Winstead, *USA Today* bestselling author of *Midnight Is the Darkest Hour*

"*Doll Parts* is a grippingly powerful journey through a woman's troubled past in college to her present postpartum experience as she grapples with the loss of her estranged best friend. Penny Zang brilliantly threads the haunting legacy of Sylvia Plath through a stunning plot that incisively unravels the mystery behind a tragic series of deaths. At once devastating and hopeful, this profound, exquisitely written suspense will wholly capture you and leave an indelible mark."
—Samantha M. Bailey, *USA Today* and #1 international bestselling author of *Hello, Juliet*

"I'm blaming Penny Zang for having me up way too late trying to fit the pieces together of her haunting dual timeline novel. Just the right blend of dark academia and psychological suspense, *Doll Parts* features ghosts of the past, fractured friendships, and the most clever use of a newsletter I've seen. With just one book, Zang has established herself as a must-read author."
—Kellye Garrett, award-winning author of *Missing White Woman*

"*Doll Parts* drew me in like a ghost to a stage light. A lyrical, haunting, and oh-so-alive ode to the loves of our lives—friends, mothers, daughters—and the stories we tell and retell and un-tell in their absence, enshrouded in dual mysteries unfolding twenty years apart. Assured, beautiful, unsettling—read this novel when the sky is heavy and the bruises in your heart are tender. Penny Zang is a monumental talent."

—Katie Gutierrez, bestselling author of
More Than You'll Ever Know

"Twisty, bold, and pulsing with the fever dream of '90s girlhood, *Doll Parts* is a genre all its own: part mystery, part dirge, part love letter to Baltimore, a postpartum story, and a celebration of fierce female friendship. Penny Zang has written a glorious indictment of our cultural obsession with dead girls, so well-written and so fun that you don't see its true depths until you've gleefully dived in."

—Julia Fine, author of *The Upstairs House*

"*Doll Parts* is one of the most unexpectedly imaginative—and soulful—suspense novels I've read in some time. Following dual mysteries, that of Sadie as she navigates motherhood and life in her husband's first wife's shadow, and Nikki, years earlier, chasing a shadow of her own, Penny Zang creates a unique world infused with deep friendship, grief, and the quiet resilience of becoming. *Doll Parts* miraculously succeeds on both a level of suspense and lyricism, which, if done well, of course, is the very definition of great poetry."

—Lee Kravetz, author of *The Last Confessions of Sylvia P.*

"Q: What should you read if you're looking for a book haunted by Sylvia Plath? If you crave an old-fashioned whodunit shot through with longing and lyricism? What if you want a book that honors

your backlog of dead girls, your long list of former selves, loving and laughing at them all at once, while getting all the best grrrl songs going like a riot in your head? A: *Doll Parts*. Nikki and Sadie will steal your heart (and your fishnets). I couldn't put it down."
—Emily Van Duyne, author of *Loving Sylvia Plath: A Reclamation*

"Utterly original and addictive, *Doll Parts* is a fever dream of a novel. The haunting dual timeline and blistering exploration of the objectification of dead girls work together to create a searing, propulsive narrative that readers will devour. A mesmerizing first novel—I can't wait for Penny Zang's next."
—Nicole Baart, author of *Where He Left Me*

"*Doll Parts* is smart, sly, and suspenseful. Zang's riveting debut offers an unflinching look at the many ways we betray girls and the bonds they forge to try to save themselves."
—Shelley Puhak, author of *The Dark Queens*

"Take a twisty tale about estranged best friends with a dark academia past, sprinkle in new motherhood woes, a relentless ghost, murder, secrets, and unsettling grief, and you have a relentlessly engaging and poignant novel. *Doll Parts* is irresistible."
—Megan Chance, bestselling author of *Glamorous Notions* and *A Dangerous Education*

doll parts

A NOVEL

penny zang

sourcebooks
landmark

Copyright © 2025 by Penny Zang
Cover and internal design © 2025 by Sourcebooks
Cover design by Sarah Brody/Sourcebooks
Cover image © Jake Wangner/Stills
Internal design by Tara Jaggers/Sourcebooks

Sourcebooks and the colophon are registered trademarks of Sourcebooks.

All rights reserved. No part of this book may be reproduced in any form or by any electronic or mechanical means including information storage and retrieval systems—except in the case of brief quotations embodied in critical articles or reviews—without permission in writing from its publisher, Sourcebooks.

No part of this book may be used or reproduced in any manner for the purpose of training artificial intelligence technologies or systems.

The characters and events portrayed in this book are fictitious or are used fictitiously. Any similarity to real persons, living or dead, is purely coincidental and not intended by the author.

Published by Sourcebooks Landmark, an imprint of Sourcebooks
1935 Brookdale RD, Naperville, IL 60563-2773
(630) 961-3900
sourcebooks.com

Cataloging-in-Publication Data is on file with the Library of Congress.

Printed and bound in the United States of America.
LSC 10 9 8 7 6 5 4 3 2 1

*To my mother, Pauline, who by teaching me
to love books, taught me everything.*

*And for Sarah, in loving memory.
The world is incomplete without you.*

Where you used to be, there is a hole in the world, which I find myself constantly walking around in the daytime, and falling in at night. I miss you like hell.

—EDNA ST. VINCENT MILLAY

Some girl a hundred years ago once lived as I do. And she is dead. I am the present, but I know I, too, will pass. The high moment, the burning flash, come and are gone, continuous quicksand. And I don't want to die.

—SYLVIA PLATH, *THE UNABRIDGED JOURNALS OF SYLVIA PLATH*

How to write about a dead woman:
   First, confirm she is dead. Dead enough not to mind.
   Hold a mirror to her cracked lips and watch for fog. Brave her wrist for a pulse. Let your fingertips linger.
   After a moment of silence, ask for her name. Find someone who knows her well—a father or boyfriend or brother or coach. How she died will seem to matter, but no one will want to talk about it.
   Do not let the reader forget that she was once alive. Search out the most telling details, like her favorite class and her favorite professor. Her favorite poet: Sylvia Plath, of course. What she liked most was autumn on campus, the vibration of cathedral bells, the smell of rotting leaf piles—everything made prettier as it died.
   Quote her old journals and old letters. There is so much to choose from. Keep digging. Go elbow-deep. Pencil in an open wound.
   Ask yourself what you can learn from scanning a dead woman's body. Did her skin stretch, leaving a trail of reminders? Did she once scrape her knees in a parking lot while fleeing an angry date who just wanted to talk? Some details are not relevant. Ignore the scars, like the one at her temple, a nickel-size divot from playing in the woods as a child. Pretend not to notice her gnarled feet. Resist fingering her palm to feel the length of her lifeline.
   We remember you, her also-dead friends sing, and you can't unhear them. Wisps of voices, flickering lights.
   Help me zip my dress, they say.
   Take my hand. We're glad you finally made it.

They stalk across campus in their black boots and sob-smeared mascara. The Sylvia Club. The chorus of them, always calling.

She is dead now. There is only so much you can do, only so much you can know. Pluck through the details at your feet to fill in the empty spaces. The songs she memorized, the classes she skipped, the poetry she etched on the inside of her wrist. The pretty future she could almost see, unspooling and endless. Desperately bright.

It is sad, yes, but here you are. Someone has to tell her story.

Subject: Self-Care the Shit Out of This Day

Wake up, slut! It's me again, your loud but lovable surrogate sister. I know it's been a while, but I'm here. It's time to get out of your rut and practice some real self-care. Consider this a message from the beyond that I waited too long to send.

Let me guess. You're exhausted, burned out, and so depressed you can't even see it. You're also haunted. We all are. The girl you used to be is lingering on the edges of every decision you make.

Same. Same.

I know what else is haunting you. And I know that everything is about to get worse before it gets better. It's time to rip off those stained yoga pants (better yet—burn them), replace your lumpy house bra with some legit underwire, and polish up your armor.

You already know what I think. I think you deserve spa days, mimosa brunches, and a personal chef who memorizes all your food sensitivities. You deserve a caramel drizzle over EVERYTHING. Go ahead and smile through your sun salutations because you earned the right.

This kind of self-care is transformative. It's a process bigger than chrysalis, bitch. And we're going on this journey together.

Your outstretched arms, your aching chest, the glitter in the corner of your eye—perfect imperfection. It's your superpower. And in case you get worried, Beauty Queen, remember that I always have a plan.

You aren't going to hear from me for a while, but you will see me again. I promise that whatever happens next, I'm rooting for you so hard that it hurts.

Weekly newsletter, c/o Annie Minx, Inc. Click here to unsubscribe.

CHAPTER 1

NOW

Sadie

The nipples bobbed and bounced on the surface, the steam rising and the bubbles mixing to form a nipple soup. I needed to sterilize the new bottles next. Eventually, the baby book said, I could use the dishwasher, though many women preferred to hand-wash. Safer that way. I didn't mind the ritual of sterilizing, the simple problem and solution of it. There were microorganisms waiting to worm into my baby's digestive system, and I was the only one who could stop them.

The floorboards creaked under my feet, and the kitchen lights flickered twice, the dream house waking and waking again. I paused to acknowledge it.

Next on Mama 101's Back-to-Work List was the laundry, the heaping basket of milk-stained bibs and snap-crotched onesies, making sure to use the special detergent without perfumes or dyes.

I stared at the coffee maker for five minutes, waiting for the rhythmic brew and grind, before realizing I hadn't turned it on. It was Wednesday before sunrise. If I checked off a few items each day, next Monday would be easier. I'd go back to work with the diaper bag stocked and the house clean enough not to feel my absence.

My tiny mug of coffee disappeared in one swig. Tiny for portion control. Too much caffeine for a nursing baby was, of course, Wrong. Right was the fenugreek tea that made my sweat smell like maple syrup. Water was also Right. Hydration. Good vibes. A quiet, stress-free environment was Right for Baby and Right for Mama. But Rhiannon hadn't slept more than two hours at a time since birth, so I refilled my tiny mug more than once.

Baby, mama, coffee, nipples.

Morning was my only alone time, and I craved that one sliver of daylight before everyone else woke, when I was no longer my old self but not the new me either. Mornings were blank. Blameless.

Outside, the crowning sun streaked the sky, brightening every new-model Lexus and every concierge-serviced security system. The professionally manicured yards gleamed. It was quiet, but not quiet enough. The wind rioted like a hundred women keening.

My throat clogged with a chewed-up poem I forgot I knew. Something about ashes and eating men like air. It was the kind of pink-hazed sky that called for poetry. Pink like the flick of a tongue, like a blushing cheek, the beginning of a fever.

A package sat at the front door, a box that must have been delivered late yesterday, and I tore it open before realizing it wasn't addressed to me. Inside were dozens of gold books, the title embossed and iridescent.

The Self-Care Cure: Healing What Haunts You by Annie Minx. Nikki's last book, published under a different name.

I could mail it back to the publisher with the words "Return to Sender" or "Deceased" scrawled across the top. Or wait until

Harrison got home so he could do whatever he did with the rest of his dead wife's boxes. Instead, I slipped it onto the shelf in the garage with all of Nikki's other untouched mail, all the things Harrison hadn't decided how to handle yet.

"For the hungry, wild-eyed poet in all of us," said the book's dedication page. My skin prickled.

On the line underneath, a second dedication:

"To my bestie: I would never leave without you. I pinkie swear."

A faded image of two girls with their fingers locked seethed behind my eyes, and I slammed the book shut.

My last pinkie swear: Almost twenty years before, the front seat of my car. Me and her. Torn cuticles, Magic Marker nail polish, music amped so loud it almost drowned out the thunder in my ears. Some storm brewing between us, our worlds about to break down the middle like a gold-plated-heart necklace.

Just like that, the silence splintered, breaking the morning's spell. Two hours after she'd last nursed, Rhiannon screamed for more. Whatever strand of thought I had started to unwind, snapped away like the tail of a kite, or like something else that never belonged to me anyway.

There were things we'd kept out of respect: the cashmere blanket draped over the back of the couch, the artfully arranged bowl of sea glass, the ceramic owls perched on a faux-driftwood ledge. Nothing moved. Nothing changed.

This is my life, I told myself, sometimes three times a day. *This is my house*. Sometimes I gagged on it.

The most exciting part of my day so far involved dropping half a granola bar down my nursing bra, like I planned to save it for later.

I snapped a blurry photo of Rhi wearing leggings with a circular print that looked like bagels. I posted it nowhere, sent it to no one. And I tried not to think about the box of books or that dedication page. Hungry poets and pinkie swears.

My twelve weeks were almost up. Twelve weeks of Mama Practice before going back to work, weeks marked by mangled lullabies and the stringent odor of diaper cream, equal parts exhaustion and tenderness. A devastating ache in my belly that wasn't there before, a hungry lurch to all my movements like a black-and-white-movie monster.

Twelve weeks in the dream house with another woman's shoes still sitting inside the mudroom, ready for her to slide them onto her feet again and clomp down the hall just to taste my reaction.

Luckily, there were things that could help New Mamas like me—exercise, rest, and, of course, hydration. Every magazine and parenting book, e-newsletter, and podcast told me so. *Get your steps in, girl. Keep drinking your water.* Don't worry about the hair falling out in chunks because it is Very, Very Normal. *Don't forget to keep yourself alive even when you don't want to,* is what they meant.

Staggered footsteps groaned upstairs, the sound of the house settling. My dry skin itched until it bled.

Harrison, in his professional opinion, agreed about getting me out of the house more. "Have you thought about running again?" he asked. "Maybe you could make some friends in the neighborhood." As if I could simply walk up to the women in Hidden Harbor and say hello. Never mind that I had never been a runner. He must have been thinking about someone else, a woman with lower body fat and meatier calves than me.

But what else was I going to do with my time? I needed a break from the sour smell of Nikki's perfume trapped in the vents and the hot currents of air that suddenly swamped each room. In three months, I hadn't gotten used to any of it.

So I scribbled "exercise" on my to-do list, spelled wrong and flanked by two crooked stars, then laced up my sneakers.

Straight on Wicomico, right on Dorchester, sharp left on Harford. One step. And then another. Clouds of gnats swarmed like they didn't know it was the end of summer, the spiky humidity hanging on longer than anyone expected. Around each turn, I remembered the box of books all over again and gasped for breath, searching for the clarity that was supposed to come with running, that empty feeling of nothing in my head except breath and heart rate, wind and ache. Sweat soaked my shirt and underwear, but I pushed forward until everything inside me burned. It was the burn I wanted most.

If my estimations were correct, I had approximately fifteen minutes before Rhi woke. Her naps were shorter in the afternoon. And when she woke up, she'd howl. I tried to be hopeful, tried to reason that once Rhi got a little bit older and we could establish a routine, motherhood would be easier. Harrison disagreed. It would only get worse, especially if I insisted on going back to work, he'd said. He should know. He had already lived through the baby stage, eighteen years before. And now Caroline was at Loch Raven College, the same college I once attended, living proof that it never got easier.

Garrett Road, Dorchester Ave., St. Mary's Court. Every street was named after a different county in Maryland, the houses all painted in the same palette of Griege, Tree Bark, and Gingerbread. But just beyond the shorn hedges and bleached driveways, the smell of decay. I wasn't imagining it. Rot in the roots, blighting the grass. I lowered my head to smell my armpit and almost retched.

By the tennis courts, a shirtless man gripped a racket and wiped his brow, his skin slick with sweat. When he smiled and waved, an old spark of flirtation buzzed below my still-tender C-section scar, and I couldn't help myself from smiling back. I imagined, for only a moment, what Old Sadie would do, all the ways I could crash my body against someone else's. How easily I could blow up my life without even trying.

Instead, I kept walking, my elastic waistband stretched against my gut and my mouth fringed with whatever I hadn't brushed away after breakfast.

I made a mental note to wait until dinner—our special anniversary dinner—to tell Harrison about my run, just to have something new to talk about when he got home. Since he had called twice between patients, he already knew how much Rhiannon ate, how many diaper changes she'd had, how much milk had been pumped and added to the freezer reserve.

I hadn't told him yet about the books that arrived.

You were right about the exercise, I would say. *I feel better already.*

Inside the stroller, Rhi gurgled a wet warning to keep moving, to not wake her a minute before she was ready. But I did stop. On the corner of Harford and Cecil, the front door at Mrs. Busy's house yawned open. One child sat on her hip, and a little boy trailed behind her, stomping on ants, singing to himself loud enough that I could hear him from across the street. The hostile straightness of her spine, her body on alert like a guard dog, was how I knew she pretended not to notice me, too.

Mrs. Busy's real name was Diana Noble. Queen of the Driveway Selfie, party host with a fondness for emojis and exclamation points. She posted daily in the neighborhood Facebook group and coordinated all the social gatherings: book clubs, yoga lessons in the clubhouse, the Labor Day pool party. In Hidden Harbor, she was the person to know. I made sure to never "like" a single one of her posts.

Just that morning, I'd received a Facebook invite to her upcoming mimosa brunch. I knew better than to be flattered by the invitation; every woman in the neighborhood was on the invite list.

It would have been so easy to walk over and finally introduce myself, the woman now living in her dead neighbor's home. I mean, I had once been likable and outgoing. I used to have girlfriends who were happy to see me. At least one.

In one long blink, I saw us there on Loch Raven's campus, just as we had always been, in tandem slips of velvet, hurtling toward each other across mossy paths on our way to the dining hall, early for the buffet line but late for everything else.

The sudden closeness of the memory made me want to stick my head into someone's recycling can. Something to hold me close instead of always feeling so exposed. Like the way I searched every dead-end court for an escape route. How it had felt for months like something was chasing me and today it finally caught up.

I found a fuzzy, unwrapped breath mint at the bottom of the diaper bag and sucked it down, desperate for a new sensation. With my thumb, I scraped the lint from my tongue.

As I turned in the other direction, a woman with perfect beach waves and a truck-size stroller charged toward me. Her rose gold leggings shimmered, and the glittery letters of her muscle tee read "#Momlife." Her sneakers were shinier than her teeth.

She looked like a goddess. For a moment, I thought she was coming to save me.

Beach Waves peered in at Rhi and grunted. "She's too young

for that stroller. The recommendation is six months for a jogging stroller. They need neck control."

It was the kind of mistake I would feel for days, maybe longer. Which discussion post had I missed? What baby book skimped on the details of stroller guidelines? A swell of nerves brewed in my chest like a cauldron, boiling over the lip. The feeling never went away, as if in the last year, I'd forgotten how to separate my emotions. So scalded and sensitive that I wanted to scream just to see what fell out. Worry looked the same as joy looked the same as burning rage.

mom life rose gold jogging stroller beach waves neck control neck control neck control

"Oh," I told Beach Waves. "Thanks for letting me know."

Before I could stop myself, I reached out to finger the colorful threaded bracelet at her wrist. We used to trade them like currency, braid them during math class, wear them as proof of friendship. We used to never take them off.

"I bought it for myself as a gift," Beach Waves boasted, pulling her arm away before my fingers hooked under the bracelet's knot and tugged. "They're sold out everywhere, but I found one on my last trip to New York."

Without a nod of acknowledgment, we watched Diana Noble back out of the driveway, her head-cheerleader vibe like a potion we both wanted to swallow. Then Rhi cried so loudly that I jumped. That was it. Time to go home.

"You're doing a great job, Mama," Beach Waves yelled as she jogged away, her fake friendship bracelet dangling. "Have a blessed day!" The sincerity in her voice only made it worse.

The long stumble home slowed toward a horizon crowded with houses like the one I'd moved into three days after giving birth. It didn't matter if home didn't feel like home or if I couldn't pinpoint whatever nameless thing waited for me there. I was going back anyway.

Past the front gates, through the swarming gnats, my feet throbbed with each step. Exhausted but not unhappy. Never unhappy. *Shell-shocked* was the word I would use. But I couldn't blame motherhood on any of that. I'd been this way since college. All the blurry Polaroids and freshmen rules and ivy-covered bricks, a mosh pit of memories, kicked me right where it hurt most.

I knew the women of Hidden Harbor watched from their clean windows as I trampled their mailbox flower beds. Women who would never be my friends. *It's a shame what happened,* they would say as they raised glasses of midday prosecco and thought about Harrison Walsh's dead first wife. *Cheers to hoping it doesn't happen again.*

Cheers to whatever I was becoming, balding temples and glazed eyeholes, fungus hue. Bottoms up. Here's to me. I'd clink my glass so hard it would shatter.

CHAPTER 2
NOW

It wasn't hard to imagine. The polished bronze faucet, the linen bath towel, the empty champagne flute. I stood in the same bathroom where it had happened and envisioned the whole scene. The same gilded drain stopper and amber-honey bubble bath. I used them just as I would if I didn't know what had happened there.

Every tube of lipstick, every salon-grade shampoo and hair serum I could never afford. All her best things, untouched and on display. Books balanced on the edge of the tub, pages bookmarked like she'd meant to come right back. Even a dark spot on the light switch cover, a stain that might have been chocolate or might have been blood. She left that behind, too.

But what she really left behind was her hair. Dark, wispy strands against white tile, clogging the drains, tumbled up in the corners. That unfussy straight hair I had once coveted, I didn't know if I'd ever stop finding it. Harrison told me that when his cleaning woman first showed up after the funeral, he'd sent her away, furious at the thought of someone moving anything his wife had touched. Eventually, I vacuumed up all her dust on my own.

Her robe, hanging from the hook on the bathroom door, was the only item that didn't seem staged for a photo op. Cornflower blue, oversize cotton terry—nothing luxe or Instagram-worthy about it. The collar smelled calm and fresh, like her rose-petal face cream, even a year later. Her mom used to own one just like it.

It wasn't an accident, I was told. Triple-dosage narcotics, plus alcohol, plus bathtub. A note left for her daughter beside the empty pill bottle. Apparently she had been depressed and distracted for months. Harrison only told me the story once and never spoke of it again. Poor self-destructive Nikki. She nearly burned the house down twice. That's how bad it got, he'd said.

It hadn't felt true when I heard it the first time, and it still didn't. Not Nikki. I couldn't believe it. She would never.

Her new best friend, Diana Noble, had found her. Diana, who was allowed to cry and grieve, who was invited to speak at the funeral, while I sat in the back of the church, a stranger to everyone but the woman in the casket. Nikki and I hadn't spoken in over eighteen years, a fact so unbelievable sometimes that it felt like fiction.

She died in the bathroom, but the office was where I felt her the most. Like an electrical charge on the other side of the door, a white heat clinging to its hinges. Except we kept the office locked like another dusty memorial.

"Don't touch anything," said the paper taped to the office door when she died. Harrison took the note as her final words, her last wish, and hadn't moved anything in the house—including the paper on the door—since. But I wasn't so sure. I thought Nikki meant the message for the housekeeper.

She spent her days in that room. "She never stopped working on those silly books," Harrison told me when I first moved in. Silly. Like working was a bad thing. It was the only thing he'd ever said about her writing, until last week when her final book hit the shelves. *Posthumous*, in Harrison's mouth, sounded a lot like *silly*.

Nikki, I sometimes whispered when the lights flickered, as if she could hear me. An act of denial, waiting for her to stumble out from the wings and show herself. *Nikki Nikki Nikki.* If I stared in the mirror and said her name three times, maybe she'd tell me what really happened.

We were having one of our little anniversaries. We both promised we wouldn't buy gifts, wouldn't make special plans. But after dinner, after Harrison put Rhi to bed with a bottle of pumped milk, after I shoveled the leftover meat loaf into Tupperware containers and the soggy asparagus into the trash can, after the dishwasher churned its comforting, clean song, Harrison slid a pretty gray box out from under the couch. I'd bought him a gift, too, and I pushed past Nikki's coats to reach the top shelf of the closet where it was hidden.

In the hallway mirror, my overstretched smile distorted my whole reflection. My eyes bulging, my cheeks pulled back. But at least I'd showered.

I knew Harrison had lost track of which anniversary we meant to celebrate. Not because we'd been together so long—a little more than a year, only three months under the same roof—but because I insisted on celebrating every milestone. New milestones meant new memories. That was what normal couples did. Where there wasn't a history, they created one. When the core was weak, they strengthened the muscle.

First kiss: At a party almost two decades before; a random night, a nothing kiss. I grabbed the back of his neck because I was drunk and he was cute, and because that's the kind of girl I used to be.

First date: The Baltimore Aquarium, where he said he loved the puffins most—those clumsy flyers—and also, he liked the Beatles and red wine and women with red hair. I preferred the octopus, I said, because they had three hearts and nine brains, and everyone underestimated their intelligence. I winked up at him and grabbed his hand, the one Nikki had once held.

I gifted him a coffee table book with illustrated lyrics of every Beatles song. Our names created a sort of inside joke. He was Harrison, as in George Harrison, and I was Sexy Sadie. He chuckled when he opened it, deepening both dimples. That smile made him look younger than he was—boyish, almost. Charming and handsome with long limbs, his height the kind that seemed programmed to make women swoon. He had a lean dad bod that would make women look twice if he mowed the lawn with his shirt off. Not that he would ever mow the lawn. We had people for that.

We had people for everything. That was how rich people lived, I'd come to learn—never worrying over the tedious parts of life like the taxes and the lawncare, the window cleaning and the car maintenance, the painting of fingernails, body-hair removal.

Harrison handed me a shoebox wrapped in paper the same color as our bedroom walls. Gutterball Gray, I secretly called it. Stylish Gray was the actual name. Last year's Color of the Year. So gray that it sometimes shone blue or beige, depending on the light. The attention to detail in the house made me dizzy. In the kitchen, the

Hughes Classic Interior doorknob set and the Morocco Green Limestone tiles. In the living room, the farmhouse ceiling fans. None of it chosen by me, of course. I only knew the details because of Pinterest. I doubted even Harrison knew how much time and research had gone into the leather poof under his ass.

He held the gift out to me, expectant. I predicted lingerie—sensible, unruffled panties in breathable cotton that he'd picked out on his own, something pretty and classy like the dozens of red roses he sometimes sent for no reason.

Instead, I opened a box filled with padded socks, toe spacers, and an informational brochure about bunion surgery. Lots of white tissue paper.

"You're always complaining about your feet," he said—his doctor voice, but smoother. "I thought it was time to do something about it."

All the nights rubbing my feet, looking at the new, raw wideness of them, frowning when I couldn't squeeze into my old shoes, neither of us ever used the word *bunions*. I blamed my years of waiting tables in cheap shoes, though apparently, according to the brochure in my hand, bunions were genetic.

He slipped the squishy toeless socks onto my feet like they were glass slippers, and he looked so hopeful that I couldn't say, *This gift makes me feel old and ugly*. I couldn't ask if toe spacers were the kind of gift he had given Nikki. Instead, I made a joke about how you could tell how hard a man worked by his hands and how hard a woman worked by her feet. Instead of saying, *This is the worst gift I've ever been given*, I held his hand and stroked the inside of his palm with my middle finger. Touching him anchored me. It was the only thing that did.

I might amble like the undead, but here he was to fix me.

I once went to a wedding where the minister joked that lesson number one about marriage was to never buy your spouse a broom or a vacuum for an anniversary present.

Next time, I wanted to say, *just get me a vacuum.*

Of course, we weren't married yet, either, so there was that.

First argument: Half-drunk, in my tiny studio apartment—after the funeral but before I moved in—when he found the old photos of me and his dead wife from high school, dressed in grubby ball gowns, our skinny arms tangled, our embrace unbroken. As if he didn't feel shitty enough.

"Oh yeah, before I forget, do you need money for groceries?" He pulled out his phone, ready to make a transfer on his banking app.

It only felt a little like asking for an allowance. I bit the inside of my mouth and tried not to sigh. My old bank account, along with my credit card and my apartment and my car, hadn't made the transition to Hidden Harbor, so I now used a debit card linked to one of Harrison's accounts. Just for now. Just until I started making my own money again.

The doorbell rang, and Harrison fidgeted with his collar, half hunching in that way tall men sometimes did. The big surprise—the real gift—was that Jo, the fourteen-year-old girl from down the street, had agreed to stay with Rhiannon while we drove downtown for dessert and wine.

I mustered a ripple of visible excitement even though all I wanted to do was steal a few hours of sleep before she woke again. It would be our first time out together since having Rhi. My first time out without her, ever. Practice for next week, I told myself. Prepare the bottles. Enjoy being human again.

On our kitchen calendar, a series of X's led to a red circle around Monday. I had already worked out all the details, precooking a week's worth of meals, all the cheesy, greasy casseroles that my grandmother used to make, before I returned to my job as social media coordinator for *Baltimore Alive!*, the local free paper that had more ads than articles.

The hardest day of motherhood was the day women returned to work, according to a web forum that usually made me feel worse instead of better. Story after story of women quitting on their first day back. They could never fully explain why. No one said that their concentration scrambled when they tried to operate email on three hours of sleep. Or that being away from their baby felt like a strangling, choking kind of panic. That wouldn't be me, I had already decided. Those other women were delirious. I couldn't wait to go back.

Cherish every moment, older women at the grocery store told me, their eyes blazing, daring me to disagree or protest. I never did.

Wiping my eyes with the back of my hand, I asked if I had time to put on lipstick and a pair of earrings. The correct answer: you're beautiful the way you are, but yes, you have time, which was exactly what he said.

I knew how lucky I was. Other women would kill for my life. Lucky lucky lucky. I wore the squishy socks to show my appreciation.

Before I moved in, I'd confessed to my friend Lucille that I didn't know if I was ready to live in a home designed by another woman. I didn't mention that I had once known the first wife, though sometimes I spoke wistfully about a nameless old friend, the kind of best friend I'd shared everything with. Clothes and makeup. Secrets.

There were a thousand memories that I had secreted away.

Slumber parties and locker combinations, school dances and late-night drives around the beltway with music blaring from our open windows.

Darker memories, too. Those had been bleeding through more and more.

Lucille had asked me more than once, "What happened between you and your friend?"

What she meant: How do best friends suddenly sever ties and never speak again?

It must have been bad, she knew that much, because whatever happened between me and Nikki had changed the course of our lives, not just our friendship. We never moved in together like we'd planned. I dropped out of school, and Nikki met the man of her dreams, the man of someone's dreams, and ended up in a community with gates to keep people like me out. Not that I was bitter; I eventually ended up there, too.

"It's too much," I had whined, my hands on my swollen stomach. "This isn't me."

Lucille knew what I meant. We had bonded over our messy family histories at work, me without a mother and her with a dead father. Dysfunctional in ways that we claimed gave us the right amount of edge.

We both surveyed the kitchen, every surface white and clean. Then she spread her arms as if to gather up the whole house in one swoop—the marble counters, the stainless steel appliances, the self-closing drawers. Worlds away from the sketchy apartments I had lived in my whole life, sleeping on ratty couches, unable to pay my rent money on time. The bugs and the leering men in the stairwells.

"You've won the lottery, Sadie," she said. "Don't you dare mess it up."

In the bedroom, I searched for shoes wide enough to fit over my anniversary gift. The new socks and toe spacers were too thick to make shoe choice much of a choice at all. No sparkly black sandals or open-toed wedges for me.

The closet was one of the many spaces in the house still filled with Nikki's things and not much of my own. My fingers lingered over a gauzy black dress with cap sleeves tailored for her petite frame. I knew from experience that the seams would rip if I tried to fit it over my postpartum rib cage. The good stuff, the colorful vintage dresses we had once lived for, were in the back of the closet, wrapped in plastic. Costume-room corsets and thrift-store pleats.

On the edge of my vision, a spark of white sliced the air. The smell that came with it: hot garbage, but worse. To say it felt like a presence would make me sound like the kind of person who believed in that sort of thing. The heat faded just as fast, leaving me unsteady against the wall.

In the bedroom doorway, Harrison took one look at my simple red dress and whistled. I had curves where I didn't have them before. His eye caught the crowned honeybee on my shoulder, but he knew I'd cover it with a cardigan. New Me loved a good cardigan.

"Ready?" he asked, taking up the whole doorframe, my handsome giant.

The sudden ringing in my ears echoed too loud to hear anything else. A thousand bees—a whole fucking hive—buzzing.

"I can't leave her alone." The words strangled me, stuttered in my throat. My hands locked into sweaty fists at the thought of Rhi waking up with someone else standing over her. The noises of the house, the creaks and groans, would amplify without me there to hear them. The doll Harrison's mom had bought her would watch her from its spot in the rocking chair; Rhi would be able to hear its heavy eyelids blinking.

Harrison sighed but said he understood. The baby blues were common enough. Just a Hormonal Thing. It would eventually go away, he'd told me more than once. None of the books or websites mentioned what I had, though—the rising dread, the way I heard things in the house that weren't really there. The constant feeling that I was never alone, even when I was. No one mentioned my fevered skin or the tremor in my hands. The way I forgot to breathe.

We sent Jo home and shared half a bottle of wine on the back deck, the baby monitor on the table between us the whole time. Alcohol was Not Recommended for nursing mamas, but I clutched my tiny glass anyway, waiting for the wine to take hold.

Later, after we checked on Rhi, preset the coffee machine for the morning, and programmed the security system, we rushed through sex, my playlist of screeching grunge tuned low enough that Harrison couldn't complain. Even still, he didn't finish. He claimed exhaustion and too much wine. A Kitty Cat, I would've once called him. Soft and sleepy, his underbelly exposed.

The sex wasn't wholly unsatisfying, though; I'd take any touch, any taste, over none at all. In minutes, Harrison began to snore beside me, grunting like a baby pig searching the air for food. I didn't bother sleeping. Rhi would wake again soon enough.

On the nightstand, his phone vibrated with emails and text messages that he'd wait to read until he thought I was asleep. If I asked him about it, he'd smile without his dimples. He'd grow cold, but just a little. He didn't want me to see what I already knew, that Nikki's final book, Annie Minx's *The Self-Care Cure*, had hit the bestseller list.

As much as he didn't want to talk about the new book, I knew it would become another thing that hung between us, refusing to be ignored. This was the last book she would ever write, the last thing she would ever create. Someone needed to acknowledge it.

My body felt all wrong, hollowed out and skittish. I tendered my forehead with the inside of my wrist, sure I'd find heat there. My exhaustion swelled. The sterilized nipples, the meat loaf, the informational brochures—it swirled up and smashed together so I couldn't decide if there was something I missed or something I forgot to do. The jogging stroller especially nagged at me. Mistake after mistake after mistake. Even after a scalding shower, I couldn't scrub the day away.

son of a bitch bunions anniversary bottles babysitter cardigans goddamn bestseller list

To my bestie. I flushed at the thought of it. She could have been referring to Diana.

But the other part. *I would never leave without you.* Wasn't that something we once said to each other? Didn't she say it as a promise?

The mention of a pinkie swear gouged me the hardest. With anyone else, it would have been a nostalgic memory, but not in this case. I knew Nikki better than that. She had written it as a reminder, the kind I didn't need.

Reminders of droning professors and dorm rooms with window screens pushed out to let in the moths. In my most fragile state, it was where I always returned to. A semester swathed in a scuzzy film. I could overdose on that place if I let myself.

I eased out of the bedroom, baby monitor clipped to my waistband, and, starving for something pasty, something thick, I scooped mashed potatoes from the trash with my bare hands.

I paced the hallway, lingering outside the locked office. I wasn't surprised when the door didn't budge. A perpetually locked room hadn't seemed odd at first, not in the midst of diaper changes and belly button stumps, with a whole new house and life to adjust to. But as the fog in my brain lifted little by little, I found myself twisting the doorknob more often. More tired than curious, I never lingered for long.

A scorpion glow winked under the door as if someone were inside switching a fluorescent lamp on and off, on and off. *Mayday, Mayday.* It stopped when I blinked it away.

Through the baby monitor, static rustled on high like a broken bug zapper, like Harrison's dead wife murmuring from across some invisible divide. *Wake up wake up wake up.*

Other times, the noise erupted like laughter, like Nikki laughing her ass off. *Get it together,* she said. *You asked for this.*

CHAPTER 3
THEN

Nikki

I t started with a rumble. Then a moan, but not the porno kind.
Onstage, an undead beauty queen staggered forward while Miss California Dreaming hobbled between the gravestones in broken heels. Her bloodied sash trailed behind her like a forgotten tampon string.

You were supposed to think the zombies were beautiful but also want to shit your pants in terror.

Horrifying you was part of the plan.

I trained my eyes on Sadie. Like the other zombie extras, she had perfected her exaggerated lurch, her arms outstretched and her bare feet shuffling beneath her mud-stained gown, before improvising a somersault she'd been practicing for weeks. She wanted me to be honest with her, to tell her if the stagger and tumble was "too much."

Sadie was always too much. It was what I liked about her most. *Go get him, girl*, I wanted to yell when I watched that scene. Whoever he was. *Go peel the skin from his stupid face.*

The play: *Night of the Living Dead, Miss World Edition*.

My job on show nights: working the ticket booth.

My job during dress rehearsal week: costume mistress (title created by me).

Ms. Gloria, who had been in charge of costumes at Loch Raven College for thirty years, claimed that it was the strangest play she had ever seen (Zombies! Dressed as beauty queens!). The costumes, though, we both agreed, were a blast. She picked me for the job because I knew how to sew but also, I liked to think, because I appreciated the clothes. I kept the hangers straight and the costumes sorted by decade. I made to-do lists of everything that needed to be fixed. I was the girl who enjoyed the excitement of broken zippers, loose hems, and misplaced tiaras.

You know, fixable things. Mysteries I could easily solve.

Costumes were my second work-study job, after touring prospective students and their families around campus. Both were necessary to pay for room and board.

Since the semester began, I had learned how much money—or lack of money—mattered. It mattered how much money I had on my meal card if I wanted to eat more than two meals a day. And yeah, it mattered that I couldn't afford a navy-and-maroon Loch Raven T-shirt like all the other girls. Everything about money mattered because I didn't have any, and yet I had purposely chosen to live among people who did, to attend a college where the yearly tuition was higher than my father's salary.

Blame it on my dead mother, the one who'd insisted on me attending Loch Raven, the kind of place close to home but not too close. It was a place without boys, which she hoped would keep me safe from date rape, STDs, and teen pregnancy.

But also a place where I needed a full-ride scholarship to pay for tuition and two jobs to live in the dorms. I had promised her, though, and, as I'd told Sadie, it didn't feel right to break promises to the dead.

People who said money didn't matter were talking out of their ass. It didn't matter to them because they already had plenty. Just ask Eliza Jackson, whom someone found hanging, almost dead but not quite, in our residence hall bathroom during Orientation Week. Rumors said her loans fell through and she could no longer afford tuition. Or her meds. It blistered my insides to think about. And it made me not want to use the fourth-floor bathrooms, where I might see her dangling forever even though her parents had taken her home.

While the rest of us suffered through trust falls, she had been really suffering. While we snuck gulps of vodka from someone's monogrammed silver flask, Eliza almost didn't make it.

Of course, we didn't know what had really happened at first. The school called it "an accident." Like they weren't allowed to say "attempted suicide" or something. It was simply an "unfortunate incident" that we were supposed to move on from before classes began.

Only Sadie knew why I holed myself in my room for three straight days after that, why the rings under my eyes grew darker and darker. Because she was the only person at Loch Raven who knew how my mom had died.

I leaned forward to watch as Miss Longest Dead and Miss Broken Neck fought over a motorist's femur at the edge of the stage. So badass. First, the silent tug-of-war; then a purposeful fall into the pit below the stage. It was my favorite part, when the zombies were released into the audience to shock and terrify all the assholes wearing designer jeans.

Sadie wasn't impressed by any of it. She had wanted to be Miss Longest Dead. Instead, I'd dubbed her Miss Do Anything to Win and cut a big slit up the side of her dress. The slit was the director's idea. The grittier and the sexier, the better, he'd said. Whatever. It all looked like the opposite of sexy to me.

From the back row, I folded up into my seat, making myself smaller until someone walking by could see only feet, arms, and a head sticking out of the floor. Like a magic trick gone wrong.

I moshed to invisible music from inside the chair, Hole's "Miss World" stuck in my skull on a forever loop.

When the scene ended and the lights faded, a second curtain opened to reveal the interior of the farmhouse, a spotlight aimed at the kitchen table. The lead actors debated over how to survive while the zombies blotted their lipstick and waited in the wings.

I watched it the same way I always did—like someone had safely trapped me behind a wall of glass. Like I could see and hear everything, but no one could ever touch me.

I didn't need to watch the other scenes again and slipped out the side door, into the costume room, where the lighting was virus yellow and there was no heat, but at least I was alone. Wonderfully, completely alone.

I liked to hide among the racks of cast-off wedding dresses and cheerleader uniforms, the matted minks and studded armor. Loch Raven's costume room was three times the size of the space our high school drama club had. There were drawers full of nightgowns and lab coats, a dreamy collection of fake jewels hanging from makeshift hooks.

All of it had come from thrift stores and yard sales and families as they cleaned out their attics. I had briefly considered donating my mom's old clothes, but she didn't have much. Nothing I wanted to give away, I mean.

I leaned against the door and listened for the actors onstage. For once, nothing. At Loch Raven, where silence and privacy were impossible to find, the costume room was my sanctuary.

It was like this: everywhere else I went on campus felt like being caught in someone else's performance, wearing some other girl's costume, reciting lines someone else scripted for me. And even though the audience didn't really care about my role, they were watching anyway. Someone was always watching. I could feel their eyes, even with no one around.

Sometimes I brought a thin journal and curled up beneath the rows of dresses to write. It was a back-and-forth journal, one page written by me and one page written by Sadie before she handed it back to me. I usually wrote much more than one page, which balanced out the times Sadie wrote much less. She filled her pages with doodles instead of words, engorged mushrooms and stick people getting it on.

And sometimes we passed it back and forth like a conversation. Hence the name.

But it wasn't just the silence of the costume room that drew me in; it was really about the dresses.

It started when I was little. I could be hypnotized by tulle and sequins, all the frills and shine. Dresses for pageants and birthday parties. When I couldn't sleep, I counted dresses—bodices and corsets, petticoats and Peter Pan collars, fringe for flappers, and starched fabric for flight attendants. As a little girl, I slept with my Barbie-doll dresses under my pillow, hoping that by morning, each miniature gown would have magically sprouted into a life-size version hanging in my closet.

Like now, how I needed to study but instead was distracting myself with a high-necked Regency-era dress with pearl buttons at the wrists. It wasn't accurate to the time period, but no one gave a fuck. I'd been eyeing the dress for weeks.

"I need a higher slit," Sadie demanded, bursting in, the train of her dress catching in the door. With leaves tangled through her hair and the exaggerated hollows under her eyes, she looked more zombie than beauty queen, but it suited her.

I had twisted myself up too much to respond. Closing the back of my dress involved a full-body contortion. The stiff fabric wasn't meant to be fastened by the wearer.

I had once told my mom that I didn't want to ever get married. Her response: "Who is going to help zip your dresses and fasten your necklaces?"

As if that was the only reason she kept my father around. I remembered it again right after she died, and I'd been remembering it over and over again ever since. Maybe she had needed better clothes that didn't require complicated zippers. Or maybe, instead of a husband to help her, she had just needed better friends.

But that was before. Before Latin 101 and halfhearted sobriety pledges. Before my mom died wearing nothing but a blue terry cloth robe and a pair of sunglasses.

Before pulsed in my memory, a cavernous opening, an echo.

"Also, we're going out tonight." Sadie ripped at the side of her dress, too impatient to wait for me to help. "I just decided."

Going out was the last thing I needed to do, and I had a good excuse: an 8:00 a.m. test that we both needed to study for.

The test: Freshman Seminar, Gender and Popular Culture. Unit 2: "Dead Girls in Literature, Film, and Pop Culture." It was a class that sounded kind of cool and provocative until you were actually in it. The test would include questions like *This poet haunts popular culture with her tragic "sad girl" appeal.* And then we were supposed to name the dead woman. That was an easy example, though. Professor Weedler had a hard-on for Sylvia Plath. Great American poets, especially the tragic ones, were his thing.

It was repulsive. How he enunciated the word *penetrating* to describe her eyes, how he pinpointed phallic imagery like it was what we should care about, too. The way he flaunted his pit stains, because talking about her made him hot.

Especially disgusting when combined with the way girls worshipped Plath around Loch Raven. I loved her work, too, but they took it to another level. They talked about her as if she were still alive, their unopened copies of *The Bell Jar* an obvious addition to every clear-plastic backpack. Just like when Kurt Cobain died and suddenly everyone had a Nirvana T-shirt, even if they had never listened to his music.

They inked Plath's name on the inside of their wrists and took turns wearing a screen-printed crop top someone found at the mall with "I'm a Sylvia" inside a swollen red heart.

Sylvia everywhere you looked. A line of Sylvia Plath Barbie dolls, one for every occasion.

Smart Scholarship Sylvia. Fashion Magazine Sylvia. Sex Fiend Sylvia. Wife and Mother Sylvia. Dark Poetess Sylvia. American Sylvia. British Sylvia. Sylvia on the Beach. Sylvia in the Library. Sylvia, Unexperienced with Men. Sylvia, Who'd Bite Off the Best One's Cheek.

Stare long enough and their painted-on smiles covered up their very different inner screams.

There was a reason, it turned out, that my classmates cared so much about Plath, besides the fact that they all wanted to catch Professor Weedler's personal attention. My eyes twitched whenever I remembered what my roommate, Eileen, had told me the first week of class.

"You've heard the stories about the girls who died here, right?" She picked at a scabby pimple on her chin, her eyes bright with the joy of teaching me something. "People call it the Sylvia Club. Every year, one freshman kills herself by the end of the first semester. We almost had one this semester already."

A rush of bile burned my throat, and I swallowed it back down. We had barely made it through the first day of orientation when we heard about the dozens of deaths on campus. Suicides, all of them, going back as far as the sixties. Sadie called it urban legend, and I tried to label it a rumor, but it turned out, according to some of the older girls, that it was at least partially true.

Calling it a "club," though—that was news to me.

"For real. My cousin went to school here and told me so," Eileen had said. Casual, like it was an everyday thing. "This whole college is more haunted than a cemetery."

I tried to picture it: girls jumping from the cathedral steeple or guzzling too many pills in the cafeteria after hours, their final words uttered without anyone around to hear them. The images glowed inside my head too easily.

"That's horrible," was all I could choke out in response. The whirr in my skull sounded like the opening of a garage door, my mom suffocating on the other side.

But it wasn't horrible, not according to Eileen, who seemed as thrilled as the other girls to dress up for Professor Weedler's class and get moony about poetry, her own unread copy of Plath's poems tucked under her pillow. She was even more excited to take us on a "Death Tour" and identify the locations where several girls had died.

We already knew about Mary, the ghost that allegedly haunted the auditorium. And Abbie, who wasn't so much a ghost as a presence, her death two years before seeping into campus like blood through a bandage. She was the reason the old dormitory was closed, the reason girls kissed their cross necklaces and said prayers I didn't know the words to.

We never learned the names of the other girls who had died. Those stories were still buried.

There wasn't much time before Sadie's next scene, but she grabbed the Polaroid camera we kept on the accessories shelf, and I posed in my usual stance, the one she taught me: hands on my hips, chest out, Wonder Woman–style.

Together, we had hundreds of photos of us modeling vintage dresses, our heads always cropped out so our identities were unrecognizable. It started as a zine we made in high school, but we ran out of patience for that. It turned instead into a floating scrapbook full of headless dresses that we thought could eventually morph into a website if we ever learned how to make one.

We'd been stealing costume-room clothes since ninth-grade Drama Club. We wore the oversize moth-torn outfits to school dances and field trips, usually matched with Doc Martens or Chucks. In high school, it made us misfits, but in a cool way. Cool-ish. In college, dressing from the costume room just made us outcasts. The poor kind.

Lately, I'd been wondering about the women who owned the dresses first. If a dress could be haunted, what would the ghost say? How much would she hate someone like me for wearing the dress instead of her?

"You look like you just crawled out of your casket to eat my brains," Sadie said, both to me and her reflection. That was how the extras complimented each other during rehearsals. Looking like hell was a good thing for zombies. Except I wasn't the one who was supposed to resemble a corpse.

In the mirror, the domed shape of my dress engulfed me, my hair flat and limp against my cheeks, my eyes red and wet. I never used to cry, but now I was always on the verge of some emotion I didn't see coming. Like a sudden growth of grief that I'd thought was dormant.

This is what happens when you don't sleep enough, I could hear my mother saying. *You're taking too many classes. You're eating too much bread.*

She wouldn't have even recognized me, how I had sunk into myself. Weird instead of ambitious. Manic doll eyes instead of open doll smile.

Damn shame, she would have said, because that was the kind of thing she used to say.

"I'm not going out tonight," I added to the back-and-forth journal, pushing the book into Sadie's hands.

She ignored my protests and wrote, "Wherever we go, I'm not washing off my stage makeup."

Then, eyeing my face for a reaction, she spoke out loud. "You and that earring."

I wore only one small ruby stud, the last gift from my mom. The other one had been lost for weeks. Sadie and I had searched everywhere, from her car to our dorm rooms. I touched the single ruby in my left ear to make sure it was still there.

When the bare bulb above us flickered, I stared at it until I had an excuse for my watering eyes. That was how I always tried to see my mother, through a temporary blindness. If my vision blurred enough, she might appear behind my eyelids. Flashing light, shooting star, shrieking ghost. I didn't know what form she'd take, but when she finally appeared, I would be ready.

After five months, I hadn't seen her once. Not in a stranger's face on the street, which people at the funeral had promised would happen all the time. I looked. Hard. I looked for a woman with her eyes hidden. Because I couldn't picture her eyes anymore. She didn't show up in dreams, and I didn't randomly hear songs that reminded me of her unless I played them on purpose.

I waited until my tears retracted, then adjusted my bodice for another photo.

"Hey, pretty girl?" Sadie reached for my arm. "You okay?"

No, I was not okay. I didn't need to say it out loud for her to understand. She knew I didn't want to talk about my mom or the almost-dead girl in the fourth-floor bathroom or Sylvia Plath and her Loch Raven fan club.

We reset our bodies like actors primed to begin again, pretending that the previous moment hadn't happened at all. She snapped a second take with me wearing long white gloves.

No point in arguing about going out. She knew I'd follow her. Give me an extra ten minutes and I'd map out our route, including where to stop for gas and how to avoid bridge and tunnel tolls.

We had already planned to live together, grow old together, die together. And after death, we'd haunt each other, too, we joked. Except we meant it. We were those type of friends.

Finishing each other's sentences: check.
Reading each other's minds: check.
Saying yes even when we didn't want to: check.
"You owe me one," I wrote in the journal.
She winked on her way back to stage, like *what's new*.

Fast forward to the next part: her car, my eyeliner, Hole's *Live Through This* CD on repeat despite every dude we met telling us that "grunge is dead." We'd rage through "Asking For It" and slide right into "Jennifer's Body," doing our best Courtney Love, fury filled and messy with rage. We would tousle each other's hair until it tangled, a headless Peaches 'N Cream Barbie splayed on the dashboard. Then the sky would bruise into darkness, the highway bumping beneath our half-deflated tires. There would be a swollen moon, I could only guess.

CHAPTER 4
THEN

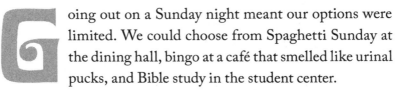oing out on a Sunday night meant our options were limited. We could choose from Spaghetti Sunday at the dining hall, bingo at a café that smelled like urinal pucks, and Bible study in the student center.

We had only gone to Bible study once. We sat in the back and tried to conjure Kurt Cobain on Sadie's grandmother's Ouija board. Big surprise, we were not invited back ever again.

But Sadie had already settled on a random house party downtown. Apparently, a dude she met at a gas station had invited her.

My plan: hang out, say hello, and if the party was lame—which it usually was—we could ditch early to eat banana splits in the campus cemetery and make it back to the dorms before curfew.

"You look cute," she grumbled as I climbed into her car.

That was her thing, fake pouting before we went out, like there was some kind of unspoken cuteness contest and she was afraid she wouldn't win. But she had nothing to worry about. With her fiery red hair and her baby doll dress—a dress I'd picked out first, a dress I would get back before the end of the night—she'd turn every head. Not to mention the zombie makeup she refused to wash off. She could reach out and pluck whatever she wanted.

I was a little jealous of the zombie makeup, so she added a few fake gashes to my cheeks at a red light.

Sadie's high school yearbook superlatives: Life of the Party and Biggest Flirt. Unlike me, who had been nicknamed "Most Organized." Which wasn't even one of the categories.

Most Organized. Or "Stage Manager," as Sadie called me, given my need to manage all the necessary details of our lives. Meaning I spent more time planning on the sidelines than actually enjoying life.

"But you put your own spin on it," Sadie had said to make it sound less pitiful. "You're my Stage Manager, and you do it with style."

Most Likely to Cry Her Way through Senior Year. That would have worked, too. Most Likely to Make a Joke about Death That No One Finds Funny. Most Likely to Write More Than She Speaks. And maybe, in a parallel world where teenagers appreciated vintage clothes, Best Dressed.

Tonight: thigh-high black boots and a very short, very silver disco dress that would fit Sadie perfectly when she was ready to switch.

Turned all the way up: "Miss World." More than once.

Campus shrank in the rearview, and our ears no longer itched with the needy hum of girls' voices. Within minutes of our drive, we were free from all of it.

Baltimore was, as usual, miserable, with scavenging pigeons and abandoned store windows. On the side of the highway, hubcaps and compacted roadkill. A man shooting up beneath the underpass. Charm City all the way.

Everywhere, redbrick row houses now looked stained with gray. I hated it in the way I hated everything I also loved. South Baltimore was where my mom had grown up, the part of the city she loved most. Driving past the Cross Street Market with the neon of the Inner Harbor at our backs bombarded me with memories. Happy memories were the worst kind.

The problem was that neither campus nor the city had ever felt like home. Campus at least had a dark beauty I respected. I could convince myself I had landed somewhere special, a place with mahogany desks and oil slicks of light. Stony paths led to headless rosebushes, and even that was charming in its own way. The city, less so.

"Whose place is this, again?" I asked when we pulled up to a chain of row houses with flat, crumbling fronts. Besides empty flowerpots and faded Orioles flags, the whole street looked deserted.

"Just some random dudes."

I started to roll down the windows but changed my mind. The city smelled like death, like the worst part of the ocean. An algae bloom, I'd later learn. The night before, the water temperature rose, and thousands of dead fish surfaced from the Inner Harbor down to Fort McHenry. The smell lingered everywhere, a stink worse than decay. Like the fish had died more than once, like they'd died and kept dying.

"It doesn't bother me." Sadie shrugged. "Death has to smell like something."

We reapplied our strawberry lip gloss and brushed hair off each other's shoulders, loose strands that floated away into the street.

Our chipped black nail polish glittered like chunks of mica worn down to the stubs.

"Slaughter me if this party sucks," she announced before knocking.

A buzz cut answered the door wearing a T-shirt stretched so tight against his chest it looked like it might rip. The way he leered at Sadie, starting at her bare legs and working his way up, I could already tell what kind of night it was going to be. I guessed he was in law enforcement or the military. He had that look about him—mean and muscled, ego for days. He reeked of it.

I peered around his shoulder to see the rest of the party, but all I saw was us, zombie girls, reflected in one of what must have been a dozen mirrors along the wall.

Baby dolls, but the cheap drugstore kind.

Haunted was the word Professor Weedler used to describe me. "You always look like you just saw a ghost," he said.

I wished.

Q: In a Pacific Northwestern town, her body is discovered, leading to a cryptic search for her killers.
A: Laura Palmer from Twin Peaks.

Q: Bilingual singer killed by the president of her fan club.
A: Selena.

Sadie would freak if she saw my flash cards. But First Year Seminar had become my hardest course, even though, out of six classes, it should have been the easiest. Weedler's lectures veered so wildly from the syllabus that I never knew what to study.

As far as I could tell, we completely skipped the chapter on women in business to focus on what he called "the pretty, dead ones." There was Marilyn Monroe, of course, Jayne Mansfield, Billie Holiday, Natalie Wood.

Dead and dead and more dead.

Except dead women weren't supposed to be an academic subject, not the way he taught. It was how excited he got, the way he turned death into a beautiful, horny thing. He closed his eyes and growled, low and rough. His heavy breathing like a phone-sex operator about to ask us what we were wearing under our dresses. And worse was the way the class responded to him, the way they batted their eyelashes, soaked up every word that leaked out of his mouth.

I kept showing up each week anyway, even though every time he introduced a new dead woman, my throat constricted with the image of my mom, her mouth lolled open, the taste of invisible gas trapped under my tongue.

When I'd found her, I was wearing a gold-star sticker at the corner of my eye and a dress she hated just to piss her off. Going to Weedler's class meant the memory never stopped festering.

"Let's switch," Sadie sang, dragging me by the arm to the small bathroom wedged beneath the stairs. The room echoed as we crammed in between the toilet and sink. "Your dress is cuter than mine."

Beneath her dress, she wore a lacy black thong and a push-up bra: underwear meant to be seen. I wore white cotton and a bra the color of my flesh.

"This isn't even your size," she said, lifting the flashy disco dress over her head. Then she stopped when she realized what she'd said. "You knew I would want to trade, didn't you?"

Of course I knew. She didn't have the ability to say no to sequins. I was surprised we'd made it all the way into the house before she asked to switch. She didn't call me Stage Manager for nothing. We switched shoes, too, because our feet had always been the same size. Twin feet, the only part of us that matched.

"Got any other surprises you want to tell me about?" Her hand hovered over the doorknob, eager to jolt back into the party.

I'd hidden Gatorade and Advil back in her dorm room, underneath her pillow so she would find them when she needed them most. She could call it stage managing, but she didn't know I did it more for myself. Switching outfits was about me, what I wanted to end the night wearing. Even the Gatorade was for me, so I didn't have to take care of her the next day.

Not that I'd ever tell her no. She knew that, too.

She gave me and my dress a last look. "Don't make me remind you to have fun."

She didn't have to remind me. We were supposed to be having the time of our lives. We were supposed to be reckless and impulsive, dim-witted enough to believe we had all the time in the world. Smart little sluts who brushed up against failure but didn't let it stick. We were supposed to spin through revolving doors like we were high on whipped cream fumes, then charm the pants off anyone who judged us. We were meant to pose for every flashing camera and kiss each other, or whoever, on command. *Fall into open arms*, the world seemed to tell us. And Sadie took the message as a challenge. *Show a little more leg. Flash your tits at truck drivers. Kiss your middle finger before you flip off every suit-wearing dipshit in the HOV lane. Make it up as you go along, and smile while you're doing it.*

The row house was narrow, and everyone crowded in the kitchen. Death metal blared from a stereo in the corner while I tried to memorize dead-women trivia. Every time I looked up, I caught a shard of silver light as Sadie drank and danced, willing drunk dudes to stare at her ass. I pulled my short dress down each time hers rode up.

We were the only girls.

"Who is Sylvia Plath?" one of the dudes asked, eyeing my flash cards over my shoulder. Besides his dimples and creased shirt, he looked like the others—taller than most and attractive in a boring sort of way. His nails were cleaner than mine. He probably played tennis or owned his own skis.

"The poet? She wrote *The Bell Jar*?" When his blank expression didn't budge, I added, "She killed herself by sticking her head in the oven?"

Still nothing. My face burned from mentioning how she'd died. It wasn't what she should have been known for. Except I knew most people associated Plath with her death. Not this guy, though. He didn't have a clue.

"Nikki looks a lot like young Sylvia, doesn't she? Over there in the corner, hiding underneath that shy smile," Weedler had asked last week in the middle of lecture.

On the screen at the front of the room, Sylvia, blond and tan, cheesed for the camera in a bikini. Not so dark and depressing after all. The opposite of how he'd described her. But my hair wasn't blond, and I definitely hadn't been smiling. All the other girls had turned to look at me anyway. The worst was the way he'd winked to let me know it was all in good fun. Gag. When I stayed after class to ask for studying tips, he scratched his stubble.

"Come to my office for a one-on-one conference," he'd said. "Let's talk."

Not a chance, pervert. I'd seen him stroking another girl's hair after class, inviting her to apply for his mentorship program. It happened more than once. Worse was how he'd literally panted like a dog, tongue out and wagging, the first time he ever mentioned Sylvia Plath. Sadie and I busted out laughing as soon as we stepped into the hallway, though it got less funny the second time he did it.

If he had any idea about my mom, maybe he'd stop gushing about how Sylvia Plath died. Knowing him, he would probably get off on all the horrific details.

"Imagine it," he crooned, slowly rubbing his hands together as we stared at the projector slides. "Her head, the oven, the tape sealing the empty gaps to protect her children. Can you think of anything more poetic?"

My classmates nodded at his every word. *Yes*, they agreed, hand to heart. *Her death was so poetic.*

At least our textbook kept it simple, summing up the short Plath section by saying, "In the end, her work is much more compelling than her death."

Weedler's one published book, something densely academic that had been out of print for years, was about Plath. He was going to fit her into the syllabus no matter what, I figured.

It was what the other students wanted, the unit they had all been waiting for. Sylvia Plath was the bridge to the stories that started during Orientation Week, ghosts in the dorms, well-dressed spirits who slammed doors and flicked off the lights while you shampooed your hair.

No one ever missed Weedler's class during his Plath lectures. Their perfume was never stronger, their mascara never thicker than on those days. So devoted that they composed their own lovesick poems in the margins of their textbook, hoping he would see.

Dimples disappeared for what seemed like only thirty seconds and returned with a glass of something fizzy and dark that burned going down. I said "okay" instead of "thank you," all my good manners searing the back of my throat. I couldn't make myself smile at him if someone paid me.

Sadie met my eyes and collapsed her face like a mime, exaggerated weeping. Her favorite party game: guessing what a man's sex face looked like. She was the expert, after all. At first glance, she could guess if he was a Weeper, a Screamer, a Rager, or a Kitty Cat. Dimples, she seemed to guess, was a Weeper: the kind of guy who cried during or after sex, who was so sensitive he ruined the mood. I focused on my lone ice cube to keep from laughing.

Q: This model and actress was pregnant when the followers
of a famous cult murdered her.
A: Sharon Tate.

Dimples, in the middle of telling me a story about growing up in a family of doctors, tipped my chin to get my attention. God, he was tall. I blinked, suddenly exhausted and bleary eyed. "Sorry, say again?"

I shot Sadie a look to say, *Let's leave soon, please. I need to sleep and study and drink a gallon of water and not be around all these creepers.* At least, that was what I hoped my face said.

But she had already moved on. She flitted through the crowd like a hummingbird, her sparkles twinkling along the mirror edges. The mirrors were affixed to every surface, creating new corners and hallways, backward doors and double floating windows. Mirrors everywhere, clear and un-smudged.

In one mirror, the face glinting back at mine was a girl I didn't recognize. Her coiled perm and head-to-toe Loch Raven colors looked like an eighties pep rally. She took her time scanning my outfit, then offered a taut, pitying smile. No eyes, only gaping cavities. I blinked to make her disappear.

Dimples squared his jaw and tapped the bottom of my glass. "Drink up. The fun is just getting started."

After that, the party traveled from room to room, level to level, the men challenging each other to chug beers and turning up the music so loud that the only way to hear the person next to me was for his mouth to graze my ear. Everyone stayed inside to avoid the death smell. New dudes entered covering their mouths and noses with stretched-out collars.

In an upstairs bedroom, where all the guys played a drunken game of darts, there were no clocks to check the time, but the pitch of the sky was too dark and muddled for stars. That's how I knew we were already late for curfew.

I found a doll-size skeleton in one of the bedrooms, the skinless, sexless kind used in an anatomy class. I painted his ribs and his arms with the gold nail polish from the bottom of my baby backpack. First his strong parts, then his fragile parts. The glitter glowed along his joints where the paint pooled.

"I am I am I am," I painted inside the medical textbook on the desk next to him. My nail polish brush feathered every letter.

"Having fun?" Dimples asked, finding me again. His hot breath left my cheek wet. I didn't mind his soft features, I decided, the baby fat still hanging on in his cheeks. "Hey, you know you're only wearing one earring?"

I stared up at a nearly shredded movie poster of Marilyn Monroe high on the wall. You know the picture—the one with her standing over a grate in her famous air-lifted dress.

"Where's her face?" Tiny craters had been pierced through every part of her dress. Her head was a black hole.

He laughed and grabbed my waist. "Target practice."

When I finally found Sadie in the bathroom, she opened the door only a crack. Her zombie wounds were smeared, and I couldn't see whoever was inside with her.

"Look, I'm going to go check out Darren's place, two blocks over."

Darren, I predicted, was the guy at the party with at least one barbed wire tattoo. Knowing Sadie's type, he was probably shortish and scrappy. A Screamer.

If Darren had a rooftop balcony, our little curfew wasn't going to keep Sadie from seeing it. A balcony overlooking the harbor was code-speak for hooking up. Even I knew that. I didn't mention that they'd have to deal with the smell. It probably didn't matter.

"Just wait for me, dollface," she said. "I won't be long. I pinkie swear."

When I tried to accuse her of "slurring," my own wobbly voice made "slurring" sound like "slurry." The room swam, though I couldn't remember finishing my drink or the one after it. My flash cards were gone, forgotten in one of the rooms or spilled outside when I'd tried—and failed—to find fresh air.

Images of dolls with their eyes thumbed shut, their plastic hands open and jointless, danced each time I blinked. Dolls in college T-shirts. Dolls for target practice. Dolls with snapped necks, broken by nooses.

On her way down the hall, Sadie grabbed Dimples by the back of the neck, kissed him hard, then walked away to leave him picking her hair out of his mouth. Clean-cut rich boys were her type, too.

We were improbable friends, everyone told us, our differences hard to reconcile. But she had been there for me every time it mattered, even agreeing to go to Loch Raven when she could have gone somewhere cheaper, somewhere with more boys and fewer nuns.

She was the one who had stayed with me while I cried and screamed and puked after we found my mother's body.

And after Eliza Jackson was taken away by one loud ambulance during Orientation Week, Sadie held my hand while I rocked back and forth. It wasn't that I didn't want the reminder of my mother. It was that I didn't want to turn into her.

> *Q: Found by her teenage daughter, this woman sealed herself in her garage and left the engine running. Her blue robe smelled like gasoline. She didn't leave a note.*
> *A: My mom.*

"You're not her. You wouldn't do that," Sadie had said, referring to the way my mom died—alone, where she knew I would find her. No note, no hint at what she had been going through.

In an attempt at humor, Sadie added, "We're Thelma and Louise. If you die, I better be coming with you."

My laugh was the bark of a wet seal. "Yeah, okay. You have my word. You know I would never leave without you."

For her friendship, I'd give her a pass on kissing whoever she wanted. She was my only real friend, and I was hers, even if I couldn't tell her what was really bothering me, how I couldn't stop thinking about dead girls. Like once I'd heard the Sylvia Club story, even if it was only just a story, Loch Raven felt like a different place, a campus full of phantom shapes and throbby wounds. Who needed zombies when you had actual ghosts? The kind who wore pearls and smoked long cigarettes because they still thought smoking was glamorous.

Pretty ghosts. Ghosts without pagers and email accounts. Ghosts who didn't know they were dead.

They were walking among us, and we didn't know it.

Sadie didn't care about any of that unless it meant having fun, and I couldn't blame her. Maybe, at least for one night, I could try it her way. Impulsive. Reckless. I found Dimples and let him kiss me, too.

He didn't ask my name, but I asked for his. Harry. It felt like something I should know.

Okay. Everything was going to be okay. That single word laced through me, and maybe I had been saying it all night.

Okay and okay and okay. Because everything had always been okay before.

CHAPTER 5
NOW

Sadie

The day I met Harrison Walsh—heart doctor, golfer, HOA volunteer, husband to Nikki, father to Caroline—he didn't remember me. Why would he? I was his dead wife's friend from eighteen years before, and we'd met only once. But there I was, at his front door. He didn't recognize me from the funeral, didn't know if I meant it when I claimed Nikki had been my family. He had no reason to believe anything I said, but he let me in anyway.

The funeral hadn't been the worst part, and neither was the day I heard how she'd died. The viewing, though, when I walked into the packed funeral home—that was hell.

We hadn't spoken in almost two decades, and suddenly it was too late. She was gone, and I couldn't believe that she'd left on purpose. Not Nikki. Nothing could convince me she chose to end her life. Anyone who thought otherwise clearly didn't know her.

No one recognized me at the viewing, which meant she hadn't

kept any friends from her old life. People whispered. Not a funeral kind of whisper. More a scandalous, gossipy kind of mumbling that I thought, for a moment, I had caused just by existing.

Since I still looked like myself but with puffy eyes, I hoped she would look like herself, too. And she did. Her hair, only a little shorter. Her skin, unblemished. Makeup too thick, but yes, she looked like my childhood friend. My Nikki. Then I understood the whispering. She wasn't tastefully dressed in that open casket. No understated black church dress to wear for eternity.

Nikki wore an orange satin cocktail dress. Tangerine orange. Inside-of-a-flame orange. Net skirt underneath, low neckline, and spaghetti straps. It was a costume-room dress that I had adopted and worn on the worst night of our lives. I thought she'd destroyed it. The stains were hidden in the casket, but I knew they were still there.

When I'd shown up at her house, I told myself I wanted to claim any other things that belonged to me and to pay my condolences during his tragedy. I'd called it *his tragedy*. After all Nikki and I had been through, surely I didn't deserve to grieve, too.

From the curb, I'd watched a petite blond woman knock on the door, dabbing invisible tears from her eyes. She wore one oven mitt to hand-deliver a casserole to the grieving widower, then bared her teeth on her way back down the driveway, disappointed, I guessed, that Harrison hadn't invited her in.

"I love your hair," he'd said, when he opened the door for me. Maybe he let me in because I didn't have a casserole or an oven mitt. The red hair, I would later learn, didn't hurt. He would also eventually tell me that the orange dress was part of Nikki's last wishes, to be cremated in it, according to a will she'd had drafted weeks before her death.

Nikki and her perfect life, the huge kitchen, the jewelry she flashed at her own funeral without even trying—how did she end up with that life and not me? We had experienced the same disastrous year at Loch Raven College, the same secrets that had led both of us to drop out of school and never speak again. But she'd ended up with the dream house. She had everything, and all I had was a roach-infested apartment and a rusted car. No family or friends except my coworkers.

I didn't feel guilty about sleeping with Harrison. The guilt would come later, too. When I saw him that day in his doorway, his pretense and good manners from the funeral finally peeled away, I understood what Nikki had seen in him: a way out.

After another sleepless night, I watched the gray-haired woman across the street shuffle to her mailbox, clutching a stack of outgoing mail. With her favorite fur wrap draped around her shoulders and her orange lipstick, she resembled a dramatic retired actress. Harrison once told me that her husband died several years before, and her only child worked too much to visit. She lived in the only rental in Hidden Harbor.

Like so many other days before, she slid her mail in the box and forgot to swing up the red flag. She reminded me of my grandmother that way. I always waited until she went back inside before running across the street to raise the flag for her, so the mailman remembered to take her letters. It had happened enough times that she must have known. She must have seen me running.

On that particular blur day, after the run between mailboxes, I let Rhiannon nap in my arms while I watched a snippet of *Charm City Brunch with V and G*.

V and G—Virginia and Georgia—had designed their whole

show that morning around one of Baltimore's own, the dearly missed Annie Minx and her final book, *The Self-Care Cure*. An instant bestseller, they cheered.

"Annie Minx—or whatever her real name was—never used to show her face. Remember that? Masks and costumes and whatnot," Virginia said, her bobbed black hair like a helmet. She was the daughter.

Nikki used to wear a curly red wig and a veil to hide her identity, but readers and internet sleuths had figured it out. Now that her last book had been released, a year after her death, the world, at least a small part of it, seemed to care all over again.

Georgia, with her identical helmet bob, shimmied her shoulders toward the camera. "For those of you watching from home, don't worry. I would never hide my moneymaker."

Virginia pretended to swat her mother, cackling the whole time. Hilarious. They were the kind of mother and daughter who looked nothing alike but tried to fool everyone by wearing matching outfits. Duplicate green blazers over lace camisoles. Identical pink-stained lips, eyebrows threaded and arched like mean-girl mannequins.

"And now her last book, *The Self-Care Cure: Healing What Haunts You*—which is fantastic, by the way—has made a splash," Georgia read from the teleprompter. "And thank God for self-care. I. Am. In. Need."

When I closed my eyes to envision self-care, something else barreled toward me: steel-toed boots and trampled grass and dog-eared pages. Ouija boards and eyeliner thicker than coal.

I'd never been much of a reader, so Annie Minx and her books hadn't been on my radar before Nikki's death. Not even a little. Still, something about the elaborate way Nikki had tried to hide her identity made me uncomfortable. The masks and costumes were clearly a marketing ploy to set her apart from the other influencers, but plenty of writers used a pseudonym. Why bother with a ridiculous wig when she could have chosen no picture at all?

First time I ever wore a wig: with Nikki in our high school production of Guys and Dolls. She helped me find a curly auburn wig, darker than my natural color, twisted up in little Medusa ringlets. "Beauty Queen," she'd called me, and pretended to add a crown on top.

All her books except the newest one were lined up on the living room shelves: *The Pretty Girl Hustle*, *Finding Your Posse*, and *How to Overthrow Your Sloppy Boundaries*. I didn't have to read them to know they weren't my kind of thing. Annie Minx's voice, unlike Nikki's, imitated an artificial bad-girl vibe doling out tough love. *Get out of bed, you lazy slut!* were the giant words that greeted you on her website.

The Nikki I knew would never have written low-key therapy for rich women; she wouldn't have cared about facial yoga and matcha mud wraps or anything that seemed more trendy than helpful. My girl was scrappy and fierce, her clothes mended with safety pins, her fishnets tattered. We would have made fun of books with *hustle* in the title.

Georgia leaned forward and readjusted her glasses as if they were real. "The wildest thing—did you hear this? That subscribers to Annie Minx's mailing list received an email from her this week. A message from beyond the grave, people are calling it."

Virginia, with a razor of aggression, added, "Yeah, the newsletter is creepy. Talk about haunting final words."

I coughed and couldn't stop coughing, like I'd swallowed something I wasn't meant to swallow. Bullshit. There were no messages from the dead. The publisher or her agent must have set up her emails to coincide with the book release. Still, I opened my phone to search for the text of the newsletter they'd mentioned. It wouldn't have come to my inbox. I had never signed up for Annie Minx's emails, barely even knew Annie Minx existed. I had never made the connection that she and Nikki were the same person. My previous life didn't involve self-help or books like hers.

It didn't take long to find the newsletter online, but I couldn't read more than a sentence at a time without stopping to slow my heart.

And in case you get worried, Beauty Queen, remember that I always have a plan.

My stomach bottomed out. Part of Annie Minx's appeal, as I now understood, was that everyone thought her message was curated just for them. All her fans wanted to be Minx's BFF. But that newsletter didn't sound like it was meant for thousands of readers.

It sounded like she had one specific reader in mind.

No. Not a chance. There was no way I'd been on her mind before she died, before she timed a newsletter to release with the launch of her last book. No matter that we used to call each other "Beauty Queen."

She'd been just as vague in the book's dedication. *To the hungry poet inside all of us. To my bestie.* Or maybe it wasn't cryptic at all. Maybe I knew exactly what she was talking about.

Self-care costume wigs fake glasses son of a bitch cure cure cure.

Rhi smiled up at me with her bright eyes, suddenly awake, all slobber and gums. I'd been ranting out loud.

I'm falling apart over here, I almost texted Harrison. Literal pieces of me dropped all over the house. My hair in the drain, my sloughing skin settled in the grout lines.

But what kind of woman did that? Not a woman still expecting a marriage proposal. Not a woman trying to prove she could manage everything in the same effortless way her former best friend, a bestselling author, once did.

If Caroline and Harrison had seen the newsletter, no doubt it would have torn their fresh wounds wide-open all over again. I'd never know, though, because they didn't talk about Nikki. They believed, like the rest of the world, that she had wanted to die. Maybe they thought the newsletter was just another suicide note she left behind.

There was no evidence anymore of the kitchen fire that had almost burned down the house, one of Nikki's reckless acts in those last months. The gas leak that could have killed them all—Nikki clearly had a death wish. That was what I was supposed to believe.

I wasn't sure what really happened, but it didn't involve Nikki making a choice that would leave her daughter behind. Not after her own mother had died that exact way. Or those tragic girls we used to tell stories about on campus.

Unless.

Unless she had been guilted by the same splinter buried under my skin, the same secret we pinkie swore not to ever talk about again. It sure seemed that she had wanted to remind me, in print, that even though our friendship was broken, our pact wasn't.

I would never leave without you.

Walk it off, girl, Annie Minx would have told me. *Calm your tits.*

The smell of decomposition, almost sweet, filled my nose, like something had died in the walls. I made myself stand up. In the corner of my eye, what looked like a muddy handprint appeared on the banister. I hadn't noticed it before.

When the woman from Human Resources called, my hands and hips held the weight of both baby and laundry basket. I slid the phone between my shoulder and my cheek until I could drop the hamper with a satisfying thump.

"Ms. Stone, we're sorry to inform you..." Her voice hollowed, faraway and fading. Then a long pause. Even her pauses sounded garbled.

My body's reaction was instant. A ticking at the base of my skull like a time bomb. I knew the warning signs. I could see the panic coming. A thick, guttural groan trapped itself in my throat. "Downsizing" was the only other word I heard her say.

"Can you repeat that?" I croaked, but she had already hung up.

I closed my eyes and counted to ten. The room sloped like my vision had been nudged off-balance.

On the mantel, a picture of a woman in matching lipstick and cardigan beamed down on me. It was the only photo of Nikki still framed at Caroline's request. The room did that tilting thing, that upside-down vertigo thing. Gulping at the air only made it worse.

I secured Rhiannon in her swing just in time.

The first time someone else noticed was at my gynecologist's office, one month postpartum, while I waited in my paper robe. Rhiannon rested in the stroller a few feet away. Was it too cold for her? I had forgotten her socks, and surely Dr. Cruz would have opinions about that; the nurses had already given me the side-eye, judging me, I was sure, for all the ways I lacked as a mother.

Heart rate: accelerating. Skin: heating. Eyelids: twitching.

Framed sailboats and hot-air balloons lined the walls. I narrowed my eyes to focus on the one with the sunset, the faded watercolor horizon. Pretty and boring. Safe.

But I hadn't mailed out the birth announcements yet or scheduled the professional family photos—all the things other moms posted about. How did they have the energy to plan it all? How did they know what to plan in the first place? I hadn't even taken Rhi's one-month photo with one of those little chalkboard tablets I'd seen all over Pinterest.

If I stared close enough at the hot-air balloon picture, the blurry people in the basket appeared to scream. They were the suggestion of people, hazy lines where people might be, their mouths open wide.

I gripped the edge of the paper-lined bed, forgetting to breathe, pasty with sweat. So much sweat. I couldn't remember the last time I'd slept. A pain shot through my middle and down my arm. Wrong. Everything. Wrong.

When the doctor finally arrived, I gasped and blurted, "I think I'm having a heart attack." Tears burned inside my eyes each time I blinked. I couldn't stop blinking.

He tapped my wrist, pulse-searching, and I sealed my lips tight until he reminded me to breathe. That simple instruction seemed so generous that I cried more. Why hadn't anyone else reminded me?

"How long has this been going on?" he asked. "Do you have a history of panic attacks?"

Before I'd had a baby, no. The old me—the party girl and occasional actress, the sometimes bartender when she needed rent money, the woman who found the best clothes at flea markets and avoided serious relationships—didn't panic about anything. But it had happened at least a dozen times since I gave birth and since I moved into the house. Loss of breath, numb fingers, clouded vision. It didn't take much to trigger me. A feverish plugged milk duct in the middle of the night or the paralyzing fear of driving Nikki's car. Sometimes I couldn't trace the root. Sometimes the root didn't exist.

But a debilitating attack, to use Dr. Cruz's words, was new. I willed him not to say *baby blues*. I hated that term. Because when I simply felt blue, it didn't feel the same as wanting to scream into a pillow until I choked on the feathers.

He frowned to make sure I paid attention. "I am going to refer you to a doctor I know. Dr. Norton specializes in this sort of thing, for new moms."

It was days before I realized I'd lost the other doctor's number. I could have called the office to ask, or I could have looked her up myself, but I didn't.

Out the back door, I dry-heaved into barely sprouted thyme and rosemary, withered and half-brown. A kitchen garden. Before I'd arrived, Nikki had planted tulips, but I ripped out the bulbs and planted herbs instead. I'd wanted to start over, even though I grew up in the city and knew nothing about plants or soil. But I'd stopped tending before I really started.

I stumbled into kneeling, my knees sinking into wet dirt, and it almost felt like praying. Or what I thought prayer might feel like: tunneled concentration and a wash of emotion, eyes brimmed and stinging with tears.

No job meant no childcare meant no chance of ever feeling like myself again. Without a college degree, I already knew there weren't many options. I had searched enough times before. Especially not options with childcare. With my own money, I had wanted to start my own bank account again, to give myself—and Rhi—a safety net. Until Harrison decided to marry me, I needed a "just in case."

I gagged until my chest hurt from the effort. Nothing came up. My mouth to the dirt, my lips caked with it. The blade of grass on my tongue not as sharp as I would like.

If I could tell myself to calm down, I would. Panic didn't work that way, though, not for me. This panic felt different, like it had real weight to it, a real middle and a real bottom. The only feeling I could compare it to was mourning. It was how I'd felt when I lost my grandmother, the woman who raised me. I wore that grief like a second skin that wouldn't peel away.

You aren't going to hear from me for a while, but you will see me again, Nikki had sent to thousands of readers. Either a promise or a threat.

For just a moment, her eyeless face appeared in the window overlooking the yard, distorted at the edges but clear enough for me to know it was her. She shook a blurry fist, her pinkie finger extended.

Inhale, I told myself. *Do not think about the past. Exhale. Pretend not to feel Nikki watching from the kitchen window. Nikki is dead.*

In the right light, every doorway curved into a pointed arch. Even chimneys looked like towers. Had Nikki seen it, too, that with enough cloud cover, a gated neighborhood could turn into a shaded campus? An unguarded house into a barred dormitory?

The sun suddenly flared, burning through the clouds, and a lazy bee bumbled near my head before moving on to something sweeter. Still doubled over, I half listened for Rhiannon through the open door. The neighbors, Mr. and Mrs. Graham, grew a garden designed for bees and butterflies to pollinate. A pollination station. I knew because Mrs. Graham had told me about it when I first moved in, though she stopped talking to me after she saw Rhi.

When Rhiannon was born, Nikki had been dead less than a year. We could all do the math.

Get up, bitch.
I channeled Annie Minx's voice ordering me off the ground, unimpressed at my melodramatic huffing and puffing. *Drink your water. Move your ass. Think about somebody else for a change*, she would say.

When my heartbeat leveled enough for me to move again, I turned the wheel on Rhi's swing to replay the weasel song, fighting the urge to curl into a ball on the carpet. Harrison would come home and find me there, an empty husk. A Sadie-shaped body, slumped and stiff-legged.

Mannis and Brill, my now-former coworkers, texted to invite me to happy hour after they'd heard the news, but I wouldn't be good company, not in my empty-husk state.

Another coffee was not what I needed, but I headed for the kitchen as if led by a string.

It took a few minutes to realize the woman slouched over the kitchen table was Nikki. She wore a peach and ivory ball gown with ruffles up to her chin, just like a Barbie doll we used to keep on the dashboard of my car. Her briny smell preceded her, like dead fish, but swampier and full of rot.

Not Real. I wiped my eyes with a dish towel. This was Anxiety and Lack of Sleep. This was Postpartum Something or Other. Exhaustion and Hallucination.

She stretched her legs out long and drew an eggplant in permanent marker on each palm.

No. I sealed my eyes tight and ignored my racing heart. *Go away, go away, go away, go away.*

"Do you have a tampon?" Her voice pierced like a barb, and it sounded so much like her, my tears hit my hand before I realized they had fallen.

"Bathroom, under the sink. But I might be all out."

She smashed her eggplant hands together to smear the ink. "If you don't have a tampon, let me have one of your bras. My tits are so saggy now." Then, as if to prove she wasn't lying, she squeezed her boobs together and sighed down the bib of her dress. "Man, I used to have the best rack."

Nikki never spoke that way. But maybe that was what happened to everyone in death—you became the version of yourself you couldn't be when you were alive. Because if I were really speaking to Nikki, wouldn't she be furious with me? Wouldn't we need to discuss what had happened since she died, how I'd moved into her house and had a baby with her husband?

At least I waited until you were dead, I would have said. It was what I had been telling myself.

Her face was blotchy with gashes, like zombie makeup. A zombie beauty queen. She looked and smelled the part. I tried to focus on her eyes, to see if rage or sorrow lived back there now, but black holes were melted into her skin where her eyes should have been. It wasn't as disconcerting as it sounds.

"We could move to a new house," I used to suggest to Harrison. The three of us could have easily started over in a new place, one without Nikki's memory oozing from the walls. But there was more sentimental value in that home than I had let myself comprehend. The house in Hidden Harbor was where they had raised Caroline. He would never move.

"It's your house now. Every room of it," she said, reading my mind like she always did.

I guzzled a cup of water and watched her through the glass as it tipped against my nose. When she yanked at a sequin on her bodice, the threads popped, and I waited for the rest to unravel.

She snapped her fingers to get my attention. "Sleep deprivation makes you weak. You can't afford any weakness. Not now."

"I'm not weak." Neither of us believed it.

My best friend. I had once missed her so badly I couldn't breathe, but eventually the absence of her friendship became part of me, too. Now all the years between us, especially the ones we'd missed, rashed together under my skin.

Her arms dissolved against each other like a watery vapor and her voice trailed, echoing through a long, bottomless hallway.

"You owe me," she said before she left.

She could have been talking about so many things.

CHAPTER 6
THEN

Nikki

Welcome to Loch Raven College, the only Catholic all-women's college in Maryland. Loch Raven was founded by Sister Mary Agnes, who originally named the school Saint Mary's Academy of Loch Raven due to our proximity to the Loch Raven Reservoir. Was it named after real ravens? The legends say maybe, but I think yes.

Notice the classical Gothic architecture of one-hundred-year-old stained glass windows and decorative finials. There are even gargoyles at the top of historic Hope Hall. Pretty cool, right?

Inside, you'll notice the long hallways and vaulted ceilings, the nuns in full habit. No, not all the professors are nuns. Just enough to keep us on our toes.

Choose from classes like Latin, public speaking, literature, and philosophy. Freshman Seminar 101 is a favorite among, well, the freshmen.

Fun fact: Loch Raven College was established in 1895. Our location, a private liberal arts college north of Baltimore City but secluded from the city's hustle and bustle, promises allergies in the spring, humidity in the summer, and frost all winter long.

I joke, but we do offer a little bit of everything.

As you journey across campus, take special note of the field hockey team, the cathedral, and the massive fountain of a swan swallowing his own spit. The students call him Seymour. Don't be surprised if you see girls all dolled up for Movie Star Monday. It's the first day of Spirit Week.

Yes, I agree, it is a stunning campus. The fountain never collects too many leaves before someone removes them. Even the statue of Sister Mary Agnes, that woman over there with her large hands cupped to the air, remains unblemished from the weather and bird droppings.

Turn left, past the dining hall, and you'll find the Sabi Clair Auditorium, where Mary Matherly overdosed, either onstage during a rehearsal or up on the catwalk, depending on who you ask. The stories say her fiancé dumped her for her older sister. She still bops across the stage for her perpetual curtain call, heartbroken and vengeful, to this day.

Keep going down the hill, past the parking lots, to the library we share with Patrick College. Every full moon, a ghost named Betsy swings from the mezzanine railing, clutching the invisible noose around her neck. She's a prankster, we've come to learn, sometimes knocking books from the shelf or flipping the pages a cute boy is trying to read.

We end our tour at Hope Hall, where everyone has heard about Abigail, a girl we would have met if we got here two years earlier. Abbie jumped from the roof, reason unknown. The mystery surrounding her death has shut down Hope Hall ever since. Perhaps only the lazy-eyed gargoyles know what really happened.

This ends our tour, folks. Thank you for spending your afternoon with us. The bookstore, for all your Loch Raven College swag, is open for another hour. We hope to see you here next fall.

CHAPTER 7
THEN

I woke up fully dressed except for one sock, sweating through my dorm-room sheets. I sat up too fast and quickly realized two things: I was late for class, and I was about to throw up.

The nausea toppled me out of bed and into one of the miniature stalls in our shared bathroom across the hall; I barely made it to the toilet. Spitting and sweating, I clutched the edge of the bowl and waited for my insides to lurch again. My pretty little party dress was trashed.

The longer I sat, my nausea on a low simmer, my skull gripped by a looming migraine, the more I felt the rest of it. My legs, mostly, my inner thighs.

Natalie Wood, the Black Dahlia, Dorothy Stratten.

I heaved again.

Q: Her death is made to look like a suicide in this dark comedy from 1988.
A: Heather from Heathers.

I slumped on the floor and remembered: flash cards, dimples, balconies, curfews. They were cusp-memories disappearing along the curve. It wasn't ridiculous to sleep with a guy at the party, I told myself. College girls did that kind of thing. Sadie did that kind of thing. Just not me.

Judging by the midmorning light, I had missed both my morning classes. I had missed Weedler's test.

Shit. Shit, shit, shit, shit, shit, shit.

When I stumbled out of the stall to the sink, I shielded my eyes from the overhead fluorescent. The only other girl in the bathroom avoided looking at me, but when she did, she flapped her hands in front of her face like a tiny bird.

"It's you. You helped me at orientation." She pulled down her headphones, and her hair bristled into staticky needles. "The cold water, remember? That really worked."

Yes, I remembered. We had both been in the bathroom during the first day of orientation, cheesy trust-building activities broken up by student-ID photos and campus tours. She'd stood at the mirror with her palms flat against the sink and her head down. Her breath sounded shallow enough to almost make my chest seize. It looked like the start of a panic attack, the kind my mom used to get in public places.

"Cold water on the back of your neck will help," I'd told the girl, trying not to draw too much attention, which I knew would only make things worse. "It's a sensory thing. Try it."

I pretended I wasn't wearing a matted dress with a puke-stain overlay. "I'm glad it helped."

The song trickling from the girl's headphones: "Killing Me Softly with His Song" by the Fugees.

When I made it back to the room, Eileen had returned. Her wet ponytail dripped down her Loch Raven sweatshirt. She didn't say anything, but watched as I tripped into the wall in search of my toothbrush and shoes. As if rushing to get dressed would change anything. My empty stomach rumbled.

There were twenty of us on my floor, a long hall with two girls in each boxy room, shower stalls at the end of the hallway. It always smelled like a mix of perfume and mildew. Houndstooth rugs covered the wooden floors, and framed maps of the Loch Raven Reservoir and Gunpowder Falls lined the halls—a polished and intentional darkness. So much of our hair collected in the corners and jammed up the drains because we were always shedding, no matter how hairy or hairless we seemed to be.

Sadie and I weren't allowed to room together. Instead, we were encouraged to live apart and make new friends, a fact of our "college experience" that I was still bitter about. Most days it was enough to know she slept only one floor away. The rest of the time, I stayed bitter.

"So, things got a little crazy here last night," Eileen said, dropping into her most dramatic tone. "Some girls upstairs found a Ouija board and were having a séance; then they started screaming, waking everyone up. It took, like, half the girls on the fourth floor to calm them down."

She crossed her arms and huffed, a reaction I recognized as jealousy over not being invited to join in.

The fourth floor made sense for a séance. It was where Eliza Jackson had almost died. And it was where a ghost named Jessie was said to reside. She was known to storm the halls right before exams. That was when she had died, stress over her finals leading to an overdose.

According to Eileen. According to the girls who lived up there. "Poor Jessie," they all said to each other through giggles and yawns before going to bed each night. It was bad luck not to. If you didn't acknowledge her, you would be the next one she'd pay a visit to.

The one time I went to the fourth floor, the cadence of their voices dripped through the walls.

Poor Jessie, poor Jessie, poor Jessie.

"It was so annoying. Causing all that drama? One crazy person starts screaming and then everyone else screams, too. It's contagious." Eileen had a voice like string cheese, phlegmy and frayed. You could peel it apart, chord by chord.

I could see it: black light and puddles of melted wax, girls having fun until they weren't. Maybe they had heard some manic weeping through the wallpaper or saw a sickle dressed in tartan plaid and wool tights.

Eileen eyeballed my smeared mascara and greasy hair, the dress that looked like I'd slept on the street. Most of my zombie makeup had ended up on my pillowcase. "What did you get into last night?"

I had stopped telling her about my adventures with Sadie right around the time she started referring to me as a "Scholarship Girl." We were never going to be friends. I had a radar for girls who couldn't be trusted, and I'd spotted Eileen a mile away.

She had turned up her nose when I suggested lining our walls with a collage of sonnets and paper dolls, but now she was the one pretending to care about poetry. Bookishly hardcore about line and meter. Enjambment enthusiast. She loved whatever Professor Weedler loved.

Things I'd learned about Eileen so far: she grew up riding horses, her family liked to vacation in Greece instead of France, and she had her own credit card. Meaning, it belonged to her, but her dad paid it off. All her new black dresses were designer goth, easily digestible adaptations that would have looked better in shreds.

I'd thought I was hiding my lack of money those first few weeks of the semester. I nodded when girls in my hall reminisced about their summer trips to Prague and Belize. But people with money could always tell who didn't have it. That was another thing I had learned, a lesson I kept learning long after.

My thrift-store outfits and work-study jobs were no match for private academies and live-in nannies. I couldn't afford the dresses that *Seventeen* magazine named trendy for fall, sheaths, shifts, and slips in "materials begging to be touched." Velvet and mohair. Corduroy and suede. There were girls in my hall who ordered sushi each day instead of eating the dining hall food. They had professional manicures and probably never ran out of money on their meal card.

It wasn't fair to call them all bitches, but I wanted to.

A wrinkled envelope from the financial aid office sat on my desk, already open, and Eileen's cucumber-melon body spray wafted up from the paper inside. If I asked her about it, she'd laugh. Like, no big deal how many times she'd opened my mail.

The first page of the letter inside reminded me of the GPA requirements for my scholarship, though I already knew them by heart: academic scholarship students were required to maintain dean's list two semesters in a row for their first year at Loch Raven. Eighteen credit hours were required both semesters, though most other girls took the standard twelve or fifteen credits. Most other girls also had moms to call and cry to.

The second page included a list of all my classes next to dotted signature lines. Each of my professors needed to record my current grade, then sign the paper to verify. Weedler's class was first on the list, and it was due before midterms.

Attending a school like Loch Raven was no joke. They regularly advertised how many successful women they'd molded: congresswomen alum, brain surgeons, and lawyers with fat pockets. My mother had seen it as yet another reason to apply. The Hall of Success, a plexiglass gallery full of every success story the college could claim, was where we all wanted to end up.

Sadie was lucky that her theater scholarship depended on a different kind of performance. Her GPA requirements were more forgiving.

Quick math. The zero for today's test, which was worth 10 percent of my final grade, meant getting an A or even a B in Freshman Seminar wasn't mathematically possible. Not even if Weedler dropped the lowest grade. Given his strict no makeup policy, I was screwed.

I couldn't attend Loch Raven—or any college—without scholarships. The financial aid letter was a necessary reminder. Moving home wasn't an option, either, mostly because there wasn't a home to return to. Right before school had started, my father packed everything up and left on a road trip with a new dog I hadn't met. If there was any money from selling the house, I hadn't seen it.

No life insurance from my mom, either, which I'd made the mistake of asking about. Not a cent. Due to the nature of her death.

My head throbbed as Eileen paced the room, lingering at my dresser, where I kept everything that didn't have a better home. Her fingers grazed the teeth of my plastic comb and the rim of an old soda can. She picked up my only framed photo: me and my mom at the Enchanted Forest theme park when I was little, both of us sitting in a giant whale's mouth, me looking sideways and her looking happy.

I gently removed the photo from Eileen's hands and placed it back on the dresser. In the hallway, voices bled under the doors. Out there, someone was always laughing or crying. I could never tell which.

"Don't forget, it's Spirit Week," Eileen said. "You better get changed."

The next time I puked, the spray landed directly on her feet.

After a quick shower, I changed into my sensible flight attendant dress with a flannel tied around the waist and forced myself over to the Humanities building to talk to Professor Weedler.

The financial aid letter, waiting to be signed, wouldn't let me rest even if I tried.

Notice how the Loch Raven campus is the very image from the college brochure. Literally. It's the same picture. That perfectly golden light. That crunching sound of leaves under your boots? You can't buy that vibe anywhere except Loch Raven College in the early fall.

Fun fact: There are so many acres of forest surrounding the campus that you could get lost here if you wanted to. Or so I've heard.

Even a hangover didn't stop the tour-group spiel from ticking through my head.

A girl wearing a pink pillbox hat and oversize sunglasses looked up at the dark windows of Hope Hall as we passed. Movie Star Monday, the first themed day of Spirit Week.

"Shoot me dead if you see me looking like *I Love Lucy* or some shit," Sadie had said when we learned about the weekly themes. We were experts at dressing up, but once someone called for school spirit, we tapped out.

The girl—Jackie O, I guessed—kissed her fingers to the crucifix around her neck. It was what girls always did when they walked in front of Hope Hall.

"They said on the news that she jumped," Eileen had told us weeks before during her campus "Death Tour." Something like disbelief in the way she'd said it. And the way we'd stared up at the roof like we weren't sure. Could someone die from jumping three stories? A pointless question because that girl, Abbie, did die.

By the fountain, girls with overworked costumes replayed the night before. The Betty Page of the group retold the same version I had heard from Eileen: Séance. Freaking out. Some weird shit happening on the fourth floor, though she didn't say what.

"What spirit did they think they were channeling?" Audrey Hepburn asked. I slowed down to listen and pretended to re-lace my boots.

"Sylvia." Betty Page practically sang it, enunciating every syllable. One word left loose on the breeze. Almost like a hymn. *Sylvia.*

Shaded by the cathedral's spires, I thought about all the girls who'd lived on campus before me. Not just girls studying for exams and lounging beneath droopy trees, but lonely girls. Girls without families or homes to return to, girls who couldn't find their footing in a place as unforgiving as Loch Raven. Not just girls who wore black and read poetry to attract a teacher or fit the season's latest trend, but misfit girls with stories they didn't know how to tell. Like me.

We knew about Mary and Jessie and Abbie. But if there really had been so many other deaths like Eileen claimed, why didn't we know those other names, too?

Before I walked on, another voice chimed in. "I was there. We were just trying to find out who's next."

A winded, pink-cheeked classmate left Professor Weedler's office as I entered. She was dressed in a white Princess Leia dress, which didn't really fit the movie-star theme, but whatever. The buns on either side of her head were coming undone.

"Wish me luck," she said, holding up an application to the Loch Raven Mentor Program that Weedler directed. I'd received an application, too. All the financial aid students did, assuming that if we needed help adapting to college, our professor was who we would want to talk to about it.

"One-on-one faculty support, lots of personal attention," was how Weedler had described it. All I knew about the program was that acceptance was highly coveted and equally selective. And that I wanted nothing to do with it. All the other girls who didn't get selected but clearly wanted mentorship or counseling were out of luck, I guessed.

He greeted me with all his teeth, looking up from a leather-bound book opened to the middle. The pages were mostly blank, and he kept his pen poised in the air as if about to write something important. His shoulder-length hair made some of my classmates— the girls in the front row—think he was hot. Or maybe it was the elbow patches on his blazers that they liked.

For the record, I didn't agree. He wasn't as old as my father, but old enough.

Also, whether we were in the same class or not, Sadie and I always sat in the back.

"Darling Nikki, there you are. Are you feeling better?"

The inside of my mouth tasted rotten, like something decaying behind my molars.

Books lined the shelves behind him, and framed photographs of Sylvia Plath hung on the wall like a fanatical gallery. I guessed the frames made them art. The way she stared at the camera seemed tragic when you put all the pictures together. Or pornographic. Like she knew something nasty was about to happen after the camera flash.

> *Bonus points: Name three beauties who died from carbon monoxide poisoning.*
> *A: Thelma Todd, Sylvia Plath, my mother.*

"I'm ready to take the test now, if that's okay," I said. Then, because it felt important to say out loud, I added, "I can't fail your class." I smoothed my dress to keep my hands busy after resting the scholarship letter on his desk.

He steepled his hands in front of his nose. The air in his office was still, and suddenly cold. "Here's what we're going to do. Instead of making up the test, you can write an essay on any of the women we've discussed in class."

"You mean, any of the dead women?"

His face flattened into a blank stare. What other possible answer could there be? Then his eyes drifted down, down, down until I crossed my ankles and clinched my bare knees together.

The C- he gave me on my last essay, a piece I called *How to Make Room for a Dead Woman*, still made my cheeks burn. "You missed the assignment instructions," he'd said. "This isn't a creative writing class."

A test would have been so much easier. But I also knew any kind of makeup work was a gift. After all, he could have said no and shut the door in my face.

"You aren't the strongest writer, Nikki, so this will be good practice for the kind of writing you'll need to do in your higher-level classes."

It hit me like a punch to the throat. Writing was the only thing I knew how to do. A teacher had never told me my work was anything less than above average. My face must have given me away, the hurt and confusion and anger, especially the anger, though he pretended not to see.

"What do you think? Who would you choose to write about?" he asked.

I knew he wanted me to choose Sylvia Plath. Instead, I sniffled and said, "Marilyn," at the same time that he handed me a stack of books and a folder full of articles.

The article on top: "How to Write about Sylvia Plath" by Kimberly Crowley.

I skimmed the first page, my eyes glazing over—not out of boredom, but stubbornness.

"For some, she highlights the difficulties faced by women as they try to juggle their desires for professional success with expectations for their domestic success. For others, she serves as an example of what was wrong with the system for treating mental illness. Still others see her as an archetype of the tortured writer."

"How to Write about a Dead Woman," the article should have been called.

"How to Survive College While in Mourning."

"How to Keep Your Scholarship and Still Fit In with the Rich and the Fabulous."

Before I could offer another topic suggestion, he held up one finger to cut me off just like he did in class. He smiled so wide I could have fit my whole fist inside.

"There's plenty of research on Sylvia—an overwhelming amount, actually. Don't just regurgitate her biography. The challenge will be if you can say anything new," he said.

Only half of his words made it to my brain: confessional poetry and Ted Hughes and *The Bell Jar*. I didn't bother pretending to care, but I also didn't tell him no. Especially after he picked up my scholarship letter and told me to bring it back later, once I had gathered ideas for my new paper.

His rolling chair skidded so damn close, close enough to smell his cologne—cool and green, like a Christmas tree—and he widened his eyes the way people did when they were waiting for you to say something smart. "Other thoughts?"

My only thought: *What would my mom say if she were here?*

She would shake her head and tell me to get my shit together. She would take one look at my split ends and tell me to buy a nicer shampoo.

"Find yourself a man who can support you," she used to tell me. Because as a woman, being able to take care of yourself was never guaranteed.

She prepared me for a lot of things, but never for people like Weedler.

I reached up to my earlobe out of habit and flinched. My ruby earring was gone. Not tangled in my hair, not buried in my lap. Gone gone.

My eyes watered and my mouth filled with saliva. I was going to vomit again. If I didn't get out of that office soon, it would get ugly.

"Let's check in on your research in a few days," Weedler offered, patting my knee. "I'm holding my office hours at the Brew Station this week, so we can meet there."

I watched his hand, up and down, up and down, until he pulled it away.

That night, I dreamed of dead women, a pageant of them, outside my dorm-room closet. Every dead woman I ever knew: my grandmother, my aunt, my third-grade teacher. And the girl with the perm, the one without the eyes, ready for her own Loch Raven Spirit Week. The gold leaf pin on her collar was identical to the one we were all given at orientation. She fronted a line of young women wearing navy and maroon. Some had headbands and bobby socks, then others with leg warmers and hair teased peacock tall. At least one wore velvet Mary Janes and colorful barrettes to clip back her bangs.

They all wanted my favorite black dress, the same one I wore underneath my cap and gown at graduation. It was also the dress I had worn to my mother's funeral.

The dead women took turns trying it on. In real life, the dress wouldn't fit any of them, but in death, it slid on each body type easily, as if elastic and seamless. They spun in front of the mirror and flattened the lace with cold hands.

I watched, terrified at first to make a noise and disrupt them. There must have been something they wanted. Maybe there was something I could give them. They ignored me when I tried.

Help me with the zipper, they all insisted in unison. A frantic, high-pitched choral refrain. Pushing and shoving. Snarling mouths.

Me, me, they cried.

Then: *You. You you you.*

The connection between them was palpable: the dress. The performance of it. Orbiting the mirror, twirling, angling their shoulders, standing on tiptoe to mimic heels.

When the dream blazed through me again the next morning, I ran to the closet to check my black dress for stains or rips, only to realize I was already wearing it.

The girls of the Sylvia Club. They wanted to be seen. Their voices echoed.

My mom was the only one who never showed up.

CHAPTER 8
NOW

Sadie

"Tell me this isn't exactly what you're looking for," Brill said, sliding a limey gin and tonic across the table.

Mannis swept his arms in the air to whoop his approval. "This is it!" he yelled. "This is exactly the thing I've been wanting all day."

This was what they did—performing the exact opposite of my mood to get a reaction out of me. And they'd had me pegged the minute I walked in the door.

"Cut the shit," I said, scanning the bar full of men loosening their ties and twisting their wedding rings. "I have too much on my mind."

In the last few hours, between losing my job and Nikki showing up in the kitchen, a fiery rage had begun to bubble over. I'd roared at the coffee machine when it didn't work fast enough and cold-cocked Rhi's baby doll just for existing. I'd punched hard enough to leave her face dented.

"Fuck you, dirty ass!" I'd yelled at her collapsed head, only mildly surprised when her features didn't bounce back.

Mannis and Brill, with their terrible shock of enthusiasm, were exactly what I deserved. We silently agreed to wait until I finished my first drink before we discussed how they still had jobs but I didn't.

Complete bullshit newsletters self-care downsizing damnit pinkie swear swear swear

Honestly, the anger felt so much cleaner, so much less complicated, than my panic. I almost felt like myself again. I had rushed through the stages of grief after Nikki's death, skipping every emotion I didn't have time for. Shock and denial, if those were two of the stages, were where I'd lingered for the past year. But maybe I didn't deserve the sweet relief of anger, either. It seemed wrong to let myself feel anything at all.

All I could do was remember.

The day Nikki died, a man I barely knew slept beside me in a cheap motel room, naked and spent. The toilet paper was still folded into a triangle, and the TV remote had never moved from its perch on the nightstand. A bug scurried across the baseboard. I hadn't planned to stay long.

A terrible ache filled my chest out of nowhere, and I considered heading home without waking the man, a clean-cut suit-wearing type.

She showed up with smooth hair and bloodless skin, scrubbed clean of all our years together. Someone's classy Barbie doll in human form. It would be days before I heard the news. We weren't in the same circles, and we didn't follow each other on social media. But later I put two and two together. She appeared in my motel room only hours after she'd died.

At the foot of my bed, she wore a black dress unzipped in the back, like she had been in the middle of getting ready but needed help with the finishing details. Ruby studs, two tiny specks of blood, dotted her ears.

I knew those earrings. Both of them.

I didn't call out her name, but I thought it. *Nikkinikkinikkinik.* I rubbed my eyes and forced myself to look away.

Then she offered her pinkie finger, bent at a broken angle. That was the moment I'd have nightmares about later. My whole body pulsated, like branches bursting into bloom, the buds crawling up my throat. I almost cried. I almost choked. I remembered it later because it wasn't the kind of thing I could forget.

Nikki didn't disappear after that, but she faded. I could pretend to ignore her looming presence. But only for so long.

It turned out that leaving the house without Rhi was much easier once faced with the vision of never leaving it again, of being chained to the house with only a baby, a breast pump, and an eyeless version of Nikki as my sidekick. The happy hour invitation that I'd first ignored suddenly felt like a lifeline, and by the time Harrison showered after work, I had ordered a pizza, changed Rhi's diaper, and pumped enough milk for the whole night. I handed over the diaper bag with little more than a peck on his cheek.

"It's for my sanity," I'd told him. "Self-care." I actually said those words when what I wanted to say was that I couldn't spend another minute in the ghost house. That's what it was—a spectacular haunted house, every crevice bursting with Nikki's memory.

"Go have fun," he'd said, recovering fast from the shock of me leaving the house without a panic attack. "I'll be fine. I've done this before, remember."

But it had been eighteen years since Caroline was a baby, and within twenty minutes, he'd texted me five times with questions about bottles and bedtime. I dulled my mixed feelings of relief and irritation with whatever drink Mannis and Brill shoved into my hands.

There wasn't much to say about work. Mannis and Brill had already told me about the other people who'd been laid off and how morale in the office had sunk to a new low. "Maybe one day they'll hire again," I suggested, but that didn't seem likely, either.

Mannis sported a new furry beard that his girlfriend probably hated and bopped his head to the jukebox. He followed my gaze to a dude so sturdy and wide-shouldered he could swallow me whole. Something about his long hair unnerved me, the way he scratched his hand across his scalp as he flirted with the bartender. Professor Weedler, twenty years younger. The goose bumps on my arms grew teeth.

"You should make a move. Might take your mind off whatever bug crawled up your hoo-ha."

Brill snorted in the direction of the bar and removed his maroon thrift-store jacket, his Thursday blazer. "Even on her best day, she wouldn't dare go after another married man. No offense, Stone. You know what I mean. One wrecked home is enough."

I groaned and buried my face in my hands. Harrison wasn't married when we'd started our relationship. How many times did I have to tell them? He was a widower. That was an important distinction. But I knew it was a technicality the women in Hidden Harbor overlooked, too. It didn't matter to them that

Nikki had died first or that Harrison and I fell for each other hard. What he offered me and Rhi weren't the kinds of things people turned down: Safety and security. Love and stability. A family.

At least Mannis and Brill were calling me by my last name, treating me like one of the guys. It felt like a hard-earned victory even if it was too late to matter. Most of the staff at *Baltimore Alive!* were men. They planned the content, led the staff meetings. I had always been the only woman at happy hour, and it occurred to me then, like a forehead-slapping epiphany, that the other women in the office couldn't attend because they had to go home and take care of their kids. Lucille quit her job to spend more time with her family—or she got fired for insubordination, if the rumors were true—and now half-priced appetizers and salty margaritas were a thing of the past for me, too.

The TV above the bar filled with a recap of the day's news: a Playboy playmate turned actress who had been strangled by her husband. All the images on the screen emphasized her cleavage or zoomed in on her arched body, posed on top of a car, like those were the only photos in existence of her. No one at the bar gave the TV more than a glance despite her beauty or her tragic death. She was already old news.

"If you grip that glass any tighter, Stone, it's going to explode in your hand."

My fingers blanched from clenching, and I took a long, burning drink so I wouldn't have to speak. *Nikki.* Her name sat on my tongue like it had been scorched. There were so many things I had meant to tell her, but now that she had made her presence known, I couldn't remember any of them.

Brill finished his drink with a flourish. "So, we know we didn't get you a baby shower gift or anything, but we do have something for you."

When Mannis retrieved a book from his messenger bag—unwrapped, with the receipt tucked inside like a bookmark—my laugh sounded more like gagging.

The Self-Care Cure by Annie Minx.

Laughing was better than the alternative. There was too much noise inside the bar for anyone to hear me if I screamed. I couldn't escape her. Of course they didn't know that my old best friend, the one whose house I now lived in, was the actual Minx. They'd probably walked into the bookstore and bought whatever they saw on the front table.

"We thought you could use a little self-help or whatever," Mannis mumbled. "My girlfriend swears by this chick."

The gift was mostly thoughtful, minus the part about them thinking I needed self-help. I punched Brill in the arm as a thank-you, then paused to appreciate the book's weight. It felt heavier than it looked.

"How about you get the next round?" Brill nudged me with his bony elbow toward the man at the bar. Wink, wink.

"Rain check." I dropped the book in my too-big mom purse and slid out from my chair. "Gotta feed the baby."

The phrase "feed the baby" was enough to make them blush. They didn't need to know I had already pumped and dumped in the single stall, buzzed from half a whiskey, a manual hand pump and my right tit hanging over the toilet.

"Did Mannis tell you about this bird theory? That they don't shit at night?"

"Everyone shits at night," I said. But I wasn't sure, not really.

They were good guys, Mannis and Brill. They had never tried

to hit on me, and I didn't have to pretend I was someone else around them. If I told them about seeing my dead ex–best friend, they'd probably yawn and ask if she was hot. Still, they couldn't understand my life. They weren't afraid to walk alone to their car. Their days didn't feel like clawing out of a grave, fingernails splitting, choking on someone else's dirt.

Baltimore at night was a goddamn joy. All the glowing neon, plus the fish/sugar/diesel/funk of the harbor. Baltimore locals with their gritty spit-and-see-where-it-lands edge, were my kind of people. Sharp wind cut through my jacket, and I inhaled the smoke from a loitering stranger's cigarette. A car blasted its horn, and a homeless man shook his cup at me while singing Bob Marley's "Three Little Birds." I didn't want to take it as a sign, but I still stopped to give him the fifty-five cents from my pocket.

On the sidewalk, I squinted up at the starless sky, and a pigeon crapped two inches from my feet. There it was: birds did crap at night. Good luck or bad luck, I could never remember what bird shit was supposed to symbolize. Either way, it had just missed me.

A yellow parking ticket sat on my windshield tucked under the wiper blades, and I considered letting it flutter away. The wind was awfully strong. For a moment there, Old Sadie was back. My jagged happy hour buzz, combined with the carelessness of letting the meter run out, felt almost right.

While I waited for the car to warm up, I stuck the ticket in the glove compartment and scrolled idly through Facebook. As much as I missed Rhiannon, so badly that my body hurt in literal and physical ways, I wanted more of that alone time, to linger on a thought long enough for it to reach full bloom before withering away.

This was Healthy. I was Taking Care of My Needs First. The

baby blogs mentioned it more than once, even if only as a footnote to all my other mom duties.

In the passenger seat, the shiny Annie Minx book cover caught a slice of streetlight. I had only gotten as far as the dedication page before, but this time, I started at the back of the book, the author's bio and photo. There she was, and wasn't. In the photo, a woman in an orange dress sat headless, holding up a mirror in the space where her head should have been.

My teeth chattered enough to shake my whole body. Even her final photo was torturous. Headless, like the pictures we used to take in the costume room. And the orange dress again. The thinnest threads of straps. Satin that wrinkled easily, so orange it glowed like a safety cone. It wasn't just her funeral dress, and I was the only person in the world who knew it.

The last time I saw that dress: A night so cold the motor sputtered. Driving without headlights. Fast, then faster. Me wearing the dress, neither of us with scarves or gloves. Before the crash, Nikki and I turned to look at each other.

Before the crash, she hooked her pinkie finger with mine. A swear. A promise.

That was it. The memory ended as soon as it began. Like waking in a room full of sun, my new life—Harrison, Rhiannon, the house—came back into focus, each detail more precise, each decision more sober, and I could almost breathe again.

On the back of my parking ticket, as ridiculous as it seemed, I channeled Nikki's list-making skills by writing all the ways it seemed like she had tried to leave me a message: her book dedication, the newsletter, and now her photo. The dress. Unless I was looking too hard for signs. If I kept conjuring her memory, anything could seem like a message.

I only leaned my seat back and closed my eyes for a second, but when I opened them again, Professor Weedler, with his long hair and dirty jeans, stood in front of my car. He slammed his palms on the hood, his eyes wild with rage.

I slammed on the gas and revved the engine to drive away, forgetting the car was still in park, my face as frantic as his.

It was only the man from earlier, the one singing Bob Marley, now yelling at me for my idling car's toxic fumes. Lucky for him I didn't charge my car straight into him out of instinct. Lucky for both of us, I guessed. It was Nikki's picture that had channeled Weedler's memory. I knew it. Somewhere inside me, they would always be linked.

Panting, I shoved the book under my purse, as if it alone had the power to summon every old spirit I wanted to forget. On the way home, I didn't listen to music. Silence, even if only temporary, was the only cure I needed.

Dry-mouthed and not entirely sober, I checked on Rhi in her crib and tiptoed through the house. I had missed dinnertime and bathtime and storytime and bedtime. Outside, the sky darkened, all the promise squeezed from the day like the dishwater from a sponge. Harrison had fallen asleep in Rhi's room, sitting up in the glider meant for rocking babies to sleep. I didn't dare wake him. No lights on at the woman's house across the street, no lights inside ours. The fleeting solitude was too precious not to savor.

Even Nikki didn't show her face. No creaking floors or algae smell.

A reminder to RSVP for Diana Noble's mimosa party popped on my phone's cracked screen:

To: Sadie Stone (+ 32 other recipients)
From: Diana Noble
Subject: RSVP for Moms and Mimosas

It's that time again—Moms and Mimosas! Please let me know if you can attend this special brunch event, the ultimate Self-Care Starter for starlets like you!
And if you haven't bought your copy of *The Self-Care Cure* yet to honor our beloved friend Nikki Walsh/Annie Minx, what are you waiting for? I read it in one day (hello Chapter 9—how do you know my life?!!?).
In the meantime, I'm over here channeling the best version of me (and so much more).
I hope to see you soon, babe! Treat yourself! You've earned it!
~Di

All the exclamation points in the world couldn't make the event sound any less like hell. Probably one of those at-home "parties" selling magnetic eyelashes or pastel handbags printed with seahorses and anchors. Maybe face cleanser that Literally Erased Your Pores or leggings that Ate Away Your Cellulite with some advanced technology that helped justify the three-hundred-dollar price tag.

I rested my forehead against the office door, searching for coolness or heat. Anything. My jaw throbbed from grinding my teeth.

Then something cracked open inside me. The sensation felt like waking up, my body on a different kind of autopilot. I'd been staying in that house as a guest, like a patron in a fancy bed-and-breakfast who had to ask for the Wi-Fi password. I couldn't move the position of a lamp without permission. And I remembered again, with a surge of nausea, that Nikki was dead. She didn't care what we did anymore. Besides, Old Me had never been the kind of person who asked for permission.

It's your house now, every room of it.

I checked the spare key ring and dug into the pockets of all Harrison's pants. His neatly hung clothes, the precisely folded shirts—I yanked and overturned them all. It didn't matter what he'd say about the mess. I couldn't be stopped.

Hair in my eyes and chest heaving, I fell against the door, laser focused as ever. Pulling drawers from their tracks, I scraped my knuckles, bent one fingernail back hard enough that blood pooled underneath. I shook his shoes upside down and, crawling on all fours, hissed when nothing fell out.

Finally, I found it hanging on an exposed nail inside his closet, a single key that I tucked inside my fingers like a blade, the way my grandmother always told me to prepare to fight back if someone attacked me.

With everyone asleep, the temptation to unlock the office was too strong to ignore. I could be quick and quiet. I could look around just a little bit.

Bracing myself against the doorframe, I pushed my body through the opening, disturbing a year's worth of dust, and stared at what Nikki had left for me to find.

Like entering another world, the office didn't match anything else in the house. The furniture was old and worn—not messy but "well-loved," as my grandmother would have said. No custom light switches or expensive rugs. Poised in the office doorway, alert for any sounds down the hall, I saw the room Nikki had meant for herself. The old Nikki—my Nikki, the creative, stubborn girl I loved—had designed the office as the one place to feel like herself.

She'd made it her own with old woolly blankets instead of the rest of the house's rigid throw pillows.

And the stretch of matted carpet, darker than the rest, from years of pacing—it looked like the house she grew up in, the patches of carpet worn down where her family had walked from the kitchen to the living room, back and forth, for decades.

An otherwise empty shelf of old Loch Raven College yearbooks were carefully flagged with sticky notes. Harrison really hadn't touched a thing since she died. A coffee mug edged with stale lipstick sat on the desk, where at least a dozen manila folders were stacked just as neatly. The room had been clean and tidy once, but now dust coated everything. Dead skin. I had to force the thought away.

Ink-pen etchings of Sylvia Plath quotes covered the nubby fabric of the oversize chair. One about tulips, one about a fig tree. And on the bulletin board hanging over the desk, an enlarged image of Sylvia Plath had been pinned to the center.

I'd always associated Plath with Loch Raven and Nikki. And Professor Weedler. It was impossible not to.

At least one of the lines of poetry was Nikki's own. I recognized it from a zine we'd put together the summer before college. I had loved it so much that I memorized it: "we pretend we don't remember the taste of our own reflection / we tighten our coats against death's perfection."

I squared my shoulders and forced myself forward. Whatever I was looking for, I wouldn't find it in the doorway.

It was the way her papers and folders and books were organized that made my chest tighten. Everything sat in little landing zones just like in her dorm room back in college. A zone for sitting, a zone for reading, a zone for working—each decorated with a sparse but intentional vignette of things she wanted to display, like a ceramic bumblebee and a paperweight with a dandelion trapped inside. The cup of highlighters was part of a vignette in that zone. The bulletin board, too.

"This is my zone for getting shit done," she had once said about the corner of her room where her desk sat.

Starting with the first manila folder in the pile, a photo of a girl named Abbie Moriano stared back at me. I recognized the name but couldn't place it. There wasn't much else besides her photocopied image. High school transcripts and a page torn out of a yearbook, a group photo of Abbie with the rest of the Loch Raven choir. She had died not long before we'd attended school there.

Each folder was the same as the first, except with different names and photos. All the girls inside the folders had attended Loch Raven, and all had been dead for decades. Everything was numbered and color coded, arranged in a way that would only make sense to Nikki. I turned pages without purpose, one ear toward the door, until I found a list of names, the same names as the girls in the folders, with the year they'd each died in parentheses. Three in 1968, three in 1985, and a handful in the years following, including one that I remembered during our year.

"Nikki," I spoke to the room. "What the hell."

Down the hall, the floor creaked, closer to the office than I wanted any ghost or human. I'd left the door wide-open like a big gaping wound in the hallway. If Harrison found me inside, he'd probably change the locks and seal up the doors forever.

My mouth went dry as I continued searching. The room wasn't exactly a shrine or a conspiracy theorist's lair, but every flagged yearbook page and notebook entry was devoted to those dead girls.

I'd only seen Nikki get that fixated once before. Not just fixated. Obsessed.

She had been researching the Sylvia Club again.

On a hunch, I flipped over all the papers and books. When I lifted another pile of folders, a brand-new spiral notebook waited underneath.

We used to leave messages for each other in a notebook just like it. After a while, Nikki had to hide it from her snoop of a roommate. If I showed up to her dorm room and Nikki wasn't there, I knew to look under the stacks on her desk for our personal back-and-forth journal, as we called it.

In this new notebook, she'd only written on the first page, her slanted handwriting both foreign and familiar at once. There wasn't a doubt this time who her message was meant for.

Sadie, To-Do—if something happens to me:
- *The old notebook?*
- *The Sylvia Club*
- *Caroline*

I dropped the notebook like it had suddenly burst into flames and whirled, sure someone else was in the room, watching. And that absence, too, the fact that she wasn't there, hurt like hell. Tears brimmed over no matter how hard I tried to will them away. It had to be Nikki's real final note. But if I was the one who was supposed to find it, how had Nikki known I'd be in her office to discover the message?

The questions wormed through me faster and faster, my brain unable to process a single rushing thought. She had left me a to-do list, just like the ones she used to make for me, her way of helping me keep track of my assignments and obligations. My Stage Manager, I called her. No matter how many times I forgot to use her lists, she kept making them anyway.

The Sylvia Club, she'd written, as if I could do anything about it. Her final research had been preserved here in the unopened-until-today office, but what could I do with photos and notes and obituaries?

And why mention our old notebook? Did she mean the one she'd promised to burn before we left Loch Raven? The whole book—and everything inside that we never wanted anyone to see—should have been destroyed.

Caroline's name on that list threw me even more. Caroline, who looked so much like Nikki it made me afraid I'd call her the wrong name. The girl who literally snarled each time she saw me. Nikki's daughter didn't belong on a to-do list, especially one written for me. Not to mention that this list was over a year old. If anything about it was urgent, I had probably missed the deadline.

If something happens to me, it said. That *if* felt suspect and, knowing Nikki, intentional. Knowing Nikki, I shouldn't have been surprised that even after death, she had a plan.

A gurgle bubbled so close to my ear that my hand came back wet when I tried to slap the sound away. I whipped around but found only mud on the carpet—a flat-footed print, still damp.

The pressure inside my brain raged into a blinding headache. I had so many questions, and the only person I could ask was too dead to answer.

My partner in crime, my ride or die. My Betty Veronica Laverne Shirley Lucy Ethel. My bestie.

Her best friend would have known what Nikki was going through. True best friends always did. My palms itched, the way they used to when I was younger, when I thought about doing something I shouldn't. I sealed my eyes tight as I hit "Yes" to confirm attendance to Diana Noble's brunch party. No matter what they were selling, I'd be there.

CHAPTER 9

THEN

Nikki

Weedler paced back and forth as he recited "Lady Lazarus," his favorite Plath poem. Puffs of chalk followed him each time he passed the board, where he handwrote the same words every class: "After-hours meetings by request."

"She tried and then she kept trying to die, you see?" He mounted himself up on the large desk at the front of the room. Fully seated, his button-up shirt strained against his midsection. With one hand, he pulled his long hair back before letting it fall again. Sadie and I were tallying his hair flips, how many times he played with a long tendril or combed his nails across the top of his skull. This was the fifth tally mark so far.

"She was the most tragic figure in literature," he said. "Anyone claiming to be a Sylvia Plath fan would need to understand that sadness deeply, don't you think?"

The front-row girls nodded, scribbling sloppy notes without

ever looking away from him, their furious pens running off the page.

My suddenly throbbing hand ached beneath the desk, my nail bed full of blood. I had mauled the skin around my thumbnail until it bled.

But he wasn't finished. "Extra credit for anyone who can connect the beauty and the despair in one of her final poems." He stood, pulling down on his khakis, and I swear he had a semi-erection. I watched Eileen's eyes go wide as she noticed it, too.

"Bulge," some girl had penciled on the back wall of the classroom long before our semester began. And now I understood.

On my way out, he stood in the doorway, taking up the whole frame, reminding us yet again that applications to spend more time with him were almost due. Everyone was encouraged to apply for the mentorship program, but it was known that spots usually went to financial aid students. Eileen had ranted about it more times than I could count.

I stepped back, afraid he would try to touch my hair or the small of my back like he did to the line of girls who left before me. Instead, his chalky fingers grazed mine as he transferred a stack of articles and books into my arms.

"We still need to schedule that meeting. Let me look at my calendar when I get back to the office. I live just up the road. That will be cozier. A bit quieter. I'll order a pizza."

Instead of saying no, I lied and told him I'd check my calendar, too.

Eileen glared at me outside his room, obviously eavesdropping. She stomped off, while two girls giggled in my direction. Matching miniskirts, turtlenecks, jelly bracelets. They could have been alive girls or dead ones. Sometimes it was hard to tell.

On the way across campus, I cut through the Admissions building to escape the rain, which meant a trip through the Hall of Success with its wall-to-wall glass cases of photos and mini-biographies.

Their photos were all the same flavor: blazers, eyeglasses, shoulder pads, and gold cross necklaces (or no jewelry at all). White women. Rich women. They were the opposite of the images of Sylvia Plath on Weedler's walls, yet just as jarring, as they stared down the camera with their arms crossed across their chest.

The real name of the Hall of Success was Hawkins Gallery, named after a dude not involved in any of the women's accomplishments. It was a quiet place, revered by all the girls. You could see them hold their breath when they walked through, like if they listened closely enough, they might hear the voices of the successful women who came before them.

This could be you, the women in the photos might have said.

Their tips for success: hard work, resilience, and not waking up with a hangover on the morning of your big test.

Q: What all-women's school did Sylvia Plath attend?
A: Smith College.

I loitered the longest at the small In Memoriam case, though these women were older, not the girls of the Sylvia Club.

It felt wrong not to remember the girls who had died here. Just like it felt wrong to listen to my classmates make casual references to a suicide club. Jokes about ghosts had turned into bets on who this year's newest Sylvia Club "recruit" would be. You couldn't walk to the bathroom without hearing their predictions.

Wet footsteps clunked behind me. Boots, by the sound of it. I peered over my shoulder, but there was no one. As soon as I turned around again, the footsteps returned with a pounding vibration, advancing through the long hall.

I looked around for a door to slide through or a friendly-enough nun to move toward, finding only the faces of all those long-gone women. The footsteps advanced, a heavy squish and squeak. Louder, closer.

It's nothing, I told myself, not sure what I was afraid of. Plenty of people walked through this building each day. Still, the raised hairs on my skin felt like a warning. If I listened to my gut in this case, it was telling me to run.

I spun around to find Dr. Gallina shortcutting through Admissions like me, shoes soggy from getting caught in the storm.

With her short, spiky hair and her concert T-shirt/pantsuit combos, Dr. Gallina was hands down the coolest professor on campus. She taught the English and mass communications classes that freshmen weren't allowed to take yet, classes like Reliability in the Media and Marketing Principles. But I had been lucky to secure a seat in her Freshman Comp course.

That day's shirt, paired with wide-leg trousers and a denim blazer: Madonna's *Like a Virgin* tour. Next to me in my loose-fitting prairie dress—another costume-room find—she looked even cooler than usual. Also, I had never, ever seen her wear high heels. Like, she just refused. So badass.

"Nikki," she said, her voice as deep and formal as when she lectured about research methods. My heart hadn't stopped thumping yet. She gestured toward the papers threatening to slide out of my arms. "Do you need a hand?"

As soon as she said it, the first book fell, and then the other folders full of Professor Weedler's stapled academic journal articles slipped, too. I wanted to drop it in the trash can, not at Dr. Gallina's feet.

"Just place it all down on the floor," she instructed, crouching beside me. "You need to straighten it out and reorganize."

I did as I was told. If I was being honest, Dr. Gallina intimidated me, but in a good way. Like I wanted to be her when I grew up. Judging by the number of girls who wait-listed her classes, I wasn't alone.

Some girls called her a bitch because they said she played favorites. Or maybe because she didn't walk around with a smile plastered to her face and she didn't sugarcoat her feedback. She'd once made Eileen answer the same question six times until she could speak without using the words "maybe," "probably," or "um."

"Plath, huh?" From her squatted position on the floor, she studied my pile of pages. "What class is this for?"

When I mentioned Freshman Seminar and the essay I'd been assigned to write, her mouth twitched, an involuntary and almost unnoticeable reaction.

Sylvia Plath was more than just a depressed, suicidal writer—that was the first thing I'd learned in my research. Weedler had classified her as only a "dead girl." Sad and dead and beautiful. Which, in my opinion, missed the point.

I understood why my classmates loved her work. I really did. She was a genius.

But the second thing I had learned: despite everything, including how much I enjoyed her poems, I still didn't want to write about Plath, especially not about her death. I already couldn't sleep, but it was harder each time I read another account of Plath's final days. Sometimes I read so much about Plath that I expected to find her waiting for me outside the dorms, dressed better than anyone else. Sometimes I replaced her face with my mother's.

But scholarship students did what they were told because any other option was too great a risk.

As dramatic as it sounded, it was true. The pressure on Scholarship Girls came from outside and from within. The number of credit hours, the GPA expectations, plus the pressure to fit in with the other girls, to make ourselves at home in a place we could never afford, would challenge anyone's first semester. I could tell a Scholarship Girl from across the room by how hard she watched what the others were doing. I suspected that if Eliza Jackson had stayed at Loch Raven past Orientation Week, she could have turned into one of us, reading every room, digesting every social cue like it was another test we had to pass.

"Well. Writing comes naturally to you, Nikki, so I'm sure you will do well," Dr. Gallina said.

I barely registered the compliment. "You grade differently than Professor Weedler. He isn't a fan of my writing."

I didn't mention that instead of researching Plath, I had decided to focus on campus resources like counseling—or the lack of resources, in Loch Raven's case. Not to mention the curriculum choices in classes like Freshman Seminar that could be seen as insensitive, given the fact that Abbie Moriano, among others, had died here.

Eileen claimed the freshman-curfew rule had been created in response to the Sylvia Club, and I hated it even more based on principle alone. A curfew didn't make sense when there were things that might actually help students. Like real counseling services instead of a tiny office that was never open.

Only Sadie knew about it, but in that horrible first week after Eliza Jackson had almost died upstairs, I tried to speak to someone at the college. I talked myself into it, built up all my nerve, and when I got there, the counseling center was locked. But I could see through the glass door that the man inside was asleep at his desk. I couldn't bring myself to knock and wake him up.

Since then, every time I walked by, the office was dark, empty. I never saw any students go in, which meant no one was able to get help, at least not on campus. If the school really wanted to keep students safe, they could do so much more.

I decided not to care what Weedler would think about this topic. It gave me more room to investigate the college in a different way, with an eye toward fatalities on campus, if I wanted. And I definitely wanted. If the college had failed those girls, the least we could do was make sure they weren't forgotten.

Dr. Gallina didn't break eye contact. "You have a real talent for writing, Nikki. I mean that. You should think about working on the school newspaper."

She didn't seem to expect a response, which was good because my mouth refused to work while we finished restacking my messy research.

As she walked away, I turned back to the women behind the glass.

Yeah, I knew the images of those women were meant to inspire. *Look at what they did, look at all they accomplished.*

But I couldn't relate. They just weren't realistic, with their perfect teeth and expensive haircuts. They weren't the students who got called in to meet with the RA and who worried about losing their scholarships. I doubted any of them were Scholarship Girls at all. If they were the model of what a successful woman should look like, I had a long way to go.

Autumn chill, drooping sun. Me, always rushing. The vapory figure of a girl wearing a shrunken baby doll tee staggered into

Hope Hall, gripping her head like it was wounded, like she couldn't walk in a straight line. Except Hope Hall was still closed. And when I approached the dusty glass to peer inside, there was no one. Just me in the reflection, looking for ghosts.

Polly, the RA, lived down the hall in her own single room. She was a junior and a competitive swimmer. Even though I'd seen her in passing many times, we'd never spoken. Her hair was known to reek of chlorine, according to Eileen, but I couldn't smell anything.

She opened her door and led me to two folding chairs she must have set up for our discussion, then launched into her practiced speech. "It has come to my attention that you have missed curfew on three occasions. Three off-campus curfew violations."

The quivering note card clamped in her hand had seen better days. I wondered how she knew I'd gone off campus, but with the nosy girls on my floor, there were no actual secrets at Loch Raven. Unless you were the one keeping them.

"I'm allowed to leave campus." It was too bright under her overhead lights. The aching behind my eyes intensified, regardless of where I aimed my line of sight.

"But you missed curfew again two nights ago, and you didn't check back in until the next morning. That's a problem. You've read and signed the Freshman Student Code of Conduct, right?"

The smell of sweet sewage drifted from a vase of dead roses on her desk. Like, really dead, the water mostly evaporated and brown. All the fallen petals crisped into black at the edges.

It reminded me of how my dad had kept funeral flowers in vases and moldy fruit baskets on the dining room table for weeks after mom died. Fruit flies swarmed and the house stank from decomposition until I finally threw it all away.

She started again; she had a script to get through. "If there are any more missed curfews, unattended classes, or other *instances*, you will have to meet with the dean. It isn't up to me."

"What does that mean when you say *other instances*?" I asked.

Her face reddened. "Other instances include the practice of the occult or supernatural activities not in accordance with the principles of the college." Her fingers moved like she was playing an invisible piano, an elaborate twitching.

Someone must have gotten in trouble for that séance on the fourth floor, and this was the college's way of addressing it.

"Possible consequences include warning, academic probation, suspension, expulsion. I'm supposed to report it if people even mention the Sylvia Plath club. It's a matter of safety. If you have a plan to bring up your grades at least, maybe some sort of special project or independent study will help show you're serious. You know, if the dean asks to meet with you."

This was the part where I was supposed to straighten my spine and promise she'd never hear from me again. Instead, I leaned forward to mimic her posture. "How's swimming going? Do you love it?"

She visibly warmed at the mention of her favorite topic. "It's the only thing that gets rid of the Dread."

The Dread. I knew exactly what she meant.

"Where's your twin?" she asked before I left. "You know, for Twin Day."

Another one of the Spirit Week themes. Girls all over campus had found someone to dress like. Identical pigtails, duplicate bucket hats, and platform sandals. Matchy, matchy.

"I don't have a twin," I said, and Polly's face filled with so much pity I couldn't look back. There was nothing more depressing at

Loch Raven than not having a twin on Twin Day. Nothing lonelier than an unmatched girl.

I wouldn't say the meeting with Polly motivated me, but I did get back to work. Back to the coed library down the hill, trying to make something out of the mess of papers Weedler had gifted me, then finally shoving them aside for a topic that mattered more, the root of all the campus stories.

My rubbery headphones, the ones I shared with Sadie, tunneled Veruca Salt into my skull.

The song on repeat: "Seether."

No matter how many times I reread the peer-reviewed articles on counseling and suicide risks for college-age students, I couldn't focus. Like my usual level of distraction, plus a thousand. I thought about my mother. I thought about the dead girls whose names we didn't know.

I tried people-watching, but there weren't any cute boys nearby and the dim lamps on each table coated everyone with dark shadows. There were only girls who looked equally hungry and sleep deprived, their faces buried in dusty books. I recognized one girl from our scholarship meeting at the start of the semester. She nodded hello, reapplied her sticky lip gloss, and returned to her notes.

Another girl wearing a maroon sweater vest, her neck rubbed raw and bruised, hugged her own body like a straitjacket, then glided through the bookshelves and emerged from the other side like vapor. Betsy, I remembered. From the Death Tour. Eileen hadn't been lying. I pinched my cheeks to wake up, thought it might be time to develop a taste for coffee.

Absently, I ran my fingers over the grooves in the old wooden table until I realized the grooves were letters. "Peg Kline, '65" someone had scrawled into the desk, maybe with a pocketknife. The letters were serrated and imprecise. Before I knew it, twenty minutes had passed with me staring at Peg Kline's name and writing down questions I could never answer.

Was she a Loch Raven student, and when did she graduate? What was her major? Where was her dorm room? Who was her roommate?

And then, surprising myself only a little, I let the questions go deeper: Was she in the Sylvia Club? How and when? Why?

They weren't unanswerable questions, at least, not all of them. The second floor of the library had a reference room, where, among globes and framed maps, they kept old yearbooks. The librarian told me I could only check out reference materials for twenty-four hours, which was all I needed. That was enough time to scratch my itch and move on with the work I was supposed to do for Weedler's class.

Before I could write an essay about the college's failures, I had to prove the severity of the issue. And if Eileen was right about the Sylvia Club, the girl who'd died each year was a freshman, a girl who'd attended one year and never again.

I scoured the yearbooks for names of students who didn't appear in the following year's list and for students who had seemingly disappeared from Loch Raven's history completely. On each of my index cards, I jotted the name of a girl who might be dead, meaning she only showed up in one yearbook but not the next one. It only sounded gruesome if I thought about it too long.

I wanted to know who they were. At first, their names were all that mattered. So far, I had twenty-six from the sixties alone.

It was too long of a list. As I half watched Betsy knock books off the shelves, I realized my mistake. Even if I found a way to verify that each student had lived past the date of their yearbook photo, I didn't have time to track down dozens and dozens of names.

Not to mention all the other reasons a student could leave the college from one year to the next. Some people just dropped out or transferred. I bet there were a few girls who'd had the dumb luck to get knocked up. Maybe even students who weren't invited back because they got caught making out with other girls or exposing their scandalous knees. The nuns would never have tolerated that.

I'd have to start with the names I knew: Mary, Jessie, Betsy. Abbie.

At least I found Peg Kline, Loch Raven College graduating class of 1965. She played field hockey and majored in home economics. She wore a fucking headband. Peg had made it through all four years. Good for her.

Trivia time: What year did Sylvia Plath die?
A: 1963.

"Pretty shoes," Betsy quipped, her warm breath in my ear. When I turned my head, she wasn't there.

A jab. My knock-off Docs were a lot of things, but they weren't pretty.

I kept staring at a group photo of Peg Kline and her field hockey team, year 1964. They had been posed in front of Hope Hall. In black and white, the building appeared older. I squinted at the image until I realized what I was looking at. On the roof of the old dorm, a blurred figure stood on the ledge, the distorted face stretched into a wide-open scream.

I pointed to the photo and asked the girl studying across from me if she saw anything.

"Just a blur," she yawned.

Every yearbook in my reach, from 1964 until the current year, had a similar picture: girls posed in front of Hope Hall with a hazy figure on the roof behind them. It looked both permanent and drawn on, added after the fact like a sticker without edges or a stamp that didn't smear.

There was my answer. I'd been searching for students, but I hadn't tried looking for information about the college. From the local-newspaper archives, I scanned the index for Hope Hall, until I found a short article about Abbie Moriano from two years before.

"Pending further investigation, Loch Raven College closes Hope Hall, their freshman dormitory, after the tragic loss of a student."

Further investigation was interesting. The following sentence caught my attention even more:

"Joseph Cantor, the family's attorney, asks the public to please respect the family's privacy during this period."

Why would the family need a lawyer if their daughter had killed herself? Unless they were claiming she hadn't jumped at all. Maybe she fell from the roof of Hope Hall and the family wanted to hold the college accountable? No other articles had been published with the results of an investigation, though. No one had cared enough to follow up on the story.

We'd been told on our first campus visit that the old dormitory was under renovation. But I had never seen any changes or repairs, no crews working on the building. Just a dark and empty shell of what it used to be.

"I'll be your twin." The sound of a woman gagging. The echo rang out from the mezzanine.

A buzzing in my brain quickly drowned out the voice. It would have been so much easier if the Sylvia Club twisted its way out of my system and let me focus on my actual schoolwork, but now all I had were more questions.

And a horrible gut-punch realization that my questions mattered.

I wouldn't call it instinct. More like an embedded hook.

CHAPTER 10
NOW

Sadie

I*am I am I am*
Those were the words splattered across a gigantic triptych on Diana Noble's living room walls. Each time a woman asked where she'd bought the painted wooden palette, she chirped, "Girl, I'll hook you up."

I couldn't stop staring, either. It was the kind of artwork that sucked up all the attention in the room, though I bet no one else caught the reference. *The Bell Jar*, that book by Sylvia Plath that Nikki and I had had to read junior year of high school. I wouldn't have remembered the quote if it weren't for Nikki. She had written it on the bottoms of her Chucks. That was before college, though. Before her mom died.

The wide-open floor plan of Diana's home reminded me of a cathedral without the stained glass, almost holy in its cleanliness. Renovations like coffered ceilings, crystal chandeliers, and better-than-builder-grade light switches screamed, *Different tax bracket, bitches*. The surfaces gleamed, waxy enough to repel dust. Most of the families in the neighborhood hired someone to clean their houses, but I guessed Diana employed a whole team. Her fresh manicure hadn't seen a toilet brush in at least a decade. I wasn't jealous, but I think I was supposed to be.

When I walked in with Rhi strapped to my chest, the room hiccuped into silence, like a sudden skip on a record, before leveling out again. I almost backed out the front door before more people saw me.

bullshit brunch self-care locked office crying baby chandeliers why why why why

What I'd found inside her office forced panic through me, hour by hour, minute by minute. I needed to focus.

"Messy bitch," Nikki had laughed through the baby monitor that morning, causing me to spill my coffee.

"Your Why determines everything. Your Why is the base ingredient in the Cure," Annie Minx declared in the first chapter of *The Self-Care Cure*. I had started reading it after breakfast, eager to understand whatever I could of Nikki's last book and to find any other breadcrumbs she might have left for me.

I wanted to know Nikki's Why. Not why she took her own life. Because that wasn't what I believed had happened. "If something happens to me" wasn't exactly hard proof that she hadn't killed herself, but it meant something. I could only make sense of her death if I told myself it was an accident. Even that thought strangled me.

Why dead girls? Why, after everything, leave a note for me to find? Beneath the research in the office, the real focus of Nikki's work—the obituaries and the yearbooks—was a preoccupation with the Sylvia Club all over again. I didn't get it then, and I didn't get it now.

My Why for showing up to Diana Noble's house was trickier. Because I had questions only Diana Noble could answer. But also because I needed friends, the alive kind. Because Harrison had smiled like a proud parent when I told him where I was going, that I was making an effort to join the other moms. He really had no idea how unlikely it was for me to ever fit into the sleek fabric of Hidden Harbor.

Thankfully, no one splashed a Bloody Mary in my face right away. A good sign, I decided, that the room would settle into passive-aggressiveness instead of aggressive-aggressiveness. All the children ran upstairs to the playroom, where Diana had hired a nanny for the event, but I held on to Rhiannon. She would be my excuse when I needed to leave.

Twelve women, including me and Diana, stood in the wide-open living room. Everyone was more interested in snapping photos of the croissant tower and posting them online than loading up their plates. Jellied pastries and mini-Belgian waffles—a dream spread. Me and Nikki would have filled our pockets with bacon to eat on the way home.

I had never been so quiet at a party. Old Sadie would have already taken over the bar, mixing drinks and telling raunchy jokes, driving the conversation. This was new territory, though. Instead of making new friends, I kept checking under the end tables for Nikki's slop. She wasn't there.

In some of my loneliest days, while Rhi slept in the crook of my arm and I stared at the wall, I had envisioned what my new life in Hidden Harbor could look like if I let it. I could almost see my new little world blooming into a bigger kind of happiness if I squinted hard enough. Playdates and joint stroller walks. Book clubs with white wine on someone's back patio. I invented mom friends who volunteered to hold my baby while I peed. It didn't sound so bad. Different from what I had once dreamed for myself, but wasn't that adulthood in a nutshell—a parallel universe lined with decisions that would make your younger self woozy with disbelief?

Our ongoing inside joke: Kill me if I ever wear pantyhose. Chop off my head if you ever see me counting calories. Bury me in some rich lady's backyard if I turn into the kind of woman who listens to pop music and goes to bed before ten.

I wanted to like the other women. I wanted to pretend I could wear the same mask Nikki had worn.

They all wore the same brand of leggings with mesh peek-a-boo side panels, and half of them held an identical style of purse that looked like a bowling ball bag. The backpack several of them wore, full of neon color-blocked triangles, could double as a diaper bag. I'd seen it on Instagram. If I leaned in and smelled their necks, I bet I would smell the exact charcoal-infused skincare products Nikki had left in the bathroom cabinet.

More than one conversation I eavesdropped on mentioned Annie Minx and the new book.

"Did you read it yet?"

"Who has time to read?"

"Well, Di read it all in one day..."

"And you know she made sure to post every page of her reading experience."

The women laughed and dabbed their eyes. But it was tragic, they agreed. Very, very tragic to know the story behind the story, they determined between mimosa sips.

I had made it through the prologue and the first chapter so far. Minx used the words "focus," "energy," "self-care," and "release" at least twenty times in those first twenty pages. She called the reader a "bitch" more times than I could count.

Bitch, you better release all that negative energy.
What did you say? You're tired? Bitch, please.
Don't be a basic bitch. It's time to sparkle from the inside out.

It was like being bullied into attending brunch. But that was another part of Minx's appeal. She said all the things a best friend was supposed to tell you but rarely did because it would hurt your feelings. Maybe only sisters were allowed to be that truthful. Coming from a perfect and faceless stranger, readers were supposed to feel a twinge of relatability. "She gets me," her fans said. "I've never felt so seen."

Coming from Nikki, I didn't buy it. If she meant the books as satire, maybe. That kind of self-help wasn't her style. It wasn't her voice. There was no grit, no sweet but grungy self-deprecation. The research on dead girls in her office, on the other hand—that was all Nikki.

Rhi slept against me while everyone cooed at her chubby cheeks and her heart-shaped mouth. They ignored me, but not unkindly. No one could resist a baby. Then the crowd cleared to make room for Diana, wearing a strapless red sundress, her hair the color of a cream puff. Very Marilyn, if Marilyn had the body of a yoga instructor. Until that moment, she had ignored me with precision.

"Harrison Walsh is your baby's daddy, right?" she asked in a tone meant to include the whole room in her question. And what a way to ask it.

There were the scowls I had been waiting for. I was the woman who'd jumped in Nikki's grave, who slept in Annie Minx's barely cold bed. They couldn't decide if they hated me or feared me. Their husbands could be next on my list, after all.

"Throw me to the wolves if I ever hide my tattoos to look 'presentable,'" I used to tell Nikki. "Seriously, I'll drown you in the reservoir if you ever get married and settle down in the suburbs."

"Can I hold your baby while you eat? I remember how hard that age can be." Diana's voice softened, but when she grazed my wrist, I swatted her away like a bug.

"No, I have to feed her."

Self-consciously, I touched the thinning patch of hair near my temples and came away with a handful of baby-fine strands. The whole room watched. We were two actors improvising their lines, waiting to see what would propel us into the next scene.

She squinted, and then, as if deciding how to read my reaction, she started down the hall. "Follow me."

Diana's forceful silence led the way. She marched forward until halting at the end of the hallway and into a room meant to be an office but clearly used for storage.

Instead of leaving, Diana closed the door behind her and sat cross-legged on the floor directly across from me, hiking her dress up over her knees. Since I really did need to nurse Rhi, I sat in a wheeled desk chair, not bothering to turn on the light.

I couldn't tell if Diana wanted me at the party or not. Maybe she let me stay because she wanted people to gossip, or maybe she wanted a good story to tell later.

"This is a nice room." I drew a breath as Rhi latched. "Very quiet."

Diana's bottom teeth caught on her lip. "Yes, I wish I got to use it more."

The dark of the room and my usual fatigue made my eyelids droop. I pinched my leg to wake up, to remember Nikki's office and all the questions I didn't know how to ask.

"So, is this brunch a book club? For *The Self-Care Cure?*"

"Yes and no. And PS, you don't have to stay for the next part."

It sounded like an invitation to leave as soon as possible.

She held up her phone and took a photo of her pedicure, red toes against white carpet. I bet she had already filled her phone with photos of herself in that dress. Most of her other online photos were sportier—upside-down yoga poses, toned arms and flat abs on full display. Her ponytail was never not swinging.

Then, after a thoughtful hesitation, she put away her phone and said, "I was the one who found Nikki that day." She said it so casually, a practiced nonchalance in her voice that didn't quiver. "It was the worst day of my life."

What she really meant was *I'm not allowed to like you.* And *I am loyal to her even in death.*

"I was her best friend, too. Once. A long time ago." My voice cracked but didn't break.

She waited a moment to respond. Long pauses were apparently her thing. It gave me time to really look at her face—at least five years younger than me—and her muscled shoulders. Strong legs. If she had once been a cheerleader like I suspected, she would have been at the base of the pyramid, not one of the flyers.

"Is that so?"

I didn't know her well enough to read her expression, but it had changed, maybe trying to conceal surprise. It wasn't like Nikki would have ever mentioned me.

Rhi squirmed against my breast then, and Diana extended her hands to hold her while I fixed my shirt. I surprised myself by letting her.

"I know this sounds random, but do you know what she was working on before she died? Harrison keeps the office locked and—"

She straightened, her eyes widening at the word "locked."

"I assumed she was working on *The Self-Care Cure*, but she never showed me her office."

It wasn't the answer I hoped to hear. But maybe, in this case, it was better that she didn't know about Nikki's work. Yesterday, I had wanted to be angry with Harrison for sealing the office shut and treating it like a mausoleum, but that anger had subsided. The way he handled his grief wasn't up to me to judge. After all, I had handled mine by not handling it at all.

Diana rocked my daughter, and I swayed, too, mimicking their movement, my arms emptier than ever. Rhi had settled into Diana's cradle so easily.

"How's Caroline doing?" She chewed on the inside of her mouth, working through thoughts she wasn't sure she should say out loud. "I never understood why she insisted on going to Loch Raven after Nikki opposed it so strongly. But I guess Harrison finally won that fight." Her voice sharpened on every vowel. Harrison's name sizzled.

Well, that was new. I had been there when Caroline moved into the dorms. There had been no indication of a fight about attending Loch Raven between her and her dad, not that I saw. At the time, it made my stomach drop to think of Loch Raven at all, but it had also made sense to me. Caroline missed her mom and wanted to follow her path. She wanted to stand on the same grass her mom had once stood on.

I could also think of several reasons why Nikki wouldn't want Caroline on that campus. Bad memories were just the start.

Nikki's to-do list with Caroline's name on it wasn't far from my mind. Had she wanted me to keep Caroline from going to Loch Raven? If so, I'd dropped the ball on that one.

First time Nikki and I saw the Loch Raven College campus: the night before high school graduation. We hadn't wanted the official tour, with someone selling us on green space and religious history. We found the big fountain, threw pennies, and spun in circles as we looked up at an old, empty building with "Hope Hall" etched into the stone. Nikki shivered, but the air wasn't cold.

"Can I ask you something?" Diana said. She didn't wait for a response. "If you and Nikki were such good friends, why didn't you keep in touch? I didn't even see you at the funeral."

She'd changed octaves, almost accusatory. I mumbled that I had been there, that I'd sat in the back at the funeral home where she probably didn't see me. The rest I wouldn't attempt to answer. I had never said any of it out loud, didn't even know if my mouth could form the words, much less let my brain revisit it.

Someone out at the party called Diana's name, and she instantly opened the door and headed out to the living room with my baby still in her arms. I stumbled to keep up.

It was a natural question. Why hadn't we stayed friends? The bigger question lived one level beneath, the question that had threaded through me since I heard that she'd died. Why hadn't either of us tried, despite everything that happened? Every few years, I searched for Nikki online. I would drink too much or wake up in the middle of the night unable to sleep, and search for my old best friend. It wasn't just boredom and curiosity; I wanted to make sure she was okay because sometimes I wasn't. And I missed her. I wasn't too proud to admit it.

Beyond those online searches, though, I remembered what Nikki's mother-in-law had told me when I tried to call after Caroline was born: "She doesn't have time for friends right now." Nikki and Harrison changed their phone number soon after.

They moved to the suburbs. She never once reached out. I always tried to tell myself it wasn't personal. It wasn't about me. It was us. It was what we'd done. She couldn't look at me without remembering.

Women carried glasses to the kitchen and dumped half-nibbled pastries into the automatic trash can. A buzz hummed through the group. Gossip, I assumed, about me.

My whole body burned hot, and my fingers tingled. I needed out. I gasped for fresh air, my open mouth searching for it.

Diana grabbed my hand, right there, in front of everyone. She slowed her voice into a yoga instructor cadence. "Breathe. Ground yourself. It's natural to feel whatever you're feeling."

What I was feeling was a quicksand kind of death. The sound that leaked out of me was more wildcat than woman.

We stood together, breathing in unison, our hands laced, until I found the rhythm and finally let a tear slip down my face. My face hurt from holding it in. Diana must have been a good friend to Nikki, I realized, even if it pained me to admit it.

"You know, the day that I found her—" She stopped herself before finishing the thought. Then, reapplying her hostess smile, she passed Rhi to my arms before rushing over to help her guests clean up.

I wanted to grab her and make her keep talking, but I strained my mouth into a fake smile to twin hers. I suddenly couldn't wait to get home.

No one asked me to stay, and I didn't turn around to see if they watched me leave.

CHAPTER 11
NOW

Harrison wasn't home after the brunch. Off came my uncomfortable nursing bra and on slid Nikki's blue robe. Her smell spilled through the vents, but I couldn't find it when I sniffed again. I rested Rhi in her crib and peered through the heavy living room curtains. It took effort to process the conversation with Diana, everything she said and didn't say.

In the weird dart of dimming daylight, and only in one single patch behind the curtain, I saw the difference in the paint colors. The alteration was only noticeable beneath my fingers, but custom paint colors were probably hard to match. I knew from experience that holes in walls weren't always easy to disguise. I had seen it growing up, the holes my uncle punched in my grandmother's walls when he was angry, and the spackle he scraped over top to hide the damage. Whisper White versus Ultra White, so subtle I might never locate that one area ever again.

Just as I reached to flip on the overhead lights, Nikki watched from the couch, her thick hair almost black.

"Shit." I tried not to yell, yanking at the curtains hard enough to hear them rip.

"It's just me," she said, holding up her hands as if in surrender. "Don't freak."

Caroline. In a saggy Loch Raven sweatshirt. She had dyed her hair two shades darker and looked more like a copy of Nikki than ever before. Same enormous doll eyes, same upturned nose. But taller than Nikki, courtesy of Harrison's genes. Less inclined to smile.

"You scared the shit out of me, Caroline." I slumped into the chair opposite the sofa, my chest on fire, my stomach queased from all the croissants I'd stolen at brunch.

Stifling a dry laugh, she turned away so I couldn't see her roll her eyes. It was like that between us. It probably always would be.

"I just came to pick up something."

With the lights on, she had the complexion of the undead—waxy flesh and half-moons of old eyeliner. A hangover, most likely. One step away from spewing all over her mother's tufted-wool farmhouse rugs.

Caroline had always been the scariest part of sliding into Nikki's life. Teenagers, especially ones heading to college, had zero patience for bullshit. I usually took Rhi to another room when Caroline came over. I wasn't proud of it, but it was easier for all of us if she didn't have to pretend to like me.

"Does your dad know you're here?"

She stood up fast. "Never mind. I'll come back another time. I don't want to wake the baby."

The baby. Her half sister. It seemed too much to hope that

Caroline would ever hold Rhiannon, much less say her name. We were so far from the family I wanted us to be. Could I blame her? She'd once had a mother and a happy family. Now she had me and a baby sister eighteen years younger. My presence wasn't what either of us had planned.

But she was Nikki's girl. Her name on that to-do list had to mean Nikki at least wanted me to have a relationship with her daughter. I had to do better.

I followed her to the door, not sure whether I should invite her to stay or not. Maybe I could make tea and feed her leftover stroganoff. That seemed like a thing a wannabe stepmother might do.

"So, what's going on? How's school? Are you making friends? Dating anyone?" I tried again. "Your dad said you were invited into a special writing class?"

In response, she flattened me with an icy stare. The duffel bag thrown over her arm knocked into a lamp by the front door, and I suddenly noticed its size. The bulky contents strained against the zipper.

"Are you going on a trip? Because if you're going somewhere, you really need to tell someone. Us. Your dad."

Instead of answering me, she ripped at the zipper and shoved the bag into my chest so I could see the contents. Nikki's old shoes and musty clothing, a silver sequined disco dress that once fit me. And a handful of headless Polaroid photos.

The first photo I ever took of Nikki: Fourth grade, a slumber party in her basement. She wore an orange-peel smile, the rind tucked inside her lips, and a pillow stuffed under her shirt. We took turns at playing the mom, though never actually holding a baby.

When Caroline finally opened her mouth again, her voice

thrummed from holding back tears. "Just some of my mom's things. Is that okay with you, or do I need your fucking permission?"

It didn't feel right to tell her that the silver dress had once been mine and that many of those photos were images of me, too. I couldn't guess where she'd found them, because I hadn't seen a shred of Nikki's old life in that house since I moved in. I hadn't seen the photos since college. The Polaroids were less sophisticated than Nikki's Annie Minx author photo, but Caroline had to notice the similarities, too. Headless and loving it.

"Come on, Caroline. You know how your dad feels about moving things around. Would you tell him the same thing if he were standing here right now?"

"I would tell him to fuck off."

That attitude, she didn't get it from Harrison. *Good girl*, I almost said, but she didn't want to hear it. The best we could do was pretend for a minute that I was no one, not even the enemy.

I'll never recover, Nikki had told me after her mom's funeral. Caroline must have felt the same way. It was true after all. She'd never be the same person now that her mother was gone. Her heart would never not be broken.

I knew people, like my friend Lucille, who got tattoos to honor their dead family, and people who still listened to voicemails of long-gone loved ones just to hold on to that voice. But how could I tell Caroline that I understood what she was feeling, because I really didn't. Not ever knowing your mother was different from losing her. My own clumsy grief over Nikki was mixed with too much guilt and fatigue to comprehend.

"There's a notebook my mom couldn't find before she died. She searched everywhere, sort of turned into a maniac about it."

Pausing, she garnished her irritation with a bitten lip. "I'm going to find it for her."

Not enough words collected on my tongue to form a complete sentence. Somewhere close by, Nikki purred, like *Finally*.

"She started looking for it after that reporter came by." Caroline eyed my face for a response, and I couldn't help but give her one.

"A reporter?" The conversation had gone south so quick I couldn't keep up.

"A journalist, I mean. Whatever they're called."

She propped herself against the front door, then focused on my robe. Her mother's robe. "Just tell Dad to call me."

The door slammed before I could ask her to stay.

No no no no no.

A reporter could have meant nothing, or it could have meant... everything. The past cycling back on us like I always worried it would.

If Nikki had been searching for our old journal after a reporter showed up, there was a reason. She knew all too well the damage it could cause.

The neighbor across the street waved me over as I strapped Rhi into her stroller for her evening walk. I had to move my body in order to think.

Up close, her smeared lipstick and caked foundation made her look clownish and severe. She had the drawn eyebrows of Joan Crawford. A tiny woman in a brown fur shrug. Beaver or maybe muskrat.

Stepping closer, the woman bumped my robe knot and spoke to my collarbone. "Want me to walk the baby this time? You look exhausted."

Her coat mostly covered the loose, thin skin at her neck. I guessed that she was near eighty, but I had never been able to guess ages. The way she leaned in, I thought she was going to kiss me. If she kissed me, I would have let her.

"Just for a little while," she said, coaxing the stroller handles into her own hands, stronger than I expected.

I wasn't ready for a walk, I realized. I needed shoes. And a bra. It suddenly seemed like so much work.

"Okay."

Okay. Just one word, but inside it, a thousand small agreements.

"We'll be back soon. Get some rest," she yelled over her shoulder, and then they were halfway down the street, close enough that I might have to run to catch up, but I didn't.

It took me thirty seconds to realize what I had done. Enough time to close my front door behind me. I'd let a stranger, a woman whose name I didn't know, take my baby.

The house expanded and contracted around me. I picked up my phone but froze before pushing the buttons. I couldn't call Harrison. He would never forgive me for losing our baby. And it might have been too soon to call the police, but when was "not soon enough"? They wouldn't believe me when I explained how I let this muskrat-shrugged woman take my daughter. How I didn't know her name. They'd find out I wasn't on the mortgage, that I wasn't married to the "man of the house." They'd take one look at me and know what kind of mother I was.

Bernadette. Bernie, I suddenly remembered Harrison calling her once. She had lived there for a year or two. A quiet renter. A neighbor whom Nikki had probably chatted with about the weather.

Ten minutes passed. I had never timed my walk with Rhi

around the tennis courts, but I guessed twenty minutes. I laced up my shoes.

Except I couldn't time a route that I didn't know, couldn't account for the woman's walking speed or if she had to stop to soothe Rhiannon. My baby. Crying without me there to help.

Thirty minutes.

I paced up and down the sidewalk, then back into the house again. I didn't dare step away from the window. There was no one to call, though my hands gripped my phone anyway.

And then, after ten more minutes, the shape of a woman pushing a stroller filled the end of the street.

"She's fighting sleep, but we're so close. I bet if I did another lap, she'd be out for a good while." Bernie smiled, her lipstick mostly chewed off and her skin red from the sun. I had never seen her smile before, I realized, but then again, she had probably never seen me smile, either.

The sky smoothed into white. Ultra White, Whisper White. The kind of nippy day that other people loved. Bees swarmed by the mailbox as if there was a secret store of nectar they couldn't reach. A dozen chunky bumbles, too many for this late in the season. They should have been wintering, but I wanted them to stay. Nikki had always loved bees.

She watched from inside the living room window. Orange-rind smile like we were girls again. Her dress the duplicate diluted blue of the robe.

You have work to do, I could hear her yell through the glass. *Get it together, girl. Knockers up.*

It hit me again, the same shuttering grenade of memory detonating behind my eyes: my car, the orange dress. Our fingers forever locked.

Except there was another part of that memory, something I'd kept buried under all the others. Us writing in our journal, passing the notebook back and forth, spilling out all the things we couldn't say out loud, things that would ruin our lives. Nikki had promised to destroy the book, just like she promised to get rid of the dress. At least she'd fulfilled one part of that promise.

I would never leave without you.

She'd said it. She'd meant it. She wouldn't have killed herself before finding that notebook. She would have searched forever.

Bernie's face suddenly looked familiar. She was someone I knew, someone whose face I recognized even when I closed my eyes. A lover of fur and lipstick and sleeping babies. Lucky me to know her.

If the old notebook was still here in the house, Caroline couldn't be the one to find it.

"Go again," I said. "Take as long as you like."

CHAPTER 12

THEN

Nikki

In the first weeks of the semester, Eileen's Death Tour had ended up as a depressing, backward version of the Visitation Day script that prospective families heard. With a single flashlight, Eileen led us to the spots on campus where she'd heard girls had died. She ended with a less-than-dramatic pause at Hope Hall.

Q: Was Hope Hall as haunted as everyone said it was?
A: Unknown.

Sadie's interest in the Sylvia Club was originally limited to its potential for Halloween costumes. But after witnessing what she called Eileen's "uninspired performance" for the Death Tour, she wanted to take over and plan our own reenactment. Costumes, candlelight, a mixed CD already in the process of being burned. Endless possibilities.

Track 1: "Pretend We're Dead" by L7.

She didn't care about the truth, that there was an immeasurable sadness rooted into every structure at Loch Raven, that people had actually died in horrible ways. And she didn't seem to notice how I looked at our classmates, searching their eyes for something I once saw in my mom's face, a certain kind of numbness. Glazed and unreachable.

My library visit had ramped me up. I started by searching for their names, and then for their stories. Instead of sleeping, I dug through more yearbooks, making lists of names and searching for obituaries. I found possible leads all around campus: a scratch of decades-old graffiti in a bathroom stall ("R.I.P Jessie Allis") and an old theater playbill for *Lysistrata* dedicated to "Mary Matherly, who left us too soon."

Poor Jessie, the girls on the fourth floor repeated each night.

Break a leg, Mary, the cast of the play started saying before each run-through.

And Abbie, Abbie, Abbie. We didn't need to call her as we passed Hope Hall each day. Her name had already settled on our tongues.

First frost, earlier than usual, and a full moon. Everyone agreed it was a sign.

Sadie took the opportunity to hold an "offering ritual" in the overgrown cemetery that we'd discovered the first week of school. She said she got the idea from a movie we watched once at a slumber party, but I didn't remember that one.

"Bring gifts for the girls," she instructed everyone on her invite list: me, Eileen, and two other zombie extras. "And you better dress up. None of your pajama pants and shower shoes."

As always, Sadie went all in. The other girls brought flashlights, but she brought candles. They wore black jumpers while she wore a cocktail dress.

When I had asked Sadie the point of the ritual, her mouth quirked. "It's either this, or we crash the chemistry study session dressed as ghouls."

Fun was the point. I didn't argue. What would I have said? I didn't know the expiration date on grief, how long I was allowed to feel swallowed up, bothered by things like conversing with the dead. I had hoped Sadie would just look at me and know.

Unless she looked at me and saw the part of me that was curious. The part of me that wanted to get closer to the girls who once lived here.

We started in the cemetery but didn't stay there long. The tombstones of hundred-year-old nuns were worn and nearly unreadable. They radiated a kind of bleakness that made us shush each other.

"Let's take a moment," Sadie said, instructing our circle to join hands and close our eyes, her sudden European accent almost comical. "Tonight, we offer gifts to the girls of Loch Raven, those spirits who linger."

Through the tree covering, the sky oozed a pitiful light. Sadie opened one eye and pursed her lips at me for missing my cue.

"Hear us, spirits. Let us speak our intent," I rasped. She had made me practice the script three times in the bathroom mirror, though I couldn't muster any enthusiasm. It was effort enough not to roll my eyes. "We offer gifts in exchange for the honor of your presence, tonight and every night."

Sadie had wanted us to chant together, but Eileen suddenly clutched her cross necklace, breaking the circle. In the thick weeds, we rested a waterlogged edition of Sylvia Plath's *Ariel*, our first offering, and headed to the next place.

Branches snapped under feet, and we synced our breath. The call of a nearby owl grew louder and louder. First, to the back entrance of the auditorium, where we could sneak in the unlocked door.

One of the zombie girls left a fake sapphire brooch on the edge of the stage. With wet eyes, she sucked her snot back up her nose and said a wordless prayer. The brooch had belonged to her grandmother who'd died two months before.

"For Mary," we all recited.

For Mary, for Mary, for Mary.

Our voices echoed through the empty theater. Even me. I played along, aware that if I really wanted to learn more about the Sylvia Club, I'd have to find the answers on my own.

Next, we headed to the library. It had been closed for hours, and we caught each other from stumbling over broken stones in the dark. For Betsy, I dropped yellow mums I'd picked from one of the Harvest Hoedown displays near the student center. It seemed that a girl who had chosen to die in the library would appreciate yellow flowers.

"My late aunt used to love mums," another girl sniffled.

Sadie had made the whole night seem like a spectacle, but the tears on the other girl's cheeks were so fresh, so hideously raw, that I made myself look away. So much loss. If we combined all our sadness, it seemed like we had enough grief between us to power the whole campus. My mom had loved yellow flowers, too.

By the time we made it to Hope Hall, Eileen's mood had infected the whole group. Cold, tired, eager to watch *Dawson's Creek* and drink something warm. For once, I agreed with her.

"Don't tell me we're going to leave some bogus gift for Abbie here." I couldn't stop myself from speaking up, gesturing with open arms to Hope Hall, no longer on Sadie's script. "She deserves better."

She deserved better because her death was still recent enough for us to find pieces of her all over campus. A red wool hat in the lost and found with her name written on the tag. Her name inside one of the used economics textbooks at the bookstore.

And what I didn't say: she deserved better because maybe she hadn't chosen to die, not at Hope Hall or anywhere else. None of us knew enough to speculate in a meaningful way what had actually happened. She had jumped, or maybe she fell. Or something worse.

What was worse than falling?

The fact that Hope Hall remained closed somehow felt more ominous than any of the other stories about campus. I didn't mention the article I'd found. I didn't need to.

Sadie raked through her hair, tugging hard enough to pull a small handful of copper curls. She held out her hand, and I got the message, adding my own loose strands to the pile.

"We gift Abbie something more," I said. "Part of us."

Everyone's hair fell easily, the dead tendrils from loosened ponytails, the debris caught up in scrunchies. Even Eileen contributed to the nest we placed on the steps of Hope Hall.

For Abbie. For Abbie.

The other girls closed their eyes and kissed their crosses. But I stared up, ready to find out how and ready to find out why.

The note on Dr. Gallina's door led straight to a classroom where the *Raven Outlook* meeting had already started. I turned to leave, but one of the girls called out, "Hey, stick around. Don't go yet." Gallina nodded from the back of the room and gestured to an empty seat. There wasn't an easy way to slide out without being noticed.

This was not how I'd planned to spend my afternoon, but okay. Anyone who had been on campus longer than me had to know more about what had happened at Hope Hall, and even though Gallina never offered to help, she was the first person who came to mind. No bullshit, no patronizing.

The classroom looked over the widest stretch of grass, dotted with yellow leaves and gnarly branches. Harvest and hayride weather. I would have rather been out there, inhaling the damp woods instead of the cold pizza sitting rigid on the back table.

The other students at the meeting were upperclassmen. I could tell because they were still dressed in pajamas, the unofficial dress code of Loch Raven College. Unless it was Pajama Day again. I'd worn a retro party dress printed with dead tulips because I wanted my outfit to match my mood.

"All right, let's get back on track. This month's paper?" Gallina started. "All the usuals?"

A girl named Aisha, a ballerina bun high on her head, stood up to write on the chalkboard. "Sports, Campus Updates, Reviews," she wrote, with names in a column to the right.

From there, the conversation volleyed, fast and efficient. The other girls took turns volunteering for the different newspaper sections, describing their plans for what to write while Gallina sat unspeaking except to moderate if the group disagreed about a topic.

Each part of the conversation relied on Gallina's approval. You could see it in the way everyone tried not to make eye contact, the way they scooted closer when she spoke. Gallina nodding at one of their ideas sparked so much pride the room hummed with it. It was an attractive kind of power. Faded Bon Jovi shirt and all.

The girls who worked on the newspaper, Eileen had told me more than once, were Dr. Gallina's pets. Every time I heard her warn someone not to take Gallina's class next semester, I bit my tongue. Eileen just didn't like that she wasn't Gallina's top choice. And yeah, maybe she treated some girls differently than others. But so did Weedler. His way was worse.

A girl named Rosemary volunteered to write the front-page news, a feature story about the stalled renovations to Hope Hall, while Hadley, who played field hockey, wrote the sports column. Aisha would tackle the faculty and student-spotlight sections.

It was a small group, but the *Raven Outlook* was a small paper—four pages total. When Gallina handed me the latest edition, I didn't admit that I had never read it before.

"What about you?" Aisha asked, pointing her nubbed chalk in my direction. "We have no one to write the advice column now that Polly ditched us to focus on swim."

My skin splotched, red and mottled under their spotlight.

Don't let those girls see you sweat, my mom would've said. Mom, with her delicate hands, her face framed in light, soft-seeming until you heard her speak. I wished I could visualize her hands holding the ruby earrings out to me as a gift, but she had simply left them on my nightstand.

"Actually, I was thinking—I mean, hi, I'm Nikki." I waved my hand in a flustered greeting. "I'm not in this club. But I was thinking someone should write about the school play. Not a review, but, you know, something about the costumes and stuff."

I ran out of air before mentioning that I was the one who helped with the costumes or that the first performance was in a couple of hours. My voice already sounded so shrill and rambling in my ear that I couldn't bear to hear myself say another word.

Aisha added "theater" on the board, but small, like she wasn't sold on the idea. "We still need the advice column, though. Can you handle that, too?"

Before I could object, Dr. Gallina spoke up. "Think about it, Nikki. Look at old issues. It's been a popular feature of the paper for years, and everyone ends up taking a turn eventually."

On the back page of the old issue was a column titled "Dear Annie" with a question printed in italics, presumedly from a fellow student. The response underneath from "Annie" wasn't long, a mostly generic template like the kind we relied on for my high school yearbook committee. Templates made it more efficient but didn't allow for much wiggle room or creativity.

"The 'Dear Annie' questions are all fake," Aisha said. Like it was a selling point. "I mean, they're based on a question that someone actually asked one of us about, but no one actually submits a letter or anything."

Dear Annie,
Please help! I'm lonely here at school, and I haven't made many friends yet. Any advice for a shy girl like me?
Sincerely, Shy Girl

Dear Shy Girl,
We all have trouble making friends sometimes. Do what I do: walk up to a stranger, stick out your hand, and introduce yourself. It's that simple! Invite her to a campus event like Taco

Tuesday or Sunrise Prayer to solidify the friendship. You've got this!

Lovingly, Annie

By the time I looked up from the page, Aisha had scrawled my name in the column next to "Annie" with a question mark. It seemed rude to laugh, so I bit the inside of my cheek and fascinated myself with a piece of imaginary lint on my dress. If they knew me at all, they would never suggest I give advice. Not even bad fake advice.

Let me redesign a new template or create a spreadsheet, I should have said. Something behind the scenes that involved organizing small details. That's where I'd shine.

"I still think someone should write a section about suicide awareness," Rosemary said, adjusting her butterfly clips, half a dozen mini braids. Her cautious tone made it sound like the issue had been discussed before. "Everything I'm researching about the Hope Hall renovation is...bleak. We don't have to mention anyone by name or whatever. Maybe just remind students about the counseling center."

"You want to address the history of Hope Hall?" Hadley asked. "Or do you want to tell the freshmen girls to calm down with all their death predictions?"

Aisha threw up her hands. "There isn't room. Just like last month."

I took the opportunity to play dumb, to pretend I didn't know what Hadley meant.

"What history?" I wanted to hear someone else say it: the Sylvia Club.

Everyone knew about Abbie Moriano, most of us had heard

about Betsy and Jessie, the same ghost stories all over campus, but what about the others? The girls in the Sylvia Club whose names were lost, whose stories no one ever talked about?

No one made eye contact. After a beat, Gallina said, "I've been told that we need to include information about Professor Weedler's faculty-mentorship program." Her tone leveled the room. "Let's move on. Rosemary, I'm working with the counseling office for a bigger event later this semester. Maybe we can run a story next month."

The room stalled into silence. No more objections from the girls. Dr. Gallina had the final say, and just like that, the conversation was squashed.

Outside, among scattered red leaves, a girl with a raven painted on her cheek flicked a lighter open and closed. She stopped only to shake a puny pom-pom at loitering birds. Straight teeth, snub nose, raccoon eyeliner. I recognized her from one of the 1980s yearbooks. Nominated LRC Princess on Spirit Day. I was seeing things again, but it seemed so real, no matter how many times I rubbed at my eyes. When she caught me staring, she stuck out her tongue and lit it on fire.

"Holy shit." I stood up so suddenly the skirt of my dress ripped, before lunging toward the door.

I didn't tell them to erase my name off the board. They would figure it out on their own. If I never came back to another newspaper meeting, no one's feelings would be hurt. Gallina might be disappointed, but she'd understand. Instead, I trekked down the hall and waited outside her office like I should have done in the first place.

The hallway was empty, but there was no denying their muffled teasing.

Wow, brave of you to wear that dress in public. I wish I had your confidence.

Loud and insistent, they taunted me through the walls.

When Dr. Gallina finally showed up, a box of leftover pizza balanced in her hands, she eyed me without much of a response. But I had seen her reaction when I asked about the campus history. There was a conversation she didn't want us to have, some rabbit she didn't want us to chase.

"Tell me about the Sylvia Club," I said as she unlocked her office door. Then I didn't leave until she let me in.

CHAPTER 13
NOW

Sadie

Nikki kept appearing to me, her now-familiar odor filling the living room right after tummy time. Her satin gown with the hand-torn slit was speckled with glitter, the kind that stuck to everything, along with what looked like stage blood. Like she chewed on blood-syrup capsules for breakfast and lunch.

It didn't matter if she was really there or not, some product of all my unprocessed grief. She kept appearing and I let her.

"Your T-zone looks like shit," she reported.

A sound lifted up from inside her dress, the squelch of mud and puddled slush. The worst of it hardened on impact with the floor, mixed with more glitter. It had been my grandmother's only house rule—none of the sparkly stuff. Not for art class, not for homemade costumes, not for looking hot. It was impossible to clean.

You look cute, I would have said, pretending to pout, if she were alive and we were still friends.

I had stayed awake all night forcing myself to remember our time at Loch Raven, things I usually blocked out. And I tried to understand. A reporter. Our notebook. Harrison didn't notice anything different about me, which either meant I was a better actress than I gave myself credit for or that the spiraling panic happening on the inside hadn't yet reached the outside.

After he left for work, I spent every waking moment searching the house, careful to move everything back where I'd found it. Harrison might not see what was going on inside me, but he would notice even a saltshaker out of place. I never saw him do it, but I was sure he examined the house each evening to make sure nothing had been moved.

Finding that notebook was priority number one. The office was my first guess, for obvious reasons. But if Nikki hadn't been able to find it, it definitely wasn't there. I tried anyway, stopping short of unstitching the chair's cushions. It wasn't hidden on purpose, I reminded myself. It was lost.

The knowledge that Nikki hadn't destroyed it sent ripples of nausea through me all over again. Because it meant that someone could have already seen it. It meant that maybe we had never been safe from what was written inside.

"Our relationships with other women matter," the audiobook narrator of *The Self-Care Cure* told me. "Women are the ones who will retell your story after you're gone. They are our anchors. We can learn so much about a woman by how other women talk about her. The only thing I've done right in this life is put women at the center. Nothing has ever mattered to me more."

I expected Nikki's chapters to detail recipes for overnight oats or tips for outsourcing your grocery duties. That's what her previous books—what I'd read of them after Harrison went to sleep each night—had prepared me for, a seemingly sincere interest in making a rich person's life easier. Almost like a parody of self-help. *The Self-Care Cure* surprised me, though. She sounded like herself, charming and sad, more Nikki than Annie Minx.

From the love seat, Nikki's jaw unhinged and didn't right itself. She surveyed the room, lingering only at new additions, anything belonging to me or Rhi. A felt book about bunny rabbits, a scrunchie the color of rust, a box of baby wipes.

I could explain away our old costumes and zombie makeup. Even her smell cloyed at my nose in a familiar way, like the Inner Harbor when the water temperatures rose. No one else would get it but me, the way I had patched her together from pieces of our friendship. Except I couldn't explain the mud. That was where my memory gaped.

The first time Nikki ever applied my zombie makeup: "How grotesque do you want it?" she asked. Then we laughed so hard the lipstick trailed past my lip line. "Make me a monster," I said.

Every few minutes, as I rifled through drawers and peered under furniture too heavy to move, I craned my neck, sure I'd find someone watching me through the window. The hollow sound of fake fingernails tapping on glass rang out while I worked. Each time I forgot it, the drumming began again, and when I turned to catch the cause, it slipped out of range. Not a branch, not the wind.

I busied myself by removing all the books from the shelves, as if our notebook could have fallen back behind the alphabetized rows.

"Wasting your time," Nikki said, then stretched her wide hole of a mouth to scream. Only gold glitter spilled out.

I kept trying to remember what Nikki had learned about the Sylvia Club all those years ago and why she would want to dig into it again, why she couldn't let it go. What I remembered was how she used to cover her research with her hand so her roommate couldn't see, or bury her index cards in her underwear drawer. She started to hide even from me. She wouldn't be able to live with herself if someone else found our notebook.

I immediately pushed the thought away. It was more accurate to say she wouldn't be able to rest until she found it herself. And now I couldn't rest, either. That notebook could ruin everything.

"I expected more chaos." She pointed a twisted finger at my throat. It sounded like an accusation.

God, I wanted to hug her. Even with the shit stench and the mud and the glitter, I really wanted to. She used to smell like rose lotion and mint gum. She used to know all the words to "I Wanna Be Sedated" and hug my neck in a loose sleeper hold while she sang it.

Neither of us spoke for a while after that, and I listened to another chapter. Fingernails tapped on the window, faster, more insistent. Seven taps that time.

Halfway through chapter four, Nikki sighed and flicked a snail off her dress. "Moisturizer. You need an ass-ton of moisturizer." Her eyeholes aimed at the dry area in the middle my forehead. "Your T-zone looks like shit."

Her voice trilled with shock and glee over her own cruelty as she repeated herself, like a doll with a pull-string in her back, the kind who knew only a handful of phrases and played on a loop. And if you yanked the string hard enough, it sounded like something breaking on the inside.

The attic, I decided, was where I needed to look next. In my three months in the house, I had never gone up to the attic. I had never needed to. The stairs seemed unstable, and a low ceiling, combined with brooding temperatures, seemed like a dangerous place for my anxiety to grow wild. All the things from my old apartment had been boxed and put away up there for a reason. They were part of my old life. Besides, Harrison had asked that we—me and Caroline—respect Nikki's memory by not rummaging through her things.

But Caroline was the one who had mentioned the attic first. The thought of her helping herself to whatever she could find was almost unbearable. And terrifying, depending on what she found. She didn't know that anything she took from the house could be the exact thing her mom didn't want her to find.

The slow window drumbeat started again, but this time I counted to ten to make myself wake up, to clear whatever floaters filmed over my vision, before jerking open the front door.

The quiet yard thrummed with daytime sounds, all the leftover birds and bugs that hadn't yet flown south for the coming winter. No humans prowling across our lawn. The street had never felt so quiet.

By the time I realized it was coming from her, the tapping of her fingernails, the bubble of giggling voices somewhere inside her sunken chest, I had pulled out a bird's nest worth of strands from my ponytail.

"Have it your way. My old books are in the attic," Nikki said.

I didn't tell her the attic was already part of the plan.

I didn't grow up with attics but had always visualized open spaces with exposed rafters, cluttered boxes and trunks overflowing with forgotten treasures. I expected enormous spiders to slide down a web made just for me, and dust that was fingertip deep.

Except Harrison had organized the boxes into neat rows, swept the floor clean of dust and dirt. No spiderwebs or mouse droppings. There was nothing he could do about the dank light and the humidity, though. Pulling myself up the attic stairs felt like wearing a face mask in the jungle, the air thick against my eyelids, clinging to my collar.

Downstairs, Rhi napped. I had maybe twenty minutes, if I was lucky. Those minutes would fly.

I headed for boxes labeled "College" first and found Nikki's old textbooks. Beneath the books, I chuckled at a collection of Sylvia Plath's poems. Of course Nikki's copy was highlighted in pink, her notes scrawled in the margins. She had been the kind of student who paid attention to details. In one poem, she only underlined the verbs with smudged pencil.

Whirled wintering breathe bunched

I had long ago decided that I wasn't built for poetry. Caroline probably already had a newer edition of the book, required reading. It was as if every sensitive college-age girl was given the same manual, especially at a place like Loch Raven. *Read these books. Worship these authors. Absorb their lessons and plan your life accordingly.*

Her old Freshman Seminar textbook jutted out of another box. *Gender and Popular Culture: Critical Perspectives.* Professor Weedler's class. On the inside cover, she had scribbled her name in purple gel pen. I couldn't believe she'd saved it, but then again, we'd been in a hurry to pack. The memory of its heft, all the freshmen girls carrying it around because he said so, did something icy to my insides.

That man. His long hair and blazers. The cult following he amassed. He resided not in my worst dreams but in a parallel place where things turned out much differently.

A folded "Loch Raven Spirit Week" flyer fell out of the back cover, and I cringed. "Never-ending Spirit Week," we called it. Because there was always always always some themed event, Sundaes on Sunday, Pajama Day, School Spirit Fridays.

Set me on fire if I ever suggest we dress alike for Twin Day.

Choke me out if I let someone paint a raven on my face and call it school spirit.

The old notes and personal bits of Nikki's life would have the highest sentimental value for Caroline, but I wasn't ready to give them up. I wanted to claim it all, as selfish as it sounded. Caroline had decades of her mom's possessions. All I wanted was one year's worth.

On second thought, I decided to hang on to the Sylvia Plath poems for Caroline anyway, a peace offering of the saddest kind. Her mother's handwriting was worth gold.

In the box of journals, a pocket-size mirror had fallen into a corner. I almost missed it. A large cursive "A" had been engraved on the tarnished silver frame. It could have been a vintage find that Nikki had acquired years before, but I didn't remember ever seeing it. I snapped it shut as soon as I opened it.

It reminded me of slumber parties when I was little, when we used to play Bloody Mary. You had to wait until midnight and be one of the brave few still awake, then decide who would go first. Everyone knew the rules, though I couldn't say how we'd learned them. Say her name three times and Mary appeared. That was how it worked. I never saw her, but one time, when I entered the bathroom alone, the mirror fell off the wall as soon as I shut the door. I had never screamed so loud. And I never played again. Ever.

"She's coming for you," one of the other girls had said. Then, in a fake-ghoulish voice: "Now she's got your scent, you won't ever lose her."

Even as I avoided mirrors in the dark, I knew none of it was real. But what if? What if you conjured a woman out of death and couldn't put her back?

Downstairs, the doorbell rang, followed by the sound of smashing glass and Rhiannon's wails. A succession of noise so fast I wasn't sure which happened first. It scared me enough to abandon the shoebox and race downstairs. I would have to go back up later to tidy it again. I wasn't ready to explain anything to Harrison. Whatever I had going with Nikki belonged to us alone.

CHAPTER 14
NOW

Downstairs, Diana peered through the glass square in the door, blonder than ever. I ran to soothe Rhiannon before scrambling to disarm the security code. Not speaking to Diana right away forced me to breathe. Otherwise, I might lose my shit on her for ringing the doorbell during naptime.

Old Me versus New Me took effort. At least until I remembered that I was the one who had invited Diana over. I'd texted her last night, eager for more face time, to hear everything she hadn't been willing to say at her party.

I'm taking charge, bitch, I would have told Annie Minx.

"What happened here?" Diana called out from the other room. She had the kind of subtle Baltimore accent that crept out when she relaxed, one family reunion away from calling everyone *hon*. I liked her more for it.

In the commotion of noises, I'd forgotten about the breaking glass. On the living room floor, a broken picture frame trapped Nikki's photo beneath the shards.

When I was little, my grandmother used to say that when a picture fell, it meant death. Someone about to die or someone already dead, I couldn't recall. I stopped short of repeating that superstition out loud.

"It must have fallen," I said, squeezing Rhi to my chest while I scanned the room for Nikki's footprints. Wherever Nikki had gone, she wasn't far.

She chuckled her disbelief. "Hmm-mmm." Then, finally looking away from the photo, she said, "I brought wine. Not for this morning, of course. Unless we're having that kind of morning." She held up a bottle of red. In her other hand, she held a plate of homemade muffins. Vegan, I guessed. She motioned to Rhi. "Trade?"

She handed me the wine and the plate at the same time I practically shoved Rhiannon into her arms. In her non-stained, non-holey leggings and sports bra, she looked like fitness royalty. Especially compared to my outfit. I had been wearing a tank top and pajama pants. But not anymore.

I looked down at a collared Polo dress that had once been white, now yellowed in spots like strategic piss zones. I didn't remember changing. That dress over lacy black tights with holes in both knees and my oldest sneakers.

Diana side-eyed my outfit so hard she almost lost her footing. "You look like..."

She pretended to stumble for words, but really, she just didn't know what she could get away with saying to me.

"I look like a preppy eighties whore hound."

"I was going to say Buffy the Shit Stirrer."

Touché. We might get along after all.

Rhi rooted her mouth against Di's cheek, a baby zombie searching for its next meal.

When Diana's body tensed and her fingers turned white, I asked, "You okay? I'm not going to need smelling salts or anything, am I?" I tried to make it sound like a joke.

I thought I knew what she was thinking, that it was impossible not to feel Nikki there. She probably hadn't been in the house since the day she found Nikki.

"Does he really keep the office locked?" she asked, her tone so low I leaned in to hear.

That quick, any plan I'd had to ask her about Nikki retreated somewhere deep inside me. A heartbroken widower with locked shrines to his dead wife would make great fodder for neighborhood gossip. Nikki might have trusted her, but I didn't. When I raised an eyebrow at her question, she raised her eyebrow right back as if to say, *You're the one who invited me over, girl.*

I offered to make coffee, but she preferred green tea. Less caffeine. Of course. I found tiny mugs in the cabinets and let the process of pouring and steeping lull us both into a natural silence.

Finally, she threw back her shoulders and sat up as if to make an announcement.

"So, the other day. You came to the party, which I was totally fine with. But I basically have two theories why you showed up." She finished her tea in one scorching gulp and returned Rhi to my arms. "Either you really want to make friends and meet people. Which would be understandable because motherhood can be really so isolating."

"Or?"

"Or you wanted to talk to me about Nikki."

I swallowed. "Third option is that I'm a sucker for torture and wanted to see how much every woman in the neighborhood hates me."

She waved my words away. "Give it another year, and people will forget all about you and Harrison. As long as you make an effort to fit in otherwise. You know, show up to social events, have common interests."

Dress like everyone else, she meant. *Read the same books.*

"Is that what Nikki did? She fit in?"

A cloud crossed over Diana's face, a thought or memory she didn't want to share. When she finally spoke, she sounded tired. "The short answer: yes. Everyone loved her."

"But..."

"But Nikki was complicated. She had an edge. It's what I liked about her." She traced the handle of her empty mug. "She could chug a beer and cuss like a sailor one minute, then outwit someone's annoying husband at a dinner party the next."

Yeah, that sounded like Nikki.

"You know, she told me about you."

Alarm bells dinged inside my brain. I didn't have the energy for my practiced poker face.

"She didn't use your name, I mean. I didn't even know she had been referring to you until you showed up and told me that you used to be friends."

What would Nikki have told her about me, or about us? Hopefully no stories from college. From experience, I knew how close to the surface our time at Loch Raven could linger.

"Was she sad? Depressed, I mean?" The words were out of my mouth before I could stop them.

The question seemed to knock her off-balance, but she knew

what I meant. How bad had it gotten for Nikki? Did she really do it?

"Well, there was the kitchen fire," she said, looking up at the ceiling like she expected to see smoke stains and water damage that hadn't already been repaired. "And the gas leak. Harrison said Nikki started them both. Maybe on accident, but he seemed to think she was so unhappy that she'd risk her family's life, too."

That biting tone again, especially when she mentioned Harrison. One of the many taut muscles in her arm contracted and made me think of professional wrestlers. The strong, glamorous kind.

She squinted at a message on her watch, then rolled her eyes. "My new nanny is a pain in the ass. Apparently, she can't even work the microwave. I have to go."

I couldn't let her get off that easy. I loaded Rhi into the stroller and followed Diana out. As always, I had more questions than time to ask them.

Outside, the sun hid behind clouds we couldn't see. Bernie stood in the middle of her lawn wearing her best fur coat, staring down at the grass. Diana pretended not to notice her.

"What did Nikki tell you? About me?" I asked.

I couldn't read Diana's eyes behind her sunglasses. "She told me that you grew up together. That you hadn't spoken in years. Since college."

I clutched the stroller handle in a panic before convincing myself to ease up.

Why shouldn't Nikki talk about college? There were good memories, too, and enough time had passed that those memories weren't streaked with poison anymore. Not all of them. It was normal for friends to share stories, I reminded myself. Just because there were things Nikki and I had promised never to talk about again didn't mean Diana knew what they were.

I rubbed my eyes, my vision stretching every house on the street to cathedral heights. Doorways curved into arches and windows warped into stained glass. Ivy and stone, lush and imperfect. Every lawn sprinkler became a wishing fountain, every rooftop crow transformed into a sharp-eyed gargoyle, watching from above.

"And Nikki told me that if her old friend showed up one day, I should trust her. She asked me to help her. To help you. She told me to be your friend." Diana's lips pinched. "I didn't understand the conversation at the time. I thought she'd drank too much pinot after taking her painkillers. But you know. She died a week later." She looked away, her voice almost too muted to hear. "I didn't listen to her. I own that."

I wrapped my arms around myself to brace against the breeze. An ache radiated along my breastbone, but also a spike of adrenaline. "What about Caroline? Did Nikki say anything about her?"

"No, actually, she said you were the only friend she trusted with Caroline. It hurt, of course. But I think I understand now. She wanted me to protect you, though I obviously broke that promise. And she wanted you to protect Caroline."

No, no, no. That didn't sound right at all.

"Protect from what?"

She cocked her head, ponytail in full swing. "When you figure that out, babe, let me know."

Diana was halfway down the street before I realized the other thing she'd said, about Nikki and painkillers. What painkillers?

I texted her right away and watched as she stopped to check the message on her watch and then pulled out her phone to respond without ever turning around.

Outpatient surgery. They prescribed her enough narcotics for twenty people.

Then, with that graceful posture, she launched into a jog as if running was the most natural thing her body could do. She didn't look back, and she didn't need to tell me the rest. That surgery must have been how Nikki got the drugs that ended up killing her. By the time I fully absorbed her words and picked up the pacifier Rhi had dropped, Diana was already long gone.

Bernie had been standing on her lawn so long, clearly waiting to talk to me, that I walked over and met her in the driveway. We hadn't spoken much since the day she took Rhi for a walk, but we waved hello more often. We'd breached the gap between our houses and had somehow skipped all the usual small talk of getting to know someone new.

"That woman is a snake. She isn't anyone's friend," she hissed. "They're all snakes. Including him. The husband."

She had thrown off her fur and the back of her wool dress had come undone, the buttons opening to her pale flesh underneath.

"Here, let me…" I reached for her, pointing at her back. The buttons stuck, uncooperative, but she let me pull and twist at the fabric until I was done.

"You're one of the good ones," she said, patting me on the arm. Her skin felt rough, like her palm was one giant callus.

One of the good ones. Nikki would get a kick out of that.

Later, Diana texted me with one sentence.

She didn't do it.

I got out of bed, careful not to wake Harrison, and sat on the bathroom floor in the windowless dark.

Say more, I wrote in response. Her pause didn't last long.

There was no way Nikki took her own life. She would never do that to Caroline.

I hadn't breathed in too long, but when I did, it felt incomplete. I couldn't exhale all the way. Instead, I focused on the cool of the tiles. Smooth. So solid.

That's exactly what I thought, I finally replied.

You think it was an accident?

But no, that wasn't it, either. Nikki had worked too hard to leave me messages for it to be a coincidence. Asking Diana to help me if I ever showed up—that was part of a long-term plan, as if she knew what was coming.

"If something happens to me," she'd instructed on that to-do list, because she knew there was a chance something could happen. That wasn't Overly Cautious Nikki. That was Scared for Her Life Nikki.

No one else had mentioned the possibility of murder or foul play in Nikki's death, but I suddenly knew. Maybe I had known all along. I tried to remember every detective show I'd ever seen. There hadn't been any burglary or forced entry, which meant that someone with access to the house could have dosed her and slipped out just as easily. Someone Nikki trusted.

It was harder to return to bed with Harrison after that. It was impossible to sleep at all.

CHAPTER 15
THEN

Nikki

Opening night was a success, mostly. A zombie's ear fell off and hit someone in the front row, and the sound guy messed up the cues in scene three. But given the gap between dress rehearsals and performance (the director's decision), it could have been worse.

Sadie, of course, was a star. She mastered her new zombie stumble and upstaged some of the actors with speaking roles. Even in a crowd of horrifying, groaning extras, she stood out. When the director wrapped his arm around her waist in the green room, he made it clear she wouldn't be an extra forever.

"Another séance, tonight, after the show," Sadie had written in our back-and-forth journal. I found it tucked under my other notebooks when I got out of the shower.

"Happy Whatever Anniversary," she had also written on a note she'd stuck to a bottle of caffeine pills.

"Whatever Anniversary" was what Sadie called random days

when she wanted to guilt me into going out with her. She meant that we had so many good memories that no matter what day it was, we always had something to celebrate.

What were we celebrating this time? You know. Whatever.

I tried to get excited about the idea of planning a night full of scares, for Sadie's sake. Dripping candles and the right ribbon of moonlight. Black dresses, veils. The curtains twisted up in the wind because of old drafty windows. It was meant to be fun, I told myself.

Sadie would retell the story of the Sylvia Club until everyone felt it in their toes. Way better than Eileen's Death Tour, she assured me. Even better than the offerings we left. I would be in charge of making sure we didn't get caught.

If I had asked her to stop, told her that it bothered me, she would have canceled everything. But we had been having fun with Ouija boards since before my mom died. That didn't need to change. So I talked myself into being okay.

Sadie's "Séance Prep CD" consisted of one song on repeat: "Pretty Noose" by Soundgarden.

Halfway through act one, when my responsibilities ended except for a few costume changes to oversee, I recessed in the quiet lobby. The lobby's preshow drama and anticipation, compared to the eerie mid-show quiet, reminded me of college in general, how all the energy and thrill of the first semester had faded so quickly.

I had run to the dorms straight from Gallina's office with barely enough time to change into the black clothes that all the behind-the-scenes crew were required to wear. I'd already planned a few surprises for Sadie's opening night but needed to add the finishing touches.

There hadn't been time to process everything Gallina had told me about the Sylvia Club, and in my daze, I'd almost walked into a moving car on my way to the theater. Knowing my luck, if someone else had seen it happen, they'd say I did it on purpose.

"There's a tragic part of the college's history that young women like to spin into outlandish stories for every new class of freshmen. Especially this time of year," Gallina had said once we were both seated on opposite sides of her desk.

As if on cue, the church bells pierced our conversation, sudden and somber. Somehow, they sounded hollower as the weather grew cooler and the days shorter. Evening bells, I had decided my first week on campus, were the darkest kind.

"So you're saying it's true, right?" As much as I wanted to know about Abbie Moriano and Hope Hall, we had to start at the beginning.

Gallina sipped from a mug that I could only guess contained cold coffee and took her time to respond. "Throughout the history of Loch Raven College—" She'd stopped herself with a hand to her mouth. "God, I sound like the administration."

She made a clicking noise and began again. "There have been deaths on campus in the past—suicides, yes, but not every year."

A cluster of suicides. A contagion, Gallina had called it. Like a disease spreading. She didn't like the term *copycat suicide*. Sometimes it happened after a famous or popular celebrity died. Someone like Marilyn Monroe or, yes, Sylvia Plath. But it didn't have to be someone famous, and not all suicides were part of a cluster.

Q: What is the Werther Effect?
A: An increase in suicide after a well-known figure dies by
   suicide; mimicry in death.

It had happened at Loch Raven in the sixties, she admitted. Then again, a small cluster in the eighties, one suicide spreading like an infection: three girls, most of them freshmen. No, it wasn't every year like Eileen had said. But still. I was just glad to hear someone at the college admit it.

"Are you okay? Nikki? You don't look well. Is this too much?" She had stopped in the middle of the story, clocking my death grip on the arms of her office chair.

Once I'd assured her that I was fine—a breathless, fevered "fine"—she told me that more suicides had happened again a few years before I arrived on campus. Including Abbie.

Nine or ten girls total, I counted as she spoke, mostly confirmation of what I already knew. Abbie and Mary and Betsy. Jessie up on the fourth floor of our residence hall. But I didn't know all their names. Not yet.

From my spot next to the vending machine, the moans of zombies bled from the auditorium. The grumble of hunger and afterlife—it gave me chills every time. The lobby bathroom's door swung open, and I looked up in time to catch a girl from Freshman Seminar in a black dress with her eyes lasered into me. She twisted her whole neck trying to get my attention. Then, with a nod, she slow-blinked twice and headed back into the auditorium.

What the hell?

Something similar had happened before the show when I worked at the ticket table, counting money and handing out little red tickets with a pageant crown stamped in the center. Two girls, also wearing black dresses, had purposely maneuvered the ticket lines so I would be the one to take their money. I hadn't dreamed the strangeness of them waiting to meet my eyes and, again, blinking twice.

Strange, but nothing compared to what had happened inside Gallina's office. It was the reason I still couldn't calm my heartbeat hours later.

I had mentioned my Sylvia Plath paper to Gallina again, how disappointing and morbid I found Weedler's unit on dead girls, given the college's history.

The more I thought about it, the more fucked up Weedler's whole class seemed.

Weeks after a girl had tried to hang herself in the bathroom above us, a professor shouldn't have tested us on dead celebrities. We shouldn't have memorized facts about how Sylvia Plath and Marilyn Monroe had died.

Gallina's mouth had twitched at the mention of my paper, just like it did in the Hall of Success when I'd mentioned it. She didn't like Weedler; it occurred to me in that moment as a statement of fact. She couldn't tell me her real thoughts, of course, but she didn't need to. Some unspoken emotion had spread across her face when I said his name. It wasn't a positive one.

"You're a better teacher than him. A better mentor," I added. If anyone should have run the mentorship program, it was her.

I had never seen her blush before, and it brought out a freckled youthfulness to her skin. "Well, someone has to help guide our sharpest students so they don't fall through the cracks."

Then, before I could ask another question, she rested her hand on my leg and waited for me to look up, patting my knee, up and down, three awkward times.

"It's uncomfortable, isn't it, to be touched against your wishes?"

She'd said it in such a way that I wanted to peel off my skin and slither under her door. But I'd recognized her touch as identical to what I had experienced in Professor Weedler's office. He had palmed my knee the same way.

"Trust yourself and your body, Nikki. Speak up for yourself. Don't let anyone…" Her voice stumbled then. "Don't let anyone put you in a position you don't want to be in."

I only realized later, planted there in the theater lobby, the potential weight of what she couldn't say. About Weedler. Not just his focus on suicide and pretty women dying, but everything else. The hair stroking, the unwanted touches, the drooling, aroused teacher prodding us to discuss phallic symbols.

But what could I do? What did she want from me?

Another girl wearing a black kimono dress waited near the auditorium doors for me to acknowledge her. But when I tried to meet her eyes, I stared into two black holes. It wasn't just good stage makeup; she was the same eyeless girl I kept seeing. I wasn't surprised when she slid on a pair of sunglasses just like my mom.

The whole lobby turned into an icy blow of air-conditioning, artificial gusts whooshing through my hair. I waited for her to fade, but she only glided up and out toward the back entrance of the stage. She had been here before. She knew where she was going.

I balled and unballed my hands, fists and no fists. I couldn't keep standing there, hearing Gallina's voice in my ear or feeling her hand resting on my knee, while this girl seemed to lead the way.

"Match me," she sang. I took it as an invitation. *Match me, catch me, find me.*

So I ran. I ran away before anyone saw me, charging through the back hallway into the costume room, running like I could run through walls. All the noises inside me, the beating and churning of my organs, as I ran and ran, tripping over my clunky shoes, breathless and bottled up.

The girl passed through the costume-room walls, her dress a gauzy shroud, thin as air. She was going to tell me something. She was going to let me ask her questions. I had so many.

"Mom?" I called, even though I knew it wasn't her. Maybe there was a portal there. Maybe she could hear me.

And then the girl disappeared. Once inside, my heart paused before jump-starting back to life. I stalked through a rack of beaded gowns, and my gasps expanded to fill the room.

Sadie ran in a minute later, her face a wash of relief at the sight of me. Like we had been apart for decades but she had finally found me. I could tell it was almost intermission from the pleading and screaming of actors onstage. The zombie beauty queens were about to turn a stay-at-home mom into one of them.

"Girl, chill your ass out," Sadie said through her teeth, looking around in case Ms. Gloria was at the sewing machine. She scanned the dresses I must have ripped from their hangers in my stupor. Hats buckled under my feet. "Miss Dead-Ass Congeniality told me you were in here flipping out."

I'd explain it to her later. The unsettling meeting with Dr. Gallina, the girls I kept seeing all over campus. My panic attack, I didn't need to tell her that part. She could see.

Now she held my hand while I heaved into the small wastebasket full of threads and empty bobbins. It took only a moment for our pulses to match, as if she absorbed everything coursing through me. Like she could take the panic away for good.

It was what worked about us. Sometimes I was the rock, but mostly her.

"There's something in the closet," I said. By now, a group of heavily made-up zombie extras pooled in the doorway to watch us. "I heard it moving."

"Oh my God, what's in the closet?" someone said. Someone repeated it after her. Nervous murmurs that made Sadie stand straighter.

What's in the closet, what's in the closet?

"Don't freak out, guys. It's probably nothing."

Cool Sadie. Fearless Sadie.

I stayed back as she opened the door to the broom closet. It was her turn to gasp. Floor to ceiling, the other extras had helped me stack cases of Dr Pepper, our favorite drink. A lifetime supply, the card on top said, though neither of us could reach it.

"Happy birthday!" the girls yelled. I had to claim it was Sadie's birthday for them to help me. A Whatever Anniversary would have been too much to explain.

Sadie glowed, pulling me in for a hug. "You even stage-managed a panic attack. Bravo."

"Wait until you see what's next."

A scavenger hunt made out of her favorite things waited back in her room: black nail polish, Dr Pepper Lip Smackers, sour candy. If only I could have included her other favorite things: loud music, short skirts, boys with tongue rings.

I'd been planning the surprises all week. Half the clues in the treasure hunt were nonsense, leading to dead ends, just because. If I made it too easy, she'd get bored and distracted. She'd end up starting a fight with Eileen or making out with the janitor. Again.

Who knew what trouble she'd get into if I didn't keep her busy?

Besides, people worked harder when they had to hit a few walls first.

Sadie doled out a can of soda for everyone as they headed back to the green room to prepare for act two.

"There really are girls following me," I confessed after everyone left. I hadn't made that part up. I described the blinking girls in their black dresses, stopping short of mentioning the eyeless one.

Sadie laughed. "Oh, those are my girls. I recruited them to join our séance. The blinks are like a code, but I forget what it's supposed to mean. We're all going to my room after the show."

My stomach knotted all over again. Not just because I worried about waking the dead or getting in trouble, but because the word *contagion* sizzled a hole in my skull.

Instead, I said the thing that had been sitting on my tongue for days. I hadn't said it out loud yet. A wet slug of a thought. I needed to know how it tasted.

For Abbie.

"I've been researching the Sylvia Club. The girls who died. I think there's more to the story. Like, maybe they didn't all choose to die that way."

Sadie's lips formed a solid line. Her voice laced with worry: "Okay, but, Nik, you won't be able to find out why they did it—you know that, right? This might be one of those unknowable things."

She wasn't talking about the girls anymore.

"It's okay. I'm fine. There's something the college doesn't want anyone to know, and I'm going to find out what it is. I don't need to know *why* they did it. I don't care about why."

Yeah, right. Of course I wanted to know why.

Hours later, we—me, Sadie, and the three slow-blinking girls—met in Sadie's room dressed in dark chunky sweaters and flowy thrift-store dresses. Except for Sadie, who also wore a long white cloak and a short veil, like some magical high priestess. She hadn't invited Eileen, which I knew I'd hear about later. But Sadie wasn't about to let someone like Eileen try to take over or ruin the mood like last time.

"Got enough candles?" I asked as she lit another tea light to place on the windowsill. Every surface in the room was filled with pillared candlelight.

She smirked. "Just don't let me catch my cloak on fire."

This séance was supposed to be different from the night we trudged all over campus. Less about giving gifts and more about receiving messages. Knowing that Sadie was just having fun, mostly full of shit, helped soothe the pit in my stomach that happened each time we tried to rile up the dead.

We turned out the lights, tilted the window half-open for the necessary chill it brought, and sat in a circle with our old Ouija board between us. We'd found the board in Sadie's grandmother's basement, so old it didn't have any branding at the bottom. The wood was sturdier than the store-bought ones, the planchette less like a flimsy game-board piece. It looked legit, and I could tell the other girls were impressed. If we couldn't channel ghosts with that board, no one could.

Sadie's mousy roommate, who never missed Bible study, left in a huff as soon as the first candle was lit. She had gotten used to ignoring Sadie's loudness, but a séance was a step too far for her.

I should have insisted that we walk the extra five minutes to the cemetery because that was where you held a séance if you wanted it to work. Never mind that none of the Sylvias, as Sadie called them, were buried there. I'd take a dead nun's presence over nothing. Really, I just wanted us hidden away from everyone, to avoid getting a citation for candle usage.

And then, to everyone's surprise, when Sadie started the séance by saying, "Spirits, please give us a sign that you are here," one of the candles by the window blew out. Blame it on the wind, sure, but girls willing to hold a séance in a dorm room were also girls who absolutely took the wind blowing out a candle as a sign. Big-time.

"Did you hear that?" someone asked, and I did—a crunching outside the window, boots treading on leaves, an accidental sound like someone who didn't want to be heard. The other girls assumed ghost.

I didn't think a ghost would make so much noise trampling dead leaves outside when they could have been inside. A ghost would scream, especially any ghost girls on our campus. They would riot. They'd break shit. The planchette hadn't even moved yet.

Then the wind blew the long curtain straight across a tea light, and we all jumped up as it caught flame. It wasn't a big fire, and it didn't last long before I threw water on it, but one fabric panel was scorched along the bottom.

The smoke was what got us. An alarm blared moments after the fire was out, and the sprinklers released. Before we had to evacuate, Eileen showed up with Sadie's roommate and yelled from the doorway, "Now we've caught you, you weirdos!"

Like she wasn't jealous. Like she hadn't been planning to rat us out the whole time.

"Worth it," Sadie said as she blew out the other candles, closing her eyes to make a wish each time.

CHAPTER 16

THEN

Q: Loch Raven College trivia time: How many students died by suicide at Loch Raven College between 1968 and today?
A: Nine.

Nine girls, in clusters. I'd been wrong when I assumed they were all variations of the same sad kind of girl. Dead wrong. They were girls with chewed cuticles and hunched shoulders, girls who stared out frosty windows, scribbled lines of failed poetry and swallowed the balled-up attempts. Scarred girls, quiet girls with daddy issues. Or not. Girls who wanted to be scientists, girls who played basketball, rode dirt bikes. Girls who won the spelling bee and had allergies. Loud girls, popular girls. Girls with ponytails and lip gloss, straight teeth undivorced parents two-car garage designer purse perfect test scores tiny waist wrists feet.

You didn't have to know them to feel their presence. Soldiering together, their ghosts huddled all over campus, haunting every nook and stairwell. This was the stuff no one told you on your first campus tour.

Betsy Zeller, in the sixties, started the first—and only—poetry club on campus. Engaged to marry a boy named Percival. Prenamed her children and pre-dreamed her home. Wore pearls for all photos. Loved Sylvia Plath.

As far as I could tell, Betsy was the first. Followed by Mary Matherly and Grace Ballard.

I had learned even more about the cluster of deaths in the eighties. It started with a student named Shea Nardman. Permed hair, amateur beauty-pageant princess, soprano in the all-county choir back in her hometown. She'd started off her first year at Loch Raven with an equal amount of promise.

She won the talent show contest held during Spirit Week. Then she organized a food-donation drive. There were pictures in the yearbook of her standing in front of a table in the student center with a cardboard box filled to the top with nonperishables. Giant grin, perfect teeth. I had every reason to believe she was instantly loved by all the other girls, or instantly hated.

She died before Halloween during her first semester. I found her obituary in a Pennsylvania newspaper from the town where she grew up. A poem in that year's literary magazine called "Noose" and dedicated to S.N. suggested she hung herself with bedsheets and was found in a classroom. Hers was the death that set off the next two, the contagion, according to the conversation I'd had with Dr. Gallina. Three deaths in the eighties.

After Shea had died, a field hockey player named Raquel Valdez swallowed a bottle of pills and seized on her dorm-room floor. Her old roommate referenced the incident in an interview after she'd become the CEO of a popular doll company. The Raquel doll had been a "fan favorite" for decades since.

The only yearbook photo of Raquel showed her sitting with two friends over a half-played chessboard in the student lounge, all three of the girls with their eyes lowered in deep concentration. I hadn't identified the other two girls.

In the midnineties, Kiki Ward, who lettered in basketball and track, and had survived leukemia as a child, died before final exams. She wore her hair short and shaved on the side. Her friends described her as "freaking hilarious," and for years rested flowers at Loch Raven's entrance gates on her birthday, though they were always promptly removed by our groundskeeper. I learned about her from an article in the *Raven Outlook*. No word on how she'd died. No why. Her friends missed her. That was all.

The next semester, Jessie Allis, winner of more than one scholarship, according to her high school's bulletin, died on the fourth floor of the dorm we all lived in now. No one knew much about her life, only that in death, her bare footsteps slapped the floors at night and the cackle of her laugh rang out at the worst moments. Like when an alive girl's boyfriend broke up with her. Or when someone had really bad cramps.

And then the following semester, there was Abigail "Abbie" Moriano. Valedictorian of her high school class. Tetris master majoring in economics. Survived by her parents, her sister, and a Pekinese named Butterball.

Her favorite class: Freshman Seminar. Professor Weedler's.

CHAPTER 17
THEN

Our next headless costume-room photo shoot: purple shimmer tights, tutu skirts, candy-hued mohair sweaters. Too much blue eyeshadow. We started with one skull-and-crossbones sticker on each hand but didn't stop until the stickers lined our arms and faces—bats, mushrooms, lightning bolts.

"Maybe you should have left the stickers back in your middle school locker," Eileen had teased the day before when Sadie applied a scratch-and-sniff strawberry to her history textbook.

"Maybe you should eat your own ass," Sadie had replied.

The soundtrack: a mix tape with Nine Inch Nails and Tori Amos. Sadie was running late for a date with a guy who only listened to the Beastie Boys.

"Small boobs, big heart," I inked on the bottom of the Polaroid.

"Kill me if I ever forget how much I love you," she said on her way out the door. "Stab me right in the fucking heart."

I swore I saw Mary Matherly flip us both off and return to the stage. Her dress was open in the back, unbuttoned where she couldn't reach.

In addition to my pile of printed obituaries, I hadn't returned the yearbooks. The stack had only grown bigger. And in that way, the former students of Loch Raven were never far away.

It was easy to slip into their stories. One led to another until I often forgot what I had started looking for. Someone had drawn a heart around Kiki Ward's picture in black Sharpie, which I especially loved. Before the semester ended, I thought, maybe I could add hearts around all of them.

I kept coming back to Abbie's yearbook picture, sometimes on purpose and sometimes the book opening naturally to that page. She looked just like the girl I'd seen entering Hope Hall, the one clutching her head.

No one at the college denied that girls had died on campus, but they never talked about why. I couldn't let it go. What I knew from my mother's death was that there was always a story behind the story. The girls who died were more than campfire ghosts and teen-movie fodder. There was a Who and a Where and a How underneath the stories.

There had to also be a Why.

I stopped by Dr. Gallina's office every afternoon on my way to the library, and even though she didn't press me for details about Weedler's behavior, her posture changed when I spoke about him. She leaned forward, attentive. Like she wanted me to know that she heard me, that she believed me.

Add it to my list of ways I wanted to be like her. Yes, I had a list.

The more I dug, the more they came to me. Dead girls, everywhere. I never saw the Sylvias inside Gallina's office, but as soon as I stepped into the hall, they mocked me in unison.

"Cute earrings," they laughed when I wasn't wearing earrings.

I wasn't the only alive student who loitered around Gallina's office or bolted out of the classroom after lecture to talk with her. The group of girls following her around never dissipated, regardless of what Eileen would have people believe. Gallina had a source of light, and we were moth-drawn. It was the way she listened, the way she never spoke to us like we were children. I watched Polly leave Gallina's office once wearing a grin so manic that she looked like the Joker. Something about a chat with Dr. Gallina left us all a little giddy.

I remembered what Polly had said about the Dread, that sick, nagging feeling I very much related to. Sometimes it deepened into a stomach pit, and sometimes it could balloon inside your chest like a shape-shifting smog.

Meaning: things weren't okay.

Meaning: something was coming, and it wouldn't be pretty.

But there wasn't much you could do about the Dread. There was no way to brace for things you couldn't see.

The Dread was also what I called my first Dear Annie column for the *Raven Outlook*. Despite my initial refusal, Gallina convinced me to give it a try. Standing behind me, her protective hand squeezing my shoulder, her sigh full of gentle impatience, I couldn't really say no.

I drafted it, and I didn't hate it:

"Girls, look alive. You never know what hand is waiting on the other side of the mirror. And when it reaches out to scrape a talon across your cheek, who would say you weren't waiting for it? Love, Annie."

I expected the other girls to say it was too much, thanks but no thanks, but no one made me change a single word. *Unconventional and eerily poetic*, Gallina called the final result. She even gave me a pocket mirror with "A" for Annie etched on the front. *Bizarro*, Aisha and the rest of the newspaper staff called it.

After burying myself in the lives of dead girls, writing advice in the voice of "Annie" felt like splashing cold water on the back of my neck. Not even Sadie knew. It wasn't a secret, but I liked keeping it to myself.

Besides the newspaper column, I had finished writing a proposal for Weedler, a detailed outline of the essay I would eventually write, but really, I had more than one project in the works. First, there was the research on campus counseling resources and the dead girls of the Sylvia Club. That was what I had planned to turn in, even if it wasn't what Weedler had asked for.

At the last minute, though, I pasted together my thoughts about the culture's obsession with dead women, notably Sylvia Plath. I wrote about how romanticizing death led to more deaths, especially at colleges like Loch Raven. Hadn't Seattle seen more suicides after Kurt Cobain died? I hadn't made that up, even if I was simplifying the issue.

"How to Write about a Dead Woman" was my working title.

My thesis statement included the phrase "sick and twisted fascination."

Weedler would hate it, but he would hate anything I turned in. I slipped the essay under his office door for approval the day before we were supposed to meet at the Brew Station. Yeah, I could have said no again to the meeting invite, but my unsigned financial aid letter dangled above every decision I made.

The Brew Station, half brewery, half coffee shop, depending on your mood or the time of day, wasn't far from campus. It sat closer to the medical school, which meant Loch Raven girls in the know changed out of their pajamas for once and showed up after class looking for a doctor-in-training.

At the window, Weedler sat with another student, a girl whom I recognized from the way she always lingered after class. She laughed into her hand, and he took it as an invitation to reach across and twirl one of her long ringlets around his finger.

While I ordered a latte at the bar, a preppy dude pretended not to stare. He paid for his drink with a credit card instead of a wad of wrinkled bills and nickels like me. Obviously a med student. The brand-new shoes and tired eyes were the other giveaways.

When he smiled at the barista, showing off the deep dimples in his otherwise average face, I realized who he was.

Oh God. The guy from the party. Dimples. Harry. He didn't recognize me at all.

He was taller than I remembered—huge, really. His chin was ruddy with stubble, and his cheeks bloomed when he smiled. Family money, he'd told me that night. Generations of doctors. I didn't remember much else. He flushed when I reminded him of the party. But not in a bad way.

"I thought you were a redhead," he mumbled, and I chose to ignore it.

After a conversation that included him asking me if I had ever been to "the" country club, he jotted his phone number on a cocktail napkin.

I didn't bother telling him he wasn't my type. Whatever my type was, it probably wasn't someone like him. Instead, I let him put his arm around my waist, thrilled to be touched, thrilled to be noticed.

The whole interaction wouldn't have happened if Sadie had been there. She would have eaten up all the attention or pulled me away from his sturdy arms like a toddler yelling, *Mine!*

I looked up and pretended to notice Weedler only after Harry had left. His frown was almost worth it.

The other girl was gone, and my essay proposal sat on the wobbly table, filled with red pen scrawls but no grade. His smile didn't connect with his eyes, which were emptied of all emotion. I'd wait for him to speak first, I decided, my gaze shifting to the scorpion tattoo on his wrist, peeking out from his shirtsleeve. Another thing that the girls on campus loved about him. The tattoo, like his hair, was his trademark.

"You need a new thesis, Nikki." Weedler slid the proposal to my side of the table. "I'm not sure about this topic or your approach. It might help to follow your friend Sadie's lead. You could use a dose of her creativity and experimentation."

I pretended to read through his comments, looking down to hide my irritation and the growl of laughter that wanted to follow. Now he wanted me to be more like Sadie, who didn't even have a copy of the textbook. He had agreed to let her perform a Plath-centric creative monologue instead of writing an essay. Apparently, she'd sold the idea so well that he didn't even ask what character she'd play or how much research she would do. She hadn't worked on it at all yet, as far as I could tell.

"He stared at my tits the whole time I talked," she'd said, adjusting her new WonderBra, which gave her actual cleavage. Then, laughing at my horrified expression, she said, "Hey, at least I didn't let him dry hump me against his desk."

Like she knew a rumor I didn't. It was better that I didn't hear the rest.

"You know, Sylvia Plath wasn't all dark and depressing like you keep telling us. She was ambitious and very social. She was a genius."
He sneered in response.
"It looks like you have been doing your assigned readings, after all. Focus on her, not on the culture's obsession with death or whatever you call it. Don't get off track."

I could have kept going, detailing the ways his lectures had shortchanged us. And her—Sylvia. Like how she'd appreciated fashion and enjoyed motherhood. She was a good mother, which no one ever seemed to talk about, at least not in Weedler's assigned readings.

Surface level, he had scrawled beneath my two-page long bibliography.

Eileen loved it when he wrote critical feedback on her work.

"It shows he cares," she once told me. "He knows what he's talking about."

She and the other girls could say they "worshipped" Plath, but it was really him. When he called for an after-hours poetry reading, they followed, french braiding their hair with black ribbon, overdoing it on the eye glitter.

Eileen had tried to create poetic "code names" for some of the other girls: Elegy, Sonnet, Haiku. She wanted people to call her Sestina, but she couldn't make it stick.

A Venn diagram of Sadness and Beauty. And all of them caught in the space between, tattooing fake tears under their eyes because they didn't have enough real ones.

"I found this piece by Harold Bloom. You may want to consider his perspective. His voice, as a literary critic, could add a smart counterpoint to your paper." He handed me another article that looked like all the others.

One sentence had been underlined: "Hysterical intensity, whatever its momentary erotic appeal, is not an affect that endures in verse."

Then he appended the bottom of the paper with his address. For our next meeting, he said.

Big fat no. I wasn't giving up on my paper, and I wasn't ever going to his house.

Midterms had passed quietly, the whole semester both slowing and speeding in ways I couldn't pin down. I had mostly stopped sleeping, existing in a haze during my library days, but it paid off. I had learned about so many of the girls, couldn't start my day without reciting their names like a chant. And I could tie Weedler to at least one of them.

It was sheer luck that I found the LiveJournal website. I had to slog to the library to use the internet, then remember my new username and password. The whole thing was a long shot to see if anyone I knew journaled under their real name. But a young woman named Jasmine had an account. Jasmine Moriano, whose older sister had died her freshman year of college.

Jasmine's avatar was the Utz potato chip girl. She posted daily, sometimes several times a day, but rarely about Abbie. And she never mentioned Loch Raven, except for one post, which described her own decision not to go to college after watching how hard it was for Abbie to fit in. College was a "wasteland" filled with "vulture professors who preyed on freshmen girls."

I held my breath so long while reading I almost passed out.

"Her favorite class was freshman orientation. It was supposed to help her adjust to college," Jasmine wrote. "Look at how that turned out."

I tried to message her through the website and ask her to meet me for coffee. I didn't tell her who I was or give away my true motives. The message went ignored. Until she wrote about going out downtown to blow off steam with her "crew," I almost gave up. By some miracle, someone in the comments asked where she was going that night.

"Brick Studio Pub," Jasmine responded. "It's ladies' night."

That was how Sadie and I ended up in Federal Hill at the Brick Studio Pub, a building large enough for three bars. Swanky, Sadie called it, when she saw the elevator. Meaning, way nicer than all the cramped bars that we usually went to, the ones with parquet floors and crumbling brick walls. Meaning, too expensive for girls like us. But she was so surprised I wanted to go out on a weeknight that she didn't complain about my choice. Either she liked the look of the bald-headed bouncer, or she was tired of freezing outside the bar without our coats.

"The good news is that I don't want to trade outfits with you tonight," she said as she tried to smear off the black "X" on her hand. She sniffed at my KISS T-shirt layered over a tank dress and then layered again over ribbed tights and boots.

"What's wrong with it?" The T-shirt was a nod to Dr. Gallina's style, true. But I didn't think it looked bad.

She ditched me right after, and I stationed myself at the downstairs bar, where a man with a ponytail and an eyepatch sidled up to the counter. He was perfect for Sadie. And if Sadie stayed distracted, she wouldn't get bored and insist on leaving before I found Jasmine.

Song playing in honor of ladies' night: "Just a Girl" by No Doubt.

I had no idea what Jasmine looked like, of course. I could guess at her approximate age. Plus, I knew what her sister had looked like, though that didn't tell me much. At first glance, it was easy to rule out the women ordering drinks at the bar. Their eyes weren't guarded enough. There wasn't a stormy sadness in the way they carried their twenty-five-cent beers.

When I was tired of sitting, I checked the upstairs bar. Eyepatch had Sadie's attention in the corner, his hands on her waist. But no Jasmine.

I could have already missed her if her friends had decided to go somewhere else. Or they could have started at a different bar with no plans to show up at the Brick Studio Pub until hours later. What would I even say to her? It wasn't like I could walk up to a random girl at a bar and ask her about her dead sister.

But then it happened. There wasn't a line for the bathroom, though the stalls were all occupied. A woman with crispy flat-ironed hair stood at the mirror to reapply her lipstick.

"Oh," I said out loud. It was Jasmine. I just knew. She had her sister's pointed nose, the same complexion. Instead of looking sad, she looked like she could kick my ass. Something about her stance. Too pretty to be a boxer, but maybe a wrestler, in knee-high socks and a shirt tied to show her midriff. A very drunk, muscly schoolgirl.

She turned to me, unimpressed. "Can I help you?"

"Hey, I think I know you," I rambled. Now or never. "I messaged you. I go to Loch Raven College like your sister..."

She stepped forward just as another girl with even broader shoulders charged out of her stall.

"Who the fuck are you?" Jasmine yelled. Her Baltimore accent was full of smoke and grit, rough around the edges like women I grew up hearing in my neighborhood.

"What'd you say about her sister?" The other woman pushed me back against the wall.

Sadie had been in plenty of fights, but not me. Getting my ass kicked by these two women in the bathroom was the one scenario I hadn't run through my head. I'd expected grief instead of anger.

We all stood frozen, panting, chests thumping like cats ready to see who would pounce first. No one removed their earrings or slipped out of their heels. Maybe we were all thinking the same thing, that the Brick Studio Pub was too fancy a bar to lose our shit in.

I apologized, mumbling that I must have been mistaken, and Jasmine turned back to the mirror, rolling her eyes. They didn't believe me, but they let me walk out anyway. I expected them to follow or for Jasmine to at least grill me a few more times. As I walked out, all I heard on the other side of the door was one of them yelling, "Freaky big-eyed bitch!"

Winter had shown up too early and the outside bar was closed, but a few drunk guys bunched together on the patio for a smoke. They stopped talking immediately to let me know I had intruded.

"I'm looking for my friend?" I said. "Red hair, short skirt." It was a vague description, but people, especially men, tended to remember Sadie. Just outside the gated patio area, a sound like hushed voices and shuffling feet—probably rats—carried over the chilled air.

One of the sober-looking guys snickered. "Your friend...is she the kind of girl who would bang a dude behind a dumpster?" he asked.

The wind whistled, and we all heard the unmistakable moan. It crept up from the alley into the breeze. The guys weren't outside for a cigarette. They wanted a show. The sober one nodded as if that settled it. His eyes dipped to stare at my chest, then back up to my face. Whatever. I crossed my arms.

I couldn't do it. I couldn't stick around to watch Sadie strut past those guys with her skirt—*my* skirt—hiked up to her thighs. Her eyes would get all jumpy and a little vacant before moving on to her next escapade.

"If you see her, let her know that her friend is waiting," I said. Then I went back inside to wait.

Ten minutes later, she found me waiting on the same barstool where I had started. I didn't want to tell her about the interaction in the bathroom or why I had suggested Brick Studio in the first place. This part of the night was mine.

"Been busy?" I asked.

She tugged at her neckline. "Who wants to know?"

"God, Sadie." I crinkled my nose as if I could smell the dumpster garbage on her. "Can't you at least find a private place to take care of your business?"

She pretended to look confused and hurt for a moment, but then the bartender handed me the bill.

Outside, Jasmine sat in the middle of the sidewalk with her head in her hands.

"That girl's smashed," Sadie said.

I looked around for her friend, and when I didn't see her, I took the risk to lean down by Jasmine's side and ask if she was okay. She looked up with wet cheeks and bloodshot eyes, sobbing harder at the sight of me. Which was better than spitting in my face.

"You knew Abbie?"

This wasn't the discussion I wanted to have, not like this, with angry tears and dubious sobriety. But I figured it was the only chance I would get. Her friend would be back any minute, ready to toss me into the gutter for upsetting Jasmine. Because that's what friends do.

I turned my face so Sadie wouldn't hear me. "The teacher who liked freshmen girls. Was it Professor Weedler? Jerome Weedler?"

Her head wobbled backward before making eye contact again. "That place. She couldn't handle that place."

It didn't feel right to pat her back or touch her at all, even as she dissolved into sobs again.

"Bullshit professors, bullshit scholarship. It was too much."

On the way back to the parking garage, Sadie and I held on to each other's arms. If we slipped on the slick roads, we'd go down together.

"Did you really have sex behind the dumpster? That has to be a new low, even for you."

It was mean of me to say, but either she didn't notice my tone, or she didn't care. She laughed so loud that strangers passing us on the street turned to look.

"What are you talking about? Who's having sex in the dumpster?" She reminded me about the guy she'd met at the upstairs bar, the one with the eyepatch, whose sleeve caught fire when he drank a Flaming Dr Pepper shot. They'd made out in the elevator, but nothing exciting.

"His abs were so hard they felt fake. Maybe he just had to take a dump." She walked ahead but paused to let me catch up.

"Shit. I forgot about the eyepatch guy."

"I figured you stage-managed him upstairs to distract me from whatever you were up to."

She knew me better than I gave her credit for. If she'd known the things I sometimes assumed about her, I would have so many apologies to give.

"Is dumpster sex a new thing? Maybe I should try it," she asked, going for a laugh. A sudden snowflake caught in my spidery eyelashes. She stuck out her tongue to catch a fat one.

We were quiet for a few blocks, longer strides, our toes numb, stopping at a corner store for two small bottles of Dr Pepper that we could later mix with the coconut rum she kept under her bed. Our favorite cocktail, so sweet and strange that no one else would drink it with us.

Besides a few slow-moving cars and one feral cat, the streets were deserted. "Darling Nikki" leaked from a car idling at the curb, and we both laughed. More groan than chuckle, remembering Weedler's nickname for me.

"Kill me if I ever play that song on purpose," I said.

"How about you kill me if I ever buy a quarter beer again." She gripped her stomach. Cheap-beer belly was the worst.

Later, we would agree that the only reason either of us should ever play "Darling Nikki" was to torture the other one. Like a joke. Like ha ha, remember that horrible teacher who didn't understand the concept of personal space?

We didn't say much else on the walk back to the car. It was a whatever sort of night; we both agreed on that. Except I'd lost my chance at learning something new from Jasmine. It was naive to expect that she'd confirm anything about Weedler or tell me about Abbie's death. But at least I had tried.

Writing a paper to blame Weedler for decades of suicides had never been my goal. He had taught at the college for less than ten years and couldn't have known all the girls who had died. But something about Abbie Moriano felt different from the others. Her favorite class was the one he taught. She couldn't handle college because of her vulture professor.

Then I remembered that Jasmine had mentioned Abbie's scholarship. It mattered. Scholarship Girls were encouraged to apply for Weedler's mentorship program.

Q: List the names of the other Scholarship Girls.
A: The three girls who died in the nineties, Kiki Ward, Jessie Allis, Abbie Moriano. And Sylvia Plath. And me.

Something stronger than the Dread filled me after that. I had gotten off track with researching suicide rates and even Sylvia Plath. My original instinct that the college was hiding something had never been stronger.

Above us, the sky looked like nothing, just a wide-open canopy, and the air smelled like molasses from the Domino Sugar plant. I don't remember the rest of the walk to our car or how long it took us to get there. With all that burnt-up sweetness surrounding us, I think we were happy.

CHAPTER 18
NOW

Sadie

"Are you sure everything is okay?" Harrison called for the second time that morning. He had started calling more frequently from work to "check in."

"Because I worry about you," he claimed. "You're so tired." He stopped short of mentioning how many times he'd found me talking to myself or lingering outside the office door.

But I knew the real reason for his extra attention: because he suspected I was up to something, something to do with Nikki, and he couldn't figure it out. Over the weekend, his constant presence, when he wouldn't leave my side, forced me to stay away from the office.

I was in front of the mailbox with Bernie for his most recent call. I tried turning my face away from her, but she still heard me.

"Has that chucklehead proposed yet?" she asked after I ended the call. It would have been a surprisingly personal question from anyone else. But it was Bernie. No filter.

"Not yet." I wiggled my bare fingers. "I think it's going to take time for him. You know, because of...everything."

She grunted. "Don't rush it if it isn't right, hon. Especially with that kind of man."

We had gotten to know each other, a little more each day. She joined me for coffee in the front yard (none of that "green tea shit") and told me about her former life as an extra on a soap opera. She had appeared in fourteen commercials, she said, before raising her family. She had a daughter whom she didn't get to see as much as she wanted, a dead husband, and no grandchildren. She used to have a cat named Rudy Huxtable. She'd once been to Alaska to see whales.

I adored her. Her grumpy attitude toward every topic, especially the neighbors in Hidden Harbor, were like a balm after listening to "10,000 Micro-Joys You Should Journal about Today," or whatever other bullshit mantras had invaded social media.

Best of all, Bernie liked to take Rhi for her daily stroller walks, sometimes two or more a day. It gave me time to myself. A complete and utter miracle. If I worried about her getting worn out, she scoffed. She liked to boast that she was strong and healthy enough to take her own trash cans to the curb every Thursday, thank you very much. And it was true. On most days, she seemed to have more stamina than me.

She had known Nikki, of course, and we wore soft treads around the topic. If we spoke about Nikki at all, I tried to make things sound light and vague. That we had been friends before, and now I spent my spare time trying to understand the work she'd left behind. Thankfully, she never pried, never asked what I did for "work."

As I continued to read more of Annie Minx's books, I learned about bone broth and DIY coffee enemas. Nothing remotely close to the research in her office. Still, it consumed both my waking and sleeping hours, the ones not in baby mode. Every glance over my shoulder was filled with a kind of urgency that had no deadline or end point.

Nikki had spent countless hours researching "suicide clusters" and the science behind something called the Werther Effect. It was why more deaths by suicide had occurred after someone like Robin Williams or Anthony Bourdain died. She had scribbled "Kurt Cobain" in the margins of one particular article. To use the word *contagious* simplified suicide in those circumstances, but that was the word she used.

I wanted to cry knowing she had spent so much time researching suicide. With her family history. She couldn't let it go. It was almost admirable. Deranged, but admirable.

If Nikki left other clues or messages for me, she hadn't made them easy to find. So far, all I had were suspicions and gut reactions I couldn't prove. But I was on the verge. I could feel it, a certain spark in the air, Nikki lingering in doorways while I searched. Sometimes she even clucked her approval.

"Most women lose the baby weight by now," she said, bending her neck so far to the side something snapped. I'd forgotten how cruel she could be when she was tired or stressed. We'd both always had so much power to hurt the other.

Her dress: draped amethyst chiffon, shirred bodice, with one thick, muddy blot on the train.

"It looks like you shit yourself," I said.

Her laughter broke a light bulb. She doubled over, drooled glittery spittle on the rug.

"Oh, girl," she said, wiping at her empty eye sockets. "Kill me if I ever…"

"If you ever what?"

"If I ever do *this* again." She lifted the skirt of her dress to reveal her bandaged foot, wrapped mummy-tight and spotless. It was the only part of her not spattered with muck or slime. In response, my own foot ached harder than before.

I turned over the office and her boxes in the attic. Still no back-and-forth journal. Nightmares of the notebook in someone else's hands plagued me each night. Nikki must have considered it, too. What if the reason we couldn't find it was because someone else had it all along? Something monstrous came over me in those moments as I dumped every box out on the floor. It helped, even if only for a little while, to feel like I was doing something. If I sat still, a cold dread took over.

I was more positive than ever that Nikki hadn't chosen to die. Someone else had to be involved. The fire and the gas leak that everyone attributed to Nikki weighed on me more than everything else. Anyone could start a fire or open a valve. My latest effort was to find the footage from Nikki's security cameras, all of it saved on her laptop, but she had obviously already gone through it, labeling files as "bullshit" or "nothing to see here." There was nothing from the day she died.

My own weariness with Harrison lately had gotten bad. The reasons piled up. Because he didn't question that his wife died by suicide. Because he kept his dead wife's office locked and preserved. Mostly because he was just so damn stable. I was dubious. Handsome and rich and kind were red flags to anyone with enough dating experience, but always in retrospect. I looked for a secret vampire fixation or a stockpile of hair dolls but found none. I couldn't even convincingly say he had an interest in those mystery shows about murdered women that the rest of the world loved.

Finding ways to search without him getting suspicious was the biggest challenge. Just the day before, he had roses delivered to smooth over a mini argument we'd had, one in which he accused me of making a mess in the attic, going through Nikki's things. I had to remind him that my things were up there, too.

Each time he touched me now, Nikki's presence beat at the edges of my mind. She snapped at the air, her teeth biting nothing. A low-level belly growl.

"Bitch," I snarled and turned up my music. Hole. Alice in Chains. So loud it drowned out the baby monitor. It drowned out everything in my head.

If Harrison started to pull away, turned off by the music or the curl of my lip, I pulled him back harder. Old Sadie. Fast, hard, hungry.

"This is for me," I said afterward, so that only she could hear me. *For me, for me, for me.*

When she wasn't around, Harrison and I didn't touch at all.

While Bernie walked with Rhi, I didn't take a nap like she told me to do. I sat by the window instead and scrolled through social media. My gentle online stalking was a different kind of research. And I thought I was pretty good at it.

First, I checked Diana's Facebook account, going back to a year before. I wasn't looking for something in particular and didn't find anything besides staged baby photos and non-sweaty workout selfies. Then I searched for Nikki's profile. Her Facebook privacy settings were locked down, only available to "friends," but it didn't matter. I learned so much more about her from her Pinterest account. Pinterest accounts were hardly ever locked from snooping eyes.

Pinterest was where I could see her aspirations and her obsessions. Crock-Pot meal planning, but even better. The items pinned to her *Self-Care Inspiration Board* were typical, I guessed, things like essential oils, celebrity-endorsed candles, and bronzer gel that I wouldn't know how to use even if you paid me to learn.

But nothing about death, nothing about the Sylvia Club. The closest thing I found were glimmery polka-dot journals with sayings that seemed like a joke but were probably not: "Back off Ted, Sylvia's coming with me!" and "Poetry Whore."

My phone vibrated in my hand. What is, Bernie had written. An incomplete message she'd sent before she was ready.

What is

What is

What is that dark blue car sitting across the stree

?

Classic Bernie. At least she didn't add twelve emojis this time. If there was a suspicious car in the neighborhood, she would make it her business to know about it.

I peered out the window to see her waving at me from the sidewalk as she circled the cul-de-sac again with Rhi dozing in the stroller. A navy-blue sedan with tinted windows sat two houses down. I realized suddenly that I had seen it before, at least a few times in the past week. The tinted windows made me think of detectives on a stakeout. That's where my brain went first.

Breathe. Exhale. No need to unravel. Even if it was a car full of cops, that didn't mean they were there for me.

What would Nikki do? I had been asking myself that each

time I encountered something in my new world that I didn't know how to handle. The better question lived deeper: What would Old Sadie do? Static hummed in my ears.

Old Sadie wouldn't slip on real shoes. She'd go barefoot. She'd march out into the cold street; she'd knock on the driver's-side window. She wouldn't hide or wait for them to make a move. She wouldn't sit back and wonder. And that's exactly what I did.

The woman in the driver's seat wasn't a detective, though. The smell of greasy fast food blew out from the darkened car as Lucille, my old friend from *Baltimore Alive!*, rolled down her window. I hadn't heard from her in months.

"Sadie, oh my God, you look great!" she shouted. "I was just getting ready to knock on your door."

Still wearing my pajamas, braless, robed, and uncombed, I did not *look great*. She was the one with her usually unkempt hair cropped like a pixie, neat and tidy. Instead of an oversize sweater and leggings, her previous go-to outfit, she wore a blazer and delicate gold jewelry.

"You scared me, girl," I said and waited for her to follow me in. She hadn't seen the dream house since before I'd moved in, that one visit when my stomach was huge, and she'd convinced me not to blow my chances at the "good life," as she called it.

"Coffee?" I asked, knowing she'd want something stronger. That was our relationship. We'd only known each other in cheap florescent overhead or dank bar lighting. We weren't coffee-in-the-middle-of-the-day kind of friends. Close up, she didn't look as put together as I first thought. Her eye makeup had been half rubbed away, and her lips were bare and chapped. She looked out of her element in that blazer. Her sturdy frame needed something tougher. Steel-toed boots and chain mail. She needed leather.

She looked up to the skylight, spinning, taking it all in. "Holy shit, Sadie. I forgot how big this house is."

"You want a tour? Want to see the fancy washing machine?" I laughed, feeling more out of place than ever.

We settled onto barstools around the kitchen island, a container of presliced cheese and a box of stale crackers in front of us.

"So, what's up?" I asked.

Something was definitely up. Besides the fact that she hadn't called first. And if I hadn't knocked on her car window, I had a feeling she wouldn't have made herself known.

"A couple things, actually." Lucille looked at the crackers like she wanted to turn them into something better. "I'm working on a new story. Thought you might be able to help me out."

A new story meant she had another job, or she had picked up freelancing gigs. I hadn't been surprised at the rumors that she got canned, though I would have believed it more if she'd simply quit. Among the journalists at *B.A.*, her ideas were always too serious or too long.

"There's an old hit-and-run case I've been trying to look into for years. A professor at Loch Raven College. You went to school there, right?"

She already knew the answer to her own question. She wouldn't have come to me otherwise. I had never told her about Loch Raven College. I didn't graduate, didn't have a degree from anywhere. I never mentioned that year of my life at all.

"This is for your new job?"

"It's this story Drouse wouldn't let me write for *B.A.* It's an old case I can't let go." She tilted her head as if to say *What can I do?*

Interests and obsessions were just one of those things. We all had them. We didn't choose them. They chose us. But the glint in her eye. A knife's edge. I hadn't seen that in her before.

I believed her that Drouse had shut down her story idea, especially if she wanted to write about accidents that were almost twenty years old. *Baltimore Alive!* couldn't exactly slide that kind of story in next to a mattress-store review.

"And what does this have to do with me?" I stared until she stared back, impressed by my ability to speak without a warble in my voice. "Just say it, Luce."

She swallowed. "I've looked at the old case. Like I said, I've been trying to work on this story for years now. Your name is in some of the files. And your friend, too. The woman who lived here before."

Old case files Loch Raven what the fuck nikki nikki

Caroline had said a reporter stopped by to talk to Nikki. After that, Nikki went frantic searching for our old notebook, one of the last things in existence that connected us to the worst night of our lives. I'd been so busy looking for the journal that I never stopped to wonder about the identity of the reporter. And if Lucille was that reporter, I had a bigger problem. It meant she had been lying to me for a long time. It meant that when she came to the house with me all those months ago, it wasn't her first time.

The ring of the doorbell made us both jump. Bernie wrinkled her nose and stood outside, holding Rhi up and away from her body, then made me promise to call her later.

I'd never been so eager to exit a conversation, but I was also unprepared to leave Lucille alone in the house to wander around. It was the one time I was glad for the lock on the office door.

Why now?

"It's a long story, Sadie," Lucille grunted through the baby monitor, and I paused mid–ass wipe. Her voice echoed, a ghostly reverberation.

By the time I finished fastening the new diaper, Lucille stepped into the nursery. The darkened room might have seemed a cozier place to talk, but the tightness could suffocate, too. Only one way out. I cradled Rhi in the rocking chair and waited for Lucille to speak.

"The truth," she said, "is that I only saw the police files a week ago. I didn't believe it when I saw your name. I never lied to you before, if that's what you're thinking."

The rest of the story, at least the part she'd decided to divulge, seemed simple enough. She had started looking into the old unsolved case and spoke to someone familiar with Loch Raven College during that time. That person, an anonymous "they," had mentioned that Nikki was the person to talk to. It was Nikki, they'd claimed, who may have known more than what she'd told the police back then. The more Lucille talked to people and looked into the accident, the more roads led to Nikki.

She didn't have the ability to say Nikki's name without a sneer. She wasn't a fan. After all, Nikki had sent her away when she came to the house to ask questions. I knew that part. Lucille tried to forget about it, quit her job at *B.A.* and let the story grow cold, colder than it was already, until recently, when one of her connections at the police department finally granted her access to the old files.

She threw up her hands, a kind of surrender. "When you moved in here, I didn't mention the old story. Why would I? What would I have said? That I had once tried to talk to the previous owner before she slammed the door in my face?"

"Sure, you could have mentioned it."

"And you could have told me that you had been friends with Harrison's dead wife. But it wasn't relevant? Or it just didn't come up?"

She had a point. I didn't have to like it, though. It still felt like she wasn't saying everything. Not even close. What did I really know about Lucille? We had always used broad strokes to talk about our pasts, our families, our wild nights.

"I have a lot to do today, actually," I said. I turned my voice to steel.

I stood with the intention of walking her to the door. Later, I'd walk back inside calmly, then turn on the shower to cover my screams. I'd ask Bernie to take Rhi for another stroll. I'd stop wasting time. Nikki hadn't feared for her life and left me messages for the hell of it. This wasn't another one of her scavenger hunts with Dr Pepper and sour candy at the end. She meant for me to figure shit out.

And for once, I had more than myself to protect. I had Rhi. And Caroline, too. As ridiculous as my new life might seem to someone like Lucille, it was worth protecting.

"Just so you know, I'm committed," Lucille said. "I'm not giving up on this story."

Old Sadie would have told her to suck a fat one. And I did.

Nikki, in a ripped prom gown with sequins on both nips, sat in the corner and applauded.

CHAPTER 19

THEN

Nikki

It was late enough to see the nocturnal animals lumber across the main road between campus and the highway. And it was dark. Weedler gave me his address twice, but the only way to get to his place was for Sadie to drive. She was the one with the car, even if she had to park half a mile away because freshmen weren't allowed parking permits. The silver Toyota Tercel looked like every other car and frequently dropped its license plate, so no one ever said a thing about it.

Which was good because that car was a lifeline. It meant we could escape campus anytime we wanted.

"I can't believe we're doing this," I said. Meaning, I couldn't believe we were driving to a professor's house. But he had invited us. Well, me. I couldn't believe there was no one there to stop us.

Sadie tinted her lips in the rearview mirror, one hand loose on the steering wheel. "Professor Weedler gets cuter the longer I look at him, you know. The long hair is kinda sexy, huh?"

"Don't even joke. We're going here to discuss my paper. Nothing else." My scholarship was riding on that paper. When she didn't respond, I pinched her leg. "I'm serious, Sadie."

Her phony cackle drowned out the radio, and she chased the silence with an indiscriminate European accent. "Sylvia, I am wearing your abandoned shoes. I am sleeping in your unchanged sheets."

"Oh," I said as she launched into what must have been her creative monologue, the one that would serve as her makeup grade for the test we'd both missed. I hadn't seen it yet. That explained why she wore her favorite orange costume-room dress, bright tangerine and painfully retro. She probably planned to use this trip to Weedler's house as her practice performance.

Give her a martini and the look would be complete.

A monologue in the voice of Assia Wevill was the kind of idea she had sometimes, a surprising flurry of creativity to prove she had been listening as I rambled about my own Sylvia Plath research.

As soon as Sadie learned about Assia, the other woman sleeping with Sylvia Plath's husband, she called dibs right away, even though we couldn't find much more than a footnote about her in all the biographies. Ted Hughes moved Assia into his house, Sylvia's house, to help take care of the children right after Sylvia died. Assia must have slept in the same bed, used the same utensils, obeyed whatever Ted wanted for his kids. It wasn't clear.

Q: How did Assia Wevill die?
A: The same way as Sylvia Plath. In the kitchen, with gas filling the room.

"I think she's misunderstood," Sadie said the last time I asked about the monologue. That was my line, the exact thing I always said about every famous woman in history.

All those tragedies. We didn't have the right language for any of it.

As Weedler promised, his house wasn't far from campus, but the long, curved road leading up to it darkened fast, suddenly lightless. So close to the city, yet so hidden. Sadie's high beams caught nothing but trees and dirt in their spotlight.

7 Year Bitch: "Kiss My Ass Goodbye."

"This is how all scary movies start." I turned down the volume before eventually turning it off all the way.

The scariest movies, I'd always said, were the ones set in the woods where no one else could hear you scream. Sadie disagreed. The most terrifying scenarios were when the monsters hid in plain sight.

Dr. Gallina was the one who gave me the idea to accept Weedler's invitation. When I had come to her office, frantic with fear over losing my scholarship because he still wouldn't sign my form, she didn't let me babble for long.

"Nikki, your grades are slipping, and some of your professors are worried. I was just getting ready to ask you to come in for a meeting." She laced her fingers under her chin. "If there's anything you want to talk about, you know you can come to me. You don't have a big support system here. Is that right?"

Her voice traveled two octaves, higher and higher, like talking to a child or an injured wild animal she worried about scaring away. Like she needed to wear oven mitts to handle me with care.

I rubbed my forehead to feel for blood but came away clean. An hour before, in the dorm-room bathroom, a girl I'd figured was Jessie Allis made me watch as she beat her head bloody against the tampon dispenser.

"Twins!" she'd shouted. "Look, we match."

And for a moment, blood had gushed from my scalp just as hard.

Gallina's frown lines deepened. She paused, as if stuck on how to proceed next.

"Professor Weedler is one of the professors who contacted me. He's worried you're going to hurt yourself."

She rattled off a list of concerns: the failed séance turned fire, a fixation on death, my moody behavior. The dark circles under my eyes. The staring off into space. An obsession with suicide.

My desperation and exhaustion bumped up against a righteous anger in that moment, though I tried not to let it show. I wasn't the one everyone needed to worry about. Part of me realized, though, that with all the talk of "who is going to be next," it would be hard for a teacher to not say something. To them, I probably looked like just another potential dead girl.

"He's overreacting. I'm fine. I'm not going to hurt myself." The lilt of my voice hiccuped into song. "I just need to pass my classes and keep my scholarships. Can you help me or not?"

She paused. "Yes, I can help. It's your scholarship form you need Professor Weedler to sign, right?"

She detailed a short plan for me to meet with Weedler and ask for an extension on my paper. I needed to write the paper he'd assigned, the paper about Sylvia Plath, and keep my scholarship. These were the facts, she said. It didn't matter if neither of us liked him, she didn't say.

"What if he tries to...?" I started, thinking about the address he had written on my last assignment, and his hand on my knee.

She stopped me again. "Do whatever it takes to get this resolved. I'm sure you can convince him to sign the paper."

She said it so fast I didn't have time to absorb what she meant. Later, I'd wonder if we had been talking about the same thing. She was sending me to the wolves, but for a good reason.

It always came down to that scholarship. So many other girls, especially the ones in the Sylvia Club, had collapsed under the pressure. It wasn't just about good grades and taking extra courses. You got into a fancy college, your whole family was watching and waiting from the sidelines, so you couldn't fail. You couldn't come home too early or explain that you were the girl who couldn't hack it.

By then, I had created a timeline of almost all the students who had died, filling in details where I could. The scholarship was one link between them, their ages another. But I had found that article about Hope Hall, too, which made Abbie Moriano's death seem different from the others. And she had known Weedler. I couldn't let that part go.

I strained my neck to look up at Hope Hall's roof almost daily now. From that view, you'd be disappointed. Maybe you would expect to see the entire world but then only be able see as far as Loch Raven's campus stretched. Loch Raven College wasn't the whole world, but it had probably felt that way for Abbie.

Sadie drove farther into blackness until his house appeared, a simple one-level box with a large porch out front. No neighbors anywhere close. If I closed my eyes, I could already envision the whole night. I already knew how it would unfold, a late night with Sadie making bad choices and me second-guessing my own.

Weedler opened his front door and stood in the peplum of light that washed the doorway. Untucked, a bottle of beer in his hand, the top two buttons on his shirt undone, like whatever. Like he invited students over to his house all the time.

"Sadie, help yourself to anything in the fridge. Nikki and I need a few minutes to talk about her paper proposal. I won't take long. I'd hate to keep you out past curfew."

The lightness in his voice—light like cotton candy and confetti—surprised me. This was a different kind of flirting. No more official-sounding dialogue because other people might hear. He had relaxed into himself in the worst possible way.

Sadie grinned, glitter-throated and neon-sheathed. "Well, curfew is in thirty minutes. How fast can you go?" She meant to tease, to make him blush. She swirled the mesh underneath her dress until it crinkled.

My discomfort looked like this: sitting on the opposite end of the sofa, my knees turned away from him, my mouth dry.

I waited for one of the dead girls to materialize and witness Weedler for what he was. Maybe they could flood his house with their rancid perfume. Maybe they could grow fangs.

The dim light of a desk lamp shone on a typewriter and a coffee mug. In the kitchen, Sadie clinked glasses and opened drawers, making as much noise as she could.

"First, let me go ahead and tell you what you already know: what you turned in wasn't what I asked for," he said, scooting closer. "It isn't the correct assignment."

With his sleeves rolled, the scorpion tattoo on his wrist almost glowed.

I'd once heard that scorpions danced before mating. That they were venomous, but not intentionally so.

My stomach twisted. If he touched me, I would retch. The

smell of beer and his pine tree cologne. This had been a bad idea. It wasn't what Gallina had in mind.

"Dr. Gallina suggested I appeal to you for an extension."

Saying her name out loud boosted my courage and forced me to sit up straighter. I'd been irritated in her office earlier, but she only wanted to help.

"And are you going to tell Dr. Gallina about the way you drove to my house late at night in a low-cut blouse to ask for this extension?"

My black sweater wasn't purposely low-cut, but it was tight. Gallina's voice in my head had replaced my mom's: *Trust yourself and your body, Nikki. Speak up for yourself.*

I didn't know it was his finger on my neck at first, his hand cradling the back of my head, behind my ponytail, and by the time I realized, I opened my eyes wider, afraid to blink, and willed Sadie to walk in. Even if she made it worse, she would at least stop this moment from going any further.

The rest happened fast. Or slow. But it happened, his lips on mine, so forceful I couldn't pull away. He had me by the neck. His other hand reached for my waist, for something below my ribs, but I suddenly remembered that my hands were free and not frozen in place. With both palms, I shoved his face away until he retreated.

Later, I'd think: I should have used my nails. I should have screamed.

Later, I'd be glad I wore pants.

That's when Sadie walked in, holding a sandwich and a beer she'd stolen from his fridge, happy as shit with herself and oblivious until she saw my face. She knew me too well. Weedler and I both panted.

"You son of a bitch," she said, her tone sharp and low. One of her thin spaghetti straps fell down her shoulder.

It must have been all those bar games, the darts and the shuffleboard and the pool table practice, because she had perfect aim. No hesitation as she threw the sandwich at his face from the kitchen doorway. A pickle slice smacked the wooden floor. The sound of bread against flesh was the soft slap I couldn't manage on my own.

He stood, so stunned by our dueling reactions—my disgust and tears next to Sadie's spontaneous, spitting rage—that he flipped a slice of onion from his collar and sighed.

"Why don't we call it a night?" Then, turning to me as if my whole body wasn't trembling on full display, he said, "No more extensions. The paper is due tomorrow."

I yanked Sadie through the door with me before she decided to throw her beer bottle at him, too. We didn't speak until our seat belts were buckled, with me in the driver's seat, the way I instinctively did any time we went out and she started drinking.

Me and my unsteady hands, my shaking shoulders—I shook the whole car.

No need to rush, I told myself. There was no chase, nowhere to be.

I made it halfway down the long driveway before slamming on the brakes and opening the driver's-side door to throw up in the gravel.

"Did that really happen? Oh my God, Sadie. What the fuck?"

I could still feel his hand tangled in my hair. No matter how many times I gagged, I couldn't untaste him. It had started to drizzle. Then a rustling, crunching, thrashing of branches. Sadie heard it, too, and pulled me back up into the car.

"It was a shame to waste such a good sandwich," she tried to joke once we made it to the end of the gravel drive.

She wasn't angry enough, I realized. The only one quivering in that car was me.

Left or right. I couldn't remember which way to turn back to school. We sat, the car idling, the heat not blasting anything but cold air.

Her slippery tangerine fabric looked like it could ice over if it got wet.

"Think we can run away forever?" I asked instead of turning.

She smiled up through the windshield at the dark sky. Like I'd asked the perfect question. "Only if you promise to drive fast."

Her Tercel rumbled into gear, and I peeled out, turning left, gravel kicked up behind the wheels, before realizing I had gone the wrong way. I needed to turn right. There were no other cars, not this close to Weedler's deserted street.

In a mile, a stoplight and a gas station waited. But here, only purple, inky night.

I slammed into reverse, spun the car, and headed back the other way, cresting the sloped road, never turning on the headlights.

My crooked pinkie finger hung in the space between us like a hook. "Promise me something."

She didn't hesitate, linking her pinkie into mine. In the dark, her hair almost matched her dress.

"Yes, I promise to keep all your secrets, for richer or poorer, in sickness and health, until both of us croak."

We had spoken the words enough times to memorize the script.

I added her favorite part. "Even in death. You would be the first person I'd haunt."

"Oh yeah? I thought you'd never leave without me?"

"Damn straight," I said, my shoulders starting to relax, but just a little. We were in this together.

The fog clotted, a heavy veil of clouds obscuring the road and shifting into half-formed shapes. A bride laced in white, a ballerina swirling into the perfect pirouette.

Then a girl I thought I knew, swimming through the mist and murk. Abbie falling into nothing. Face-first.

We passed Weedler's street again, headed now in the right direction. Sadie didn't watch the road. That was my job.

The thud shocked us into silence. Thud on the hood of the car, smash on the windshield. We skidded to a stop, and everything else, everything outside the car, stopped, too.

I couldn't hear anything over the thunder in my ears. *Thud. Smash.* A deer, I told myself. Whatever it was, we couldn't ignore it.

Her orange fabric slipped from my hands as I tried to stop her from getting out to check. I already knew. Deep down, I knew. It wasn't a deer. I counted each breath like a petal on a flower, and when thirty seconds passed, I stepped out of the car, too. I had to see for myself.

The crooked body lay motionless, face down on the pavement, where he shouldn't have been walking. Sadie crouched beside him. His jeans looked different in the dark, and unreal, the way one leg bent at an irregular angle. The other one flat where it shouldn't have been flat.

She twisted his wrist like she meant to feel for a pulse, and her thumb covered the scorpion's stinger. Nothing beneath the skin, though. She felt nothing.

"No no no no no no no no," she cried, her voice barely making a sound.

From inside the car, Courtney Love crooned.

"We have to move him," I finally said. Behind us, somewhere in the woods, a small animal scurried. "We can't leave him here."

We could debate later what we should have done. At least I had a suggestion. She couldn't move off the ground. She might have crouched frozen there until daylight if I hadn't moved into action.

But we couldn't lift him. Me at his feet and her at his wet shoulders, his hair darker with blood. I gagged again, this time throwing up on his shoes. So we rolled his body to the shoulder. He'd be hidden until daylight. I didn't think he'd stay undiscovered on the roadside for long.

The headlights from another car, driving too fast, soared past us on the other side of the road, and I yelped. If the driver saw us, he didn't slow down. He didn't even tap his brakes. At least Sadie's car looked like every other car. I wore all black, shadowed, I hoped. Even with a drizzling mist and thin haze, Sadie's orange dress smoldered, luminous.

"Now. Nikki. Go," Sadie called, waking from her trance, already climbing back in the car, this time with her in the driver's seat. No squealing tires, but she drove fast, both hands planted on the wheel.

Neither of us spoke. Every ragged breath said it all.

"Headlights," I reminded her once we hit the main road spotted with other cars. Then we drove farther, away from campus, past a gas station and a church, past the rehab center where Zelda Fitzgerald once stayed. "Do you think he was…?" I asked.

She shushed me. It wasn't until we merged onto the highway miles later that I noticed the fissure in the windshield, the kind of crack that would spider out if it wasn't fixed.

Even if she didn't say where she was headed, I knew the roads to her grandmother's house by heart.

Heavy tears pooled in her eyes, waiting to fall loose, and I worried she couldn't see the road. "We can go back. It was an accident. It isn't too late. Right? Nikki? Right?"

My mother's middle name was Margaret. My favorite doll's name used to be Rhiannon.

Every song on Hole's Live Through This, *in order: "Violet," "Miss World," "Plump," "Asking for It," "Jennifer's Body," "Doll Parts," "Credit in the Straight World," "Softer, Softest," "She Walks on Me," "I Think That I Would Die," "Gutless," "Rock Star."*

Marilyn Monroe died in 1962. Sylvia Plath died in 1963.

The last day to withdraw from fall classes was the thirtieth of October.

And the one thing I knew for sure: girls who killed their teacher didn't end up in the Hall of Success. Even if it was an accident.

"Nik, we have to do something. Please tell me you know what the fuck we're going to do." Her voice, low and quivering, sent another vibration through me. "It was an accident. You didn't see him there. We'll tell the police it was dark and we got scared…"

I curled my fingers into my fists, bloodied my palms with my fingernails. "I'm not ruining my life over that asshole. It was dark, like you said. An accident. Except that no one will believe us, not after everything that happened this semester. The séance, broken curfew. He told Dr. Gallina I was disturbed. It isn't going to look good."

The fog lifted just enough to see the highway signs. No matter how far we drove, it didn't feel far enough.

"We shouldn't just disappear. It will look fishy. I have someone we can call. Someone to give us a ride back to campus. We can't drive this car again."

Sadie didn't ask who I meant. Harry's number sat in my pocket, though I hadn't used it yet. I would call him from Grandma Ruth's house and ask him to pick us up. He was no one, and that's exactly what we needed—someone who didn't know us and wouldn't ask questions about the rest of our night.

"I'm staying at my grandmother's."

I didn't try to convince her otherwise. But as the miles passed and more tears clung to the ledge of her chin, her face tightened in a way I had never seen before, not even when she'd gotten into that hair-pulling fight in the tenth grade. Not even when she threw the sandwich.

"We aren't going to tell anyone anything," she spit out. "We tell no one."

I nodded, certain. "We never speak about this again."

"We can't even write about this," she said, a promise we meant to keep. When she said "we," she meant me.

It hadn't sunk in yet, but it started to. She would need to change out of the orange dress. A stain bloomed at the hem where she'd kneeled over his body. My chin crusted with drops of vomit that my sleeve couldn't wipe away.

Sylvia Plath in the kitchen.
Marilyn Monroe on her bed.
My mom in the garage.

I couldn't blame Weedler for any of them. But at least now there wouldn't be anyone else to fall into his web.

CHAPTER 20
NOW

Sadie

The fondue restaurant flickered electric, full of attractive young servers with half-heartbroken smiles and smooth hands. Just the way a restaurant should be. Tonight was the night. Harrison was going to propose. I knew it when I'd dressed for the evening. Why else would he take me to a quiet, fancy restaurant for no reason? I wasn't sure how I felt anymore or what I wanted, but when he put on a tie and then Caroline showed up to babysit, I couldn't say no.

Fondue was trendy again, he'd told me on the drive over, but I didn't care. Lucille staking out the house seemed a little more important than skewering fruit into melted chocolate.

The more I thought about Lucille's visit, the bigger it grew. A crime almost twenty years old. Someone, most likely from Loch Raven, pointing a finger at Nikki. Lucille could have knocked on the door and asked me directly about what had happened all those years ago. She could have called. It wasn't like I would have freaked out on her. Much.

Me, the tired mom fighting with her breast pump for better suckage—I wasn't worth staking out.

I replayed that conversation in the nursery again and again until it still chafed at my nerves but not as raw. I had never worried that Nikki told anyone what had happened back then because I knew Nikki better than that. She had been more hard-assed about that promise than me.

If only Lucille's visit was the worst of my fears. I couldn't stop watching Harrison with a new set of eyes. A new suspicion took the tiniest shape inside me. It stayed undercooked and out of reach while I swirled expensive wine and stabbed strawberries.

I wanted to trust him. The moments when I trusted him were the simplest kind of bliss. Weeks before, all I had wanted was for him to weigh down my hand with a diamond. And, honestly, a large part of me still wanted him to ask. Down on one knee, ring sunk to the bottom of a bubbly glass. The promise of something solid and committed.

But I didn't intend to be the dumbass in a late-night true crime reenactment who married a shady widower without ever suspecting a thing. I'd rather be the dumbass who almost married him but finally put the pieces together before it was too late.

I would rather him not have anything to do with Nikki's death at all.

The bartender wiped down his station, the busboy yawned, and the hostess, her hair in lumpy pigtails, daydreamed out the window. My years waiting tables surged over me. I couldn't resist the urge to listen to threads of conversation as it escaped through the swinging doors of the kitchen, where everything was, I remembered, slick and warm, loud and easy. I noticed we were one of only three tables in the whole restaurant, and asked Harrison what time they closed. He eddied his wine until it looked like a cyclone.

He wanted to hear about Rhi's new expression, with her brow furrowed as if deep in thought and her nostrils flared like a bull. Caroline made the same face, he said.

"I read a new study about the dangers of giving children milk at bedtime. The sugar will build up on their teeth overnight and cause rot," he said. "Maybe you've already read this."

I quick-yanked a strand of hair at the root to make myself concentrate. "But Rhi doesn't have teeth yet."

I conjured up an image of a cartoon character whose teeth fell out like the glass in a windowpane. Teeth spilling out of my mouth like tiny plastic pebbles. Harrison frowned, sorry he brought it up.

Every long pause between us stretched longer and longer as we sipped our bottle of Riesling. It was too sweet to finish, but I didn't want to hurt his feelings.

I'd gotten pregnant so early in our relationship that I'd never gotten to enjoy all the excess and luxury that his life seemed to promise. These were the kinds of nights that once filled Nikki's life, too. Champagne and hot tub vacations or writing bestselling books and building a faceless empire. Though, actually, instead of living a life of luxury, during the day while Caroline was at school, Nikki had holed up in her office to research dead girls.

I needed to stop calling them that. If I remembered anything about Nikki, she would insist on knowing their names. They had stories to tell, they had lives. No one should be known only for the way they died, she used to say. And that's what I had spent the morning on, learning their names—Shea Nardman, Betsy Zeller,

Abbie Moriano. If I couldn't find anything new, I could at least try to understand the work she'd left out in the open.

Harrison's shoe brushed my calf, and I hummed the words to "Miss World." Even with all my suspicions, a simple touch was all it took to get me going. My brain, my body, needed a break.

After his text about going out for dessert, I had spent the rest of the afternoon trying to feel sexy, a little like my old self. I wore my hair in my eyes like a Playboy Bunny with a comb-over, drank ice water out of a wineglass, shaved my legs during Rhiannon's second micro-nap. I blared Hole until the windows shook and I could no longer hear Nikki singing along.

It worked, too; by the time Harrison got home from work, my body tingled at even the thought of being touched. I looked alive. My nose wasn't filled with crusted mud. I almost forgot about gas leaks and snarky zombies and Lucille sniffing around. The air felt so rich, so smooth. Harrison would look at me and never suspect anything was wrong.

Under Nikki's bathrobe I even wore the underwear Harrison gave me on Valentine's Day, which were comfortable and cotton, nothing like what I would've picked out for myself.

I gave Caroline the rundown of bottles and diapers, but I really just wanted to remind her not to get into her mother's shit. Harrison was standing right there, though, for once looking like he wanted me more than he wanted his grief, so I didn't say anything.

While we waited for the key lime–rum fondue, I told a story from my old days as a server. Some of my coworkers had a dessert-eating contest, and since the key lime pie hadn't been selling, we laid every slice in a line by the drink station. "You should've seen me," I told him, shoveling pie into my mouth like a beast. I didn't mention the way my vomit had looked like antifreeze afterward, though it was the best part of the story.

Our dessert arrived on cue, and Harrison suffered with a smile. I must have told that one before.

There weren't many other stories from Before that were worth repeating. Nothing about my family, and definitely no stories about Nikki. We both knew that topic was off-limits. Instead, I redirected my stories to the in-between years when I wasn't in college but still looked like I should have been. Wild girl with the wild hair, making it on her own, bound for mediocrity—that's the version of me Harrison preferred, even if he wouldn't admit it. Nikki was the smart one. Classy and a little broken. I'd tried those angles for myself but couldn't make them fit anymore.

Halfway through dessert, he no longer seemed nervous or excited like a man about to propose marriage, and I relaxed. I asked if his parents would visit soon, but he dodged that question with expertise. They most likely hated me. The one time we met, after Rhi's birth, they left every room as soon as I entered. Harrison never implied that with enough time they would learn to love me. We just stopped inviting them to visit.

He had grown up in Maryland like me, though it could have been another planet, for all our differences. I couldn't comprehend his family of doctors with lucrative stock market investments. They owned horses. They only flew first class. His mom could afford to use her husband's hard-earned money on international travel and injections that kept her skin baby-doll smooth.

He couldn't understand my world, either: a mom who ran off and left her baby to be raised by a grandmother who cleaned houses until she was eighty. Together, we looked like no one he had ever known. My lack of "life experience," as he called it, meant I had never traveled outside the country or eaten steak tartare.

"Don't worry," he promised when he learned I didn't have a passport. "I'll take you everywhere."

Our first slow dance: "Wild Horses," by the Rolling Stones, in a cheap hotel with a leaky faucet, because at the time, I still felt guilty about sleeping in Nikki's home. While we danced, I thought of a thousand ways I would fuck up my life if I stayed with him. Now, when we heard the song, we both got misty-eyed, but maybe for different reasons.

He eyed me over his glass as he savored the tiniest taste. "I was wondering...have you gone into the office, by any chance?"

I counted in my head before responding. Better to tell a partial truth than lie completely.

"I did unlock it once, actually. Not for long, though. Just to vacuum. But I did see that big stack of folders on the desk. Anything worth filing away or preserving?"

If he knew what Nikki had been working on or where she hid her old notebooks, now was the time to tease it out of him. The risk of him throwing everything away did something wretched to my stomach. There were plenty of reasons for Harrison to continue keeping the office locked. The obvious reason being that he wasn't over Nikki.

The other obvious explanation was something sinister that I wasn't ready to look at head-on.

With Lucille investigating our past and his fierce need to preserve everything Nikki had ever touched, I'd be stupid not to wonder. Diana said Nikki wanted me to keep Caroline safe. That didn't seem like nothing.

If I asked him outright, he'd wall up and pull further away.

Just like when I'd asked about his late-night texts. An eyebrow wrinkle or an involuntary twitch could give him away if I handled my questions carefully. But the only change in his face was the pulsing vein in his forehead.

"Let's keep it locked. It's what she wanted."

So cold. So full of charm but also so quick to frost over. It wasn't his best quality. I knew Nikki would have thought so, too.

"Do you still like your anniversary gift?" he asked, to change the subject. He dabbed at his mouth corners with a square of clean linen, never taking his eyes off me.

I lowered my voice and leaned in to pretend we were talking about crotchless panties instead of toe spacers. "I'm wearing them right now."

Under the table, my feet throbbed.

"You know, there's a surgery for bunions," I said. "I read about it online. Might be something I could look into."

I didn't mention that I'd found the information on Nikki's computer.

He grimaced. Hard.

"No. Surgery won't be necessary." He said it like an accusation.

Ever since Nikki lifted her skirt and showed me her bandages, I had suspected that her "little outpatient surgery," the one that Diana had mentioned, was for her foot. And now Harrison all but confirmed it.

His phone chimed with a message from the hospital even though he wasn't on call. He excused himself from the table, muttering into his phone that it wasn't a good time. Our conversation was already forgotten.

Our server dropped the check with two gold-wrapped mints and said, "No rush at all," which really meant, *Please get the hell out of here soon.* He smelled like a cigarette break cut short. It wasn't late, but then again, it was a weeknight.

At least I didn't have to worry about how much of a tip Harrison would leave; he was always generous, regardless of the service. Lucky me. Which meant Nikki had been even luckier.

Nikki and I had once toasted to tipping, back in the dorms after I'd gone on a date with a guy who said he didn't believe in gratuity.

"Let's marry big tippers," we vowed, raising our spiked Dr Pepper bottles. Because tipping well said a lot about a man. We thought we knew so much.

From her seat at the bar, Nikki held out a glass of muck.

Cheers, bitch, she mouthed.

And even though my glass was empty, I toasted her anyway.

Harrison drove home through the city, bouncing through potholes louder than the radio. His silence filled the car like gas, and instead of prodding, I ignored him right back.

The radio voice crooned about power ballads. Requests and dedications. He twisted the stereo knob, searching.

"Has anyone ever dedicated a love song to you on the radio?" I asked.

He nodded. A surprise. "In a different life. 'Eternal Flame.'"

"Good song. Lucky you."

Really, I couldn't think of a better song. I was a little jealous. I tried to remember if anyone had ever dedicated a song to me but could only come up with memories of myself in front of a jukebox, playing all the songs me and Nikki loved.

Before our exit out of the city, we stopped at a red light where three college-age girls waited to cross. They were equally adorable and foolish, maybe just a little older than Caroline. One girl shouted into her phone and the other girl laughed wide enough that we could hear her through our closed windows. The one wearing the knee-high boots paused to light a cigarette.

"Ahhh," I said, remembering. "I know those boots hurt."

Her exhale probably tasted like a stranger's sour kiss. I tasted it, too. Most of their skin was exposed, and they didn't wear coats. I could see three pairs of hard nipples from the car window.

"Nips ahoy," Harrison joked. I forgot that he could be funny.

Their heels looked so uncomfortable that I shifted in my seat. My feet remembered: dancing on a bar top, ignoring the pain in my feet, concentrating on the glow of a stranger's lit cherry.

"I used to be one of those girls," I blurted out. It sounded defensive, the way I said it, like I could read Harrison's mind, the way he frowned at these girls. I said it again. "That could be me."

"Which one?" His voice flattened, and I realized I didn't know him well enough to tell if he was amused or serious. I had never been able to tell.

One of the girls wore red lipstick and had a fake tan, a shirt so tight and low-cut she probably called it her "boob shirt." Another girl waved at a car full of guys, her feet thrust into a pair of banana-yellow pumps, a tattoo of the moon on her ankle. The third one, dancing in place to keep warm, wore a denim skirt so short her pockets hung out the bottom. She tucked in the first girl's tag. The action was so casual and intimate my tears surged.

The girls adjusted their bras, shouted into their cell phones, laughed out loud as they waited for the light to change. They all looked completely, utterly happy. And cold.

"All of them," I said. "Me and Nikki. We were all of them."

Yes, I had thought about going back to the side of the road where we'd left him. Sometimes I dreamed that we didn't instinctively roll the body into a ditch. Back and back, over and over, I kept rewinding.

What if we didn't, what if none of it ever

My car didn't have a crack on the windshield and blood in the grille. We didn't write a confession in a spiral notebook and save it for two decades.

Rewind further.

What if I didn't drip snot onto his collar or leave a fingerprint in his kitchen. What if Nikki didn't puke all over his shoes and a car didn't drive by while we fought on the side of the road about what to do.

What if what if what if

I didn't throw a sandwich at his head. He didn't assault my best friend. I didn't eye the knives in the kitchen with the impromptu thought to use them as a prop in my monologue. I didn't finger all their handles. I didn't fantasize about his smooth, academic hands tangled in my hair a moment before I saw those same hands at the back of Nikki's neck.

Not me doing the wrong thing. Not me jumping without looking for a safety net.

Or further back.

A parallel universe where we never attended Loch Raven. We never found Nikki's mom in the garage with the engine running. We never braided each other's hair in eighth grade when we should have been listening to the teacher, never got in trouble for passing notes during Spanish class.

We didn't keep driving. We didn't fall apart. When I said it was an accident, she didn't flinch and give herself away.

At home, the blue sedan waited across the street—closer now, just waiting. I rushed ahead of Harrison, eager to nurse Rhiannon before Caroline gave her another bottle. Rhiannon was already asleep in her crib, belly full and lips pursed. Nothing more for me to do.

Formless blue light and the hum of the TV were the only other signs of life. Caroline had fallen asleep with a zombie movie on in the background. *Night of the Living Dead*, the original. The muffled volume sounded like a lullaby. Harrison slumped onto the couch beside his oldest daughter to finish the movie together like the Good Dad that he was.

Besides an empty glass by the sink and fresh garbage in the trash can, Caroline didn't leave a crumb. The attic stairs weren't unfolded, and the hangers in the closet weren't crooked. The office door remained undisturbed, mostly because I had hidden the key in a new place that only I knew. It didn't mean she hadn't been looking around, just that she had covered her tracks.

After the movie ended and Harrison retreated to the bedroom, Caroline and I collided in the hallway. She wore a full face of makeup that I hadn't noticed from before. Nikki's eyeshadow and lipstick. Definitely her perfume. Underneath it all, she still looked like a little girl. She had Nikki's childhood frown. Something about her large eyes, another trait from Nikki, gave her a beautiful bug-like quality, like she could sprout antennae and I wouldn't be surprised.

The duffel bag on her arm was stretched to capacity like before. She wasn't too shy to crack the bag open and let me glimpse inside. More Polaroids. A bag full of them. She had found the mother lode.

I glanced over my shoulder to make sure Harrison wasn't nearby before pulling a photo from the bag, a headless image of a girl wearing a fringed flapper dress and dirty white sneakers. "See that?" I pointed. "That tattoo?"

If she still didn't know that I had been best friends with her mother, it was time she found out. I pulled down the neckline of my shirt to show her the queen bee tattoo on my shoulder. Nikki's bee tattoo had lived on her thigh.

Caroline squinted at the photo, then gasped, eyes instantly welling. Many of the photographs she seemed to love were really pictures of me. Her mother had held the camera, though, and I thought that was just as important. If she had questions, they hadn't traveled down to her mouth yet. Part of me enjoyed watching her revise what she thought she knew about me. Though I knew she'd eventually land on hating me more than she had before.

An oversize turtle pendant gleamed around her neck. It was a cheap piece of costume jewelry I'd worn to almost every formal event throughout high school. It had belonged to my grandmother. One of her Avon purchases.

First time I met Nikki: Third grade, on the playground. We didn't have the same teacher, but she saw me lurking near the dodgeball game, deciding if I wanted to play. "I like your necklace," she said, pointing to the turtle. She made me a threaded green friendship bracelet before the next day's recess. I still had it, still carried it to each new place I moved.

"I think you went through my boxes instead of your mother's," I said. "That necklace used to be my grandmother's."

She covered the pendant with her whole hand and shook her head so hard her dark tendrils threatened to tumble loose from her sloppy bun. "No. The box said 'College.' It had my mom's name on it."

"Because we were best friends."

Because everything she had was mine and the other way around. The inside of my few college boxes must have looked the same as Nikki's, a mix of things we both owned together.

"Look, anything you want to take, I need to see it first. Period. I know you hate me, Caroline, but it's complicated. I loved your mom, too." It hurt to say it out loud. I wouldn't blame her for slapping the words from my lips.

No response for a moment, especially not to deny hating me.

When she didn't respond, but also didn't move to walk away, I thought of what Diana had told me at her party. "Why did you choose Loch Raven, anyway? There's no way your mom wanted you to go there."

The last part was meant to jolt her, jabbing at the tender flesh of the last arguments she may have had with Nikki. It worked. The pink under her skin flashed to red, a wounded sputter where words wouldn't fit. I almost reached out to touch her arm. No way she would let me get that close, especially not now.

I had already learned more about the situation on my own. Her grades, I knew from Harrison, had suffered in her junior year of high school. The absurd donation he and his parents had made to Loch Raven College was meant to safeguard her admission into at least one school. Judging by the way Caroline's face crumpled, there was more to the story. I remembered from Nikki—when eyes that big filled with tears, it looked like a flood was coming.

Instead of telling me to screw myself, she managed to say, "I thought I would feel closer to her by being there."

It was a broken kind of confession that made complete sense. She wanted to understand her mom's life, to stay in the dorms where her mom had slept and dreamed and laughed, her little life before Caroline existed.

She sipped air through her teeth. "Also, I don't hate you."

Then she stomped out of the house. That was it. Not a victory, but a tiny step forward. I'd take it. She texted me before she even left the driveway. **Tell me about the dresses sometime, ok?**

The message included a link to her Instagram account, the Dress Cure. The photos she'd taken of herself in a mirror looked nearly identical to our old Polaroids but with better lighting and more filters. She wore the same dresses in some cases, the same headless pose. #facelessfashion #headlessdresses #afterannieminx

It was the sweetest memorial to Nikki I had ever seen, even if her bag of photos reminded me of everything I hadn't found yet. There were still so many spots in the house for secrets. Maybe, just maybe, Nikki had hiding places somewhere she knew I would look.

I gave myself another hour before bed to search, pausing to listen for Harrison, tiptoeing in my socks to avoid the creakiest floorboards. I searched pockets and dresser drawers, the inside of book jackets and picture frames, before I ran out of steam all over again. Nothing.

The more I looked, the more of Old Nikki I found in the house. Little things. Things no one else ever noticed. A glazed decorative bowl that was really a gas station ashtray she'd painted to look fancy. A pink haircomb shaped like a gun. A cat-head stapler with fangs that bit down hard.

She had drawn eyes at the bottom of her dresser drawers and affixed black heart stickers to the underside of tables and the pipes under the sink. She'd hidden all Caroline's baby teeth in a pill case shaped like a conversation heart.

Sunshine-yellow candy with pink lettering: "Either way we're fucked."

I slouched to the garage fridge, where we kept the Dr Pepper cans Nikki had ordered. A whole case had been delivered before she died that no one ever touched. Harrison and Caroline hated the soda, but it had been at least half of our favorite drink. Coconut rum and Dr Pepper, a concoction we never named, had filled senior year and the summer before college. I didn't think I could smell that brand of rum, let alone drink it, without drowning my senses.

That was it. Places Nikki knew I would look.

I had to stand on a chair to find the rum in the back of the highest cabinet, dusty and ignored. Way to go, Nikki, for keeping a midsize jug of coconut rum. Except it was empty. No sloshing sediment legging down the inside of the bottle. Cleaned and unsticky.

At the bottom of the bottle, a USB drive waited.

CHAPTER 21
THEN

Nikki

Not everyone lit a candle for Professor Weedler's memorial service, but everyone wore black. I took one look at Sadie in her pink pleather pants and made her go back inside to change.

"Match me," I told Sadie, gesturing to my shapeless black dress. All the girls were in mourning now, not just playing at sadness, and we had to look the part.

I didn't know who'd found Weedler, but thanks to the local news, everyone knew the basics: he was hit by a car outside his home, and they didn't bother with the shock-trauma helicopter because he was already dead.

The whole student population emerged from their dark rooms to crowd the fountain, where Eileen led a moment of silence, followed by a poetry reading instead of a prayer.

First, his favorite, "Lady Lazarus," hoarse and fumbling through Eileen's tears.

It was almost the end of the semester, and we had lost "one of our own" after all. We were one candle lighting and moment of silence away from a collective realization of the kind of man Professor Jerome Weedler had been. Or so I hoped.

More rage and less grief would have been easier—for me and Sadie, at least.

Then, as if conjured from my own blur of memories, Eileen recited "Dirge Without Music" by Edna St. Vincent Millay, the poem I'd read at my mother's funeral.

"Into the darkness they go, the wise and lovely. Crowned with lilies and with laurel they go; but I am not resigned."

Open weeping all around me, the girls with their hands locked, their sweaty foreheads pressed together, their pale lips puckered. But I stiffened. I remembered how Sadie had to help me read the poem that day, how my voice had cracked at "wise and lovely."

Sadie reached down to scratch at her fishnets but ripped them instead, a shredded tear identical to my own. Beneath our dresses, our boots were unlaced. Our knees shook and we blamed it on the poetry. We blamed it on the wind.

And. And. And.

A police investigation.

Tension hooked into Loch Raven College like thorns, the questions and rumors whistling through the halls as we watched the police cruise into the "No Parking" spots in front of the administration building.

First, Sadie and I needed to pretend our fears away, to keep acting normal. Normal-ish. Like we were curious because, you know, Professor Weedler was our teacher, too. But not too curious. We waited to speak about it from the safety of her grandmother's minivan, with the windows rolled up and the doors locked, away from anyone's eyes. Sadie left her Tercel in her grandmother's garage. Grandma Ruth never drove.

Thankfully, Sadie had never registered the car with the college because she wasn't allowed a parking permit. We were banking on the car blending in enough that no one remembered it. I stuffed the orange dress in the back of my closet. We would need to get rid of it all.

The presence of the cops gave me the biggest spike of fear. I refused to consider being caught. Nope, not us. Sadie and I hadn't crawled out of the worst night of our lives just to get caught. We had to stick to our story.

Our story, though—we hadn't really sorted out that part, either. I didn't want to use the word *alibi*.

Even the Ouija board spelled out the word *friend* when I asked to speak with one of the girls of the Sylvia Club. Which wasn't helpful, but made me feel like I was doing something important.

I ended up practicing my story with Gallina before I ever talked to the police.

"Nikki, I'm so glad you stopped by. Everyone is so devastated by the news." Her tone bobbed between brittle and sharp. She gestured to the chair where I usually sat, on the other side of her desk. "How are you doing? I mean, really? How it's going?"

But I didn't want to sit. I didn't move from the doorway.

"Abbie Moriano," I blurted out, jamming the meat of my hand into my eye socket. "I'm close to some real evidence here."

She shut the door so fast behind me it brushed my backside.

"Slow down. Take a moment. It's been a tough semester, I know."

No shit. My unwashed, unbrushed hair was matted on one side, electrocuted with static on the other. I glanced down to see I was still wearing my pajamas, a matching set of rainbow polka dots, instead of one of my usual dresses. And I wasn't wearing shoes.

I laughed so I wouldn't cry. Stress could do that to me. Just like not sleeping for forty-eight hours could make me see silhouettes in the stairwells; could make me pace the halls all night, listing the names that I knew, piling facts on top of each other until my tongue dried out.

Grace Ballard, who'd wanted to study education.

Kiki Ward, who had once trained for the Olympics.

Shea Nardman, who had placed second in a Miss Autumn Glory competition.

Q: What girl, who was later made into a bestselling doll, tried to seek out counseling only to find the campus didn't offer it?

A: Raquel Valdez. And me.

My hands shook from nervousness, and my teeth chattered. I didn't mention my theory that Abbie didn't die by suicide, because I couldn't prove it.

"I have to say, I'm worried about you, Nikki," she said.

"I'm fine. Really. My mom died. I mean, before I was accepted to Loch Raven, she died. I'm just adjusting." I didn't look up while I swallowed down a sudden spurt of emotion.

"Oh, Nikki." Gallina shook her head. "I had no idea."

The look of pity and concern quivering in her chin was why I didn't tell people. From her window, one side of Hope Hall was visible. I couldn't see the roof, but I saw Abbie. Each time I looked for her, I found her, dropping again and again.

Thud. Smash.

"Were you his last appointment? I know we talked about getting your financial aid form signed... The police said he had an appointment in his calendar that night."

The line between me and the door: five steps long.

The length of the *ummm* in my pause: thirty seconds too long.

I had forgotten about his calendar. He was one of those adults who kept a datebook.

"I didn't meet with him." It was the only lie I knew how to control.

She frowned like she didn't believe me. Like my face mimicked the sludge filling my brain. I didn't realize the police had already talked to Weedler's colleagues.

"Me and my friend hung out together that night, and I lost track of time. Missed the appointment."

The less I said, the better. I turned for the door, eager to find Sadie and make sure our descriptions of that night matched. If Weedler wrote down my appointment in his calendar, the police would track me down for questions next. All I could do was brace for it.

Gallina didn't say more. Instead, she pulled me in for a bigger hug than even Sadie gave me when we were drunk and sloppy at the end of a long night.

When she tightened the embrace, I let her. Even when she grasped a lock of hair, a gentle tug between two fingers, and said, "You need better shampoo."

My eyes welled. She sounded like my mom, dishing out the kind of hard love that was meant to toughen me up and prepare me for the world.

"You think I'm crazy." I pulled away and wrapped my palm around the base of my neck, surprised at the heat on my skin.

Gallina smiled, a parent placating her over-sugared kid. Which made me feel much, much worse. She pressed her thumb into my bottom lip, like testing the firmness of raw dough, but only for a second.

"I think you're tired," she said.

I found Sadie and Eileen locked in a staring contest in my dorm room.

"She thinks I'm going to steal something," Sadie said without meeting my eye.

Eileen faked a yawn. "I just didn't want her to set our room on fire, too."

On a normal day, we might have fed off this conversation for the rest of the night, replaying, obsessing, complaining until we used up every inch of it. I needed to tell Sadie about the conversation with Gallina, though. The calendar. The police.

But now, on principle, neither of them wanted to leave the room. Stubborn bitches. I couldn't even get mad at Eileen anymore. She was too sad, still talking about the mentorship program that Weedler had apparently accepted her into—the day before he died.

I grabbed our back-and-forth journal and flipped to a new page. "My appointment was in his calendar." My letters were less like cursive and more like broken lattice.

Sadie only read it after I shoved the notebook in front of her face and handed her my pen. I already planned to rip out the page and burn it, shred it, piss all over it, and flush it away.

"You think the police know?" she wrote.

By then, Eileen had grown bored of watching us and flipped on the TV to a rerun of a sitcom I had never liked. She had no plans to leave.

Me: *I think we need to agree on our story.*

Her: *Just say you didn't meet with him. His calendar isn't proof we killed him.*

Me: *We need an alibi. We'll say we were together. But nothing they can prove. At the park?*

Her: *Let's say we just drove around.*

She winced, realized how it sounded, and pulled the notebook back to her lap to scratch it out.

Her: *Let's say we ~~just drove around,~~ had another séance. In the cemetery.*

Me: *In Hope Hall. You and me. It's weird, but we're weird. It fits.*

Her: *What about the guy who picked you up from my g-ma's house?*

Me: *No one knows he exists. He doesn't know we killed our professor.*

Cringing, she added: *You better burn this notebook. And you better sleep with that guy to make sure he remembers you fondly.*

She didn't know that I already had, the night of the party, which felt like years ago. And also the night after he picked me up at her grandmother's house. Me and Harry, it was becoming a thing. He kept calling and I kept answering.

Me: *I pinkie swear.*

After Eileen left for another moment of silence and Sadie slouched down to her dorm to take a nap, I had the room to myself. I squeezed my skull until the light behind my eyelids spiderwebbed into neon beams.

The roaring in my ears needed relief. This was the end. I thought it because it seemed true all at once. The semester wasn't over for everyone else, but maybe I had reached a limit. This was as far as I would ever go.

It took effort to push my heavy window open, the scream trapped inside me expanding, ready to release. I opened my mouth, but nothing squeaked out, not a sound. The afternoon's rain had slowed to a drizzle, and the sun burned through the clouds, the kind of cold autumn sky that couldn't promise much.

What a beautiful bullshit place we lived in.

Looking down and down and down, the stench of dirt and leaf decay almost choked me, but then I leaned out farther to take it in. It wasn't a far drop. Anyone who seriously wanted to die might choose so many other places to jump from.

The photo of me and my mom sitting in a whale's mouth tipped over on my desk with such force I pulled myself back inside. I couldn't remember that day with my mom anymore. Another memory smothered it: Me opening the garage, the car still running. Her blue robe.

The urge hit me so fast, I didn't have time to think. I grabbed my binder and ripped out everything, all my notes from Weedler's class. Jayne Mansfield, Billie Holiday. I tore out my notes from English class next.

See you later, thesis statements. Fuck off, logical fallacies.

My room overlooked girls sitting on the edge of the fountain, planning their future, tolerating the rain. Dreamers and sluts and zombies, every one of them. I didn't know anymore which of them were real and which were ghosts.

When I dropped my papers out the window in long shreds, it didn't exactly look like snow, but the girls stared up at the sky in amazement anyway. I tossed out more sheets from my student handbook next, feeding each page into the air to see where it would land.

The wind picked up, floating a few sheets of paper back into the room. I left the sheets in a pile on the windowsill. Let the wind decide where they'd go.

This was my gift to the girls below, the girls all over campus, even the dead ones. They didn't need to look so bored anymore. Something was finally happening. Words were falling from the sky, and I hoped they remembered it forever.

CHAPTER 22
THEN

The next part—you should have heard it.

Wind whistled through glass; it rustled, then roared. I tried to ignore it, until one night, when I had been awakened again by the sound of a squall, and I padded down to the dorm's foyer to check the windows. The trees outside stood motionless. Not a breeze, only a frosted sky full of stars. A shout broke the silence—more like wolves or cats, or something wild crying.

During daylight, other girls began to notice it, too. "Do you hear it? What is that? It sounds like something dying."

Between study sessions and taco nights, prayer groups and midday naps, the cries became our backdrop.

Meaning, it didn't take long for me to name it. The Sylvia Club. Of course. It was the sound of girls screaming into muffled pillowcases, shrieking on the way down from a high drop, a creeping sorrow that could infect any of us. After Weedler died, the air was ripe with it.

In the costume room, I tried to hide from the sound. The fall show was over, and the next one wouldn't start until the following semester. The girl from the auditorium, the one who ran through walls, found me, though. She sat crisscross beneath the hat rack, wearing an old Loch Raven cheerleader uniform. A megaphone rested at her feet.

Hell, I decided, would be Never-Ending Spirit Week. Eternal Twin Day.

Kill me if I ever use spirit fingers.

The moan that crawled up from the cheerleader's throat locked me in place. Her clothes shifted. A bandage dress, tight and acid yellow, then a bubble-skirted prom puff, tunics, and skirt suits until she finally switched to a satin bridesmaid gown identical to two others that had been donated a decade before.

Icy winter blue, fur-lined cocoon shawl.

She only stopped moaning when I put on the matching version. The fur smelled like gasoline.

The stories started sometime after that. Rumors at first, and then scheduled meetings with the college administration. Students came forward to say Professor Weedler had been "inappropriate" with them. That was the word they used. *Inappropriate.*

Flirting, roaming eyes, sly touches. Stroking hair. He told a dirty joke about Little Red Riding Hood lifting up her dress, one girl said. He gave uncomfortable compliments. Kissing. Fingers up a skirt, reaching, reaching farther.

No one claimed my same experience, an invitation to his house or special meetings to discuss their writing, and I didn't plan on adding my story to the mix.

Sadie and I said nothing. I knew she said nothing, because I knew her. We minded our business at the Meatless Monday buffet in the cafeteria, our trays heavy with falafel, and we went to class. The world felt too tame and too restless. It wouldn't last long.

Then the messages showed up. All over campus, pieces of plain, white paper cut into sloppy snowflakes, asymmetrical and jagged, edges ripped as if someone had used their teeth instead of scissors.

They were the same kind of snowflakes we had all made during Orientation Week, a craft project to hang on the bulletin board in the dorm's foyer, a way to demonstrate how we were all so different. Each time I left the building, I avoided looking at the one with Eliza Jackson's name. It hung right in the center. Except now it was gone. The pretty delicate ones we'd all made started to disappear just as the new, haphazard ones made an appearance.

Snowflakes appeared on the sink ledge in the bathroom, tucked under desks in our favorite classrooms, even peeking out of library books and hidden beneath stacks of lukewarm plates in the dining hall. Instead of our names, there were penciled messages written so softly on the white paper that you had to squint to decipher the letters.

"I need help," one snowflake said.

Another: "Is anyone listening?"

The worst ones said nothing at all.

The police, it turned out, were really two detectives with bellies that flopped over their belts and a whole shaker of salt sprinkled throughout their hair.

Thankfully, I already knew what they were going to ask. They asked me outside the dorms, not loud enough for anyone to hear but their presence obvious enough for girls walking by to wonder. Sadie had gone in to take a shower, but if I delivered the story right, they would find her later to verify. That was how it worked in the movies, at least. Give an alibi and the cops would have to confirm.

"Which night? No, I lost track of time and totally forgot that appointment. Me and my friend Sadie were here. On campus."

The taller cop took notes, and the one with the bigger flop-belly squinted as I told them about me and Sadie attempting a séance on the first floor of Hope Hall on the night in question. Then I added the kind of detail Sadie could repeat to give our story texture. "No, we didn't see any ghosts, but this one creepy thing happened. A bird flew inside and tried to escape out a sealed window. It died hitting the glass too hard."

Sadie and I had snuck in to visualize the place together, to make the story real. We'd left our shoe prints on purpose, and I etched my name in dirt on one of the old desks. When we went in to scope out the supposed séance area, we found the bird among the broken shards of glass and the fallen wooden beams.

"Do either of you girls have a car?" Tall Cop asked.

I hadn't planned on that question, but I told the truth. Freshmen weren't allowed cars on campus, but sometimes Sadie borrowed her grandmother's barely used minivan. As far as the state of Maryland was concerned, Sadie didn't own a car.

She claimed that the Tercel was taken care of. It was a car one of her uncles had found and fixed, never registered in anyone's name. We'd never have to see it again. It had never existed.

What I knew deep down: Sadie and I were not okay. We'd never be in our current situation if it weren't for me. I'd dragged us to Loch Raven College, and I'd made us go to Weedler's house that night. It was me who'd hit the gas instead of swerving.

We needed a place of our own, a place with inflatable furniture and beaded curtains, poetry taped inside the cabinets. A place without the voices of girls infecting every corner.

It felt dangerous not to look forward. If we slowed down for even a moment, if we let ourselves think about everything that had happened, I was sure we'd fall apart completely, one piece at a time.

Insert my new plan. A surprise solution to the growing gap between us.

Instead of pinching myself awake through my afternoon history class, I begged Sadie to drive us off campus. I didn't have to beg hard.

We drove the long way, past the Brew Station, past the famous cemetery where Edgar Allan Poe was buried, deeper into a part of the city where we never usually went. She didn't mind driving as long as I told her where to turn.

The summer before college started, I had planned surprise trips to tattoo parlors and graffiti murals, anything to distract me from the empty house without my mom. Sadie had always acted amazed at my ability to organize and make plans. Like it was so hard. I only had to know her and what she craved to surprise her completely.

I directed her to stop on a street with faded shop awnings and parking meters. The only people outside waited at a bus stop. They hunched and smoked and avoided eye contact with each other. Before then, I would have said no one else in the world looked more tired than me, but I was wrong. It was a neighborhood some people might have called "rough," people like Harry and Eileen, who had property to safeguard. Harry would lock his car doors and move his wallet to a different pocket to feel safer.

"Where are we going this time, Stage Manager?"

"You'll see."

We parked and paid the meter, then walked a block in the

cold to a corner bar that hadn't opened yet. The faded sign read "Charmer's."

Sadie snorted. "A bar? I mean, okay, but I thought you were taking me to a sex dungeon or at least to get my nose pierced."

I knocked three times and winked, cheesy-like. Like, *wait until you see what's next.* But I liked it there. Or I told myself I liked it. The ad in the paper hadn't given me many details.

A wall of smoke blasted my face from the open door. The woman on the other side addressed Sadie with narrow eyes. "I didn't think you were going to come."

Her dark roots bled into the bottom blond half, fluffy and feathered, the way my mom used to style her hair in old high school photos.

"Marge." Sweat puddled beneath my sweater. "We spoke on the phone."

She wheezed. I didn't know what she'd expected, but it wasn't us, with our dark eyeliner and clunky boots.

"You okay? You're breathing kind of fast." Sadie gripped my elbow to steady me.

"Just excited." The chirp in my voice was new, too. Good thing she couldn't feel my pulse. It raced without warning lately, in the middle of the night, in the middle of everything.

We followed Marge past a claw machine filled with cheap stuffed monkeys. Our boots stuck to the floor, but the lighting was too dull to see what we were stepping in. It wasn't as narrow as most row houses. More like someone had stretched the bowling alley width into a double-wide. My eyes couldn't take it all in fast enough.

"Go on. Take the tour." Marge let us pass with a wave of her cigarette.

In the back of the bar, Charmer's opened up: a tiny unisex bathroom, a pool table, a back door leading into the alley. And a wood-paneled pocket door I had almost missed.

"Come on up," I called to Sadie. She was already popping quarters into a jukebox older than us.

The dark, narrow staircase led up to an apartment with a living room, a bathroom, one bedroom, and a kitchen overlooking a tar-papered roof. The whole apartment was cold and empty, but Sadie looked ready to burst with excitement.

I peered into the bare cabinets and tried not to touch the surfaces tacky with years of cooking grease. If I had been by myself, I would have turned to leave. With Sadie, though, I kept my face steady, even as she stood in a square of sunlight and spun, both her arms stretched as far as she could reach.

"This is the surprise, right? An apartment. Above a bar!"

It was a long shot, but I had already talked to Marge about the rent, and for a minute there, I thought we could swing it. After seeing it in person, I wasn't convinced.

Thud. Smash.

I flinched each time I closed my eyes. That sound on the windshield. It rocked through me, eclipsing my mood. Clouds covering the sun. My enthusiasm emptied out completely.

"I don't know if it's actually feasible; I mean, it only has one bedroom. I was just dreaming."

She didn't care about the logistics.

"We spend so much of our financial aid money on room and board. You did the math, remember?" Sadie reminded. "We could use our student loan money to pay rent and still have money left over."

She spun her own web, how our life could look next semester

with us living off campus and commuting each day for class or play rehearsal. We could get jobs at night. We could live on our own and throw parties every weekend. We'd become regulars in the bar and make this shitty apartment shine.

The violent flapping of pigeon wings near the window broke the fantasy, and it was impossible not to see all the flaws and potholes in our plan, the hundreds of ways it could go wrong.

Like how she never followed through with anything. Like how she wouldn't pay rent, or we'd fail all our classes.

Yeah, it had been my idea to go there, but I could see in person what I didn't want to admit before. We weren't ready. I had to figure out what I was going to do now, and then later, and later after that. Every time I shook my Magic 8 Ball, it said, "Reply Hazy, Try Again."

"Let's get lunch and keep talking about it," I told her to get us out of there faster.

Her face fell before perking back up. I knew what she was thinking—how easy it would be to convince me. "I'll follow you anywhere," we made our shadows say to each other in sixth grade. "I'll find you in the afterlife." Our pinkies linked in promise before we even knew what we were promising.

An apartment was the last thing we needed. I hated to say it after all my scheming. I didn't know if what we needed even existed.

Marge stared up at the TV mounted in the corner, a weather report dotted with clouds. Sadie spun one of the barstools like she had been waiting to send it whirling since we walked in.

"When do you need an answer?"

The TV noise almost covered Marge's husky voice. "Tomorrow. After that, I put out an ad in the city paper."

She searched for an ashtray but ended up ashing on the bar top anyway. Her red press-on nails looked unstable. She had already lost two.

My interest flew to the off-color paint on the wall near the claw machine, a spot most likely punched in by a drunk dude and covered with spackle.

"Why are we rubbing the wall?" Sadie joined me, palming the dirty wall beside me, mimicking my motions.

"I could punch this in. It's soft."

Not that I would ever really do it. But I had been at Sadie's house years ago when her uncles got into a fight and punched through the drywall. They covered it up with spackle only to push someone's shoulder through the same weakened spot a month later.

"If walls could talk, or some shit," she said.

Marge eyed our wall touching, and in case she could hear us, I whispered, "If we lived here, this is where I'd hide our precious jewels."

Sadie's eyes glinted. "Yeah, I could punch the hole and you could cover it up."

She saw it perfectly, our whole life full of heists and secrets and hidden passages.

See, this place has character, she'd tell me later when I needed more convincing. *I'm sure it's not that loud at night,* she might say if I wondered about drunk laughter floating up through the floorboards while we tried to study.

In Sadie's head, we were already there.

"What song did you play just now? On the jukebox?"

She had forgotten already. "Three B. Whatever that was."

We didn't stick around long enough to hear it.

On the way home, with my eyes clamped shut, I tried to forget, to erase my mind, to start over, fresh and blank and empty. No handsy professors, no dead girls following me, no dead moms, no confusion over what to do next.

But I had my classes to think about. The teacher who took over Weedler's classes said that Weedler had already entered a "zero" for my essay in his grade book. I could still pass the class if I got a perfect score on the final. Which was mostly impossible. Anything less wasn't enough to keep my scholarship. But at least the new guy signed my form. It was late, but given the circumstances, no one in the main office said anything about it for now.

"Next time just be born into a rich family," Sadie tried to joke. When I didn't respond, she added, "Come on, at least I didn't suggest marrying a rich guy."

I was quiet for a while after that. We weren't angry at each other, but for the first time in our lives, I didn't know how to talk to her. I was afraid to say anything.

At least we had each other, though. In our beautiful, chaotic, messy lives, we were as safe as we could ever be. Even if it was only an illusion of safety.

Subject: Don't Forget Where You Came From

Hey, Beauty Queen! It's been a while, but I promised I wouldn't send you on this journey alone.

By now you've hopefully read my new book, *The Self-Care Cure*, all about healing from your haunted past. As I've said before, we're all haunted by something. One part of the Cure that I didn't include in that book involves revisiting our old crash sites.

Where are the places you once fell apart? What campuses and neighborhoods and stretches of highway helped you become the person you are today? Imagine setting up a cross and little plastic flowers to create a memorial in that exact place where you once stood.

Let's revisit that place if you can. Not just metaphorically, but literally. Don't get all resistant on me now, bitch. This is where some of the most powerful healing happens.

If there's a map of your life, it's full of crash sites and landing zones, especially the places where you almost landed, almost crashed.

For me, one almost-crash site was a bar. A true dive bar with yellowed walls from years of smoke and sticky floors. I can still hear the jukebox spinning Billy Joel (don't laugh, I know it's old-school). It's a place that could have had so much greater significance. My life could have gone so many other ways.

If you're ever in Baltimore, check out my favorite dive: 307 Fort St. The old name was Charmer's, but whatever it is called now, it's still got that old neighborhood feel. It still feels like a place to hide all your secrets.

It's time, girl. Play song 3b on that old jukebox and pour one out just for me.

Weekly newsletter, c/o Annie Minx, Inc. Click here to unsubscribe.

CHAPTER 23
NOW

Sadie

Almost morning, the still-dark sky consumed everything in its path, and I reached for Harrison only to find his side of the bed empty. I worried for a moment that I'd left the office open, and I pictured him inside, sitting in a circle of Nikki's papers, setting them all on fire just to spite me. But no. That wasn't it. I never left the office open. He must have left for work, but how had I slept through it?

With a sudden jolt of fear, I jumped. The silence had woken me, not Rhiannon. Something was wrong. Too many hours had passed without her waking or crying or eating.

SIDS. Spontaneous Combustion. Kidnapping by Serial Offenders.

In her crib, she gazed at me with soft eyes. The rise and fall of her chest, a marvel. My breasts ached for a release, but that wasn't why I cried. For the first time since she was born, I had slept at least seven hours, and she had slept through the night, too.

Fully rested, we smiled at each other through her diaper change. We couldn't stop smiling. Focus and self-care and intention all seemed possible. One coffee might suffice.

I might even be able to concentrate on the USB drive. It contained Nikki's last manuscript, a rough and unfinished draft of her research on the Sylvia Club. The pages were full of partial notes and half-coherent paragraphs, with a dash of her poetic style mixed in. Over three hundred pages, all written under her real name. And it would never be published.

It wasn't the kind of thing you could sit down and read front to back, but I skimmed enough to know it was exactly what I'd suspected. Before she died, she'd started writing a book about the Sylvia Club, the true story of suicide clusters that were mishandled at Loch Raven College.

"How to write about a dead woman," she'd written on the first page.

"First, confirm she is dead. Dead enough not to mind. Hold a mirror to her cracked lips and watch for fog. Brave her wrist for a pulse. Let your fingertips linger. She'll have that bright smile, you know the one, instead of the perpetual grimace she developed at the end. You will hug her, oblivious to everything that once flared up between you, and for a moment it will feel like the world is a time machine.

"She is dead now. There is only so much you can do, only so much you can know. Some stories will never be told. It is sad, yes, but here you are. Someone has to tell her story."

Why she went to such lengths to hide the document was beyond me. Her notes were scathing in some sections, especially when it came to Loch Raven, but she didn't point fingers at anyone in particular. She hadn't gotten that far. The messy state of the manuscript was another piece of proof that Nikki hadn't planned to die when she did. She would have never left an unfinished piece of work behind like that. She'd hidden it, though, and left it for me to find. I just had to figure out why.

A quick search of the document didn't find a single instance of Professor Weedler's name, which didn't surprise me. He had never been part of her research, as far as I knew, though his involvement sure felt linked to my memories of that time. There was no central thesis, not one that I could see. Nikki's conclusions about the Sylvia Club and the college were either unresolved or buried between the lines.

I spent weekdays in the office now, moving from the typed document to her handwritten notes, always searching for the wordless messages in the edges of her sentences. I tried to only touch what I needed. Bursts of delayed grief made me want to preserve her fingerprints since they would never exist again.

There were so many things she had missed. Elections. Celebrity deaths. Wildfires and tsunamis. Her daughter going to college. When I thought of it that way, with Nikki's ghost shuffling through the house all night full of longing, I felt both better and worse.

I would never leave without you.

What she'd meant was that she'd never be a part of the Sylvia Club, and even if everyone else in the world believed she had been depressed or that her marriage was falling apart badly enough to end her life, she knew I would never believe it. She wanted to make it clear that if something happened to her, I should be suspicious.

So I kept looking.

It turned out that one night of good sleep wasn't enough to trick my brain into forming complete thoughts. I skimmed through the manuscript until my eyes burned, until I found a footnote toward the end of the document that referenced a podcast Annie Minx had been interviewed on. Just as I picked up my phone to search for the episode, it buzzed in my hands with a text from Diana.

Want to go for a run?

Run? No. I'd never keep up. But I wanted to talk, and she had declined all my invitations to come over again. I needed to find out more about Nikki's last months. I wanted to know all of it.

When she arrived, I left Rhi with Bernie and told Diana to get in the car. She arched an eyebrow but didn't argue. Now, at least, she couldn't run away before we were done.

I didn't have anywhere to go, so I lingered at stop signs and yellow lights to give us more time. Her hair fell into soft blond waves, never not looking like someone's favorite Barbie.

"Is this a kidnapping?" she asked, amused at my second spin around Hidden Harbor.

"Tell me about Nikki."

Her pause was so painfully long I didn't know if she'd ever speak again. But then she was ready.

When she'd found Nikki, the scene looked staged, she said. An empty pill bottle on its side, which rested on top of a letter that just said "Dear Caroline" in shaky handwriting, very un-Nikki-like. An empty champagne glass sticky with pulp sat close by. Nikki was in the bathtub, but there wasn't any water.

"She wasn't even supposed to soak her foot for another week after the surgery," Diana mentioned. The memory made her remove her sunglasses and rub at her eyes.

"Bunions," I said.

She didn't correct me. "Harrison's idea because her feet always hurt."

He had gotten weird when I mentioned surgery, like he couldn't stomach the idea, but he had also bought me a box full of bunion paraphernalia. Unless he hadn't bought the toe spacers for me at all. My tongue went thick with the realization that it could have all belonged to Nikki.

"A classic overdose, they said." Diana snorted. She used dramatic air quotes to emphasize *they*. "They said she had been unhappy in her marriage, depressed about her career, which wasn't true. Not all the way true, at least. And you know how I feel about that fire and gas leak. Harrison clung to those weird accidents like they were proof of everything."

Weird accidents, she called them. She didn't say what I was thinking, that more than one thing could be true. What if it wasn't intentional but also not an accident?

We didn't speak for a few moments; then she added, "There was no other explanation for the cause of death, I guess. No one asked me what I thought."

"What if someone spiked her drink?" I finally said. Many strong pills mixed with alcohol would do it. I wasn't sure if you could taste narcotics mixed into a mimosa, but I figured one glass might make her senses fuzzy enough not to taste all the drinks after.

The real question was why. Why would someone want her dead? Why would she hide her USB drive or leave notes and clues for me? It had something to do with Lucille and something to do with Weedler, but I couldn't puzzle it together. That part wasn't anything I could talk to Diana about. The why was for me to figure out on my own.

I had already forced myself to consider Harrison's harshest angles. With his hands around Nikki's neck or standing over her with a bottle of pills, ready to shove them down her throat. I tried again, but none of the images fit.

For a moment, I tried to imagine Diana mixing drinks in the kitchen, too. All it did was make me want a drink of my own.

She reached over and plucked the fallen strands of my unwashed hair. "Nikki always said Harrison had a thing for redheads."

Nikki and that goddamn red wig. In her author photos.

Diana laughed when I pulled into the drugstore half a mile from the neighborhood, even as I rang up the cheap box of Blond-a-Thon with Harrison's credit card.

"I'm dying," Nikki deadpanned.

Dying of laugher. Caroline would have inserted a skull emoji. Dying. Already dead.

I hadn't read the directions on the hair dye, hadn't considered that bleach might be better for the job. The end result was more like faded pink, half-orange at the bottom where the dye ran out. Deranged clown.

"Slutty clown," Nikki corrected.

Nikki's spangled wrap dress almost resembled a hairdresser's smock. When a chunk of her scalp fell, she covered her head with the curly red wig like a crown.

A new Annie Minx newsletter dinged in my inbox. After the last newsletter, I had signed up for Minx emails, just in case there would be more. This one, like the first, was sent to her whole mailing list but clearly meant for me.

"Hey, Beauty Queen," it started.

Mannis and Brill had invited me to several happy hours since the last one, but I'd declined each time. This time, I chose the location.

Bernie agreed to continue watching Rhi until Harrison came home from work, even though Diana offered, too. Friends. I almost sorta kinda had friends. I wanted to run into the street and scream it for the whole suburbs to hear.

Harrison would've preferred I build a stronger friendship with Diana or the other moms in Hidden Harbor, but he accepted that, in Bernie, at least I had someone to talk to. She had been a good neighbor to Nikki, too, he'd said. She kept her personal life to herself, which I appreciated because it meant she didn't pry into my business, too. *My daughter and I are very close*, she'd told me once, but I didn't believe it. No one ever came to visit her.

The address of the bar I texted Mannis and Brill wasn't anywhere near our usual drinking spots, but it was the exact address mentioned in Nikki's newsletter. "If you're ever in Baltimore, check out my favorite dive: 307 Fort St.," she had written. I didn't make the connection until I pulled open the front door of the bar. I'd been there before. With Nikki. We had almost moved into the apartment above the bar.

It smelled exactly the same, like old beer and leftover smoke, even though smoking hadn't been allowed inside for years. It smelled like a back alley or like a long night I wanted to forget.

Mannis sat alone at one of the high round tables up front, close enough to feel crisp blasts of wind with every swing of the door. "What happened to your hair, Stone?" he yelled.

Slutty, deranged clown. So be it.

He had shaved his beard since I last saw him, and gray hairs sprouted into his patchy stubble. It didn't look bad on him, but I'd never admit it out loud.

"Where's your sidekick?"

He peeled the soggy label off his beer bottle. "Brill sends his regards. He's got diarrhea real bad."

All around us, bottles clinked and music hummed. Phil Collins crooned through the staticky speakers. Before that, Guns N' Roses. The music was as outdated as ever, but outdated in a good way. The old relic of a jukebox that I remembered from before had been replaced with some sleek updated machine that probably relied on an app instead of quarters.

"Why did you choose this place?" Mannis asked before belching and ordering two more beers. The slap of balls on the pool table sounded like thunder. I could pretend we had entered through a portal if I wanted to, a time machine to a world without cell phones or Google. A world where if I wanted to confirm the lyrics to "Sweet Child O'Mine," I didn't have the internet to consult. I just had to listen really hard.

My phone screen lit up with a message from Harrison. **Working late, Caroline will get Rhi.**

I texted Bernie to let her know.

We drank in silence for a few minutes until I had enough booze in me to willingly talk about what was really going on at home. The short, vague version—my dead best friend and her unfinished research about a campus legend. He nodded, seemed to swallow it all down. I left out the parts about Lucille. I left out a lot.

Even if I didn't say anything remotely close to secretive, it felt good to talk it out. On instinct, I looked over my shoulder more than once, sure I'd find Nikki, or maybe Lucille, hanging out by the door, watching and waiting.

If there's a map of your life, it's full of crash sites and landing zones, especially the places where you almost landed, almost crashed, Annie Minx had written in her newsletter. Yeah, that sounded right. Jukebox, beer, stale memories. We had almost crashed there.

"Sounds like you're haunted," Mannis said, raising his voice to talk over a loud conversation at the table behind him.

I wheezed, my tongue foamy with beer. "Excuse me?"

"You know, burnout and fatigue. It's haunting, am I right?"

Neither of us knew what to say after that. I almost asked him if he was on drugs until he laughed and covered his eyes with his hand.

"I just heard how that sounded coming from my mouth. It's this damn e-newsletter thing my girlfriend reads. She prints them out and hangs them on the fridge. I can't avoid them."

I laughed, too, but my insides had gone cold, a chill spreading inside me. "What the hell, man?"

"You heard of that author Annie Minx? The one whose book we bought you? Lena's a superfan. Cult level. She's obsessed with her newsletters, the ones that keep coming out even though the writer is dead. I must be absorbing them without realizing it."

I chugged my beer and let myself sit and process what he'd just said. The sensation that I was missing something filled me, some detail just out of reach, and if I sat long enough, it might reveal itself. I let him order another round while I unlocked my phone and read the newsletter again.

The old name was Charmer's, but whatever it is called now, it's still got that old neighborhood feel. It still feels like a place to hide all your secrets.

It's time, girl. Play song 3b on that old jukebox and pour one out for me.

"Fuck."

I reached up, leaned across the table, and smoothed my hand against the wall, overwhelmed by the memory of me and Nikki standing in that exact spot. We were supposed to live there like characters in a lighthearted comedy, one ridiculous adventure after the other. Even as I remembered it, I knew it was wrong. We were never lighthearted enough to forget the horrible things that had happened. But we did have a whole life to look forward to, a path we were supposed to stumble down together.

This is where I'd keep my hidden treasure, she had said about this wall. Something like that. I didn't remember everything, but I remembered that part. The soft drywall underneath would break easily. The paint colors were still mismatched, the spackle still rough under my fingers.

dry wall, spackle, hidden jewels, dive bar, newsletter, jukebox

Nikki had thought of everything. It was stunning to realize how much trust she'd had that I would ever see the newsletter or find a USB drive somewhere in her house. What a gamble. Just in case she died. It was one hell of an insurance plan.

"Move," I instructed Mannis, pushing him out of the way before I punched the wall. Once, twice, three times before it cracked.

"Stone!" he yelled, no longer amused. A few of the drinkers at the bar turned to watch, but most people didn't care. It was the exact kind of bar for not caring.

"Play song Three B, Mannis. Now." He knew better than to ignore me, and he had an app on his phone to make the jukebox sing.

I didn't really think there was anything inside the wall, but I pounded and pounded until Prince's "Darling Nikki" boomed from speakers I couldn't see.

I wanted my hand to ache and my knuckles to bleed. In the end, the wall was so soft it didn't hurt at all.

There wasn't anything in the wall in the bar, but I rushed into the house, barely remembering to turn off the alarm code before I made it to the living room.

Us and that song: outside, coming from somewhere cold, "Darling

Nikki" blared from a car window and we both died a little inside. Weedler had called her Darling Nikki, ruining the song for us forever.

"Kill me if I ever play this song on purpose," one of us said.

The implied response: *If you play this song on purpose, I'll know you're up to your usual bullshit.*

I ripped the curtains off the rod and found the exact spot I needed by the time Caroline ran in. The paint-color difference, White and Other White. Nikki had been pointing me to it all along. I punched the wall a half dozen times before Caroline grabbed my shoulders and forced me onto the couch. She smelled the way she always smelled, like she'd doused herself with Nikki's honeyed perfume and rose-petal lotion.

"Are you drunk? What the fuck, Sadie!" she panted, the struggle between us over but still shocking.

Instead of trying to explain my reasons to Caroline, I sniffed the air. Wherever Nikki was, she wasn't there. The glitter and mud matted into the carpet meant she'd be back soon enough.

"It feels good to hit something. You should try it."

When Caroline side-eyed the suggestion, I added, "I'll take the blame. You can be the one to tell your dad I did it."

Her cheeks flushed only for a moment before she joined in, punching the same spot in the wall until a hole appeared. I wanted to pretend she was Nikki, just taller. Sweat on her forehead, crooked smile. She didn't need to tell me I was right, that sometimes the best feeling in the world was hitting something that could break.

I reached my hand inside the hole, down into the wall.

"What are you looking for?"

I ignored her, reaching around more, clawing, dirt caking beneath my nails. After a few minutes, I pulled out my empty hand. Nothing. A lot of effort for nothing more than a hole in the wall and a torn set of curtains. I peered out into the dark street and found myself wondering if Lucille could see me, if she was watching.

The thought of Harrison's face when he saw what I'd done to the wall would have terrorized me before. Now it lit up in my stomach like a tiny firefly. He needed to get used to me at my worst, which was arguably also my best.

Caroline eyed my head. "He's going to lose it when he sees your hair."

Hours later, Harrison pulled at his necktie and asked if I was crazy.

"Do I even know you anymore?" he asked, as if I had changed the shape of my face or revealed a secret identity instead of dyeing my hair.

It was a good question. And the answer was no. He really didn't know me.

After Caroline left, after Harrison wore himself out from talking about my hair, after Diana texted me a link to an article called "Faceless Fashion, the Newest Insta Trend, Inspired by Late Author's Photo," I returned to the hole. I had felt it before, of course, the edge of a plastic bag. If it was the back-and-forth journal, I couldn't let anyone else see it, especially Caroline. I'd burn it like Nikki should have done years ago.

The gallon-size plastic Ziploc contained another bag and then another. Bags within bags like misshapen little nesting dolls. Inside, a thick wad of cash curled in on itself, bound with a rubber band. The note tucked between the bills read "To get you started when it's time to leave."

CHAPTER 24
THEN

Nikki

"Counseling services," I said at the next newspaper meeting, our last meeting of the semester. No one had suggested an article about Professor Weedler yet, but I knew it was coming. "Dr. Gallina, didn't you say you were working on an event with the counseling office?"

A couple of the other girls nodded. This seemed like a good time to revisit the conversation of mental health and suicide awareness, we all agreed without agreeing. The upcoming holidays might be hard for a lot of girls.

I didn't hear students wondering anymore about "who was next," but the question had bled into our walls, still lingering, even as Weedler's death took center stage.

Gallina stared expressionless out the window like she hadn't heard any of us. I missed her old rants about how important it was for us to be strong women. The way society wanted us to be small, helpless victims was a variation on a theme that she often repeated.

Rumor had it that she'd once told Polly she shouldn't date anyone in college because our reliance on men made us weak.

"Should I coordinate with the counselors directly?" I asked, this time turning my whole body to face her. It helped to have something to focus on. It helped to not think about my first Christmas without my mother, or where I would go during the semester break. Sadie had already volunteered her grandmother's house, and I didn't have a better option.

"Yes, call them. That's a good idea." Her shoulders shook in a way that wasn't related to the draft creeping through the windows, then stood up. "Finish the meeting without me. I have to step out."

Aisha continued her columns and rows on the board while I slid closer to the window to see out, then down. The same two detectives climbed out of their car. Their presence had become a daily occurrence, an unfortunate fact of our semester.

Gallina must have had something to say to them, the way she rushed out of the room when they drove up the hill onto campus. My constant worry was that she would tell the police about my issues with Weedler, that she'd give me away without realizing it.

But it wasn't Gallina who stepped out of the building to talk to the police. Sadie was the one they stopped. A mass of red hair fountained on top her head, and despite the cold, she wore a thin black leotard and gauzy pink skirt with her sneakers, like she was channeling *Flashdance*. All she needed was leg warmers.

Every other girl who walked out of the building hunched forward into the wind or stared down at their shoes. The ones with better posture glared at the hazy brightness and rushed off to wherever they were headed next, careful not to brush the detective's shoulder. Not Sadie. From above, I watched her cock her hip and smile at the detectives like she was happy to see them, like she had been waiting for them to give her the time of day.

It was time for her to tell her story, the one that matched mine.

Two girls stopped chatting to kiss their crosses in front of Hope Hall—*For Abbie, for Abbie*—and this time, I lingered by the wooden front doors to wait for her, to see what my mind would conjure this time.

When she emerged from the side of the building, her head still wrapped, I had nothing to offer. No books or nests of hair. No crucifix or black dress.

She took one look at my long dirty-hemmed skirt, the puffy cloud sticker on my hand, and fluttered her eyelids like she couldn't be bothered with a full eye roll.

"You look awful," she growled before lowering her mouth to a handful of melting chocolate soft serve. It dripped through her fingers, onto her shoes. Someone must have fixed the ice-cream machine in the dining hall.

Maybe I thought she'd look different after Weedler died. Fixed, somehow. And thankful. She looked more pissed than ever. Constantly grabbing at her head with her ice-cream hands like she didn't know it was still bleeding. Always teetering, close to an edge I couldn't see. I'd seen her that night, an apparition in the fog. Before the thud.

"Are you coming or not?" she asked. She reached toward me as if to give me a gift, and I pretended like she didn't hand me anything at all.

While Sadie was busy, I used that time to visit the counseling center, a tiny office that smelled like stale coffee. The door was actually open for once, and the only man working there hadn't heard from Dr. Gallina since Orientation Week, but he got excited about distributing flyers next month to the dining hall if he could get it approved.

Whatever, dude.

"We were thinking of some kind of event for suicide awareness. And encouraging students to seek out your office's services if they need help," I told him.

I had gotten better at pretending I knew what I was talking about. And as I said the words out loud, I believed them. This mattered. More than Weedler's memorial service and the police investigation, the college had an obligation to its students. If another student was out there considering self-harm, maybe we could help her before it was too late.

The counselor grimaced. "It's only me here. Don't send me a bunch of students all at once. But flyers. I've got some good flyers."

Unimpressed and half-deflated, I told him I wanted to write positive messages and his office's number in sidewalk chalk. He puffed his cheeks. "Not sure that Student Activities will approve it, but go ahead and give it a try if the spirit moves you."

All I heard was "go for it."

On the way out, he shouted, "Tell Dr. Gallina she can come back any time she's ready to help again. The students really connected with her."

Sadie and I had just finished writing giant numbers to advertise the counseling office's location in sidewalk chalk when Aisha trotted down from the dorm steps.

"You guys better get out of the way. Someone is coming around with a hose to spray all this off."

I stood up and wiped my blue hands on my skirt.

"You didn't get approval. You can't even hang a poster on the bulletin boards without approval."

Aisha lingered there with us while Sadie and I waited for the groundskeeper to wash it all away in colorful swirls. "You heard what was going on, right?"

Probably something else about Weedler. The latest rumors ranged from analyzing his death (*maybe he intentionally jumped in front of a speeding car*) to gossiping about his sordid life *(did you hear the one where he had sex with a freshman in the bathroom?)*.

Aisha's face was hard to read. "Polly is gone. Missing. Didn't you see the police?"

The wind gusted so fiercely it punctured something in my skull. But the sound was only us. We were the ones with our mouths to the sky, letting it all out.

Q: Where did Polly write her goodbye note?
A: On the edges of a paper snowflake.

Everyone was sure they wouldn't find Polly alive, but I refused to add her to the Sylvia Club list. Not until the police finished searching the grounds and the wooded area, not until we knew for sure. I cringed at the thought of flashlights aiming their beams in the dark and dogs searching for a scent. I didn't want to hear anyone calling her name, waiting for an answer. And after all the speculation about who would be next, I wanted to blame them all.

There was no way to concentrate after that. Not in the library or the cafeteria. Not even in my own room, where someone had rifled through my clothes and taken my black funeral dress.

My skin crawled with invisible bugs each time the dead girls gathered outside the dorm. Huddled together in the cold, dancing to their own songs, lighting candles and dripping the wax across each other's palms.

Join us, they called.

Help me with my zipper.

I heard bells that no one else could hear, and when I asked Eileen if she heard it, too, she said, "Sounds like you need to get your sorry self to church."

Her bitten-down nails and wastebasket full of crumpled tissues told me I wasn't the only one struggling.

"You're really taking this hard," Sadie told her when she burst into my room and saw Eileen's swollen eyes from crying all night.

In a voice thicker than usual, she huffed, "I wouldn't expect you to understand."

She seemed to have moved on from poetry. She was always in the hallway talking about the world ending on New Year's Eve. Sometimes she moved from the hall to her AOL messenger account (name: HolySpice99) to post Bible quotes. A WWJD bracelet replaced the smudged Plath stanzas from weeks before.

After Sadie left, she locked the door.

"Nikki, I like you. So let me give you some advice." She wiped her eyes. "Your friend Sadie is a troublemaker. A bad egg. You know it, I know it. Everyone knows it. And I've seen that new boyfriend of yours. With the nice car?"

I didn't confirm or deny Harry's existence.

"If you invite Sadie to an event with his family, they'll know you're…"

Trash. I waited for her to say it.

"They won't let their son marry you. And that's the plan, right? If you plan on leveling up, it's time to lose the deadweight. You can thank me later."

I didn't have a plan to get married or go to Harry's family events. It had become increasingly difficult to plan anything at all. Each time I thought about the future, it went from hazy to blank.

When our phone rang, we both jumped. It never rang.

Eileen listened to the person on the other end and smirked, finally passing the receiver to me.

"It's the dean's office," she said. "What did you do this time?"

CHAPTER 25

THEN

Dean Blankenship had a thing for clocks. Old-timey, ancient-looking clocks ticked on every wall, dozens of them.

"Ms. Vale, you have read the Code of Conduct, is that right?"

Séance, missing curfew, failing more than one class. That was how he started the meeting, with my crimes. If he only knew.

I shouldn't have been there. This wasn't how my first semester of college was supposed to unfold.

"Yes, sir. I have read the Code of Conduct."

I hadn't, but I could remember enough from my meeting with Polly.

The gist of it, if I had to paraphrase, was that students were not permitted to conjure spirits on campus. If students were caught lighting candles for any reason besides church, they must confess their sins. All students were expected to treat their body like a temple. Students should not burn that temple to the ground.

"You have missed several classes, and your grades are slipping." A clock on the wall tolled with a gong, and he paused until it finished.

At least I wasn't dead, I wanted to say. Death seemed like a thing that could have happened to me already. Laura Palmer, all frigid and violated. The Black Dahlia, bisected on the grass.

The clocks did nothing for my nerves. Someone should have told him that it sounded like a ticking bomb inside his office.

My restless knees jumped, which he thankfully couldn't see beneath the large desk. He couldn't see my chewed-up cuticles if I tucked them under my seat.

"I understand that you have been asking about an unfortunate part of Loch Raven College history. More than one faculty member has mentioned it to me."

Professor Weedler must have said something before he died. Dr. Gallina was the only other professor who knew.

"I called you in today because it seems that your, um, let's call it a fixation, on this story has now become potentially dangerous. Do you know what I'm referring to?"

He was referring to the Sylvia Club, of course, but also the séance and the fire, I guessed. That was the line I had crossed. I knew Eileen would tell her family about it. Her father was one of the college's big donors. Even if Dr. Blankenship could ignore the teachers' complaints, he couldn't ignore big-ass donor money. Maybe Eileen had tried to warn me in her obtuse way. If I wanted to stay in this vine-smothered, wrought-iron world, I had to think and act like one of them.

For a moment, his professional, strict demeanor fell away, and he looked almost sad. The effect aged him at least ten years.

"College suicide is unfortunately not uncommon. Statistics show it is on the rise across the country. Loch Raven College cares about its students. This semester has been especially difficult, but fixating on tragedy does not help the situation." He paused for emphasis. If he was referring to Polly, I wished he would just say her name. "I'm sure you know where this is going, Ms. Vale. We cannot let this disturbing preoccupation continue, not without disciplinary action."

Meaning: I needed to stop digging.

His message was clear. I straightened my spine and turned into a mannequin, my arms stiff and my legs locked. I'd been practicing this face in the mirror—the blank stare, that refusal to give away any emotions.

"Dr. Blankenship, my concern is that out of the nine students who died by suicide on campus, several of them were on the same financial aid scholarship as me."

He knew which scholarship I meant, the one with the nearly-impossible-to-maintain standards.

Q: Name the ways a student could lose her full-ride financial aid scholarship.
A: Not completing her community service hours, not meeting the GPA requirement, not taking enough credit hours both semesters, not falling in line.

I waited until he nodded. "The pressure from that academic scholarship may have been the catalyst for the girls who died. Is this something the college has considered? I think larger news outlets would be interested in this kind of story, as well as the *Raven Outlook*."

He stammered, pushing papers around on his desk as if looking for something. He hadn't expected me to do anything but apologize in our meeting. Because that's what Scholarship Girls did. He didn't need to know I was bluffing, that my research was incomplete and I had nothing concrete.

Since I was on a roll, I just kept going. "Some might say it's irresponsible for a college to let a professor teach a class about dead women when so many women have died on campus. It romanticizes suicide. Especially when there aren't strong counseling services in place. Some might say."

There was nothing more to discuss as far as I was concerned. My stomach churned, a wave of nausea that promised to linger.

"I will only say this one more time, Ms. Vale. To be clear, whether it's part of a research paper or an article for the school newspaper, you are not permitted to write this story. It would be disrespectful to the eight families involved. Frankly, we have enough to deal with this semester already."

Another clock chimed. A translucent hand pressed against the outside of his office window. Written on the palm in black marker: "Look alive." The hand twisted to flip me off.

"Nine," I corrected him, realizing what he'd said. "Nine families are involved." But suddenly I wanted to redo my math.

Ten, if you counted Polly. I didn't count her, though. I didn't want to.

His face pinched into pain and disgust. No one wanted to have this conversation, especially him. "One of those deaths was inconclusive. The figure is technically eight."

Confirmation, finally, of what I already suspected. Abbie Moriano. Her family had hired a lawyer because they didn't believe she jumped. It was possible, of course, but something else was possible, too. *Inconclusive* could mean so many things.

A police investigation would uncover a professor's inappropriate relationship, for one. It was also the kind of thing a family might sue over. The kind of thing a college would cover up.

Detectives would have to consider the other option. If she didn't fall and she didn't jump, someone must have pushed her.

I ran straight to my room afterward, ignoring the cold rain that soaked through my jacket. Their chants followed me the whole way.

Poor Jessie.
Break a leg, Mary.
Me, me, me. You, you, you.

The unreturned yearbooks were right where I'd left them under my bed. No matter how many times I read her obituary or stared at Abbie's smiling yearbook photo, the information didn't change. The truth of what had happened was still out of reach.

Survived by a sister. It had been her sister's writing online that made Abbie more than a name on a list. Jasmine's grief oozed like an infection. Like a living thing. It made Abbie knowable, it kept her alive in whatever parallel realm the dead sat waiting for us.

I didn't have an autopsy or a family statement to prove how Abbie really died. All I had was her sister to ask.

Jasmine's updates on LiveJournal had been sparse in recent weeks, and I hoped it wasn't because of our encounter. I hoped she wasn't writing because her life was rich and filled with flings and wild nights. A little orange dot next to her name indicated her online status.

This is the last time, I told myself. I didn't mean to upset the Moriano family, but the need to know clouded over me and refused to let me move on. If I wanted to finish the semester, I needed to study and pass my classes, not chase down stories about dead girls forever.

The college says your sister's death was inconclusive, I typed in the message box. I had to use Eileen's desk computer and hope she wouldn't return to see me.

Jasmine messaged back within seconds. **There were other injuries. I can't talk details. My family is suing the school. We think she was pushed.**

My pulse quickened. There it was. Had I known all along? Had Abbie tried to tell me? **By another student? By Professor Weedler? The dead guy? That's one theory. You should watch who you trust.**

Then she signed off and the orange dot turned white.

I shivered inside my wet coat. It sure seemed like Jasmine had someone specific in mind, and I doubted the family would sue the college if they blamed a student.

Murder and lawsuits—no wonder the college had closed Hope Hall for "renovations." By establishing strict rules for freshmen and hiring exactly one counselor, the college meant to show they had taken action. They could claim they didn't sit back with their thumbs up their ass.

Abbie's yearbook photo took on a different sheen then, her smile more genuine instead of pained. Like a girl enjoying her freshman year of college. Like a girl with friends or a girl in love. I couldn't unsee this new life for her, or this new death.

The other photo of Abbie that I'd missed the first time: her seated in front of the fountain with a group of girls, posed with the choir, and then, beneath that, another group photo of her with the Journalism Club.

The faculty adviser with a hand on her shoulder was Dr. Gallina.

I didn't know we'd ever had a Journalism Club. Abbie had majored in economics, I thought.

Another idea struck me, and I opened up a faculty directory from two years before, one of the many outdated documents I'd nabbed from the Admissions office. Next to Professor Weedler's name, his contact information was listed, but there were no clubs or activities assigned to him. Next to Dr. Gallina's name, there was more.

Dr. Isabel Gallina: Journalism Club Adviser, Loch Raven Mentorship Program Director.

When Sadie burst into my dorm room, the open yearbook rested in my lap like a stone. I ripped out the page and shoved it into my desk drawer with my lip gloss and a Polaroid of me and Sadie in matching drama club T-shirts for a car wash in the tenth grade. Not headless, just happy.

"They found something in the woods," she gulped, short-winded from running.

"Damnit, Sadie. I'm trying to think here."

A spindly thought rolled away, and I didn't reach out in time to catch it. She never let me just sit there and think.

The Cranberries played from my CD player: "Zombie."

Girls in the hallway yelled and joked about their dinner plans. It was Lasagna Night.

I used the pen stuck in my ponytail to write on the last lined page of our back-and-forth journal, though there were so many empty pages in the middle. One word, one reminder of the thing I didn't want to forget, the bothersome little splinter under my nail. Then I tucked the notebook away somewhere safe until trash day.

"Did you hear me, Nik? Cadaver dogs. They found Polly's gloves."

When I met with Harry that night at a twenty-four-hour diner, it was scarily easy to pretend that everything was okay. He didn't ask many questions, and when he did, he accepted my vague answers.

Mostly, I let him talk. He told me about his interest in cardiology and that even though he was so tall, no one else in his family was especially gigantic. He told me how his mom was stubborn and a little snobby, only wearing particular designers and eating food made by particular chefs. He laughed when he said it, a forkful of his diner eggs hanging over his plate.

"I'd like to bring her here just to see her reaction," he joked, though he was the only one of us laughing.

"What would she think of me?" I was convinced she would never actually meet me.

Harry chewed, considering the question. "If I love you, she will grow to love you, too."

If only it was that simple.

He didn't know about the dead girls or that I was always one meal away from running out of funds on my meal card, or that my dad called my dorm-room answering machine last week and left a message saying, "Sorry I missed you. I will call again on Christmas." Like the dorms weren't kicking us out after finals, leaving me with nowhere else to go but the basement of Grandma Ruth's house for two and a half weeks.

Together we drew our future, though neither of us called it that, on the back of my paper place mat. He made the house—a chimney billowing smoke, a tree with a tire swing—and I added the stick people. Me grinning, him tall, and a third, curly-haired figure that I meant to be Sadie visiting for cocktails. He assumed she was our future child. A daughter.

"You would be such a good mom," he said, taking my hand. He

meant it. I could tell by the way he smiled at me, the way he saw past me to someone he thought I could be.

"I almost forgot." He jumped up and ran out to his car to retrieve a bag. Inside the bag was a leather journal that he said made him think of me. The cover was yellow, a lattice of honeycomb etched into the fabric.

"What's this for?" It was beautiful, the kind of journal I never bothered to covet because I knew it was too pretty to be cheap.

He dabbed a piece of toast into the leftover yolks on his plate. "For your writing. You've got stories to tell, I just know it."

That wasn't all it took for me to love him the way he already loved me, but it certainly helped.

CHAPTER 26

NOW

Sadie

Not all the time, but sometimes it felt like I knew what I was doing. We fell into a routine—sleeping better, eating our veggies. I could wake with Harrison, help make his coffee, and pack his lunch while he showered and shaved.

I had been right that he hated my hair more than he hated the hole in the wall. He hadn't touched me in days.

"Too much change," he said, then went gray-faced as if suddenly hearing his disembodied grief taking over. He hadn't commented on the mud crusting every room, though. He didn't seem bothered by the smell she left in her wake.

Rhi and I stared up at the "I Am I Am I Am" triptych, identical to Diana's, that I'd hung in the living room. He didn't say anything about the new artwork, and there was no way not to notice it. Either Harrison knew that Nikki would have approved—though I doubted that he understood the reference—or he was finally starting to relinquish control.

A new dish towel in the kitchen. A new candle to replace the old one, burned down to the wick months before. I even toyed with the idea of starting to buy a new wardrobe and slowly replace the items in the bedroom closet. Except for Nikki's old dresses. Of course we'd keep those. We'd keep anything that had been important to her, anything with clear sentimental value.

There were so many ways to memorialize her.

As one of the passages on the USB said, "How to Keep a Dead Woman Alive: Frame her portrait and hang it high. Wear her gemstone around your neck and tattoo her zodiac sign into your softest flesh. Lace a lock of her hair into your braid. Talk to her. Let her whisper her secrets into your mouth. Say her name. Say it daily."

But I wasn't trying to memorialize her daily. I needed to plan my next move.

I still didn't understand the purpose of the money. I hid it in one of my boots for safekeeping because I had to do something. Nikki had left me so many messages that the least I could do was try to unravel her meaning. Most women, including Diana, wouldn't have punched through a wall to find a dead woman's hidden clues. It had to be me.

My thoughts were so tangled I almost didn't flinch at the sight of Lucille's car again. I had lost count of how many times she sat out there. Surprising that a neighbor hadn't called the cops yet. That's what they usually did when a strange vehicle showed up. If I gave Bernie the suggestion, she would have the vehicle towed without hesitation.

Are you just going to keep stalking me? I texted Lucille just to see what she would say.

She didn't respond right away, though I could see she had

read the message. When enough time went by that I figured she wouldn't respond at all, she asked, **Want to meet for breakfast?**

Bernie wasn't home and Diana had a "thing," but I doubted Lucille would mind if I brought Rhi with me. I had the perfect place in mind.

Annabel Lee's was one of several Edgar Allan Poe–themed establishments in the city. It met all expectations: servers with fake Poe mustaches, punny Poe menu items, and tables polyurethaned with his writing. It was the kind of kitschy place Nikki would have loved. Full of poetry.

The walls were designed to look like a cheap diner / ancient castle. Gothic gray-and-purple wallpaper, fake tapestries, and what I thought was deliberately spilled ink but was really a syrup puddle. Ravens everywhere, though that wasn't unusual for Baltimore. I waited at the front podium under one of the giant taxidermy birds, his mouth open mid-caw.

Lucille sat alone in a booth wearing a corduroy blazer with elbow patches. Before she noticed me, she gloomed into her coffee, both hands circling the mug as if seeking warmth. *Damn girl*, I wanted to say. *You look as corpsey as I feel.*

She greeted Rhi with a halfhearted wave, the way people do when they don't know how to talk to babies, then shook her phone awake to check the time. "I can't stay long." Tiny shrug. Casual. "Are we going to have an actual conversation this time?"

In response, I eyed the menu. The daily list of specials included Waffle House of Usher and something called the Tell-Tale Chicken Biscuit. I used to order Fortunato's Western Omelet, but I didn't see it listed anymore.

When I finally spoke, I kept my voice level. "Look, I'm not

really eager to revisit something that happened almost twenty years ago. I have a lot of bad memories from college. Things that have nothing to do with your story. I can't help you in this case."

Rhiannon fussed and I picked her up, bouncing her on my lap until Lucille said more. Listening was hard enough with a crying baby, but responding was even harder. The only surefire way to stop the tears meant feeding her. I had forgotten my nursing cover, but no longer cared. When I pulled down the top of my shirt and lowered Rhi to my chest, at least three people, including Lucille, wide-eyed my boob before looking away.

At least she isn't crying anymore and interrupting your coffee! I wanted to yell. *If you want a quiet baby-free café, don't be surprised when I whip out my tit.*

"Remember how I said there was a witness statement from back then? Don't you want to know what it said? Your friend certainly wanted to know." She watched my face as if just noticing how different I looked. "What happened to your hair?"

"Just spit it out already, Lucille."

She nodded down at my chest where Rhiannon had fallen asleep, milk drunk, leaving my boob completely exposed. Just hanging out. I waited a beat before covering.

"The tip reported seeing a young woman with big red hair and an orange dress standing on the side of the road where the victim was found."

All heat dropped from my skin. I waited for her to mention the car, but she didn't. Someone had seen a woman with red hair. Nothing else. Which meant they didn't know who the woman was.

All at once, it made sense. I understood why Nikki had made such intentional funeral arrangements. Her written instructions told Harrison to cremate her in the orange dress, but not before everyone saw her wearing it. Even her old author photos showed a faceless woman wearing a curly, red wig that was now gone from the house, too. She had thought of almost everything.

nik nik nik nik nik nik nik nik nik nikki

"I'll take the blame," I had tried to tell her that night. Because she was my friend. Because that's what friends did. It wasn't like either of us had sisters to practice pointing fingers at.

"No," she had said. "Neither of us is going to take the blame, but if it comes down to it, it's going to be me."

It explained why the cops had questioned me more than Nikki back then, why they went to my grandmother's house. I had never even considered the possibility of a witness. Lucille's brain must have lit up when she read that report. With Nikki dead, there was no one else left to ask or blame but me.

The day Lucille showed up outside the house, hadn't she also said that she'd recently spoken to people in the know, people who'd pointed a finger at Nikki?

"Who did you track down from Loch Raven?"

I couldn't remember anyone's name except Eileen. There were a few teachers I could picture, maybe a few other girls from the drama department. Even my own roommate was a blank spot in my memory, some girl who participated in every themed Spirit Day like her life depended on it.

"You'd be better off asking why *they* tracked *me* down." Lucille scratched at her arm. "This story, Sadie. It's taking over my life. Feels like I'm living inside its house but none of the light switches work."

She pushed up her sleeve to show off her newest tattoo, fresh and red around the edges. A black scorpion. She watched as I made the connection. It wasn't a perfect match to Weedler's, but close enough.

Weedler's death wasn't famous enough to inspire obsessive admirers, and he hadn't lived long enough to go to jail and acquire fangirls. No, Lucille's connection ran deeper. I could see it now, complete with the professor blazer.

Our shared connection, our bare family trees. Me without a mother and her with a dead father. He would have died when she was just a girl.

Which meant she had a good reason to not give up on finding out the truth.

"Ask if she has a boner for Sylvia Plath like her daddy?" Nikki's voice rang out in my head.

I covered my mouth, afraid of what I might say next. Or what I might have already said before. Maybe she had always chosen to hang out together in dark bars because she didn't want me to notice the way she played with her hair like him or how she also cocked her head sideways when she was curious the way he used to do. I noticed it, of course. I just hadn't known what I was noticing.

When Nikki had gone frantic about Lucille showing up, it wasn't just about the notebook. There was no way she wouldn't have noticed the resemblance.

Caroline texted me on the way home. **So, I have been pleading with the college to add my mom to the Hall of Success, and they're finally doing it. Sending you a link.**

Her email included a link to RSVP for a belated memorial service for Nikki Walsh, a.k.a. Annie Minx. Beloved writer and Loch Raven alum.

The invitation included a short schedule of events. The introduction to the memorial would be given by Dr. Isabel Gallina, esteemed professor of journalism, returning to Loch Raven after more than a decade as the new head of the communications department. Very fitting. Nikki had adored Dr. Gallina.

I waited until I got home to press my face into the couch cushions. It was all too much. Lucille and Weedler. The witness statement, but also the memory of that moment, how I must have looked on the side of the road. Light rain, patchy fog. A dress that could be seen from space.

But the good news, too, Nikki's Hall of Success induction, piled on top of everything else like the heaviest weight. Funny, as in not funny at all, that Nikki had to be dead and famous for the college to claim her as alum.

All I texted back to Caroline, though, was **You did good. Your mom would be so proud.**

She responded with a link to her latest headless-fashion post. Moody poetry and headless dresses were all she posted lately. The aesthetic was both comforting and disturbing. Her most recent post featured a green velvet slip dress with her head Photoshopped out. When Nikki wore the same dress, she'd added a baby doll T-shirt underneath and—always, always—her black boots.

The caption: **"A dress so powerful you could chop your head off and the dress would wear you." #thedresscure #facelessfashion**

In the photo, Caroline wore my gold-plated turtle pendant on a new gold chain. It blended with the green fabric, the turtle's shell rounded with fake jade. Who knew why she liked that cheap necklace so much, but I had loved it without reason, too. It had been one of my grandmother's favorite Avon treasures. She gave it to me before college, along with a roll of quarters to help me do my laundry.

I had accused Caroline of sorting through the wrong box, but maybe she hadn't. It wasn't like I had seen that necklace since college. Nikki could have been hanging on to the fake-jade turtle simply because all our things got shuffled at the end, the same way she took the orange dress.

It didn't matter back then, and it wouldn't matter ever again. She had carried my things around for years, the same way I carried hers.

I opened my mouth to utter the words as they congealed in my head, but my feet were faster. I raced up to the attic with more purpose than ever before. Yes, I had searched Nikki's things, but how had I not thought to look through my own boxes? What if the reason Nikki couldn't find the back-and-forth journal was because I'd had it the whole time?

There weren't many containers filled with my things, but they were where Harrison had left them, never touched by Caroline or anyone else. I had been lugging the old containers around for years. Some of the boxes hadn't been unpacked since high school. Programs from my first shows, ticket stubs, notes Nikki had passed to me in school.

Focus focus focus

It didn't take long to find the tub from college, mixed in with a collection of old coffee mugs, half of them chipped from not wrapping them in tissue paper like a more prepared woman would do.

Compared to the things Nikki had saved from Loch Raven, my collection was small. The programs from *Night of the Living Dead: Miss World Edition* were wrinkled and torn, but I was glad I had thought to save them.

Then I found it: the edge of a canvas tote bag peeked out from underneath a swath of gauzy ivory-colored fabric—a costume-room veil we had both once loved. Inside the tote bag was a spiral notebook that I recognized right away. Thinner than I remembered, its edges worn and the spiral about to unfurl from age. But it was ours.

Erratic noises from downstairs rose up through the insulation. A bottle popping—no, a bottle breaking. Celebration and destruction.

Whatever she was going through, I felt every bit of it.

Instead of turning to the confession, which I couldn't bring myself to read quite yet, I flipped through other pages of our old notes, our doodles and jokes, how casual and how easy it had been for us to be friends, until I got to the last page. Nikki had written one word. No date, no context or detail. Just one word to end on before she'd closed that book forever.

Gallina.

I couldn't tell anymore which details were merely coincidence and what was part of Nikki's long game, but Nikki had written that name almost twenty years before. This wasn't a new clue she'd meant for me to find. And yet. All of it seemed to hold the same prickly, unbalanced weight.

The first time Nikki ever told me about Dr. Gallina: In the dining hall after our first day of classes. Her, English; me, Acting Arts 101. We hadn't heard good things about Dr. Gallina as a teacher, but Nikki had been impressed.

"I think it's going to be a good semester," she said, the first hopeful words I'd heard from her in months.

I agreed. We were going to have the time of our lives.

I texted Caroline, hoping the goodwill from our earlier conversation hadn't already faded. "That writing class you applied for, is Dr. Gallina the teacher?"

"Yes!" she confirmed. "But I didn't apply. I was invited. Just me. Isn't that cool?"

CHAPTER 27
NOW

I had been foolish to think my daughter was now a "good sleeper." She slept through three nights. And then she didn't.

Harry canceled all his appointments one day, claiming he was concerned about me. My blank stare in the middle of conversations, my struggle to focus on the smallest tasks like pouring a cup of coffee or starting a load of laundry. That was the morning he found me sitting on the floor outside the closed office in tears, slapping my face to wake up. To get it together.

"Take a nap when Rhi naps," he suggested. The usual advice.

As if she ever napped for long. Or I could afford using my time alone to sleep.

I needed my time to myself, but by staying home, he kept me in his sights. Like a babysitter.

The worry lines on his forehead brought me the tiniest bit of joy, at least. He deserved to worry.

Despite my exhaustion, I knew what I had to do next. I had to find Dr. Gallina. She wasn't on social media for me to message, but I planned to show up to the address listed online as her home. She wouldn't be able to tell me why Nikki had written her name in the back of a book or what Nikki had been thinking before she died. But maybe. Nikki could have reached out to her and prepped her for my visit like she did with Diana.

The address listed online was only a trip around the beltway with my eyes trained for the right exit. "The longest of shots," I said to Rhi, who had fallen asleep in the back seat. I knew I should have been grateful because she needed the rest, but if she slept in the car, she'd wake up as soon as we parked.

In the passenger seat, Nikki wore a strapless bridal gown and popped a wad of cinnamon gum.

"You weren't invited, by the way," I told her. We sat outside Gallina's house with the engine running. Rhi hadn't awoken, and I wasn't ready to rile her up.

"Neither were you."

A seeping band of moss spread across her chest. Just like at the end of the play when instead of another undead pageant queen, a zombie bride emerged on the steps of the farmhouse. She wasn't the grand finale, but she was close. Nikki had helped cover the actress in green stage makeup that was supposed to resemble moss, even if the audience couldn't see that close to appreciate it.

I needed quiet to think, and, besides snapping her gum, she obliged me by not talking while I ate a drive-through cheeseburger, my first since moving in with Harrison. It tasted as good as I remembered. No gourmet burger with a brioche bun and arugula could compare.

Nikki watched the house from her window. "Looks like a rental. I bet the window gaps are drafty."

"You think it's a rental?"

"I said it looks like a temple." A slurry of dirt and clay caked her lips, her voice broken-sounding. She drenched the seat with her mud. Always the mud.

An old Tori Amos song hummed through the speakers, and I thought even Nikki, eyeless as she was, might cry. It was the kind of music we used to memorize. We played it so often that it seemed to belong to us. That was the way it was with music anymore. The saddest songs were now the ones she had loved.

I waited until Rhi stirred, then lifted her car seat and headed up to the front porch. Dr. Gallina opened the door like she had been waiting for my arrival. She must have been watching me from the windows while I ate my cheap cheeseburger and talked to myself.

The recognition on her face almost concealed the real emotion hiding there. Disappointment. I wasn't the person she wanted to see. She let me in anyway.

"Welcome," she sang, heading deeper into the house in a way that invited me to follow. She sat down at a desk and gestured to the chair across from it as if it were a student conference. Once a teacher, always a teacher.

I probably wouldn't have recognized her out in public. Not because she looked different, but because she hadn't been my teacher. My vague memories of her involved Nikki beaming at her from afar. Gallina had always worn dark trousers and blazers, T-shirts and Chucks. The cool professor. She had aged well. Gray streaks threaded through her short hair, and the skin around her eyes and mouth had softened.

Only as we sat across from each other, with my baby cooing herself awake in the car seat, did I realize I hadn't introduced myself.

I hadn't said anything at all since she opened the door. That was the mesmerizing quality Gallina had, or so Nikki had led me to believe. Her presence made it hard to speak.

"You won't remember me, but I was a student at Loch Raven College over eighteen years ago. I was best friends with one of your students, Nikki Walsh. You knew her as Nikki Vale."

She stiffened, her sharp inhale like scissors snipping. She remembered Nikki. The way her eyes looked past me, clotted up in some old memory, I guessed the news was still fresh for her. She hadn't had enough time to process, to grieve.

"I remember Nikki. She was one of my favorite student writers. And you look familiar, too. Drama club, maybe?"

"You have a good memory." I sank back in my chair, heavy with relief to talk to someone who remembered Nikki the way I did, who could picture her in all her creative, smart, weird glory. Rhi softened back into sleep, lulled by the scent of sandalwood from a burning candle on the desk. Whatever tension I held in my stomach started to unknot itself.

"I know this is random, but when was the last time you talked to Nikki? Before she died, I mean?"

Gallina frowned and her hands flew to her mouth before traveling back down to her neck, then the desk, then her lap. "No, I didn't speak to her after she left campus."

"I'm guessing you know of her daughter, Caroline Walsh, who also attends Loch Raven. You invited her to some independent-study class thing."

I collected my voice into a facsimile of composure. Gallina didn't react to Caroline's name. She wasn't ready to move on from talking about Nikki.

"Nikki was a sad young woman. She was in mourning. The sad

girls always found me. That was my gift and my curse as a mentor, I suppose."

In mourning. An interesting way to describe Nikki. Sometimes I forgot how sad Nikki had been about her mom that year, all while I acted like we were indestructible. I had let her research dead women when she was mourning her dead mother. I made her come to séances and tramp around the campus cemetery. What kind of friend did that make me?

"I was also hoping you could help me remember these old campus stories people used to tell about girls who had died there. The Sylvia Club. Nikki had been weirdly obsessed with it back then and..." I debated telling her that Nikki had never let go of that obsession, that she kept researching it, kept writing about it up until her death. "I mean, it wasn't just a story, right? It's part of Loch Raven's history."

Gallina nodded, an agreement on all counts. The Sylvia Club wasn't the kind of thing you could forget, especially since she had been there as a teacher for at least a few of those deaths.

"I told Nikki to stop working on it. Especially after Jerome Weedler died. Her interest didn't seem healthy."

Flames shot through my middle at the mention of Weedler's name. Even Lucille had danced around his name without saying it directly. Him. The victim.

Gallina caught the change in my demeanor, the gag I worked to suppress.

"When did you transfer out of Loch Raven again?" she asked. "I'm trying to remember where else I recognize your name from. Not just from the theater production."

Something had shifted. A tonal slit in our conversation, an inflection in her voice I recognized as pandering. She didn't try to disguise it or hide that she was lying. After all, she couldn't recognize my name because I hadn't given it to her.

"Nikki and I were there for a year." Vague on purpose. I couldn't decide where to steer the conversation next. It hadn't been a full year, we left partway through the spring semester, but I didn't mention that, either. The smell of soil snared inside my nostrils. The candle couldn't mask the scent. Nikki's mossy ghost sat in my car, but maybe I wasn't the only person she had decided to haunt.

"Nikki was pregnant. That's why she left, right?" When I didn't respond, she nodded like my silence told her everything she needed to know. "It all makes sense now."

"What makes sense?"

"I thought she had left after Jerome's accident. I used to think Nikki was disturbed by that accident and that was why she left school. But I suppose she had other reasons to leave."

I held up my empty hands, palms toward the ceiling. "The pregnancy. Our friendship. It's a long story."

"Oh? I assumed she got worried about being caught."

My chest constricted, the panic propelling me into the kind of haze I couldn't see through.

The gargoyles on the top of Hope Hall. The cathedral, the tower, the cemetery, the fountain. A beautiful, haunted place. The place where I'd made some of my hardest decisions. Some part of me hoped all my secrets were buried with Nikki, that they would vanish with time. A naive thought. Secrets never stayed buried.

She didn't smile, but she wanted to. "I told that reporter what I knew. About both of you. She tracked me down about a witness statement I gave back then. The detectives never figured it out, but I did."

What she knew.

weedler sandwich orange dress dark road scorpion semester smash thud

Had I reached the part where even Nikki hadn't put the pieces together? Had Nikki known that Gallina was the witness and the one who had spoken to Lucille? And if Gallina really knew what had happened, why wouldn't she give the police more than a vague witness statement?

I wouldn't have been able to respond if I tried, my mouth sealed shut. Acid rising. It was time to go. Somehow, I didn't collapse as I jostled the car seat out the front door. Gallina didn't follow, or if she did, I didn't turn around to see her.

Bitch, Old Sadie would have yelled back at her to get the last word. But I didn't have the energy to speak.

Whatever she knew about that night, Lucille knew it, too. The question was if Lucille believed her. She was smart enough to realize there was more to the story, but that didn't mean she would wait to tell it.

Nikki wasn't waiting in the car when I returned. I turned the key in the ignition and half expected the engine to burble and bubble, underwater, the way I felt. Gallina wasn't watching from her window when I pulled away. She didn't need to see how fast I fell apart.

Sad girls, Gallina had said, always flocked to her. Did she mean girls like Nikki or girls like the ones in Nikki's folders?

Raquel, Betsy, Kiki, Abbie.

Not to be confused with the women we'd learned about in Professor Weedler's class.

Actresses, poets, mothers.

In my head, I had separated That Night from the Sylvia Club.

Two very different and unrelated puzzles. What if they were part of the same puzzle? What if Gallina had talked to a reporter about Weedler's death because it was the only card she had to play?

My guess, knowing Nikki, was that she had an even bigger card.

Diana texted me an old picture of her and Nikki from a cookout in someone's backyard. In coordinating denim shorts and jewel-toned silk camisoles, they looked like sisters.

Any updates? Di asked.

I zoomed in on the photo, but the smiles were tight. Forced. I'd wait to write back. Maybe even respond with a better picture than hers. Instead of fake smiles, I'd find one where Nikki and I looked feral.

There had been a podcast interview with Annie Minx that I meant to look up, mentioned as one of the footnotes in her big Sylvia Club document. *The Boss Bitch Retreat*, the podcast was called. Cute. Very Annie Minx and very un-Nikki. I searched for the episode on Nikki's old laptop, guessing correctly that she already had it bookmarked.

I knew I didn't have time to listen to the whole interview, so I found the transcripts instead. The episode had been recorded six months before she died. Most of it was pretty typical: questions about Annie Minx's books and her writing process, advice for working moms.

About halfway through the episode, a weird exchange:

Host: Can I ask what you're working on next? How long do we have to wait for the next book?

Annie Minx: Well, my next book is called The Self-Care Cure. *We're probably looking at another year before publication.*

Host: How exciting! Any other fun projects in the meantime?

Minx: (pauses) I'm also working on a book about a series of deaths at an all-women's college. I'm pretty deep into the research, so I don't want to say much about it yet, but it is very different from my other work.

Host: It sounds like true crime? Is it? Because I know our listeners love true crime.

Minx: Yeah, I guess you could call it that. It's really looking at a couple big topics. Like the culture's fascination with dead women and also the way death, especially suicide, can be romanticized. And then there's this college story, a cluster of suicides with a possible murder mixed in. There was a professor who pretended to be a mentor and advocate but really should have never been a teacher at all.

Host: Oh, wow. That sounds juicy. I'm guessing there are some people at that college who really wouldn't want you to publish a book like that.

Minx: Yeah. I know what you mean.

I let the words sink in. Two days before, I would have sworn the teacher she was talking about was Weedler, but buried beneath the episode's comments, Anonymous389 had written, **Liar. You just want to ruin someone's career. You'll pay, bitch.**

A clear threat. Weedler wasn't who came to mind. Gallina was the one who was still alive with a career to lose. It certainly wouldn't have taken much for Nikki to make the kind of insinuations about Gallina that would get her fired. Not that I thought Gallina had the time to write anonymous comments on a podcast with hardly any downloads.

"What now?" I asked on a fresh page in the old back-and-forth journal. I didn't expect Nikki to chime in.

The garage door buzzed to life. Caroline had texted to say she was on her way over. I closed Nikki's laptop, but not before I glimpsed the virtual folder on Nikki's desktop called "Threats." I paused, and at the last moment tucked the laptop under my arm, then rushed to get out of the room before Caroline found me.

But it wasn't Caroline's footsteps in the hall. Just as I turned to leave, Harrison lurched in, his body the biggest thing in the room. I'd left the door open to listen for Rhi.

His face turned swollen and purple with an expression I'd never seen before. Anger—true, undeniable anger that he usually tried to hide. I stepped back until I ran into the chair, and I thought again of Nikki in her empty claw-foot bathtub. Harrison looming above her, huge as ever, his hands ready to cover her nose and mouth, to let her die.

I wondered if she felt him above her like a dark cloud, if she ever saw it coming.

Then he fell to his knees, his whole face wet with tears. "Nikki," he choked between violent sobs. His shoulders hunched in a way that looked painful, like something inside him had finally caved in.

I stood too far away to touch him. I wasn't going to move closer, though, in case he was playing me. If I reached down to console him like he expected, he could rear back and attack.

Except he only sobbed harder, flattening himself into the dirty carpet. Fragments of her glitter stuck to his pants like cat hair. "Oh God, I miss you," was all I could make out.

Not anger, only grief. The office locked to preserve her last wishes and the house he refused to redecorate. All along, he'd been a grieving husband. Nothing more. There was no way he would ever hurt her. She would never have brought me there if she had worried he could hurt either of us.

And she had definitely been worried about someone hurting her.

Harrison wasn't the one.

CHAPTER 28
THEN

Nikki

ust a studio apartment, Harry said. Just a "little shack" to live in while he finished school.
And he actually believed that it wasn't anything special.

"You have a doorman," I said. "And a dishwasher and your own laundry machine. This isn't just a 'little shack.'"

The holidays had passed in a blur of fake Christmas trees, too-sweet cookies, and the musty basement space at Grandma Ruth's house. At night, the only way Sadie and I could fall asleep was with zombie movies playing in the background.

Harry picked me up each day and dropped me off each night. Sadie and I never talked about where I went. We never talked about anything. Without saying it, she had made it clear that she wasn't interested in hearing about the Sylvia Club anymore. Which meant there wasn't much left to say. Even after my suspicions about Abbie's death had been confirmed, it didn't matter. No one would ever be able to prove what really happened on the roof of Hope Hall.

"You're so cute." His dimples deepened, quarter-size craters. "Marry me now."

Whether it was a joke or not, I laughed every time he said it. As if the me who had zero experience with fork etiquette and country clubs wasn't too young, too weird, too poor for his world. Me in my thrift-store dresses, without a passport, showing up to brunch with his mother.

But I only said, "Let me finish school first."

I didn't say no because I didn't know if I'd one day need to hold on to every offer that came my way. The police had stopped questioning me, but that didn't make me feel any safer. Besides, I loved Harry. Even if it wasn't passionate, obsessive love, I felt it all the same.

By then, I knew something had started to grow inside me. It was the size of a blueberry, I had read, or a quickly sprouting lentil. I wasn't sure when to tell Harry, but it wasn't time yet.

He overexaggerated a groan and fell back in his leather sofa. "Guess that trust fund will have to wait."

Even when he joked about his family money, it had a ragged edge. He wasn't quiet about his anger at his grandparents for setting up a trust fund that he couldn't access until he got married, and then by only half. The other half of the money would be available after his first child's birth. It didn't sound bad to me, but after he mentioned it, I had to ask Eileen to explain trust funds.

So we talked about marriage even though he didn't know my best friend and he definitely didn't know about my mom. Part of me thought it was inevitable that he'd get to know Sadie, eventually, but it seemed too risky. She devoured men when she wanted to. And I didn't want Harry to be her prey. Didn't most men want a certain kind of good girl to marry while secretly lusting after something spicier? So, without even realizing it at first, I kept them apart.

With Harry, it felt like starting over sometimes, the way he didn't know me at all. In a good way. I wasn't Studious Nikki or Misfit Nikki. I was just his.

He did this sweet thing where he set up candlelight takeout dinners that we ate naked on his floor while listening to whatever music I wanted.

My music selection: Mazzy Star, "Fade Into You."

"You're a dream," he said.

No one had ever loved me so simply.

More than anything, I loved sleeping at his place, which I only did if he set an alarm and returned me to campus by curfew. The soft, clean touch of every surface reminded me of a fairy tale. And when I was there, I stopped having nightmares about dead women ransacking my closet, pinching me awake. I slept without jolting awake at every sound. There were no sounds. No loud wind or church bells. No police waiting in the bowels of Hope Hall holding a dead bird. And for the first time in the past year, I felt safe.

Let me tell you: if you haven't tried feeling safe, I can't recommend it enough.

When they found Polly's body, no one talked about where and how. Just the confirmation of what we already knew, that our classmate was gone.

I cried so hard, silently heaving and throwing up in Harry's bathroom, that he wasn't sure what to do. Even when I explained it to him, he was surprised that it wasn't on the news. The local stations barely covered the story.

He'd seen the news about the dead professor, of course. Everyone had heard about that.

Fact: I couldn't afford to stay at Loch Raven College.

Everything else felt like a branch I couldn't reach without stretching. Already spoiled futures weighed down each limb. Graduate school somewhere far away, somewhere warmer. A year in London, tea instead of coffee, the Tube instead of the beltway. Writing a novel about our time at Loch Raven. A house full of expensive dresses. Me and Sadie growing old and living together like *The Golden Girls*.

Between Harry's offer, the lentil growing inside me, and my inability to keep my scholarship, my choice wasn't much of a choice. I'd grab on to whichever branch I could reach, and never let go.

The world outside was brittle with frost-tipped grass and iced-over pathways. The sky blanched in preparation for the inevitable snow. With steamy breath, we layered our sweaters and settled into the new semester.

I kept going to class out of habit. It never occurred to me to stop.

Mr. Sable, the new teacher hired to take over literature classes in Weedler's absence, made the mistake of calling on me in class. For thirty minutes, he had stumbled through a lecture on "women in the arts," half of which must have belonged to Weedler and half of which he made up on the spot. I couldn't remember what the focus of the class was supposed to be, but if Weedler had designed it, I expected more death and, knowing him, more Sylvia Plath.

"Ms. Vale, tell us your favorite woman writer from last night's chapters," he said, waking me out of my daze.

A moment before, I gazed out onto the back side of the campus with glass in my throat. Raging nausea, combined with heartburn, felt like I had swallowed burnt crystal.

"'Woman writer'?" I asked instead. "Can't we just say *writer*?"

This was the kind of almost-insight that Dr. Gallina loved to get sidetracked by in her classes. But Mr. Sable didn't smile. He wasn't charmed.

"In this case, no. We're at a women's college, reading a book about women in modern literature, so..."

His tone—slow, like talking to a child—made me twitch. I didn't want to argue. Really. I just wanted everyone to stop looking at me. And I wanted him to shut his mouth.

"Well, you can move on, then, because I don't have an answer for you."

One of the other girls snickered. I thought I heard someone gasp. I'd never been so disrespectful in class, never been the girl who said what was on my mind. Even Sadie would have made up some answer on the spot. To her, Mr. Sable was just doing his job. He wouldn't have been worth the trouble.

"It's essential to complete all course readings if you want to pass this class, Ms. Vale. I insist on following the syllabus, as presented." He moved closer and closer to my desk while everyone watched.

My stomach churned and my armpits dripped. He loomed over my desk. "Do you understand? Or is this going to be a problem?"

I'd seen my mom have panic attacks enough times to know what was going on with my body—the racing heart, the tunnel vision. My chest tightened, and I gripped the edge of my desk so I wouldn't slide out onto the floor.

He should have walked away. He'd made his point, and the other girls wouldn't likely make my same mistake. Loch Raven girls passed their classes and worked for that A.

But he didn't walk away. "Ms. Vale? Are you going to answer me?"

If I closed my eyes for too long, I smelled Weedler's aftershave, I felt the shade of his wingspan engulf me in the same way. My hands suddenly flew up, knocking books from my desk. Mr. Sable jumped back.

"Fuck you!" I screamed, horrified at the way his face distorted into anger.

I grabbed my bag and sobbed my whole way out the building, huge heaving tears, no air in my lungs.

A wave of nausea rolled through me so hard I had to grip the nearest tree.

Laughter bellowed. All around. Up from the dead grass, radiating off the scraping tree bark. Girls laughing and laughing.

I couldn't remember the last time I'd eaten.

Look alive, girly. Whoever said it, said it hard.

My sudden and blazing hunger guided me to the cafeteria, which was empty after lunch. As long as they kept the salad bar open and as long as I didn't have to pay for the leftovers, I kept refilling my plate. The only thing left were toppings and garnishes: chickpeas, slivered almonds, cucumber slices, little squares of cheese. It was how I had survived the first weeks of school, when I realized there wasn't enough money on my meal card for three meals a day.

I had missed a lot of meals lately. My dresses hung loose from the nausea. Skeletor, Eileen called me. As I overloaded my tray, my hands shook. I only paused to let myself cry harder.

"You're late for the buffet."

I wasn't sure who said it. All of them waited at one of the long tables, a spot open in the middle of their bench just for me.

Mary held an unlit cigarette, a stage prop, in her gloved hand. The shine of Betsy's patent-leather purse matched her Mary Janes. Brigitte Bardot and Audrey Hepburn dressed for Movie Star Monday.

The space they saved for me widened. No one except Sadie had ever invited me to join her table at lunch.

I ignored their expectant faces as I took my seat. They smelled like spilled perfume.

Raquel flipped her feathered hair and readjusted the gold pin on her oversize lapel.

Kiki patted her shoulder pads, then yawned in my face, unhinging her jaw.

Dress for Success Day.

Ten girls, I counted. Including Polly. She was the only one wearing jeans and sneakers, and I understood from the way the other girls angled away from her that they didn't approve.

She sighed and squeezed in beside me, her knees bumping the table, sending a few grapes rolling to the floor. When I didn't acknowledge her, she exhaled again, even louder. The hair at her temples stuck out, the frizz left behind from wearing a hat in the cold. She didn't need eyes for me to see her exhaustion. The skin around her graying mouth wilted.

"Where's your twin?" Shea Nardman trilled. A taunting chatter aimed at me. "It's Twin Tuesday."

Jessie grabbed one of my cucumber slices and Grace reached across to nab the rest of my grapes. Metallic maroon and navy foil strands hung from their ponytails, like walking pom-poms. I willed myself to stand up and walk away, to yell until someone heard me, but I couldn't move, not even to wipe the tears as they streamed down my face.

At the end of the table, Abbie stood and unclogged a thick mucusy strand from her throat. She had attempted to cover the seeping bandage on her head with a headband, but it didn't fit, and she ended up throwing it to the floor.

Everyone watched her, waiting for a big announcement, even the headless girl at the end. Not just eyeless—headless. I didn't know which one she was. No matter how many times I silently named the other girls around the table, I couldn't place her.

Another dizzying swell of exhaustion, another spark of pain inside my skull.

Abbie twirled in her rust-colored corduroy dress, identical to the one my mom had bought for me at the mall two years before. Hers was open in the back to reveal hand-shaped bruises.

"Help me zip my dress!" she yelled, louder than she needed to be.

Like a doll with only five sentences programmed into her plastic head. I'd heard that one before.

She had the shouting voice of someone wearing headphones who didn't know how loud they sounded. Soon, they all matched her tone. Every voice at once, endless.

For you, Mary squealed as she shoved olives into Betsy's mouth.

For me, Jessie demanded and pushed Polly off the bench.

Help. Me. Zip. My. Dress. All of them shifting, ramming, thrusting, breaking open the seams of their dresses, freeing every zipper and button.

The headless girl couldn't scream. She only banged her hands against the table over and over.

My own screams didn't drown them out. Even with my hands over my ears, I couldn't make them disappear. Not until I shut my eyes and crouched onto the floor did I make enough room in my head to think clearly.

I was done. With this day, with this semester, with this whole place.

Nope.

I said it out loud, but no one heard me. It didn't matter.

No thank you. No more. This is over. I'm out.

No one was there when I opened my eyes, just the spilled contents of my food tray.

I didn't worry about the textbooks falling onto the floor on my way out. I wasn't going to need them anymore.

The tears cooled my face, tears of relief for the realization that I didn't have to decide anymore. My indecision over what to do next had never been much of a decision anyway. I didn't want to be a Loch Raven girl.

I figured I had twenty-four hours, maybe forty-eight if I was lucky, before someone from the college asked me to leave. Of all my violations, I was pretty sure that cussing out a teacher was the most inexcusable. I wasn't coming back from this one.

But first, there was one other rabbit hole I hadn't completely lost myself in yet, one more girl I hadn't added to my list.

The headless girl. I needed to know her name.

Q: Fill in the blanks with the names of the three girls who died at Loch Raven College in the eighties.
A: Shea Nardman, Raquel Valdez, and _____.

Nine deaths, according to the dean and Dr. Gallina. Ten now, including Polly. I knew all their names except one.

Anonymous Girl, 1985. Gallina said there had been a cluster of suicides, three deaths, in the eighties. I only knew two of their names: Shea Nardman and Raquel Valdez. I'd been puzzling over that final name for weeks, resigned to the fact that I might never figure it out.

It had always felt important to know their names. They weren't Sylvias. They weren't just fragmented, cautionary stories. They had their own lives and identities. They had lived. To lump them together meant getting it wrong, all of it. It was the thing I realized since my mother's death: parts of her life were unknowable to anyone but her, and there was nothing I could have done to save her.

Still shaking, I lurched to the library computers. My knees wobbled, and my brain fired with the kind of blinding headache that would soon knock me out completely. But I had one more idea.

In the comments of Jasmine Moriano's LiveJournal, random people often posted requests for money or "free pix." **Please send money to our country**, one comment read. **We need your help, Miss.** I'd seen a similar scam in my school-issued email account before.

One of the old comments said **Support the Zara Wilder Scholarship Fund**. Nothing else. A phone number showed up when I clicked "Show More." Whoever had posted it no longer had a LiveJournal account. But I could see their other two posts, each time posting the same phone number and "scholarship fund" message.

In addition to commenting on Jasmine's page, they commented on an account about Suicide Prevention on College Campuses. The other post they commented on was by someone called Baltimore Lover, an account that regularly posted reviews of restaurants in the Baltimore area.

It was almost like the Zara Wilder Scholarship people had

chosen at random where to ask for donations, but in their randomness, I saw a pattern: suicide, college campus, Baltimore. And Jasmine, who sometimes referenced her sister's death, a sister who'd died at Loch Raven—she was the other link.

Another search for the Zara Wilder Scholarship only pulled up one result, an outdated website that looked like someone made it and forgot about it shortly after. A blurry photo of a young woman with auburn hair and a port-wine birthmark appeared through a trippy strobe effect.

Zara Wilder, beloved daughter, we miss you.

Year of death: 1985.

She had been eighteen.

I didn't need to call the phone number listed. Returning to the 1985 yearbook gave me all I needed. That photo of Raquel Valdez playing chess with two other girls was the answer. Raquel had a distinctive hairstyle—feathered locks hanging in her face, barely covering an overbite. I couldn't see the eyes of the girl across from her, but the large birthmark on her face that I originally thought was a shadow, was now obvious.

They had been friends. Zara and Raquel. But the other girl in the photo wasn't Shea Nardman, who had also died in 1985. The caption didn't list any of them by name. The closer I looked, the more my body reacted. Faster pulse, shakier hands.

The student had curly hair and hair-sprayed bangs. The spiky peacock kind. It was a shitty photo. But I could make out the words on her shirt. Madonna's *Like a Virgin* tour. Dr. Gallina still had a shirt just like it.

It must have been traumatic. It explained why her face fell when I mentioned the Sylvia Club. She didn't want me to keep researching it because it hurt too much for her to think about. But wasn't it weird that she'd been friends with two girls who had died? And then taught a few others who died in a similar way?

Like, pretty damn weird.

She had never told me she went to school at Loch Raven. Just like she hadn't told me she used to be the professor in charge of the mentorship program. Two years ago. Replaced, it seemed, by Professor Weedler.

I glanced at the clock on the library wall and sprang up. Harry would be there any minute. There wasn't time to keep searching. Not anymore. I was done with the Sylvia Club. I had to be. I had used up all my resources, reached the bottom of what was available to me. This place. The stone walkways, the fountain full of wishes, the beautiful, haunted buildings where I had never belonged.

As I packed up my purse and jogged over to the parking lot, where Harry waited in his shiny car, I thought about Gallina and all the questions I still hadn't answered.

I added Zara's name to my list of girls who'd died at Loch Raven and told myself to be satisfied with where it ended up. Except that I couldn't forget. Their twisted figures and unzipped dresses already lived inside me.

CHAPTER 29
NOW

Sadie

Another blur day, another walk around the same streets, turning onto my same cul-de-sac. A few porches were styled with pumpkins and mums, but no one in Hidden Harbor really decorated for Halloween, no skeletons or spooky lights. I didn't see a single fake tombstone.

Home was tense and silent, Harrison's grief loose and filling each room. When he wasn't home, Nikki marched the halls in silence like she couldn't be bothered, her glittered flesh breaking open, stripes of shiny black tar running down her chin. My own restlessness was plenty for me to live with. I didn't need to live with their anxiety, too.

When I'd had enough and needed to pee, I swallowed as much brisk air as I could and went back. If it still felt stifling, maybe I'd open all the windows and let the house clear itself.

The snap of a branch on the side of the house stopped me cold. I felt myself teetering between the ledge of unreasonable paranoia and valid terror. *Let's go see, Rhiannon.* The words didn't make it to my mouth. *Let's explore. A squirrel. A bird.*

As I walked up, a woman wearing high-waisted leggings pulled the back door shut and zipped her cheetah-print hoodie. Blotchy around her smeared mouth, skin red as if rubbed raw from rough stubble. Her crooked ponytail hung limp, recently undone.

She looked up at the same moment I heard Harrison lock the door from the inside. I recognized her as one of the early-morning runners from the neighborhood but didn't know her name. Her eyes met mine, and for the smallest second, I hoped she had black holes instead of pupils. I wanted her to be another ghost. No such luck. She fled as soon as she saw me.

"Oh," I said.

The first time I realized it was over: Late fall, at the back door, wishing I said more than "Oh."

I'd read this script before. I knew what happened next.

Harrison sat on the couch and looked up from his phone, fully dressed and composed. No alarm or guilt on his face despite the fact that a woman just secretly left out the back door. His skin wasn't flushed and his pants weren't unzipped. I bet she hadn't ruined the mood by talking to his dead wife or playing Nirvana loud enough to worry the neighbors.

"How long?"

"Pardon?" He shifted his position, the tiniest indication of his discomfort.

I rested Rhi gently in her crib because I didn't want her to hear me yell.

Harrison walked to the kitchen and poured a mug of coffee. So calm. His hands so clean. "Want a cup?"

"Harrison. I saw her."

He focused on the mug, leaving room for cream. He was thoughtful like that. Since he never drank coffee in the middle of the day, the cup was for me. It didn't matter that too much caffeine was Bad for the nursing baby, one of the many gentle suggestions he'd guilted me into following. Not now.

"Just tell me. How long? God, how many?"

"Can we sit?" He gestured toward the chairs at the breakfast bar, but I refused. I wanted to stand until my legs stopped holding me.

"Is it always going to be like this?"

The question surprised us both, but his lack of response offered no surprise. Yes, our relationship would always be like this. Hadn't I known it all along? Or, more accurately, hadn't I tried to ignore it all along?

"Are you even happy here, Sadie?"

I wondered if that was what he would have said to Nikki if she had confronted him. But would he have cheated on her? And would she have cared?

"I'm not happy when I'm with you." The truest words I could speak. "This was all one big bad idea."

"You think?" The smell of something wet and rotten tainted the air, and he twitched his nose.

Everything between us felt like a blink, a brief moment despite the longer thread of history connecting us. He started a relationship with me because he was lonely and in mourning. He moved me in to his house because of Rhiannon, because he thought it was the right thing to do. And I said yes to all of it. What other options did I have? A woman in love who had already made so many mistakes, I wanted to think I wouldn't choose differently even if I could go back and do it again. Nikki had wanted me here. I couldn't forget that.

I snatched a pillow and a blanket neatly arranged in the hall closet by the much more organized woman who lived there before. I'd sleep on the couch or on Rhiannon's floor if I needed to. Better yet, I'd sleep in the office. I needed distance between me and Harrison to think clearly.

The office was unlocked. Untouched, but unlocked. I stilled, pausing to hear if he had followed me down the hall. Nothing.

Then I noticed what was different. The spiral notebook I'd left on the desk beneath the manila folders, the back-and-forth journal, was gone. I hadn't destroyed it when I had the chance. Because what if it held some other earth-shattering message? I'd meant to. I was going to.

"Where is it?" I yelled, unable to control my volume. "Where did you put it?"

He didn't know what I meant. He refused to cross the threshold into the room at all.

It sounded like a storm alarm, the roaring in my ears. Harrison called for me to wait as I stumbled toward the front door.

"I need air," I said. "Don't follow."

Diana opened before I knocked but didn't invite me in. Her weak attempt at a smile told me she had already heard. The other woman, Miss Cheetah Hoodie, might have texted her. Maybe she had known all along.

Karma's a bitch, the neighbors would say with their mouths full of expensive cheese.

"I should have called," I said. I hadn't grabbed my phone in my rush to leave the house.

Her face filled the crack in her latched door, and I told her about the fight, how my head felt like it would split open. Before I finished speaking, she pursed her lips and closed her eyes.

"You can't stay here. I'm sorry, babe."

Even our shallow friendship had limits, she seemed to say. Bernie's words echoed in my ear: *They're all snakes.*

"I don't know what to say, Sadie. The good news is that you get half of everything. Unless you have an iron-clad prenup or something."

A bruising jab. Anyone could see the jewelry I didn't wear. I gave her the pleasure of hearing me say it out loud. "We were never married."

There it was: the acknowledgment that I'd never had a stake in this world.

"Family? Friends?" How little she knew about me.

"No."

She waved her hand out to me. A farewell. "Bless. There's nothing harder than what you're about to do."

Wrong. Wrong wrong wrong wrong wrong wrong

It would be hard, but I had endured worse. At least I would have enough courage to make a clean break. I'd take Rhiannon and I'd make a plan. I stood on Diana's porch until I heard her latch click. My mistake for thinking she didn't harbor all sorts of resentment toward me.

Bitches, I could hear me and Nikki mumbling under our breath during orientation. *Kill me if I ever act like one of those girls.*

"Those girls," like her roommate Eileen. Fake nice. Pretend friends. The kind of girl who didn't have your back. Diana wasn't the first, and she wouldn't be the last.

I didn't need to walk anymore. I needed a friend. If Bernie really watched from her window as often as she said she did, she already knew about the woman leaving my house. Maybe she had seen that same woman several times before but never told me. I'd excuse the betrayal if she opened up her door and invited me in, embraced me, and let me cry. She was as close as I had to family. I had no one else.

I tempted a peek in her mailbox to find several days' worth of catalogs and junk mail. Her porch light was on, but even from the front steps, a sullen void made the house feel abandoned.

From the window as I peered in, I could see that the house was empty, a bare shell where furniture left indentations in the carpet. I didn't bother knocking.

I picked the Amazonian Motel because it was close and cheap, but also because I'd been there before. The last guy I'd dated before Harrison used to meet me there. The Dollhouse, was what I called it because of its sloped dollhouse roof and dirty pink shutters. In my memory, the motel wasn't so bad, but now, between the man shooting up under the streetlight and the sign at the check-in window that said, "No refunds after 15 minutes," I nearly got back in the car.

A large moth circled the only light bulb near the bed, and I smashed it with the palm of my hand. At least it wasn't a cockroach. But the motel had those, too. Small bastards crawling all over the bathtub. I spread out one of Rhiannon's blankets and grabbed another from inside the car to cover the bedspread. I didn't want anything in that room to touch my body or hers.

I had already checked in when I realized I should have gone somewhere nicer. I needed to sleep away from Harrison, though. I needed space to think. Even though I had Nikki's money from the wall, I didn't want to waste it. It looked more and more like I would need every bit of that money as I decided what to do next. She had known I would.

Harrison wasn't ever going to marry me. It was so obvious now.

I opened up Nikki's laptop with her folder full of threats, all of them emailed or messaged to her over social media from online trolls or disappointed fans. They ranged from simple anger (**You're a hack.**) to terrifying violence (**I'll slit your throat if you call yourself a boss bitch one more time.**) and, scariest of all, at least to me, were the messages from stalkers, from people who wanted Nikki to know they were watching.

I know where you live, several messages said. **I like that tight blue sweater you're wearing** and **Those waffles looked tasty this morning.**

That only included the virtual threats. She had taken photos of other physical messages that must have been left at the house. One photo file labeled "Windshield" said, "You can't hide forever" in pointy letters. Another labeled "Doorstep" said, "Burn, baby, burn." I checked the date. Two days before the kitchen fire that Harrison thought she started.

He could say she accidentally started a fire in her carelessness and depression, but the gas leak? No one had ever given me the details except to say the house filled with gas from a burner left on, and they all had to evacuate.

Yeah, she was terrified. And it wasn't clear if she had ever told Harrison about the messages. The folder also included a receipt for updating the house's security system using her own credit card.

It all seemed to ramp up after that podcast interview. Nikki knew someone was after her. Not Annie Minx. The threats were addressed to *her*, long before the public learned her real name. And she planned her last weeks accordingly.

I created a new document to organize all my jumbled thoughts and untangle the events of the last few days. For once, I understood part of Nikki's need to write. It was how she made sense of the world. Maybe it would work for me, too.

What I knew: Diana hated me. Bernie was gone. Harrison

had another girlfriend. These were the less relevant things that I couldn't afford to worry about. I wrote down those facts anyway to get them out of my head.

What else: Nikki had continued researching the Sylvia Club, and she'd thought it was important enough to hide her final manuscript where only I could find it.

She'd helped me by leaving me money and making sure I had friends waiting with open hands.

She trusted me, according to Diana, to take care of Caroline. She didn't want Caroline to go to Loch Raven.

She had feared for her life.

Our journal was gone. I didn't want to suspect that Caroline took it, but besides me and Harrison, she was the only person with access.

Dr. Gallina was behind Lucille's renewed interest in Weedler's death. She knew something about Nikki and me. And now she was giving a speech about Nikki to induct her into the Hall of Success. She had invited Caroline to a journalism seminar with no other students.

Even with everything I knew or thought I knew, it seemed like I knew nothing at all.

The panic didn't crest and fall like a surging wave. No peaks and no valleys. It rocked through me all night and long after. My usual tools to cope only made it worse. Add in sweating, dizziness, ears ringing, nausea, and hyperventilating, and it became a one-woman panic party. I double-checked the lock on the door and cried myself to sleep, no longer caring about the bugs and the horrible room or the sound of people arguing in the parking lot.

People always said to sleep when the baby sleeps. Bullshit advice that made zero sense to a new mom who had milk to pump, bottles to sterilize, and spit-up-covered laundry to wash. But for the first time since Rhiannon was born, I didn't have a single chore or responsibility except to keep us both alive.

Nikki rasped from the chair, syrupy stage blood spewing into the lap of her tight leather dress. *Mine*, I wanted to say. That dress wasn't one of her zombie theater costumes. It had been mine.

The room turned into an outside place, prickly cold with the stank of fermentation. Dark water rose from the floor and my bed became an island. Spiraling in the rushing water, a bottle of coconut rum, a knotted friendship bracelet, a blue notebook.

"You're fucking clueless, you know that. You always have been." She reached down into the water and grabbed a compact mirror with "A" engraved on the outside. "Pretty," she said when she held it up to her face.

I was done with the riddles and the costumes. I'd already punched holes in two walls looking for her clues.

"I deserve every bit of this mess, right? Isn't that what you want to say?"

She rubbed her temples with two fingers. "You don't even know how to grieve right, bitch. You never did."

Dead and full of rage, she sounded so much like herself that it broke my heart.

I pressed my hands over my ears to drown her out, but she was already in my head, the same way I would never not have the smell of her mud in my nose.

"Maybe you should just come clean. That would stop everything."

She had eyes again. Dark marbles, rings of hazel. Just the right amount of eye glitter. A gold-star sticker at the corner.

My tears fell and I didn't try to wipe them away. I pulled my knees to my chest, shaking so hard the headboard knocked into the wall.

"Stop," I growled. And she did.

The room transformed back to its original state, another place I didn't want to be.

Nikki clawed at her mouth as if to stretch it wider, to let out something huge and horrible. But then she smiled. A smile that no one else in the world could claim. "Your daughter is beautiful. Don't forget about mine, too."

CHAPTER 30

NOW

My phone chimed loudly in my hand, waking both me and Rhiannon. No messages from Harrison, but three texts from Bernie.

Did u come by? she messaged. **House being renovated.**

Then the second text when I didn't answer the first, **Where r u? R u ok?**

A third said, **This is Bernie,** as if I didn't already know.

Despite not wanting to talk to anyone, I chuckled. She could spell out "renovated" but not words like "you." When I told her where we slept, she typed, **Not ok. Meet for coffee?**

I needed the biggest coffee.

After I packed our things and flipped off a creeper in the parking lot, I drove to meet Bernie at a small café near Hidden Harbor. She bombarded me with questions the minute I stepped out of the car.

"Can we get coffee first?" I moaned.

She pressed her lips together after that and surprised me by not asking any more questions until I swallowed the first sip of coffee. I tried not to think about how we wouldn't be neighbors anymore once I left Harrison for good.

"Tell me what happened. Was it that a-hole? Did he get caught with his pinocle out again?"

Her sincere anger on my behalf made me shake my head and pull down my sunglasses to cover my eyes, at least until the tears subsided. *Again*, she had said. So, she had known after all.

I avoided all conversations about Harrison—there wasn't much left to say—and stuck to the other story, the one that involved Nikki's research. The way Nikki had hidden clues for me to find. For so long, I had tried not to talk about it with anyone, but I wasn't sure why anymore.

"It's almost like Nikki knew I would end up in her house even though we hadn't spoken in decades. How is that possible?"

Bernie sipped a mug of milky tea, silent, before asking, "I think she knew you well enough to know how you'd react. Me and my daughter were like that."

"Like she orchestrated this whole thing?" Me with Harrison, me moving in, me unlocking the office and finding all her clues. "That doesn't even make sense."

Her mug landed with a thud on the table. "It makes complete sense. Nikki was the craftiest woman I've ever met."

She said it with a twinge of regret. I hadn't considered that Bernie and Nikki had been close enough for her to feel a similar kind of loss. Then again, Nikki left an impression on everyone.

"Yes," I agreed, though *crafty* wasn't the word I would have used. "Nikki was so smart, so talented."

Except Nikki had missed something big, too. She couldn't piece together every part of her own puzzle, which was what she needed me for. I still didn't know what the Sylvia Club had to do with Dr. Gallina. The answer itched at my palms. Something was there, just out of my range of vision.

I had dominated the conversation for long enough. "So, you're renovating your house?"

"Tearing down walls for an open concept. Something I've been meaning to do for a while. That's not interesting, though." She waved her hand away, her eyes shiny with tears. "You know, I dreamed about Nikki last night."

I knew how that felt, to find her and lose her all over again.

"What did she look like? In the dream?"

"She looked like herself, but angry. And she was wearing that weird little dress of hers with the dead flowers on it."

The dead-tulips dress was always one of her favorites.

We finished our drinks quietly, both of us trapped in thoughts we didn't need to share. As much as I hated the thought of going back there, I was eager to get home.

"What you need to do is this: force yourself back into that house until you have a better place. Harrison is an a-hole, but he doesn't have the you-know-whats to kick you out. Don't you dare take your baby back to that motel, Sadie."

When I asked her where she was going to stay during her home renovation, she waved me away again. *Don't worry about me*, she would have said if she was the type to waste words.

Harrison wasn't home when I went back. A small relief. He had left a note in the kitchen that read "I'm sorry. Let's talk about the next steps."

Somehow the written note meant more than a text or phone call. It meant he expected me to come home, if I could even call it that anymore. I appreciated the apology as much as I noted he wasn't asking for me to forgive him. He wasn't asking to work things out. It felt like as much closure as I was going to get.

Once Rhi sat smiling and laughing from on her swing, I searched the office again for the spiral notebook, just in case I had dreamed its disappearance. When I still couldn't find it, I opened up Nikki's manuscript document. I had searched the document for Weedler's name before, but never Gallina's name. Gallina was the connection I needed to understand most.

References to Dr. Isabel Gallina were sparse, but they were there. I kept coming back to one page of Nikki's document: page 717. It didn't make sense because the document wasn't seven hundred pages long. 717 lived somewhere in the middle of the document, out of order.

July 17. My birthday.

Except the information on that page looked the same as the rest of the document. Notes, biographical information. Nothing new.

It took a while, but after staring at the screen long enough, I moved the cursor and found what Nikki had hidden. When I hovered over Abbie Moriano's name, a link popped up to a locked online document. Locked to everyone, unless you had the link.

The new document was a police report for Abigail Moriano, Loch Raven College freshman, 1997, whose death had been listed as suspicious.

Professor Weedler was her Freshman Seminar teacher and Dr. Gallina was her mentor, adviser, and journalism teacher, Nikki's notes said underneath the police report. Abbie had switched majors and signed up for "independent study" with Gallina midsemester.

Professor Weedler took over the mentorship program shortly after Abbie's death, if the dates were correct. Weedler didn't just take over the program; it looked like Gallina had been removed from her duties. Nikki had typed each detail on a new line, like a list of facts, each one worth emphasizing.

Abbie fell or jumped from the top of Hope Hall. Some of her injuries might have happened before the fall. Bruising and other marks of self-defense led the family, and briefly the police, to wonder if she hadn't jumped on purpose at all.

A murder among the suicides, just like Nikki had said on the podcast. It wasn't just a fun fact or an odd detail buried in all the others. Abigail Moriano's death was the part Nikki couldn't let go of.

I clutched the closest couch cushion, prepared for the room to spin and for my panic to knock me sideways, but everything seemed to slow instead. I tasted coffee on my inhale, felt my chest expand when I exhaled. I didn't fall apart. I couldn't give Nikki or anyone else credit for that small miracle. I had remembered how to breathe on my own.

If the college stripped Gallina of the mentorship program, there could have been so many reasons. It didn't mean they knew she was involved in Abbie's death—her possible murder. The more I turned it over in my head, the more it made sense.

Gallina wanted Nikki, and now me, to stop digging into the Sylvia Club. Why else would she seek out Lucille about the night of Weedler's accident? She wanted us to get caught to take the pressure off her, the pressure that was heading her way. And she knew Lucille was the only one who would care enough to see it through. Unlike the detectives who had given up.

The last sentence listed a phone number.

"Jasmine, Abbie's sister. Text her. She won't answer if you call."

I didn't hesitate. Jasmine hadn't been warned that I might contact her, but she responded as if unsurprised.

"I talked to Nikki several times. She wore me down. I think I was just glad someone still cared to look into my sister's murder. It was so long ago. People stopped caring."

That word again. *Murder.*

Knowing Nikki, she would have wanted to figure out every detail of what happened. I could see us arguing over this very point. All I needed to know was who to blame and who to trust.

"I'll tell you what I told Nikki: Abbie had been hit with a brick or something like that before she hit the ground."

"Did you or Nikki speculate who was responsible?" I closed my eyes and let the memory of Hope Hall grow, a Gothic castle full of horrible secrets.

"Well, she had a strong bond with this professor named Weedler. I think she had a crush on him. He was the guy who died a few years later. And her adviser was strange, too. Dr. Gallina?"

Three dots. Still typing. Her rapid-fire texts were a relief. Finally, someone willing to talk.

"She creeped me out," she wrote. "Abbie didn't like her, called her a vulture. She said she thought Dr. Gallina was doing more harm than good. She got too involved with everyone's lives. But for what it's worth, Dr. Gallina was also the only person from the college who ever contacted my parents to offer condolences."

I didn't know what to do with that information.

After a few minutes, when it was clear the conversation with Jasmine had ended, I reopened Nikki's manuscript with a sudden but hazy memory:

Me and Nikki walking around campus at night while her old

roommate pointed out the places on campus where girls had died. Eileen had some kind of insider knowledge from a sister or cousin who'd attended Loch Raven. And she'd told us something else. She'd mentioned that by second year, everyone knew to avoid Professor Gallina's classes.

It wasn't a rumor so much as fact back then. Professor Weedler had a mentorship program to help struggling students, which made him beloved but also predatory, as Nikki and I knew. But Professor Gallina, Eileen had said, was a bitch. She played favorites. If you didn't work on the school newspaper, you weren't worth her time.

It had never mattered. Not to Nikki. Because she was one of Gallina's favorites, too.

I searched Nikki's document for Eileen's name and sure enough, found a transcript from a conversation dated not long before Nikki died.

"I had a thing with Professor Weedler. A thing for him, I should say. A lot of girls did. I knew he was divorced and had a daughter he never saw. He had a first wife who made his life hell. Or so he said. I knew his first book about Sylvia Plath was out of print, and he had horrible writer's block trying to write a second."

Nikki's notes indicated a long pause in the conversation before Eileen started again.

"But there's this other thing. My cousin graduated from Loch Raven in 1997, and she always told me to watch out for Dr. Gallina. Remember her? I warned everyone I knew not to take her classes. Being teacher's pet in college was not a good look. But later, like years later at some family thing, my cousin told me more. Apparently, that girl who jumped from the top of Hope Hall had been Dr. Gallina's only mentee the year she died. They'd been inseparable."

I could almost follow Nikki's train of thought. She suspected one of the deaths—Abbie Moriano—was a murder. So did Abbie's family. Maybe she suspected Weedler at first, but then Eileen reminded her of the simplest facts, a thing we knew but overlooked all those years ago: Gallina chose favorites.

Nikki did the research, reached out to families, but wasn't as quiet as she could have been near the end. If Gallina had heard the podcast and knew that Nikki was onto her, she'd have a reason to keep Nikki from ever speaking again. Gallina's career was on the line.

If any of it was true, I was the only other person who Nikki could ask for help. I was the only one Nikki could go to, and she couldn't even make the call.

The reason why Gallina would kill a student in the first place was the part where I got lost. Abigail Moriano had been hit with a brick. It took rage to hit someone. And if she could kill someone before, it wasn't a leap to think she could do it again.

I wrapped my arms around myself tight. The pieces sort of fit. Even if not completely, it felt like enough to know that Caroline shouldn't be alone with Gallina.

I opened the calendar on my phone and winced. Nikki's memorial service with Dr. Gallina as the presenter was only a few days away.

I couldn't just charge up to campus and call her out, though that was exactly what I wanted to do. She knew too much, or thought she knew too much, about me and Nikki. It was why Nikki had never spoken up, either. They were locked in a staring contest, and both of them refused to blink first.

When Lucille picked up her phone, I didn't have time or energy to tell her everything about the Sylvia Club, so I gave her the short version. It was much bigger than a hit-and-run accident, I explained. She listened even if she didn't sound convinced.

And then I said the best part, the part I had been waiting to say out loud: "Dr. Gallina is at the heart of this whole case. Going back decades."

It hadn't started to gel until I saw where Nikki had written Gallina's name in the back of the journal. Like a reminder to herself that something wasn't right.

She had been Nikki's favorite teacher, the person she trusted. And she was the one who told her to do whatever she needed to get an extension on her research paper. Nikki should never have been alone with Weedler, though. He was a horrible man. The college replaced one bad mentor with another horror show. Though I didn't dare tell Lucille what I really thought about her father.

We couldn't blame Gallina for what we did, but I didn't know if the accident would have happened without her pushing Nikki in that direction.

It was all there in Nikki's document for someone who could read between the lines. Suicide clusters plus a mentor/friend who was always a little too close to the women who died. Not that she killed them all, but she also didn't try to stop them. Was that unfair to say? Who could stop someone who wanted to die? If it wasn't for Abbie Moriano, maybe Nikki would have let it go.

Lucille huffed. She didn't believe me, but she also didn't want me to hang up.

"Come see for yourself," I told her, before texting the information for Loch Raven's planned memorial.

Even as I searched the house to tell Nikki that I'd figured out the last of her clues, that I had a plan, I knew she wasn't there. No smell, no eruptions of glitter, no beautiful eyeless woman mucking up the furniture.

The service wasn't for a few days, but Nikki was already on her way.

CHAPTER 31

THEN

Nikki

Sadie had been driving for thirty minutes when I finally asked where we were going.

"You'll see," she said and turned up the CD.

Tori Amos: "Silent All These Years."

It was our last night at Loch Raven, and neither of us wanted to hang out on campus. That whole place was fucked.

I hadn't told anyone except Sadie that I was leaving. Despite how little we talked lately and despite how awkward we were together since the night at Weedler's, she started packing immediately. I was the one who "verbally assaulted" a teacher. I was the one eating lunch with dead girls. But we came together, and we'd leave together. She'd said.

When we pulled off the highway, I sat forward. Every now and then, Sadie could surprise me. Tonight was apparently one of those nights. She's made me promise to hang out with her instead of "Big Money," as she called him.

She never said she hated Harry; she didn't even know him. But her whole face curdled every time I mentioned going to his apartment, as if I were abandoning her.

"I think this is it." She bit her lip, slowing into a grassy lot away from all the traffic and noise.

Wordless, I followed her out of the car. I kept following, following, through dead grass and mud that would probably freeze overnight. For now, it was an inch of muck that we couldn't avoid walking through. She stopped in front of a chain-link fence and held her arms up high above her head. V for Victory.

"I give up," I said. "Where are we? What are you up to?"

From her coat pocket, she retrieved two flashlights and handed me one. "Tell me when you see it."

I flipped on the light and mimicked her aim, my boots squelching deeper. It smelled like sewage, like trash day in a swamp, but I held my breath and focused on our double beams. It had been a wet winter. There was so much mud.

Trees. Dead stumps. Farther away, more fencing. A bench. And then I gasped as my spotlight clung to the wide-open mouth of a blue whale. Willie the Whale, like the photo of me and my mom from my desk. We were at the ruins of the Enchanted Forest. It had been shut down for years. Sadie had found the one place you could see the old amusement park attractions.

She giggled with glee watching my face as I figured it out.

"How in the world?" A hook caught in the space between my words.

She tugged on my sleeve. "Knock it off. No crying. Oh, and guess what? I found a hole in the fence on the other side."

First, we grabbed a bag full of snacks and a thin blanket from her trunk (she had come prepared, another Sadie surprise); then we trudged back through the sludge, weaseling through a hole we had to stretch to fit through. Her coat snagged on the wire.

"Who's the stage manager now?" I joked. I could practically hear her smile.

After a while, I didn't even notice the cold or the smell.

It all came back to me in slivers, the kind of patchwork memories that probably saved me from feeling too much all at once.

A tarnished spoon and dish smiled through flaking paint. My mom had pretended once to shake their hands.

A crooked, discolored gingerbread man, now face down in the mud, had sparked my parents into a playful argument about the real words to the gingerbread man rhyme.

All the abandoned fairy-tale structures looked like haunted houses waiting for residents. No one cared to trespass there but us. I almost made a joke about us moving into Cinderella's castle and hanging a disco ball. I wasn't in the right mood to commit to dreaming, though. Memories had me stuck somewhere else, my hand clasped in my mom's. For once, I didn't push them away.

This had been a good place. This had been our place. That it was shut down and nearly destroyed didn't hurt as much anymore. It felt fitting. Like this place couldn't hold any more new memories at all.

When we finally circled around to the whale with the open mouth for sitting, Sadie waited for me to enter first. We spread out the thin blanket across his tongue and huddled together for warmth while we tore open a bag of Utz crab-flavored chips, the kind that left our fingers tingling with Old Bay seasoning.

"This is perfect," I said, her head on my shoulder, neither of us scared by scurrying animals and falling leaves in the dark. It had been too long, us together, believing everything was going to be okay.

She grunted. "I did good."

Yeah, she did. She did so good.

She had been with me when I bought a pregnancy test, though we never spoke about the results. The not telling, the way I pushed away her flask of vodka, said it all. We'd talk when it was time. A night away from conversations about school and scholarships and unborn babies was what both of us needed.

We spoke instead about how some other freshmen girls were getting scared about the props moving around onstage. Mary Matherly up to her tricks again. Those other girls clearly hadn't attended the Death Tour.

"That's an easy fix," I said. "Set up a ghost light. It's a no brainer."

Theatre 101: What is a ghost light?
A: A common theater tradition/superstition, leaving one bare bulb lit on an unoccupied stage to keep the ghosts at bay.

When I replayed it all later and tried to identify the real end to everything we'd started, it always ended there, away from the dorms, smelling like wreckage. The mud, the mud, the mud.

I was waiting for a new start without realizing everything new had already begun. Of a thousand endings, that night was the real end. Me and Sadie, testing the limits of our tether.

We waited until we were back in the car, headed toward campus on dark streets, to discuss the cops. They had been lurking less since the new semester started, which somehow worried me more. When I thought about what they found in Weedler's house, proof that someone else had been there—the remnants of a sandwich, maybe threads of my hair—my insides went cold.

"They showed up at my grandma's house," Sadie said.

We both knew what that meant. They wanted to ask about her minivan, see if she had any other cars.

"Did she let them in?"

Sadie laughed. "Hell no. Grandma Ruth is from the streets. She knows they need a warrant. But she probably said it in a way that made them think she was still a sweet old woman."

"And the Tercel is gone?" I asked.

"Gone." She didn't want to tell me more.

After a few more miles I asked, "Would you ever go to a country club?"

"Only to burn it down."

Kill me if I ever belong to a country club, we didn't need to say. *Push my head underwater if I even mention it.*

Never mind that neither of us had never been to a country club. I could only envision some eighties-movie version of a rich-people hangout, golf carts and white blazers, exclusive entry. To punctuate her feelings on the subject, she sped up just to flip off a passing BMW. Rich assholes. We were both thinking it.

Eileen had been right about one thing: I couldn't take Sadie anywhere. It was her best quality.

The responsible side of me could see into a crystal ball that the rest of my life might not go the way I wanted, but if I was careful, it would go the way it needed.

I liked that realization. It felt like the kind of epiphany I would have paid a lot of money for a therapist to help me figure out. Therapy, by the way, was on my list of things I'd be able to afford if Harry's offer—that future we drew on the place mat—hadn't expired.

Q: List the things you don't need but really want.
A: A washer and dryer, non-scratchy sheets, extra batteries when the other ones die. One impractical pair of shoes, a library full of books, and a space to write in that no one could enter but me.

I wanted it fucking all.

Which meant making the kind of decisions I'd been avoiding.

I didn't know how to tell Sadie that she couldn't be part of my decision-making process anymore. We couldn't move in together, we couldn't have sleepovers every night, we couldn't live above a bar. She wouldn't be surprised, but she would be devastated. I needed to think of myself as a "we." And the second person in that "we" was no longer Sadie.

But me and Harry and the lentil wouldn't be a complete family, either, because without Sadie, I would always be incomplete.

Back on campus, after Sadie went to bed, I climbed to the top of Hope Hall without my coat. My last night. I wanted it to keep going.

Hope Hall had only been closed for two years, but with its icy openings and weathered floors, it probably needed renovation long before that. The stairs weren't so bad—cold and rickety and three stories tall. My lungs opened on the way up, and I drank the cold air in like I couldn't get enough.

I wanted to look down from the top and see the descent. I wanted to see the whole campus from a different vantage. I thought about Abbie Moriano, of course, but I had more pressing things on my mind.

When I made it to the roof, someone was already there. A

woman's figure stooped, her eyes cast down over the ledge. She stepped closer and closer to where her shoes balanced between air and cornice. Abbie.

My heart thundered, a scream stalling on my tongue, until I realized it wasn't a student. Dr. Gallina extended her arm to pet one of the gargoyles, her spiky hair gray in the moon's dingy light. She smiled like she had a joke all to herself.

My footsteps shocked her upright, and she stumbled too close to the edge before righting herself.

"Nikki. You scared me. What are you doing up here?"

I stepped toward her but didn't speak. I couldn't. The sky up there opened darker than dark. It smothered my thoughts instead of calming them.

We hadn't seen each other much since the start of the new semester. I'd been busy and preoccupied. But the real reason I kept my distance was that there wasn't much left to say. We weren't going to talk about Weedler anymore, not with the cops in the picture, and I wasn't going to ask her about the Sylvia Club now that I knew she had lost friends. She had her own grief and trauma to deal with. The less I said around her, the better.

"Please don't tell me you came up here to have a séance like those other girls. I already sent them away," Gallina said. No softness in her voice, no pleading for me to step away from the edge. Mild irritation radiated off her oversize concert tee. If I had headphones, I'd play the song.

The Ramones: "I Wanna Be Sedated."

"Aren't you worried I came up here to jump?" I didn't recognize my own voice or the crackle in it. A taunt and an accusation all in one, a joke wrapped in bandages. If I stayed at Loch Raven, I'd turn into one of them, I had realized on my way up to the roof.

Meaning: Loch Raven girls had better opportunities. They made better choices.

Meaning: Loch Raven girls, unchecked, could turn monstrous. Or tragic.

But I wasn't staying.

"If you wanted to jump, that would be your choice. You have to make the right choices for yourself, Nikki."

I almost asked if she was drunk, but she sounded high more than anything, her ideas lolling under the surface, probably brilliant and logical in her own ear. She lowered herself onto a grimy patch of roof and gestured for me to join her.

"The decision to end your life is not one to take lightly." Her words fell away in a slow tilt before she found them again. "If you take the leap, you have to be sure."

"I didn't know I signed up for counseling." I tried to make it light.

She craned her neck and sealed her eyes to the sky. Sadie would never believe how my night had ended.

"Life is precious, but it isn't for everyone." Gallina's voice sang more than preached. Breathless sigh on top of sigh. "Did you know that when Sylvia Plath died, the public didn't know it was suicide for years. Everyone thought she died of pneumonia at first."

Another fact that Weedler had never mentioned. A tendril of crimped hair fell out of my topknot, and I let it drape over my eyes, tuning her out as she sputtered on.

I had misspoken on my campus tours. There were no castle turrets or arched beams to tunnel myself under. Up close, the gargoyles looked like scared dogs. Not a romantic place to die, though I never thought, not even for a minute, that death was romantic. My mom had chosen her station wagon, her messy garage filled with old Christmas decorations.

Her last meal: a bowl of oatmeal.

Her death cloak was nothing but a blue terry cloth robe.

If Abbie Moriano had walked up the steps of Hope Hall with the plan to jump, she probably didn't care about the architecture. She would have wanted silence.

"You've got to give up on that story," Gallina mumbled, now almost half-asleep while sitting up. I didn't realize the conversation had shifted.

She wasn't wrong. I knew I had to move on. Having a baby changed everything.

And to become part of Harry's world, I'd have to change my clothes and my hair, my hobbies, my interests.

Not everything would make the move to whatever dream house waited for me on the other side. College. My writing. And Sadie. I'd have to leave her behind. It was the worst thing I'd ever thought, even worse than what we did. But safety and security might not invite me in again. And I knew our friendship would always be waiting.

It has to be this way, I'd tell her. *Not forever. Just for now.* We'd find our way back to each other eventually.

I didn't say it was my best idea. It was just the only one I had.

Gallina's hands on my shoulders didn't surprise me. She always found a way to let me know she was there. I rested my cheek against her hand and almost forgot that she'd spent the last ten minutes trying to convince me to jump, too.

CHAPTER 32
NOW

Sadie

Twenty-five miles away, Loch Raven College looked exactly the same. It had always been small and quiet, almost holy. The campus was sheltered and surrounded by a wooded area despite its proximity to Baltimore city limits. I waited for a panic attack to settle in as I drove up the hill, the chapel in full view. The numbness I felt instead offered a false sense of calm.

Judging by Nikki's research, two of the suicide clusters at Loch Raven College—in the eighties and nineties—were connected. She could link the same friend/mentor to six of the deaths. In several cases, this same person also found the bodies. Dr. Gallina. First as a student, then as a professor.

Nikki's theory, if I grasped her logic, was that Dr. Gallina pushed susceptible students to the edge. She'd done it to her friends when she attended Loch Raven. Then, as a professor, she did it again. You couldn't blame her for their deaths, not exactly. Except for one: Abigail Moriano.

And now she was coming back to Loch Raven with Caroline in her sights. It sounded dramatic and disjointed, but it also made sense, even if I couldn't prove it.

In front of Hope Hall, I half expected to find a group of girls dressed in black, eyes heavy with liner, in front of a Ouija board summoning the spirit of a dead poet. But the girls at the fountain all looked well-adjusted and, of course, well-dressed. Girls with straightened hair and nails sharpened into stilettos. They sipped expensive coffee, posed for selfies, and scrolled through apps on their uncracked phone screens.

I walked past the theater building and braced for a stab of memory that never came. That had been another life. Another girl.

"Sadie?" Caroline shouted. "What are you doing here?"

My relief bloomed at the sight of her. She wore a heavy bookbag that sagged on one shoulder, and she stopped walking, forcing me to backtrack and catch up to her. Her dark hair hung in a long braid down her back, not a single flyaway.

"I'm meeting with the alumni foundation," I said. Making up lies on the spot had once been my superhero skill. "I was going to see if you wanted to get lunch, but I figured you were in class. It's just a quick trip."

She frowned. Lunch with me? She would never. "You didn't even graduate. How does that count as alumni?"

Damn. Too smart, just like her mother.

"It's actually a job interview. I'm looking into some new options."

It was the kind of lie that could unravel at any moment. I wasn't sure that an alumni foundation existed.

"If you're here for my mom's event, that's fine. Just say it. You're early, but whatever." She eyed my rumpled clothes and asked, "Where's Rhiannon?"

It was the first time I'd heard her say her sister's name.

"With the neighbor. But hey, did you take a notebook from the office by any chance? Your mom's office?" I lowered my voice, a new habit, like I always anticipated that someone was listening.

The immediate confusion in her eyes told me no. She didn't have any notebook. And I was in deep shit. Her whole face contorted when she realized what I was saying.

"Is that the notebook my mom was looking for?"

I squeaked when I really wanted to scream. "Yes. No. Probably. It doesn't matter now."

We sat on the steps in front of the newly remodeled Hope Hall, renovated to make more room for student housing. The building had grown two more floors, the old stone facade replaced with sharper corners, more windows. The effect looked more modern than I remembered.

Caroline sat beside me. "What are you wearing for the event? And don't say you're wearing your ripped yoga pants and a hoodie with baby puke on your shoulder."

The joking tone of her voice threw me off guard. She wore faded jeans and an oversize sweater, but I guessed she planned to change, too.

It stung again and again to see Nikki's contours on Caroline's face. Especially there in the place where I remembered her last. A sudden surge of tenderness trapped me in place.

"There's so much I want to tell you. About your mother, among other things." I hadn't planned to say it, just like I didn't mean for my voice to break.

She looked away, no doubt to avoid crying, too.

"Look, Caroline. You need to stay away from Professor Gallina. It's a lot to explain, but you need to trust—"

"Stop." Her voice sharpened, one level below shouting at me. "You don't get to suddenly act like you have a say in my life."

Clearly whatever bridges I thought we had built, she wasn't ready to cross over them. She had never wanted me to have any role in her life, especially not a motherly one. But Nikki wouldn't have wanted her around Gallina, either. She didn't even want her at that school. When I started to speak again, she held up her hand.

"I know more than you think I do," she said, almost inaudibly. Whatever she meant, she didn't explain. Instead, she sucked her tears back in and stood up, looming like her father. "Let me know if you need something to wear. It's almost showtime."

Down the hill and past the library, I tried to remember her, whoever Nikki used to see, the outline of a girl in a maroon sweater and a pearl necklace, the swing of her long skirt. The sun in my eyes, I kept walking.

Our residence hall's stone structure was yellower than I remembered. Upstairs, through an open window, you might hear the girl on the fourth floor. Her bare feet slapping tile. Pounding her head against the tampon dispenser. Nikki told me that one. We never went to the fourth floor alone.

We left them poetry and clumps of our hair. We left them jewelry. But they were Nikki's ghosts. I never saw them. I never knew them like her.

The good thing about old colleges was that sometimes they never changed. A building might get remodeled or renamed. The student population might change, but at Loch Raven College, the location of the theater department and the costume room was one thing that had stayed exactly the same. Same location, same unlocked door in the hallway beside the auditorium. I peeked into the auditorium to see the bare bulb gleaming upstage. The ghost light. It brought me a tiny ache of joy to see it.

I had been wrong before about not missing this place. It was the girl I had been here who I missed.

I waited for someone to say hello or ask if I was lost. Nothing. I strode into the costume room like I belonged there and closed the door behind me.

Nikki sat on the floor beneath a rack of cheerleader costumes, like she had been waiting for a while.

"I didn't smell you this time," I said. Years of perfume and deodorant were trapped in those garments.

She was home. And maybe that was why she no longer smelled like dead fish. She had mud caked on her boots as usual, though. Boots beneath her long black dress.

There were things we would have never said back then: *I'm scared, I'm not having fun, I need help. This isn't working.*

"This is the place," she said. "They took most of the black dresses. Good luck finding one."

I found the only remaining black dress on one of the back hangers. It was a little much. Leather bodice and satin skirt. High in the front and long in the back like a mullet. It looked like the wedding dress in a Guns N' Roses video, but black. Kind of badass. Caroline would kill me if I wore it.

"Fuck it," I said. It was Nikki's memorial, and she would have loved it.

I angled and arched in the mirror's reflection, twisted to make sure nothing ripped when I sat. A pair of knee-high vinyl boots in the "shoe corner" were only a half size too big.

I strained to close the back of my dress, and the room drew a breath with me, like hundreds of girls gasping all at once. Nikki reached out like she wanted to help, but I didn't need it. I handled the zipper on my own.

"Any words of advice?" I asked.

I wanted her to tell me to *give 'em hell* or to *light 'em up*. Something strong and powerful to send me out to the wolves. An Annie Minx kind of mantra. *You got this, girl. Don't back down.*

She laughed instead. "You should have shaved your legs."

As usual, she wasn't lying.

Despite the cold, the event was set up in front of the swan fountain. A few dozen white folding chairs sat in front of a podium, and an enlarged photo of Nikki rested on an easel. I grabbed a program from one of the students and scanned the order of events.

First, the dean of humanities would introduce Dr. Gallina.

Then Dr. Gallina would give a small speech honoring Nikki Vale/Walsh/Annie Minx before leading the whole audience through the Admissions building and into the Hall of Success. Nikki's photo and biography would already be there, I assumed, trapped behind plexiglass.

A small bio on the program listed Nikki's books, as written under her pseudonym. It didn't include the fact that she never graduated from Loch Raven College. The Walsh name carried a lot of weight, it seemed. It was a fact Gallina must have known, too.

The bio for Dr. Isabel Gallina was much longer. Her degrees and awards, her teaching history. The college wanted to celebrate her return after more than ten years away. She wasn't just the new communications department chair. Her name was on a new scholarship fund for promising freshman writing students. She planned to reinvigorate the old mentorship program, and she had a forthcoming book about the retention of financially disadvantaged students in higher education.

I sat in the back and watched. Caroline arrived alone, wearing a tasteful black sheath and kitten heels. She had wrapped up her braid into a crown around her head, a hairstyle Nikki had worn for her college ID photo. She met my stare before rolling her eyes and laughing at my dress. When Diana texted, I ignored it. She hadn't apologized yet, and I didn't have the energy to talk.

The chairs filled and Dr. Gallina was the last to file in. Lucille waited on the edge, scanning the crowd. If everything went right, I'd get her a new story to report on so she could leave her father's memory in peace. Gallina clocked both of us.

The next minutes crept by. Waiting, waiting. When Dean Collier stood to introduce Dr. Gallina, Caroline also stood and moved to the aisle. I couldn't take my eyes off Gallina. Her speech about Nikki would surely start pleasant and insightful enough. I had to be ready for what else she might add.

Nikki had always called me Chaos, but I had thought through the event enough to know if I stood up and shouted when Gallina began, I would be removed from campus. That would be that. I didn't want that kind of chaos.

Instead, I planned to beat her to the podium. If I took wide enough strides, I could get there at the same time as her. Maybe even get a head start. I needed to speak first.

I didn't even get a chance. No sooner did Dean Collier lower his lips to the microphone, did an off-key wailing erupt from the back of the crowd. From the swan, I thought at first. No, it was Caroline. She opened her mouth wide and howled. I pressed a hand to my lips. Then another wail rang out. Louder and louder, a droning sound from all directions.

Students emerged from behind the fountains, from around the trees, some even strutted out of the Admissions building. All of them bellowing, all of them wearing black dresses.

The moans released like a heavy wind, something dying and coming back to life. Many wore scowls and clenched jaws, but more of them openly cried. Not just a cry, but a keening. A collective aching so loud a small child in the audience covered his ears.

The students marched up to the small platform, surrounding the podium. They outnumbered the members of the audience. I didn't pretend they were all crying for Nikki, a woman they didn't know. But they knew grief all the same. It showed on their faces as they cried out for their lost mothers and sisters and friends. Their grandmothers and neighbors. It was the kind of public grief that we all shoved down each day, now on full display. They were crying for themselves maybe, too. Wasn't what we all did at a memorial?

My eyes stayed dry. It wasn't that I couldn't cry. In the past weeks, I had cried plenty, usually hot, urgent tears full of rage and regret, the kind of tears that could be wiped away and ignored in order to finish loading the laundry machine or answer the front door with a smile. Never an open floodgate, though. And never like this, with so many people around.

When I finally started crying, I didn't think I would be able to stop.

Dean Collier's horrified face quickly turned to concern as he stepped off the platform. Loch Raven College wasn't a place used to performance art or peaceful protest. Whatever this keening wanted to be, the crowd didn't know if they should join in or applaud. They watched in rapt silence anyway.

I dared a glance at Lucille. She stood erect, stepping forward, like she wanted to join in. Only Gallina turned in her seat to watch me rather than the young women dressed in black. I couldn't read her expression, somewhere between amusement and boredom.

After five minutes, the church bells rang, off schedule, and the women quieted. Whatever had just happened in front of all of us, couldn't be ignored, even as we tried. The reverberation of their cries lingered. If I could feel it, I knew the others felt it, too.

CHAPTER 33
NOW

Campus security showed up after the fact. They followed the crowd inside, waiting to see what happened next.

I still had time to take over the crowd and bypass any announcements or speeches Gallina planned to make, but she didn't make a move to walk inside. She angled her hand over her eyes as a shield from the last dip of sun.

I finally checked my messages. Three calls from Diana. The one text message said, **Sorry I was a bitch. Call me.**

I texted her instead. **We can talk later. At Loch Raven College. A lot going on.**

She would understand the gravity of the situation without me saying it. This was about Nikki. It was always about Nikki.

How can I help? Let me take Rhi for a little while. I saw Bernie walking her around the tennis courts for the fifth time in a row.

Long story but Bernie's renovating her house, I typed with one eye still on Gallina and Lucille. **Everything is fine,** I added.

Lucille turned her gaze from me to Gallina to Caroline, who was red-faced from her efforts, as she descended the platform stairs. And in Gallina's hands was the back-and-forth journal. Blue spiral. She clutched it to her chest.

I couldn't begin to process how she got ahold of it. All that mattered was that it ended up back in my hands.

Another message from Diana buzzed in my hand. **Doesn't Bernie have a rental?**

I stared at Diana's message, too paralyzed to respond. Too many things had happened, were still happening, all around me.

The last time I saw Nikki alive: Here, on campus, in this exact spot near the spitting fountain. Plastic bags filled with whatever we could hold. I didn't know it would be the last time. I didn't know that wherever she was going, I couldn't follow.

When I looked back up to find Caroline, she had disappeared. Just like that. Lucille and Gallina were gone, too. Had Caroline gone with them? She didn't know that her future teacher wasn't someone she could trust. I should have tried harder to warn her.

mother daughter bullshit keening campus don't cry don't cry don't cry

Gallina had the notebook and was probably on her way to the police. But that didn't make sense, either. If that was her goal, why would she bring the notebook here? She wasn't interested in talking to the cops. After all, she had the confession Lucille had been looking for.

With shaking fingers, I texted Bernie. **Everything okay?**

No response, but sometimes it took her a while.

I twisted my body, searching for Caroline. I didn't want to go inside the Hall of Success and get trapped in the crowd. That wasn't where she had gone.

As the gathering shifted, blocking my view of the Administration building, I turned and scanned the rest of campus, the parts I could see. The auditorium, the Humanities building. Our old dorms.

Hope Hall.

My eyes traveled up until I found the roof, where two women stood. They were nothing more than hollow profiles, but I knew. Gallina had taken Caroline to the place where she had killed Abbie Moriano. Caroline, who looked so much like her mother she couldn't scrub away the resemblance if she tried. I ran without thinking. If Gallina lured Caroline to the roof to trap me, it worked. There was no way I wouldn't follow.

I didn't brave the elevator, running up the stairs instead, misjudging the number of flights. By the time I reached the top, my lungs burned and my cheap costume-room boots chafed my ankles. My dress was damp with more than leaking breast milk. I couldn't think about Rhi, though. She was safe with Bernie. Diana had seen her. Everything was okay okay okay. Nikki's baby was the one who needed me.

The door to the roof slammed shut, and Caroline turned to face me, relief and surprise mixed together in her expression. Gallina didn't turn. She stood near the edge and stared down, one hand still gripping the notebook.

"You okay?" Caroline asked, stepping closer to me as I doubled over, trying not to heave. "Sadie?"

She angled her head, pointing without pointing to the corner of the roof. Another person was there. Lucille stood alone, watching the whole scene. She wouldn't make eye contact, not with me.

Lucille directed her questions to Gallina. "That's the notebook your mother found?"

Her mother. I was always so slow, falling five steps behind at every curve. If Gallina's mother had been in our house to steal a notebook, that meant someone close enough to walk right in.

I didn't have enough breath to gasp. Bernie.

My daughter and I are very close, she had told me.

I looked for a railing or a wall to hold me but could only lean into the wind as my brain caught up. Caroline's face went pale, her eyes the size of moons, as we realized all at once. The whole time—Bernie. The fur-coated neighbor across the street. She was Gallina's mother.

I didn't want to believe it, that she had stolen the notebook for her daughter. And yet it seemed immediately, horribly true. Every time Bernie had mentioned Nikki, each time she had offered to take care of Rhi. It was all a ruse. Remembering how Bernie brought up Nikki's dead-tulips dress made my stomach curl. Only a few people would have remembered that dress. Gallina must have told her mother all about it.

She could have slipped in the side door that Harrison kept unlocked for his other girlfriend. She could have found the key to the office, or maybe I left it unlocked. It was a lot of work to shield an adult daughter, but it was also just unhinged enough to make sense. Part of me understood that level of commitment.

The things we did for our children. Or, in Nikki and Lucille and now Caroline's case, the things we did for our parents, to hold on to them, to never forget that they existed.

I looked down at my phone again and texted Diana. **I need you to find Bernie. Now. Get Rhi. Can you do that? Call Harrison or the police if you need to.**

Gallina's laugh cut through my panic. "There's a confession in here, you know," she said to Caroline, waving the notebook over her head like a prize.

Lucille grimaced and Caroline's eyes darted from one side of the roof to the other, neither of them speaking.

"Thankfully, my mom came through," Gallina said. "Moving her across the street from Nikki into that ridiculous gated neighborhood was the best choice I ever made."

And there it was: Bernie was the part of the larger story that Nikki never figured out. Once it was clear Nikki wouldn't let the Sylvia Club story go, Gallina planted a spy. Her grumpy, harmless mother.

Please let her be harmless, I prayed to myself.

Gallina never came around to visit her mom, so Nikki wouldn't have pieced that relationship together. Bernie must have earned Nikki's trust like she did with me, enough to make Nikki tell her things about her research that Bernie then used to alert her daughter. Over a year ago, right after the podcast episode. That's when Lucille showed up to question Nikki. Right when the threats started. Right before Nikki died. But also right after Nikki created an insurance plan that involved me.

Gallina and Bernie hadn't planned on me.

Clearly I had made the same mistake as Nikki, telling Bernie too much, half of which I didn't remember.

Gallina handed Caroline the notebook. "Take a look." Then, turning to me, she added, "I think we'll know when she finds it, huh?"

With each step Caroline took, closer to Gallina, closer to the edge, my breathing stalled. The sky wobbled as I forced my heart to keep beating. At least I could step away from the edge and its new little safety railing, but that moved me closer to the glass panels, the new skylights added to brighten the atrium of the building. They didn't look like they could hold my weight.

Caroline flipped through the notebook, taking her time on each page. Each moment she didn't look up at me felt intentional, like she couldn't stand the thought of meeting my eyes again.

"Allow me to say the one thing that I think needs to be said out loud," I announced. It was how I would have started a speech at the podium if I had gotten the chance.

I cleared my throat again. "This is the place where Abigail Moriano died. It appears she didn't die by suicide. She was hit by a brick before she fell. Right, Dr. Gallina?"

The USB drive nearly burned in my pocket. I envisioned tossing it to Caroline if Gallina or Lucille attacked me, but I shoved it deeper into my pocket instead. Too much could go wrong.

Gallina's eye twitched. "The group of young women everyone called the Sylvia Club had one thing in common: they wore their troubles like a gaudy piece of jewelry. That kind of weakness makes the rest of us look bad. Abbie Moriano was different. She was scrappier than most of you financial aid princesses."

I saw my opening. "Abbie knew something about you. Did she threaten to tell the college about the way you latched on to students? What did you call them? 'Sad girls'?"

It was the best guess I had, and she didn't disagree.

"As a mentor, I've always wanted to be surrounded by the best and the brightest minds. I've made it my mission to take promising first-year students under my wing and guide them toward their success, which sometimes involved a bit of light therapy. Self-help, if you will. I served in this unofficial role as a student as well. I often think I should have gone into counseling."

It sounded like a job interview, like a scripted lesson plan recited from memory. Or a classroom lecture.

"I'm asking about Abbie."

"We didn't see eye to eye. But I liked Abbie. She was a fighter."

"Just like Nikki."

At the mention of her mother's name, Caroline looked up.

The wind almost drowned out Gallina's voice. "If you're going to try to suggest that I killed Nikki because of what happened to Abbie Moriano, you've got at least a few of your facts wrong."

None of us had mentioned Nikki being killed. I wanted to grab Caroline and tell her to run. She didn't need to hear any of this. She could go home and help Diana with Rhi.

Rhi had to be safe. I couldn't consider anything less. But I trusted Diana to get her back.

Reaching for Caroline wasn't an option. I considered instead how I could pin Gallina down to the ground. She wasn't big. I could take her. Except there wasn't enough space to get "scrappy." If she went down, I'd go down with her.

Lucille shifted her balance and bit down on her already chewed bottom lip. This conversation with Gallina was for her benefit. At least partly. She needed to hear the real story, and it wasn't about the hit-and-run accident.

Caroline looked up then, her skin an unhealthy pale. "What did you say, Dr. Gallina? About my mother being killed?"

"I'm saying I didn't do it. I don't know. Whoever did it probably only meant to knock her out."

I wanted to cry. "Bernie."

It was the only thing that made sense. I knew Harrison and Diana too well to believe they could be involved. Their grief was too raw. Bernie had access. Hell, Nikki had probably invited her in to help after her foot surgery. Loopy from narcotics, Nikki might have said more than she meant to.

And if Bernie's daughter had asked her to knock Nikki out and search the house, she could have easily laced too many of those painkillers into a pitcher of mimosas.

She also could have done it on purpose.

A similar realization hit Caroline like a bullet in the gut, her realizing that the otherwise blank "Dear Caroline" note found beside her mother's body wasn't written by Nikki at all. She recovered quickly, only a slight tremble in her voice. "Why?"

It always came back to why. Why kill Abbie? Or anyone? There were always so many whys.

Lucille spoke up, her scorpion tattoo in full view. "I want to know, too. This is part of the story, right? And it involves my father?"

Gallina's eyes were suddenly darker. Exhausted.

"Abbie claimed I had harassed her, that I was obsessed with her. She told Jerome Weedler, your father, about me—apparently, she trusted him more than me. Imagine that. Trusting a predator like him. I'm sorry, my dear, but he was a horrible man. I tried to report him so many times. But Abbie wanted to get me fired instead. She called me a vulture." Her voice trailed. "It all happened so fast."

I reached for my phone to record the conversation but paused to read the incoming message from Diana. It was a selfie of her and Rhi, their big heads filling the whole screen.

"Bernie disappeared before I could ask her what was going on," her message said. "She just ran away. But I've got baby girl."

That was all I needed to know. Anything else Gallina told us, I could handle.

"I only wanted to help young women. Do you think it's been easy for me? Write about that. I found the bodies of my two best friends. Do you know what that does to a person?"

I considered Diana's heavy burden from finding Nikki. And

I had almost completely repressed the memory of me and Nikki opening the garage with her mom dead inside. Still, I wasn't going to let Gallina claim the role of martyr in this case. She didn't deserve my sympathy.

Caroline spoke up before I got the chance. "You found their bodies, but didn't you push them, too?" She had been right earlier when she said she knew more than I realized. She hadn't missed a beat. "Wasn't that your thing? Nudging girls close to the edge?"

I didn't know if it was true, if you could convince someone to take their life. If someone wanted to die, maybe they would always find a way. But Abbie Moriano hadn't made that choice. Neither had Nikki.

With all that wind, it was hard not to tremble.

Caroline shook the spiral notebook like a Magic 8 Ball, her face blank again. "There's no confession here. You're all full of shit."

Lucille reached out and ripped the book away from her, thumbing the pages so fast, the edges ripped under her fingers. "It was there. Didn't Nikki tell your mother there was a confession?" she yelled at Gallina. "Which one of you tore it out?" Her voice lowered into a terrible growl, the voice of someone who had reached their own private pit of hell.

She'd spent her whole adult life piecing together what happened to her father. That was a lot of time and effort only to realize she wouldn't get a resolution. Not the one she wanted at least. It seemed unbelievable that Nikki told anyone, even Bernie, about that night. Yet Bernie knew what she was looking for long before I did. The notebook. The confession.

But maybe Nikki had needed to get it off her chest. I could picture it, the way the alcohol and the drugs loosened her tongue.

Gallina glowered. "My mother didn't have time to read it. She gave it directly to me."

I hadn't torn out those pages, I knew that much. But Caroline had access to the house, too. She was the only other one. The brightness in her eyes, wet with tears but also victorious, nearly made me fall to my knees with gratitude. She did what Nikki or I somehow never could.

Gallina pointed at me instead of Caroline, which was good because Caroline could barely hide her smile as she held up her phone and hit "Stop" on the recording. "I made a copy of the USB, too," she said.

So much for me hiding anything from that girl.

Only a second passed before Gallina turned on her heel and charged at Caroline. She stumbled and caught herself at the last moment, almost slamming through one of the glass panels.

"Give me that phone, Nikki." She cringed at her own mistake. "I mean, Caroline."

"Run." I didn't need to scream it for Caroline to hear the urgency. "Don't worry about me. Get the police." Caroline started to hesitate, her eyes flicking from me to Gallina to Lucille, like she wasn't sure which one of us to listen to or which one to fear most.

Then she ran, faster than I ever would, easing her way across the narrow walkways to the only door, the only safe way out. Gallina waited until the door slammed to lunge for me, and before I fell, I watched Lucille reach out to stop her. But she was too far away to stop whatever was going to happen next. Lucille, at least, didn't want anyone else to die.

I fell to the ground beneath Gallina, my head pounding the roof pavement while she held me down. She clawed at my face, cursing me, cursing Nikki. "Bitch," she spat.

The pain in the back of my skull made it impossible to open

my eyes. My whole body shuddered. A sinking feeling, like falling asleep. A curtain closing.

Wake up, Nikki's voice brushed against my ear.

With all my energy, I thrusted to kick Gallina off me. Her grunt meant that I got her somewhere good. My face stung with a different pain from the back of my head, and when I reached up to touch, my fingers came back red. More than a scratch.

I couldn't wait to tell Nikki all about it. *You'll never believe how it all turned out.* I had to stop myself from saying it out loud.

"I'm sorry," I said instead.

No apologies. I loved every minute.

Closing my eyes around her voice was my last moment of peace before Gallina leaned on top of me again, rolling both of us not toward the edge, but toward the glass.

With a raised palm, I got one good hit. My knuckles hit teeth before we both fell and kept falling.

CHAPTER 34
THEN

Nikki

The last time I saw Sadie: in front of the dorms. Her holding a trash bag full of clothes, me wearing the baggiest clothes I could find to hide my bloated belly. Half of our things were mixed up, in each other's bags, not sure what belonged to who. We could have set our bags side by side and we wouldn't have known the difference.

She clipped her old pager to the waistband of her jeans. I hadn't seen it since last fall. One of the many things discovered while packing up on our rooms.

The semester wasn't over, not even close, but it was over for us. It had been decided for me the moment I'd screamed at Mr. Sable, though maybe my fate had been sealed long before that. Rewind to the night at Professor Weedler's house, rewind all the way back to orientation.

"Hey," she said, her face brighter than the situation required.

Without campus housing or an apartment to move into, she was headed to her grandmother's.

She dropped her bag and reached into her pocket, retrieving a tiny red stud. My lost ruby.

"I forgot to tell you I found it."

She clasped her palm into mine to transfer the earring, our hands as familiar as sisters. That feeling was what I would remember later. We didn't need blood oaths to be connected forever. Our lifelines had already merged and there was no going back.

"I owe you," I said, slipping the earring into my pocket. "I found the other one. Did I tell you? It was in Eileen's jewelry box."

"Bitch. At least now you match."

We surveyed campus, empty because of the cold, and because everyone else was still in class. No wind, no girls in bunny slippers for Pajama Day, only silence turning the sky two shades of white.

White and Other White, we would have joked if we were in a joking mood. The joke lived between us, though. That was the sign of real friendship, I had always thought. You didn't need to say the joke out loud because the other person was already thinking it.

"I have to go," I told Sadie, but neither of us moved.

I half expected to see Dr. Gallina or Eileen, someone who cared enough to ask where I was going. I gave campus one final look, the words to my tour-guide spiel fading and fading, useless now, everything tangled up in a permanent knot as I peered up at Hope Hall and then at my own dorm.

That's when I saw her for the first and only time. My mother. She stared down at me from my dorm-room window, the only face appearing in all those squares. Just a blank expression, what I hoped was a look of wonder, as she watched me leave. I lifted a hand to wave, but she was already gone.

Harry's car shone over the hill toward us. There was so much I had to tell him. I shielded my eyes against the light, and Sadie walked away to give me that moment to myself because she was always the better friend. Whatever bag she picked up wasn't hers.

At the last minute, while packing up my room, I had shoved my Freshman Seminar textbook and the old library yearbooks into my bags. It felt like they belonged with me, even if my time with Sylvia Club had run out.

For Abbie, girls said when they passed Hope Hall.

But now there was also Polly. If I had a cross necklace, I would have kissed it just for her.

Polly and the rest of the Sylvia Club would live inside me, I knew that. Even if I didn't hang on to my old writing, even if I made myself stop thinking about their deaths. So many deaths. Before I left, I fed my pages to the wind in long shreds, and it felt good.

How to Keep a Dead Woman Alive by Nikki Vale.

Frame her portrait and hang it high. Wear her gemstone around your neck and tattoo her zodiac sign into your softest flesh. Lace a lock of her hair into your braid. Talk to her. Let her whisper her secrets into your mouth. Say her name. Say it daily.

Remember how she used to mourn her dead, relentlessly, her whole body under siege. She could crumble at the opening notes of an old song. Sometimes she stopped driving, pulled to the shoulder to let the dead wreck her all over again.

This is how she would want you to feed her memory, with your own private fanfare and a violence that looks like love. She would accept nothing less.

Build a shrine layered with dolls she once bathed and cradled.

Plastic-headed dolls. Dolls whose eyes never closed. The nearsighted one. The velvet-frocked.

Name a new baby in her honor. Or a building. Cry real tears at the ceremony.

Go to her home and hang a plaque. Raise a historic marker. Search the grounds for her burial dress. She stripped it off after the service and kept running. The dress is in the tree, dangling on the wind, warped beneath the sludge. When you hand-wash the fabric, ignore the frayed threads and the broken stitches.

She left other messes, of course, but you get to decide if you want to clean them up.

Inside Harry's car, I waited to tell him about the pregnancy until we left campus, until I felt like I could hear myself think.

Yes, to that thing he had said about marriage. Yes, to the trust fund and a new last name. If the offer still stood, I told him, we could have a family.

What I didn't say: we—me and the baby—needed a safety net.

The other truth was sweeter. I loved him. I loved his goofy dimples and his rumpled hair, his loafers and his stodgy leather furniture. I would have loved him without medical school and summer houses and trust funds because I loved the way he looked at me. Like I had arrived from another planet, and it was his job to tour me through his world.

And a baby, it turned out, didn't complicate things for him or his family. A baby in my world was a disaster, a liability, a dead end. In his world, though, no one was worried about one more mouth to feed. No one had to choose between paying rent and buying diapers.

I waited for him to ask me all the questions I had practiced responses for:

Question: What about college?
Answer: I can always go back later, after the baby is old enough to go to school.
Question: Have you told your family?
Answer: My father isn't in the picture. We'll send him a postcard.
Question: Didn't you want to be a writer? Won't a baby hinder your progress?
Answer: Let's face it, I'm not writing a bestseller at age eighteen. I can wait a few more years for my masterpiece. Babies don't turn you into mindless zombies the last time I checked.
Question: Shouldn't we at least invite your friend? Sadie, the one you always talk about?
Answer: She can't make it. Whatever day we do it, she won't be there.

I couldn't tell him that my best friend wouldn't approve, that if I saw her on my wedding day, I knew she'd convince me to run away and change all my plans. We'd drive off like Thelma and Louise over the cliff. Or even better, we'd slip on our costume-room dresses and wigs and find a better place to start over.

I knew we needed a break from each other if either of us wanted the kind of life we were destined to lead. That was what I made myself believe. Her, an actress. Me, a mom turned writer. Or a writer turned mom. Either way.

Question: What kind of ring do you want?
Answer: I don't care about jewelry, but I love rubies even more than diamonds.

He grabbed my hand and didn't end up asking a single question at all. It wasn't romantic or sentimental. Neither of us cried.

Fiona Apple on the radio, a serenade. Song: "Shadowboxer."

He bought the ring the next day.

Poetic justice. If I finished this story, that's what I'd call it. But I ran out of time.

Sadie was the worst loss. You can't re-create a friendship you started when you were seven years old. I tried making new friends, but that shit was hard. There's no way to start from scratch with someone new when history has already been written.

What happened between us wasn't new. Fierce friendships often get sidelined for marriage, children, jobs. Death. I took the blame, even if Sadie never got to hear me say the words. She was friend and sister and first love. You don't get over first love.

And you never find friendship like that again. I know that now.

The hardest part wasn't the end, because we never really had one. We didn't know that the portals we stepped into would disappear behind us.

A damn shame, my mom would have said.

If we didn't even recognize ourselves anymore, how could we expect to find each other?

In the end, it would only be this: me, gone; her, fighting for both of us. I hoped. I planned a lot of things, but I couldn't plan it all.

I started writing again when Caroline no longer needed a babysitter. I chose a pen name that reminded me of my time writing the advice column at Loch Raven College. Not because of fond memories, but because that was the last kind of writing I'd taken pride in. Self-help wasn't what I'd ever dreamed of writing, but it worked out. Ish.

I should have been happy. People say it: *Just be happy*. It doesn't work like that. I started to hear the keening again, that sound that had haunted me at Loch Raven. It was my mom's memory creeping just out of reach, I thought at first. Her voice, her smell, things I had made myself forget. But it was the Sylvia Club chasing me down all over again.

I didn't realize how much the body remembered. I could force memories away, but year by year, their names wriggled behind my eyes when I tried to sleep. Between bake sales and book clubs, making dinner, mapping out a new garden, and, of course, my own part-time writing career, the Sylvia Club lived in the margins.

The chorus of them. Always calling.

Back then, I wanted their names. But later, I wanted to tell their stories. The friendships and broken engagements, the clubs and sports, their majors, their bright futures. How they styled their hair and what they wore to class. Every class had their own Spirit Week, their own Twin Day fraught with insecurities I couldn't understand. Because I always had someone to twin with. Even if me and Sadie weren't the school-spirit types.

I didn't want them to be someone's dead muse, some vague and morbid statistic about suicide on a college campus. So yeah, I buried my head in one tragedy to avoid thinking about my own personal shit.

I didn't know what I was looking for back at Loch Raven, not really, but then I found a piece of it. Before I left campus and married Harry, I found that yearbook photo of Dr. Gallina sitting with two girls who'd died that year. It didn't click until years later how suspect that one fact sounded when I said it out loud.

She knew them all.

Not including the girls from the sixties, of course. They were in a cluster of deaths that we would never understand.

Gallina had been friends with the girls who died in the eighties. She had been the teacher of the girls who died in the nineties. And then one of them died in a way that didn't make sense. Pushed instead of jumped. The wording mattered.

Apparently, she had once wanted to study psychology and go into counseling or social work. Instead, at the prodding of her parents, she studied journalism and English at Loch Raven College. That didn't stop her from offering her own free counseling to classmates and students, usually freshmen girls who followed her around like a puppy. Eventually, she led a mentorship program targeted to financial aid students.

I knew you couldn't just whisper in someone's ear to make them down a bottle of pills. But an influential figure like a mentor or a friend might, over time, encourage someone already vulnerable to change the direction of their life. I could see it.

And I remembered Gallina's singsongy voice on the roof of Hope Hall with me. It had sure sounded like giving me permission to end my life. If I had been in a different headspace, who knew what I might have done?

And that wasn't the part that had haunted me. It was the questions surrounding Abbie Moriano's death. Someone had killed her. The family knew and I knew. I was pretty sure the college suspected it, too. Why else would they remove Gallina as a faculty mentor? Her tenure saved her teaching job, was all I could figure. But why would she kill a student? I left that question simmering, almost forgotten, burning at the edges of my skull like a casserole crust.

I kept writing. While Harry slept with every unhappily married neighbor and Caroline became a moody teenager, I had more time. I reread all Sylvia Plath's poetry—not to analyze it or worship it, just to enjoy it. Shame on me for judging the other girls who loved her. They were discovering poetry. They were loving something that deserved to be loved. If I could go back in time, I'd appreciate that part more. I wouldn't let a teacher ruin her for me.

And then I recreated my Sylvia Club research from scratch.

I got so excited about writing a book under my real name, uncovering the truth of that horrible place, that I slipped up and mentioned it in the most public way.

The podcast interview. I hoped no one would hear it. But they did. And someone didn't like how hard I'd been digging.

By the time a reporter knocked on my door to ask about Weedler's death, I knew it wasn't a coincidence that while researching the Sylvia Club, my worst secret came back to haunt me.

It took me too long to realize who Lucille was, that she worked with Sadie. Not a real reporter but catch her in the right light and you'd see how much she resembled her father. All of it meant two things: she had personal reasons to never give up her search, and she was closer to the truth than I could handle.

The handwritten threats were what filled me with so much horror. Lucille wanted a confession, but the threats came from people who wanted me to never speak again. They wanted me to stop talking forever.

The fire in the kitchen? That wasn't laziness or depression or self-destruction.

The gas leak that could have killed all of us if Caroline hadn't smelled it? Not an accident.

Harry didn't believe me, not when I worried about the same car driving by the house each night or my absolute certainty that someone had followed me to the grocery store. There were eyes on me everywhere. I felt them.

So I prepared. I might die and I didn't want everything I knew to die with me.

A lawyer friend was able to track down a witness statement from Weedler's case (I told him it was for research purposes). The other vehicle that had driven by that night saw a redheaded girl in an orange dress on the side of the road. Suddenly, I knew. We had never been safe.

In the event of my death, Sadie stood to get in the most trouble. She didn't have a lawyer or the money to buy one, I suspected. She didn't have anyone to ask for help.

I already had the wig. I had used it for my author photos for years, a nod to the girl I had always idolized. Harry's weird attraction to the wig was a fact so strange and messed up it made my insides cramp.

And I still had Sadie's old dress. I'd die with it. "Cremation, please," I added to my will. It was one less thing they could trace back to her.

Tracking Sadie down was easy enough. I tried to call more than once, but her voice ached in my ear each time. I called again and again, listening to her voicemail greeting, memorizing the new tones and inflections of her adult voice. Suddenly, I didn't want her to see how I turned out. I couldn't bear an awkward meeting where we didn't know how to talk to each other anymore.

Instead, I knew I'd have to set up a life for her that gave her safety and pointed her in the right direction.

If and when Sadie needed to uncover the truth about the Sylvia Club and Gallina, it would be there for her. Or maybe she'd put her head in the sand and never even make it to my funeral. I couldn't force it, not with someone like Sadie. I wanted her to want to find the answers. She didn't have to pick up my torch, but I left it there with barely glowing embers just in case.

I hid my research in a place only she would look. If someone else discovered it, they might find it strange, but they wouldn't "get it" in the same way Sadie would. She could have chosen not to look. It was up to her.

I left her a message in my office that she could have ignored or never found. I would have left the message in our back-and-forth journal if I knew where it was. I hoped she was the one who ended up with it, our belongings intertwined as they were. Another gamble. But here's the thing about knowing someone that well—it happens in marriages, it happens in families, and it happens in friendships as close as ours—you can guess each other's next move. You can do more than predict; you can make plans.

The page number only she would notice. The money in the wall that would save her ass when she needed it. A safety net of friends who would help her: Diana, Bernie, even Caroline.

There were some surprises so intricate, she would never figure them out. I liked it that way. When she used to call me Stage Manager, she understood that my job was to hide the seams.

The whole plan, every last bit of it, depended on me knowing Sadie well enough to predict how she'd move. I had to bank on her showing up to my funeral or my house after my death. Her attraction to men like Harry and her inability to not flirt probably hadn't changed. His grief mixed with his red hair fetish equaled the perfect storm.

To make sure he noticed her, I mentioned her at least a half dozen times in his presence, my old friend, the one with the red hair. I had been thinking about her lately, I told him. I wondered where she was, wished we could reconnect. If she showed up, he'd know that she mattered, even if he didn't know why.

It didn't make me sick—not much—to think about them together. What did I care? I'd be gone. He had already slept with half of Hidden Harbor anyway. Diana was the only friend who saw through his dimpled smile.

All I wanted from Sadie in return was to shelter Caroline from the same Sylvia Club fate, the Dread, the horrible thing that my mom had never been able to shake. Sadie was exactly who Caroline would need in my absence, even if she wouldn't admit it. Sadie had been the one who always saved me, after all. I couldn't have her in my life anymore, but at least my daughter could.

"Caroline, I need you to do me a favor," I'd told her one day while Harrison was at a hotel with another woman, a secret he thought he had kept so well. "No matter what happens, no matter what people say about me, there is a woman out there who knows the truth. You have to believe her."

She had just gotten out of the shower, her hair wrapped in a towel, and she smelled like roses. I'd try to leave her a folder full of notes, too. That was my plan in case Sadie never showed up. I'd try to explain what I couldn't explain in person.

"You're freaking me out, Mom."

"Her name is Sadie, and you will want to hate her. But don't hate her. Believe her. Help her. Make sure she has everything she needs."

Caroline pulled away from my grasp, my fingers clinging to her wrist until she mumbled "Okay, whatever," and slammed her bedroom door. I didn't take it personally. Growing up is like that. I did the same thing with my mother.

How to make room for your dead woman: Let her in. Let her wander around your house at night and rummage through your closet.

Let her keep dying. Let her leave and come back as many times as she needs.

Remember everything, but not all at once.

They say your life flashes before your eyes before you die. But there isn't time for your whole life in that flash. And you don't get to choose. It just happens.

For me, only one memory reappeared, that night at the ruins of the Enchanted Forest. Not even the whole night, just the moment outside the chain-link fence, me and Sadie with our flashlights, the squelching mud, the horrible smell in our noses. Everything was beautiful and ruined, muck snatching at our boots. So much mud. I never forgot it. The way we laughed as we stumbled, then grabbed on to each other for balance. I never had that again with anyone. No one else could make me laugh like that, could help me find my balance, could show me exactly where to aim my single beam of light. Grinding my teeth, gripping her hand. I remembered it all.

Give me a second, I should have told her when it was time to leave. *I'd like to stay here a moment more.*

CHAPTER 35
NOW

Sadie

The new apartment was small, but plenty big enough for me and Rhi. We had our own bedroom with the crib crammed up next to my bed, a bathroom, a small but functional kitchen, and a couch that Diana claimed she was planning to give away anyway. There was enough room for friends to come over and feel comfortable, even if a little cramped. I had windows and a fireplace that didn't work, so I could fill it with baby toys or whatever. And I could change the curtains whenever I wanted.

"Bonus: at least it not haunted," Caroline said, her dry sense of humor the biggest blessing to come out of this whole mess. Just the fact that she visited me at all made it feel like we had our own imperfect little family.

She joined me for a weekly movie night even though no one made her. We were especially fond of zombie films.

Harrison got to take Rhi every other weekend, and I hated

it every time. According to my therapist, I had trust issues. Go figure.

What I couldn't tell Caroline was that it wasn't her home that had been haunted. Her mother's ghost didn't live within the confines of that gigantic house in Hidden Harbor. It was me. I was the haunted one.

I hadn't seen Nikki since that day. Maybe I never would again. Grief fades, all the self-help books claimed. They were full of shit.

Nikki had given Caroline an incomplete folder filled with her Sylvia Club research before she died, and Caroline had been working on her own to figure out the puzzle Nikki left behind, too. She had been on her own journey with a different set of artifacts and different questions along the way. Just in case I didn't come through, Nikki would have thought. Or maybe she wanted us to work together, me and Caroline. That was probably what Nikki's to-do list meant, but I'd never know.

The worst part was realizing all the things I'd never figure out.

Thirteen stitches. A concussion. A broken collarbone and a scar like an asymmetrical star embedded into my hand from whatever I hit on the way down. We hadn't fallen all the way to the bottom, and wherever we landed, Gallina landed first. She served as my cushion. No one asked me why I didn't fight back harder. I got one good hit, after all.

"You could have killed her," Caroline said. But I wasn't a killer—not anymore. I wanted Gallina in jail. Assault was a start. The rest of the charges, I hoped, would come later, thanks to the recording Caroline made.

In her only comment to the news, Gallina, in a wheelchair with a broken leg and an irreparable spinal injury, said, "I helped so many girls by giving them the confidence to make decisions on their own, decisions that were right for them. I served as a mentor and, in some cases, a mother figure. I am proud of my work at Loch Raven College."

God, I wished Nikki could have seen it.

I thought I saw Bernie once at the hospital, waiting outside my room. Someone had given her pink lipstick instead of her usual orange color, and it looked good on her. She was gone by the time I screamed loud enough for the nurses to come running. With Gallina in custody, I guessed that Lucille was helping Bernie evade the authorities. She still wanted someone to pay for her father's death. She had every right.

My lawyer told me that if the police reopened Weedler's case, we could claim Nikki had killed Weedler by accident, or even in self-defense. Any proof they had of me at the scene of the crime meant nothing, he said. If it came to that. I wasn't worried anymore. No one except me and Nikki would ever know what had really happened.

"Tell me again about the black dresses," I asked Caroline while Rhiannon practiced rolling over on the carpet. She rolled from one side to the other and laughed through her nose when I sang the song she had been named after. A little Fleetwood Mac never hurt anybody.

"The girls in dresses were beautiful." She told it like a haunted fairy tale. "All of them wore black like I asked them to. They cried so loud it sounded like an incoming train."

"It was something," we both agreed.

Each time I remembered the sound of them crying, I tried to understand. I had been a part of it, hadn't I? I asked it over and over again until I reassured myself that yes, eventually, I cried just as loud as everyone else.

I was there. We all were.

Collective grief. Public mourning. I didn't know what to call it. Caroline had planned it as part of the memorial for Nikki. Because keening, as she put it, felt more appropriate than empty words in a long-ass speech. I didn't disagree. Caroline assured me that the hint of protest beneath the cries, the rebellious keening was just the beginning of students rallying together. The way the college handled so many deaths—people were catching on.

I usually waited after Caroline left to open social media. Today, my feed filled with headlines about Dr. Gallina's imminent murder charge. Another girl came forward, said she saw the whole thing back in the nineties, the way Gallina had pushed a freshman from the roof of Hope Hall after slamming the side of her head with something heavy.

I didn't want to know more. At least Abbie's family would have resolution. I could only hope.

Annie Minx has started a live video, Instagram alerted me. I twisted the single ruby pierced into my lobe, one of the last things I took from the house before I moved out. Nikki died wearing the other one.

And there she was, the wig a little off-center, her face covered with a veil. I followed all of Annie Minx's accounts now just as Caroline took possession of her mother's old wig. The new Annie Minx read the script the old Annie Minx had left behind. Her final newsletter had reached our inboxes that morning.

"'I planned for a lot in my absence, but I couldn't plan everything,'" she began, reading her mother's words.

Girl, I whispered.

I had never missed anyone so much. The way she bopped her head to cheesy songs on the radio, how her smile lingered on her face, fading but not faded. Her laugh, like bells. I remembered every bit of our life together. How much sense we made together and how little logic my life had without her. I'd never recover from that realization. We wasted so much time. Because any time in our short little lives that we didn't spend together was incomplete.

Me in a life without her, unfinished and unfinished and unfinished.

I kept my gaze wide while I listened to Caroline read, one eye on the door, like if I waited long enough I'd see my friend again.

Subject: I've Clogged Up Your Inbox for Long Enough.

I planned for a lot in my absence, but I couldn't plan everything. I hope you found all my messages, and I hope you don't hate me for any of it. I hope the right people ended up smiling. I hope you got everything you deserve.

This is my last newsletter, so I figure I can say whatever I want. There isn't much left. Leave the ghost light burning, and we can both use it to light the stage. Tag me in your favorite poem, and let the likes pile up.

Begin again, people like to say. Like it's that easy. As if there are all these possible lives and we can simply swap one out for another.

In one version: me and you wearing black boots and dusty dresses, our matching tattoos with their own pulse, speeding down the highway. A life full of library books and homemade CDs. Artifacts like meal cards, spiral notebooks, glitter, and shower shoes. A life filled with hopeful nights and so much longing, we'd never not feel bruised by it.

Another life: duct tape, clear nail polish, and energy-saving light bulbs. Cheerios. Pap smears, baskets to hold magazines, towels rolled for decoration and not for function. In that life, the rings beneath our eyes weren't from sleep-worn mascara or stage makeup. But there were also clearer skies and layer cakes served by somebody else. Unbroken windshields and undisturbed sleep. Dresses that were only ever worn by us.

If there were two versions of our lives, I straddled the line between them. The possibilities for sweetness on either side have always been endless. That's what I imagined for your life, too. One step over that line probably felt impossible, but you did it anyway.

Just like me, when you were ready, I know you surprised them all.

Weekly newsletter, c/o Annie Minx, Inc. Click here to unsubscribe.

AUTHOR'S NOTE

As an English professor at a two-year college, I've always been fascinated with the life and work of Sylvia Plath. When Plath showed up in my fiction, I didn't question her presence.

Playing the role of fan more than scholar, I devoured *The Bell Jar* and her poetry, but also literary criticism centered on Plath, her published letters and diaries, and numerous biographies about her life and work. As I also learned about Assia Wevill, the woman known most for her affair with Ted Hughes and her similar death by suicide, it made sense that my characters were as captivated as I was.

While *Doll Parts* is a work of fiction, not intended to take the place of scholarly research, true accounts of Plath and Wevill lived in the back of my mind as I wrote. The more explicit references to Plath's writing will be noted by all readers. Other references, from bees to dresses to the all-women's college and "Scholarship Girls" are sprinkled throughout the novel.

To learn more about Sylvia Plath and Assia Wevill, the following reading list, in addition to Plath's own work, is a great place to begin.

RECOMMENDED READING

The Bell Jar by Sylvia Plath

Ariel: The Restored Edition by Sylvia Plath, foreword by Frieda Hughes

The Letters of Sylvia Plath (Volumes 1 and 2)

Red Comet: The Short Life and Blazing Art of Sylvia Plath by Heather Clark

The Haunted Reader and Sylvia Plath by Gail Crowther

Pain, Parties, Work: Sylvia Plath in New York, Summer 1953 by Elizabeth Winder

Reclaiming Assia Wevill: Sylvia Plath, Ted Hughes, and the Literary Imagination by Julie Goodspeed-Chadwick

Lover of Unreason: Assia Wevill, Sylvia Plath's Rival and Ted Hughes' Doomed Love by Yehuda Koren and Eilat Negev

Loving Sylvia Plath: A Reclamation by Emily Van Duyne

DOLL PARTS: THE PLAYLIST

"Miss World"—Hole
"Seether"—Veruca Salt
"Pretend We're Dead"—L7
"Doll Parts"—Hole
"Killing Me Softly with His Song"—Fugees
"Darling Nikki"—Prince
"Jennifer's Body"—Hole
"Wild Horses"—the Sundays
"Just a Girl"—No Doubt
"I Wanna Be Sedated"—the Ramones
"Sweet Child O' Mine"—Guns N' Roses
"Pretty Noose"—Soundgarden
"Eternal Flame"—the Bangles
"Silent All These Years"—Tori Amos
"Fade Into You"—Mazzy Star
"Asking for It"—Hole
"Shadowboxer"—Fiona Apple
"Sexy Sadie"—the Beatles
"Kiss My Ass Goodbye"—7 Year Bitch
"Zombie"—the Cranberries

READING GROUP GUIDE

1. Nikki and Sadie were best friends until they went their separate ways abruptly during their college years. What are the reasons their friendship ended, and how did the rift between them affect their characters, especially Sadie?

2. *Doll Parts* is not only inspired by poetry but also by music, as Nikki and Sadie bond over their favorite grunge songs. If you were to have a soundtrack to your life, what songs would be on it?

3. Both Professor Weedler and Professor Gallina have inappropriate relationships with students but in different ways. How do both characters abuse their power throughout the story and ultimately play a key role in the Sylvia Club mystery? How do the issues that both Weedler and Gallina represent affect students on college campuses today?

4. Loch Raven's campus is riddled with ghost stories and lore about former students, some of it fact and some of it fiction. What role does storytelling play in this novel? When you were in school, were there stories that circulated amongst the students like the ones in *Doll Parts*?

5. What does Sylvia Plath symbolize for the girls of Loch Raven, and what do Sadie and Nikki think of this? What might the dangers be in romanticizing rather than just appreciating this kind of "sad girl" aesthetic?

6. Throughout the story, Sadie becomes plagued with visions of her old friend Nikki. What did you think of Nikki's appearances in Sadie's chapters, and what might it say about the grief that Sadie was experiencing about that loss of her friend?

7. Much of the story is inspired by some of the real events that occurred in Sylvia Plath's life. Did you know much about Plath's life and work before reading the story, and if not, are you interested in reading her work now?

8. What role does the Annie Minx newsletter play in the novel? Were you able to catch any hints about the mystery within these sections? If so, what?

9. What was the relationship like between Sadie and Harrison, and how does motherhood affect the ways Sadie views her relationship? Were you surprised to learn that this relationship was in part inspired by Assia Wevill and Ted Hughes?

10. The end of the novel concludes with an ultimate twist, proving that among the many deaths in the story, some of them were indeed murders. As you read, what theories did you form about the mysteries that were happening in both Sadie's and Nikki's timelines? Were you right?

A CONVERSATION WITH THE AUTHOR

Doll Parts **is an inventive and evocative story of friendship, grief, motherhood, and the abuse of power. What inspired you to write this novel?**

There were so many points of inspiration for *Doll Parts*, but this story started in the years following the death of a close friend, who seemed to visit my dreams every night for a very long time. That grief happened to coincide with my almost-obsessive interest in research about Sylvia Plath and Assia Wevill. As a mother, as a woman who once attended an all-women's college, and as someone whose life has been shaped by her friendships, the rest of the story had probably been brewing inside me for much longer. It took many drafts to layer and combine all of these elements, but I am so proud of the way it came together.

The story is filled with grunge music, ghosts, dark academia, and all sorts of imagery that evokes girlhood. What movies, books, or media might have inspired the general feeling of the book?

Too many to name them all! But yes, of course, Courtney Love and Hole are a part of the vibes, though, if I'm being honest, I may have listened to more Tori Amos when I was Nikki and Sadie's age than any other artist. *The Bell Jar* absolutely lives inside these pages, as well as Donna Tartt's *The Secret History* and Daphne du Maurier's *Rebecca*. Other inspirations include everything from years of devouring *Seventeen* magazine, making zines with my friends, playing with Barbie dolls, and watching a lot of zombie movies.

Why do you think Sadie and Nikki's story is important to tell, and what do you hope readers take away from the novel?

I wanted to tell a story about friendship—not the toxic kind but the kind of friendship that can matter more than any other relationship. For me, that is what *Doll Parts*, through its many drafts, has always been about. A large part of this story also centers on how our culture romanticizes dead women with the focus on Sylvia Plath and how she is taught and remembered. I hope that readers can puzzle through these ideas just like Sadie and Nikki must do.

Nikki and many of the girls at Loch Raven College struggle with the weight of unbearable academic expectations. Do you have any advice for college students or anyone else who is trying to manage the weight of academic achievement?

As a college professor, my suggestion would be to reach out and ask for help, to use campus resources when they are available. As a former student in similar situations, I also know that asking for help is one of the hardest things to do. That weight can feel crushing, as Nikki especially learns. The most practical advice I ever got about surviving college was to make sure you show up. As simple as it sounds, I didn't always follow that advice. For a long time, I wasn't the best student, but I eventually learned that everyone is on their own path. It takes the time it needs to take.

Do you have a writing routine? How do you get to the page and write an entire novel?

While I have to adjust my writing time each semester depending on my schedule, the one consistent writing routine I have is working very early in the morning before anyone else is awake. I join the 5 AM Writers Club nearly every day to make sure that I prioritize writing first thing in the morning. Some days, that is all the writing time I get. But you can write a novel this way, in those slivers of time, page by page.

ACKNOWLEDGEMENTS

So much of writing can feel like a solitary experience, but everything that happens afterwards, when that draft gets all sparkly and starts to find its roots, takes a team. And my team really kicks ass.

Danielle Egan-Miller, the dream agent, who makes it feel like I won the lottery: This book would have been a very different beast without your guidance, support, and enthusiasm. You understood the heart of this story from the beginning. Thank you for helping to make my dreams come true. Thank you to the whole Browne & Miller team with a special shout-out to Mariana Fisher for reading and for seeing. You helped make this process a true delight.

To Liv Turner, the perfect editor for me and for *Doll Parts*, your vision for this book took it to new levels and truly made it shine. Thank you for encouraging more music, more poetry, and more of the weird. What a journey! I'm so thrilled that we got to do it together. We are both the girl with the most cake.

Thank you to Cristina Arreola and Kate Riley, the Landmark marketing team, for answering all my questions before I even knew to ask them. I have loved working together. Thank you to Jessica Thelander and the whole production team. To everyone at Sourcebooks Landmark who helped bring this book to life, thank you. I'm beyond grateful and excited that *Doll Parts* found a home with you.

This experience would not be the same without my teachers

and classmates over many decades. In particular, thank you to Gail Galloway Adams, Mark Brazaitis, Jeana DelRosso, and Mary Elizabeth Pope. Your support has been invaluable. Thank you to the English Department at Notre Dame of Maryland University and the Creative Writing MFA program at West Virginia University.

Enormous thanks go to Shelley Puhak: Without you encouraging me to pursue writing, I am sure this novel wouldn't exist. You saw me, a full-time waitress and part-time community college student, and convinced me I had something to say. It is a gift to know you.

Thank you to the English Department at Greenville Technical College and to my colleagues/friends at GTC through the years. April Dove and Becca Clark, for getting my sense of humor and for always checking in. Lori Bongiorno, my ride-or-die, I am so lucky to have found you. And to the OG Nerdlympians, my bookish friends who cheered me on every step of the way: Catherine Blass, Emily Weathers, Kathryn Hix, Katie Stewart, and Kendall Lentz. You are all my dream team.

I couldn't write my acknowledgments without including the support and camaraderie of the 5 AM Writers Club, a group of individuals too large to name you all. Special recognition to members of the 2022 UCIJ Cohort and participants in each Journey to Jupiter retreat. I can't say enough kind words about Ralph Walker and Julia F. Green—thank you for your kindness and book-loving enthusiasm. I'm so honored to be part of this amazing crew.

For a novel about friendship, I am somehow at a loss for how to properly thank my posse, the friends who know all about late nights and pinkie swears, tears and laughter—so much laughter. Jack, Rain, K, and Mel Mel (Jackie Napier, Lorraine Eakin, Katie

Showalter, and Melanie Benton): Thank you for all of it. It is easy to imagine that Sarah is still here in the mix with us, that we're all stretched out together on someone's floor drinking Dr Pepper and eating Pixie Stix. We really did, we had a time.

No one knows how hard and how long I've dreamed of publishing a novel as much as my family. To my parents, Pauline and Mike Patrick, for all of the continued support. My mom bought me a typewriter when I was seven years old! I've been writing stories ever since. Thank you to my siblings: Angela (the bestest stair-sister), and James and Sonia Zang. I am also incredibly lucky to have such supportive in-laws. Thank you to Patricia and Mark Poole, as well as Christina, Joe, and Michelle Wilcox.

And for my son, Desmond, my favorite person: Thank you for just being you. You are my best.

Finally, none of this would be possible if it weren't for my husband, Jeff, the Idea Generator, who has never stopped believing in me. I am so glad we get to travel this world together.

ABOUT THE AUTHOR

Credit: Mila Wilson Photography

Penny Zang is an English professor and holds an MFA in creative writing from West Virginia University. Her work has appeared in *New Ohio Review*, *Louisville Review*, *Iron Horse Literary Review*, and elsewhere. She lives in Greenville, South Carolina, with her husband and son. Find her online at:

Website: www.pennyzang.com
Instagram: @pennyzang
Twitter: @penny_zang
Medium: @pennyzang
Substack: Mourning Pages